ECLIPSE
OF THE HEART

ECLIPSE
OF THE HEART

ADAM ADRIAN CROWN

Knight-errant Press

Eclipse of the Heart
Copyright 2016 by Adam Adrian Crown

Published by Knight-errant Press
1045 Coddington Rd Ithaca NY 14850

Cover Design by Richard Turylo

ISBN-13: 978-0997445909

ISBN-10: 0997445904

For Dulcie, Kelsey & Mouse

Up a narrow flight of stairs
in my narrow little room
As I lie upon my bed
in the early evening gloom
Impaled on my wall
my eyes can dimly see
The pattern of my life
and the puzzle that is me.

"Patterns," Simon and Garfunkel

Ain't no sunshine when she's gone.
It's not warm when she's away.
Ain't no sunshine when she's gone
And she's always gone too long
Anytime she goes away.

("Ain't No Sunshine," Bill Withers)

Just So You Know

Let's understand each other.

I'm not really writing this for you; I'm writing this for me.

And actually, I'm not even writing it for me as much as I am for Marlo. I'll tell you about her sometime, maybe. Not right now. For now, all you have to know is that I like having her around. I like it a lot. And I want her to stay.

Forever.

But I only want her to stay if *she* wants to stay. It has to be her decision, her own free choice. The thing is, she can't freely choose to be with me if she doesn't really know me. So that's what this is about.

I want her to understand who I am, what I've done, and why. All of it. The good, the bad, and the ugly. I'm just going to tell it as honestly as I can. I don't want to make any excuses, justify anything, rationalize anything. I'm not looking to censor or soften, exaggerate or embellish, or make myself come off any better than I am. On the other hand, I'm not apologizing for anything, either.

But I'm also not stupid. Writing all this down is a little risky and that rhymes with whiskey and I could use one. I'm changing some of the names — mine, for example — and

1

places, little details like that. Little things that don't really matter. I know all about statutes of limitations.

In going back over things, trying to fit all the different pieces together so they make some kind of sense, I discovered one thing for sure: I've got a lousy memory.

With this kind of thing, you can't go by feelings. Some things that happened twenty or thirty years ago are so vivid they seem like yesterday. And sometimes yesterday feels like a thousand years ago.

I don't know about you, but if it weren't for particular events in the world that serve as markers, I'd never be able to figure out where what happened or when or in what order. I remember such-and-such and that *had* to be at this time, because I remember a certain thing happening at the *same* time. Sometimes it's a major event – lots of people say they remember exactly what they were doing when President Kennedy was murdered. But often it's a movie that was around or a song that was popular at the time. Something like that.

I don't know, maybe that's the way you remember things, too.

Hell, maybe that's how everybody does it.

Maybe, when I'm done writing all this up and I show it to Marlo, it'll be too much for her. And she'll leave, get as far away from me as possible. I wouldn't blame her if she did. I'm either the absolute best man for her to be with, or the absolute worst.

Tough call.

Either way, I'd rather she leave because she knows me than stay because she doesn't.

So it is what it is what it is.

PART ONE

Adam Adrian Crown

Somebody, somewhere
In the heat of the night
Looking pretty dangerous
Running out of patience

("Passion," Rod Stewart)

CHAPTER ONE: DWI

Imagine you're on your way home from a big family dinner with your parents and your husband's parents, plus a few siblings and their kids too, all to celebrate the birth of your new baby girl. Your husband has drunk a few toasts tonight, so you're doing the driving. Your two sons, ages three and five, are in the back seat, for some odd reason behaving like perfect little gentlemen. Your baby is cradled in your husband's arms and he coos to her in a slightly inebriated way that makes you chuckle.

You're only two blocks away from home. You stop at a red light, wait for it to turn green. When it does, you check left and right and then you start into the intersection.

You have no idea where the other car came from or how it came up on you so fast. There's just the sudden glare of headlights, the jolt of the collision, the ear-wrenching scream of twisting metal.

The next thing you become aware of, you're in the hospital, a half dozen masked-and-gowned strangers darting around you like honey bees. You can't feel your legs.

While the trauma team fights desperately to save your life, your husband and two sons are already on their way to the morgue. Your baby, having been sheltered by your husband's body, is miraculously unharmed and in the care of a pediatric nurse. The driver of the other car has suffered only a broken finger and a minor cut on the forehead requiring four stitches. Still reeking of alcohol, he is being treated by an ER resident.

It's more than you can bear.

The loss breaks your heart, and if it weren't for your infant daughter who still needs her mother, you might find a way to assuage your grief — permanently. Your parents and your husband's parents, despite their own grief, are at your bedside in shifts virtually every minute of the day and night. Like the ghosts of Christmas past. Friends come by too, God bless them, but you scarcely notice them. When the doctors tell you that you will probably never walk again, it hardly seems to matter.

You learn that the other driver has been charged with DWI — driving while intoxicated — and vehicular manslaughter in the second degree. He faces as much as 7 years in prison or as little as 5 years on probation.

It is not his first DWI arrest.

Or his second.

Or even his third.

It is his *sixth*.

The prosecutor explains to you that previous arrests mean nothing in court — only previous convictions can be considered, and he has never been convicted. He supplies all the king's horses, knows all the king's men, and they always make sure he gets off again. On two other occasions he has injured innocent people — thank god, not seriously. This is the first time he has killed.

It's a long time before the case comes to trial — almost a year. You learn that the man's lawyer will very probably work out a plea bargain with the prosecutor's office. He will be required to "voluntarily" enter an alcohol rehabilitation program — this would be his third time in such a program. After that, he would be on probation. He would serve no time in prison. In as little as five years he could be completely free.

6

In five years your family will still be dead.

You consider filing a wrongful death action in civil court. But he has enough wealth and enough power to be represented by one of the largest and most prestigious legal firms in the country. The prospects of winning are poor, and they would drag the case on for years. And years. And you don't feel you have that much strength left.

Then one day you're going through some of your late husband's things. An idea comes to you, and you suddenly find you have a purpose. A reason, if not to live, at least to delay dying. Something that, for the moment, anyway, dulls the sharp edge of your pain. You begin to make subtle inquiries. It takes a while, but eventually, it leads you to The Judge.

And that leads to me.

-II-

I met her at her parent's home in the Vista Terrace area. Her parents were out.

I guessed she was around thirty and, in happier times, had been a very attractive woman. Now, her blue eyes were sunken in shadow. They had the hollow look of having cried all the tears they were capable of crying, never to cry again. She seemed frail, not because her body was small and weak, but because it was no longer animated by living spirit.

She led me to a sunny spot on the porch — she had become very adept at managing her wheelchair over the course of the last year — and invited me to sit down. She held a small book on her lap like a sleeping kitten. I couldn't see what it was.

"I would like to hire you," she said simply.

I nodded that I understood.

"I don't know how much you know — or what you need to know..."

I let her tell me the whole story in detail. It was painful for her, but in a distant way, and she got through it as if describing the result of a disappointing sporting event.

"You know," I told her, "Sometimes people think that taking a step like this will make everything better somehow. It won't. "

"My husband was a teacher," she said. "Tenth grade English. Do you know Edgar Allen Poe?

I did.

"He was my husband's favorite author. I always thought he was too — creepy — myself. I found this among his things." She held up the book. "There was a bookmark in it. Do you know where?"

I didn't.

"The Cask of Amontillado," she said. "Do you know that story?"

I did.

In it, Poe sets out a formula for revenge. The person being punished has to know who's punishing him and why he's being punished. And he has to know that there's not a damn thing he can do about it.

"Can you do that?" she asked.

I told her I could.

"Then I definitely do want to hire you," she said. "I don't know what you charge for — your services. I have my husband's life insurance money." She told me the amount. "Is it enough?"

"You'll be needing that, won't you?" I asked. "You're going to have more expenses. Your daughter will need..."

"My parents will take care of Sherie." She pronounced it Share – EE. Rhymes with Paris and it's all comin' here to River City.

And the way she said that, her tone, told me she didn't plan on needing the money personally. Her grief had carried her away from living like a riptide pulls even the strongest swimmer gradually away from shore. Now she was caught in the undertow of soul-sapping despair and she was too exhausted to strike out for the surface.

"Also, there's some coming from the sale of... our house. That should bring..."

"If I can help you with this, " I said, "I'd like to be a little flexible on the fee. It's hard to know what the expenses will be. Suppose we wait until it's done, and I'll bill you then. I can guarantee it won't be more than the insurance money. Is that agreeable to you? You just pay whatever fee I ask afterward?"

"All right. Do you want a — retainer — now?"

"Not necessary, but thank you for asking," I said. "Just give me your hand on it."

We shook hands. Her hand was cold and limp. It reminded me of a little girl, in another life, whom I pulled from floodwaters a few minutes too late.

-III-

I went right to work on it.

But there was no particular hurry. I had plenty of time to study the subject, learn his patterns and routines. I already had a sense of how this should be handled. It was just a matter of ironing out the details.

The subject — I'll call him "D.M." — was Caucasian, male. Age 52. Height: six feet. Weight: 225 lbs. Eyes: blue, Hair: brown, straight, hairline receding. Divorced for nearly six years, he had a son, 16, away at a boarding school, and a daughter, 18, in college, both of whom lived with his ex. His drinking had been a major cause of the break-up. His alimony/child support payments were much more than most people pull down in a year, but that was just chump-change to D.M.

He was represented by Kline, Williams, Goldman and Associates. This was a firm with former judges and governors and senators on the letterhead and current judges and governors and senators among their clients. D.M. could afford them, had been their client a long time, and knew some of those past and current judges, governors and senators personally. He'd gotten out from under previous DWI incidents with a combination of sharp lawyering and simple bribery.

D.M.'s company was not far from the top of the Fortune 500, and awash in tax-payers' money for the development of a new fighter plane. I guess the old ones didn't kill fast enough. The project was currently $100 million over budget.

Guys like D.M. never do time.

He had a substantial life insurance policy; his children were the beneficiaries. Since the divorce, he'd sold the family palace and now lived in a luxury townhouse in a nest of luxury townhouses called Kingsmoor Armes.

Yeah.

"Armes." With an "e" in it.

His townhouse had two floors, kitchen, dining room and sunken living room on the first floor. Bedroom, study and master bath on the second floor.

D.M. was a whiskey drinker and judging from the dead soldiers in his garbage, it didn't seem as though recent events had nudged him toward sobriety at all. At least he drank the good stuff. Single malt, lovingly crafted in the Highlands.

His Mercedes had been totaled in the accident. That left him with just a Lincoln and a BMW. I wondered if he would drive even though his license had been suspended. It didn't surprise me to discover that he did.

I had to arrange a few things, but it was all relatively easy.

The security where he lived was an expensive joke. There are only two security devices that matter. The first and best is a large, loud, well-trained dog. You can't scare a dog, you can't fool a dog and you can't bribe a dog. You can kill a dog, of course, but that's not so easy to do, either.

The other security device to respect is a gun if it's a .38 caliber or heavier and if it's in the hand of a person who's ready, willing and able to use it effectively. That narrows it down considerably. A lot people would be better off *throwing* the damned gun.

Alarm systems and security services are generally a grand waste of money. They might make you *feel* safer. But so might hiding under the covers.

I let myself in and found the subject alone in his study. I used a stun gun to temporarily disable him, and then taped him up, careful to tape over his clothing to avoid leaving any trace on his body, though it probably wouldn't matter.

I then explained to him who I was and why I was there. In a strange way, he seemed almost to have been expecting me. Maybe his conscience was bothering him and he knew he had it coming. Maybe he was a fundamentally decent human being, as are most people. Maybe he was also an inveterate fuck-up — as are most people.

Or maybe he was a psychopath who was incapable of feeling empathy, or remorse, didn't give a fuck about the little ants he casually stepped on, and he was just trying to play me.

But I don't play that easy.

Not anymore.

He could have quit drinking, but he didn't. He could have quit drinking and driving, but he didn't. He could have pled guilty, but he didn't. He could have voluntarily made some arrangement to care for the family of the man he'd killed, but he didn't. Now the Piper was due a staggering sum, but he, himself, had called the tune again and again.

I was the Piper's collection agent.

Expecting me or not, as soon as he was able to talk, he tried to cop a plea, as I suspected he would. He offered me money. A lot of money. A *whole* lot. He offered me "anything." Name my own price, he said.

Too bad.

He could've used that money to take care of the people he'd hurt, picked up the medical bills, at the very least. Lots of things he might have done to make whatever amends he could make. Now it was too late. All that money in his wallet, all that money in his safe, all that money stashed in overseas accounts where he wouldn't have to pay taxes on it. And it was as good to him now as toilet paper.

It was tragic.

And I told him so.

I force-fed him his favorite brand of whiskey until he passed out. Then I got some more into his stomach with a tube. Not too much. I had calculated how much to use, given his bodyweight.

I wrestled him outside, put him in his Lincoln and drove out to the spot I'd selected. It was a hairpin curve at the bottom of a hill, overlooking a steep escarpment. It was picketed by rickety guardrails, about as adequate to the task as were elderly bank guards. It was a dangerous spot even for a driver who was cold sober.

I pulled him over behind the wheel, left a whiskey bottle in the front seat with him, steered the car toward the drop, and bailed out just before it went over. If he survived the combination of alcohol poisoning and the crash it would be the most impressive act of god since Charlton Heston parted the Red Sea. That kind of miracle doesn't come cheap.

I knew that wasn't going to happen.

I limped up the road — I'd cracked my damn knee on the pavement vaulting from the Lincoln — to the place I'd left a "borrowed" motorcycle and rode it to where I'd left my rental car.

Then I went home and put ice on my knee.

-IV-

She was sitting on the porch, the bright sun making her skin almost glow. She opened her eyes when she heard the floorboards creak faintly under my feet. I pulled up a chair and sat down beside her.

"It's done," I told her.

12

At that moment, she seemed to become almost weightless. I had the feeling my announcement had cut her tether and I was about to watch her leave her body and float away. She was relieved the way a dying person is relieved to know that everything is squared away and they're free to go.

"Thank you, " she said.

"You're welcome," I said. "Now there's just the matter of my fee."

"Of course. I have the insurance money. Just tell me how much you want and how you'd like me to...."

"What I want," I said, "is an invitation."

"I beg your pardon?"

"An invitation. From you, personally. I want to sit beside you at your daughter's high school graduation."

"What?"

"I've never been to one. I'd like to see what it's like. That's my fee. You *did* agree to pay me whatever I asked. That's what I'm asking."

She looked completely bewildered. And irritated. I was pulling in her tether.

"I don't believe you're the kind of person who breaks their word, " I said. "Am I wrong?"

"No," she replied icily after a long pause. "No, you're not."

"I didn't think so."

I was wrong about her having cried all the tears she could cry.

Maybe it would have been kinder to take the money.

Adam Adrian Crown

When the moon is in the seventh house
And Jupiter aligns with Mars
Then Peace will guide the planets
And Love will steer the stars.

("Aquarius," From the American Tribal
Love-Rock musical, "Hair")

CHAPTER TWO:
EL PASO SQUEEZE

They say you never forget your first time. I know that's
true for me. The first time, I was just a kid, not quite eighteen.
It happened like this.

It was 1968.

Hell of a year, 1968.

The whole world had its bowels in an uproar. The war in
Vietnam was in full swing, with the Tet offensive launched by
the North Vietnamese in January. We wouldn't find out about
it for a while, but in March, American soldiers under a
Lieutenant William Calley, murdered around five hundred
innocent people, including elderly, women, children and
infants, at a place called My Lai.

It was the year that women's libbers engaged in "symbolic
bra-burning" to protest the Miss America Beauty contest. At
the summer Olympics in Mexico City, two African-American
medalists raised their fists in the Black Power salute during
the playing of the "Star-Spangled Banner" at their award
ceremony. It was the year that civil rights leader Rev. Martin
Luther King was murdered in Memphis; and presidential
candidate Robert F. Kennedy was killed in California.

To most, if not all, of this I was completely ignorant. I was off doing my own thing, as a minor rock-and-roll hero, living every teen-age lad's fantasy life.

I'd quit high school at 15. It was a pointless waste of time for me and I think they were just as glad to be rid of me since no one seemed to notice I was gone. My parents were oblivious. So with just my Gibson guitar, my instinct for survival and a great set of fake ID's for which I'd paid a bundle, I hit the road, Jack, and don't you come back no more, no more.

Before you could say Jumpin' Jack Flash ten times fast, I was living la dolce vita, getting my money for nothing and my chicks for free. During the day, I was a martial arts gypsy working out at different dojos – karate, ju jitsu, aikido, tai kwon do, moo goo gai pan, you name it.

At night, I played rock 'n' roll and made an obscene amount of money doing it, too.

Sometimes, I pulled down more in one night than my old man made in a week as a pick-and-shovel jockey. I had a little apartment that was a palace compared to the places I'd grown up in. I had a '57 Chrysler convertible, with fins the envy of your average Great White shark. I had cool clothes. And let's not forget the part about chicks for free.

Thanks to my part-time room-mate, Stede, I had access to a steady supply of grass, too, though frankly, I always preferred hooch to hash. Chacon a son gout, daddy-o. So it was a sex, drugs and rock 'n' roll merry-go-round, and you might think I'd have been content.

And indeed, for a time I was.

But lately, I had fallen into a deep existential funk. It was largely due to a lingering spiritual hangover, the sour taste in my soul left by the Democratic National Convention.

I had grown up in and around Chicago and knew it to be a corrupt and brutal place. But the city had out-done itself on this one.

That August, ten thousand political demonstrators — most in their teens and early twenties — came to the Windy City to protest the war in Vietnam and to voice support for Eugene McCarthy, an out-spoken critic of the war, in his bid for the Democratic Party's presidential nomination. Some people then — and some even now — refer to these protesters as "hippies," or "yippies" or far less charitable terms.

But that's not true at all.

A hippy was a drop-out, someone who disdained social and political conventions, trying to resolve inner conflicts and attain spiritual peace, usually with the help of consciousness-altering drugs. Drop out, tune in, turn on.

These demonstrators weren't drop-outs; they were more like push-ins. They were idealistic activists who were deeply concerned about the future of their country, and had the courage to take to the streets to change the world into what they thought it should be instead of what it was. They wanted to end the war, make the government more representative of and responsive to the people, ensure justice for the powerless and disenfranchised.

They were the best of their generation, my generation.

I wish I could say I had been one of them.

But I only went to Grant Park on that sultry August night to get laid.

I had met a girl named Heather who was a couple of years older than I, and who was deeply involved in the peace movement. I feigned political interest only for its aphrodisiac effects.

I didn't know a thing about the issues. But I did know that when cops show up by the busload, backed up by the National Guard, and they put on their gas masks and take off their badges and their name tags, then nothing good was going to happen after that.

Truth is, once the cops charged into Grant Park, it was such complete chaos that I only have blurry impressions of what happened — extra blurry because of the tear gas. Just a few mental snapshots. I do recall one guy, one of the demonstrators, to whom I took an immediate disliking. He had longish, scraggly hair and wore an OD green army jacket and was talking a lot of incendiary bullshit. Why he was aching for a confrontation, I didn't know, considering that the tactical odds were clearly in favor of the Pigs — derogatory slang word for "police" that they more than earned on that day. In any case, there was something wrong about this guy and I wanted to be as far away from him as possible. A short time later, it was this very guy who brought down the American flag that flew near the fountain, giving the cops the flimsy pretext they needed to attack.

I remember that just before the police moved in on us, someone nearby said, "Come on, this is a peaceful demonstration. They can't just attack us for no reason..."

File that under "famous last words." Right after Custer's shout-out to his men at The Greasy Grass: "Hurrah, Boys! Now we've got 'em!"

The cops came raging in, swinging their riot clubs wildly, indiscriminately.

They beat people who tried to protect themselves by covering their heads with their arms; they beat people who didn't try to protect themselves. They beat people who put their hands up. They beat people who lay down on the ground in submission.

I saw them beat a guy in a wheelchair.

I saw them beat a clean-cut young veteran who was proudly wearing his medals at the time.

I saw them beat a girl who looked so pregnant she might've given birth any minute.

They went after anybody with a camera, too, smashing the cameras, pulling out the film to expose it. No evidence, see. That kind of back-fired on them. Bad idea to piss off the press. Back when we *had* a press.

There were a bunch of med students there, not as part of the demonstration, but as volunteers who had pledged to render first aid to anyone — protester or policeman — who needed it, should there arise a need. They wore whites so that they could be easily identified.

That turned out to be a big mistake.

The cops went after the medics in particular. I saw three cops beating one medic who was curled into a tight fetal ball on the damp grass near the fountain. Beat him long after he lay limp as a pile of old rags.

I stood in the middle of it all as if I were invisible, at the center of the storm, watching the devastating winds swirl around me. I was too stunned to move, to think, even. Some part of me couldn't believe what I was seeing, didn't want to believe it.

Then two burly cops ran past me, almost knocking me over. They were chasing a young girl. One of them caught her by the hair and she fell to her knees. They dragged her by her hair over to some bushes and started swinging their clubs. The sound of that first stroke hitting her head was like the sound of a hammer hitting a side of beef.

I saw one of those cops reach way up high to cock another swing, and the next thing I saw was somebody's foot connect with the cop's crotch from behind. The cop let out a grunt and forgot all about swinging his club.

His buddy turned and looked right at me.

Somehow, I had lost my invisibility.

Somehow, it had been my foot.

The second cop came at me fast and hard. I ducked away from a couple of swings and fired a few kicks in return, going for the knees and the nuts, but I don't know if I connected with much. I think it surprised hell out of him, though. No doubt, he'd been expecting an All-Pacifist Revue. In a moment of slapstick counter-point, the second cop tripped over his still-prostrate pal and fell on his ass, the two of them becoming a flailing, cursing amoeba of cop. I grabbed the girl by the arm and we hit the thorny bushes, forced our way through to the other side, putting those bushes between us and the end of the world.

Thorns tore some nasty gashes in my bare arms, but those scratches added up to nothing compared to what people were getting back on the other side.

I pushed my companion down to the ground and started crawling along that hedge, pulling her with me, staying low to avoid being spotted. I don't know why, but I headed north and east, toward the lake.

I don't know how long it took.

I can remember hearing the screams and shouts from all over the park as the assault continued. I tried to focus. Getting us out of there was everything. I was operating on instinct.

Then I remember suddenly stumbling out onto Lake Shore Drive, half-dragging, half-carrying the wounded girl — and I almost got run over by a big yellow taxi. The driver was a short, fat black guy with the remains of a short, fat stogie dozing unlit in the corner of his mouth and a blue Cubs baseball cap on his head.

I can imagine how we must have looked to him. We were dirty and disheveled, eyes red and swollen from the gas, the groaning girl's face streaked with blood, her honey-blonde hair matted with it.

"What the fuck?" the cabbie growled, pretty much summing up my own feelings, too.

"Got to get her to a hospital, man," I told him. "She's hurt." You say stupid shit at times like that.

"No shit," the cabbie said. He got out and helped me put her gently into the back seat.

"Get in, son," he said to me.

"I'm okay."

"Boollshit."

Apparently some of the blood was mine. I hadn't been quite as clever at evading the policeman's swings as I had originally thought. A wave of dizziness hit me then.

I got in.

"What the fuck is going on?"

"I don't know," I told him.

It was the truth.

At Mercy Hospital, they put six stitches into the side of my head and took the girl from the ER right upstairs, to do what, I don't know. I have no idea what her name was; I really don't know what she looked like, either. Sometimes I try to conjure up her face, but it's no use. I just hope she came through it okay. I wonder if she ever wonders about me.

They wanted me to hang around "for observation," but I had just assaulted a cop — with luck, *two* cops — and, not knowing who was on whose side, I decided to split.

Some things seem better in the morning.

This wasn't one of them.

As I said, I had always known that Chicago was a corrupt and brutal place. I had seen cops beat people up for no reason before. But this shit was brutality way off the cop-ometer scale. No rules, no limits. I later learned that the cops would not allow ambulances into the park to pick up injured people,

Even in a war, you let the enemy come out and pick up his wounded.

The message was clear: America had declared war on its children.

Mayor Daley sent out the call for "law and order." The irony of sending out the hue and cry for "law and order" in a city where the mafia got a taste of everything that moved, and crooked politicians and cops on the take were as common as semen stains in a porno theatre, was just the ironic frosting on a bitter cake. I think I actually laughed out loud when I heard that. It was somewhere between a horselaugh and a wail. Sometimes you have to either laugh or cry. And if you start crying, you might not be able to stop.

The real personal kicker was this: I heard it through the grapevine that the sleazy guy who had pulled down the flag was an undercover cop sent in as an agent provocateur. The whole putrid mess was a set-up. I guess that was about that last time that sort of thing ever surprised me.

After that, the entire world seemed to go sour as I fell prey to a chronic migraine soul-ache. I couldn't seem to get the riot out of my head. I'd see people on the street, regular people doing their regular thing, business as usual, and I'd want to grab them and shake them and scream in their faces "Don't you know what happened? Don't you care?"

But I didn't do that.

I guess I didn't want to know the answer.

Or maybe I already knew.

My latest band, The Saints, broke up. Our drummer got drafted and our bass player was talking marriage now that his girlfriend was pregnant, and he was slowly ambling towards the musical gallows that a square job would mean. I tried hard to give a fuck, but couldn't quite manage it. My music seemed suddenly childishly trivial and I just didn't feel like playing silly shit for people to dance to, rockin' and rollin' while Rome was burning.

I also said a fond farewell to my latest lady love, a blonde, beach-bunny dream-girl named Gretchen. Her boyfriend was returning from the Army, as manly a hero as ever a glorified shipping clerk has been, and, suffering from an unexpectedly recurrent fever of fidelity, she was stoking up home-fires, long left untended. It should have wrenched my heart, but it didn't. When she broke up with me, I even laughed a little.

She probably thought I was nuts.

She was right, of course.

By November, it appeared that winter was coming in early and coming on strong, promising a cold more bitter than I could bear. When the wind comes off Lake Michigan, it's like a giant razor blade coming down the street — especially the streets that run perpendicular to the lake. It's not very much buffered by the buildings on the parallel streets either – they just squeeze the breeze into a tighter space so it blasts around the corners and cracks into your face like an icy whip. It can turn your sperm to slush in a heartbeat.

So when Stede suggested, one evening shortly before Thanksgiving, that we go someplace warm and sunny, I found it difficult to think of reasons why not. I was staggering around like a zombie with arthritis and a bad attitude, and I figured a change of scenery would do me no harm. But you know what they say: you can run but you can't hide. Not from yourself, anyway.

I hadn't learned that yet.

Stede already had some contacts in the great Southwest, since he was currently producing, directing and starring in the road show of Easy Rider, smuggling big bags of cannabis up north via connections in Juarez and El Paso.

On Monday we decided to split, on Tuesday we packed our meager belongings into my black ragtop Chrysler (fins like a pair of roving sharks), and lashed his bike to the back. On Wednesday morning before dawn, we were gone.

We drove almost straight through, taking turns at the wheel, scarcely taking time out to piss or choke down crapburgers at a roadside greasy-spoon.

When we hit Alamogordo, New Mexico, the desert ahead of us lay so flat and the air was so clear that I swear we could make out the glow of the lights in El Paso, eighty miles away. The Emerald City.
Just follow the yellow brick interstate.

The newspaper in El Paso featured a little box up in the right-hand corner of the front page. It said something like, "Today is the 2003rd consecutive day that the sun has shone in beautiful El Paso." They prided themselves on bonny weather. Tourism, you know.

I bought that newspaper in an all-night drugstore at about 4:30 a.m., just as we hit the city limits.

Just as it started to snow.

SNOW!

What the *fuck*?

They hadn't seen snow in El Paso in 47 years. The day we arrive, they get six inches. I didn't know for sure whether to laugh or cry, but I'm pretty sure I said "fuck" a lot, even for someone speaking Chicago-ese.

The El Pasonians went completely goofy over it.

Snowball fights erupted on every street-corner, involving some of the most unlikely combatants you've ever seen. And, of course, they had no idea how to drive on the stuff, so Stede and I spent a lot of our first day in paradise leaving people awestruck at the ease with which we got their cars unstuck.

Like: "Who was that masked man?" "I don't know. And I wanted to thank him..."

By the next morning the snow was all gone, except as a topic of conversation. But the entire episode struck me as an omen stirred up by some malevolent deity seriously on my ass. I could practically hear him rubbing his palms together with glee, chuckling out, "You ain't seen *nothin'* yet, muthah-fuckah!"

Stede's main connection in El Paso was a minister's daughter by the name of Amy.

She was possibly the plainest and the nicest girl I ever met, bright, gentle, and utterly without guile. She could have been the flower power poster child. When we first met, she beamed at me so sweetly that I assumed she thought I was someone else. But I was wrong. It was just her way. It was as if when she looked at me she could see a better person than I, myself, ever saw in the mirror, and it made me a bit uneasy. Besides that, she hugged me and I'm not a big hugger. It was a real hug, too, not one of those phony hippie-handshake hugs. I recall how, at that moment, the warmth of her seemed to seep into me, the way a hot mug of coffee held in your frost-nipped fingers warms you up all over just by holding it. The pressure of her breasts against me seemed incongruous with her little girl innocence. It put a huge knot in my throat, and restless stirrings elsewhere.

Amy's tragic flaw was that she believed that people were basically good, saw virtues in people that they might not actually possess and I knew right away, in my gut, that as a result of that, something terrible was bound to happen to her.

In the meantime, we became friends.

She introduced me to several young women, determined to help me find the "right" one so I could be really happy. It was a notion typical of her conception of the world and I could no more point out the holes in the idea than I could kick a puppy. So I suffered a series of hilariously disastrous blind dates with "nice" girls for her sake.

When Stede was away, making a delivery without her, I was her confidante, and she mine, on long walks through the rugged desert. I told her things I'd never told anyone, absolutely certain that if she could not understand them, at least she would accept them without judgment, and keep them in complete secrecy.

Now, smoking dope wasn't my thing.

The fact that Amy was a marijuana cheerleader did nothing to tarnish her character in my estimation.

It was against the law, but it wasn't *my* law.

It was William Randolph Hearst's law.

And it had nothing to do with protecting people from a dangerous drug — which marijuana isn't — or even a Puritanical prohibition against people getting high. Cannabis is one of the most beneficial plants on earth. It can be — and was — used in making dozens of medicinals and other products. It's hardy, grows anywhere, grows fast, and is particularly good for making paper. But when you're a rich prick of the Hearst variety, you don't care how beneficial it is; you just concern yourself with the old bottom line. And when you own not only the newspapers, but the mills that make the paper and the trees that supply the pulp, you don't want a bunch of cannabis farmers upsetting your financial apple cart, do you? So you coin the term "marijuana" in your newspapers

to play on people's anti-hispanic bigotry. Then you get a close
pal appointed the first "drug czar" and he starts warning
White folks that marijuana-crazed, jazz-playin' negras were
going to take advantage of their marijuana-crazed jazz-listenin'
daughters.

Before you know it, it's "Reefer Madness" time.

I had to hand it to him; it was a great scam.

It had already come to my attention that what's legal and
what's right are only rarely the same thing, so the illegality of
Amy's using weed didn't bother me. I think it's fine to relax
with a joint now and then just to take the edge off, if that's
your taste. But what discontented me was that she seemed,
perhaps naturally given her background, to be ascribing almost
religious dimensions to the practice, and I just didn't believe
in Saint Mary Jane. I don't think you can hitch a ride to
enlightenment; I believe you have to walk.

Maybe it was because of her semi-religious attitude toward
pot-smoking, or maybe it was because I was beginning to have
some feelings about Amy that weren't exactly fraternal. But I
started spending less and less time around her and Stede, and
more and more of my time south of the border, in Juarez.

Mexico was the perfect place for me. Completely and
openly corrupt. No more crooked than Chicago, but a whole
lot less hypocritical. It was a place where you could get
anything you wanted, provided you could pay the price, a
place where life was cheap, dope was plentiful, and the police
were so easy to bribe they might as well have had a rate sheet
pinned to their chest. My family was dirt poor, but the poverty
in Mexico made it seem like I'd led a life of privilege. It was
so crushing that a few American dollars went a long way, and
most people would go an even longer way to get yours. One
long way or another.

Hell is a place made for the wicked, according to Don Juan,
and the wicked are perfectly comfortable there. So I felt right
at home.

Thanks to an American Indian grandfather (on my father's side) I'm pretty dark. Nearly black hair, dark brown eyes. Most people guess Italian or Spanish. And thanks to the heterogeneity of my old south side neighborhood, I had picked up a repertoire of handy Spanish vulgarities along with a few simple common phrases.

Armed with these and my Gibson ES150 — double cut-away, blonde full body — I was able to start sitting in with some of the innumerable border-town bands. I adopted the local styles, from fancy-stitched high-heeled cowboy boots (good place to hide a straight razor) to straw fedora, and sunglasses, usually worn even at night. Very shortly, it would have been hard for your average gringita to pick me out as American.

I couldn't resist having a little fun with that.

On one occasion Uno Boob Gringo Touristo, straight from central casting, and reading from his Berlitz Guide to Indecipherable Spanish, stopped me on the street and asked me where a particular restaurant was, in the process, doing to the Spanish tongue what the Allies had done to Dresden. "Dandy Astair Uh Buoyant Restrain," he said.

I rattled off directions in Español and I could tell by his vacuous stare that he hadn't caught a bit of it. Didn't think he would.

He asked me to repeat it, poor favor.

So I said, "If you'd like to sample some excellent local cuisine, I'd recommend the El Presidente, two blocks down and make a left. Very reasonable prices, too."

"Well, grassy ass," El Touristo stuttered in awe. "Your English is VERY good."

"Gracias, Señor," I replied, grinning bashfully. Oh, Pancho! Oh Cisco!

He offered me a five.

Fuck it. I took it.

I made the acquaintance of a certain Antonio Garcia, who played the t-sax pretty well, which means that by local standards, he was John Fucking Coltrane. Tony was a shady character who had several dozen even shadier relatives, by which means he was privy to everything that was going on anywhere near Juarez or El Paso. He could lay his hands on anything from women with low morals to guys with high explosives, and on damn short notice, too.

I started playing gigs with Tony's band, Los Musteños. His daughter, Estrella was the singer and star and she could make any scene from a croon to a wail. She and I sang a smoldering duet of "Besame Mucho" that never failed to bring down the house. It's a great song and easy to riff away on guitar.

And the lyrics are so good they hurt:

> *Bésame, bésame mucho*
> *Como si fuera esta noche*
> *La última vez*
>
> *Bésame, bésame mucho*
> *Que tengo miedo a perderte*
> *Perderte después...*
>
> *Quiero tenerte muy cerca*
> *Mirarme en tus ojos*
> *Verte junto a mi*
>
> *Piensa que tal vez mañana*
> *Yo ya estaré lejos*
> *Muy lejos de ti*

Beautiful song. The lyrics don't translate well, though. For example, "besame mucho" literally means "kiss me a lot," or "kiss me many times." But what it actually means is more like "kiss me passionately." Kiss me as if for the last time, as if this were our last night together. Kiss me with all the desperate hunger of our first kiss, one more time, because I somehow know this *is* our last time together. So I want to hold you close, see myself reflected in your eyes once more. Because tomorrow may find us far apart. Forever.

Yeah, man. I really dig that tune.

It came to pass that I did Tony a little favor, and he wasn't one to let it go with just paying me my cut; he had to take me out and show me a good time, on him. It hadn't been that big a deal, really. Several soldiers stationed at Fort Bliss had done some business with him, only now they'd decided they weren't going to pay the freight. I covered his back while he persuaded one of them — the biggest and loudest one — to reconsider. Immediately thereafter, the others they coughed up their fair share without a peep and that was that. No big deal.

But the way Antonio acted, you'd think I'd saved his life in the war.

He insisted on taking me to one of his favorite places and providing me with an experience he was certain I wouldn't soon forget — and in a way, he was right. His favorite playpen turned out to be a place that was called — like about a hundred other places — "Casa del Gato."

Yeah, real subtle.

And like about a hundred other places, it featured beaded curtains, Aztec murals and re-cycled beer, served to bleary patrons hunched around tables the size of a poker chip, while a variety of "dancers" stripped to the buff onstage, and, accompanied by an out-of-tune combo, appeared to fuck Claude Rains. But this particular dive, Antonio assured me, had something the others didn't have.

This one had Rosa.

Apparently, Rosa was reputed to be the most talented and enthusiastic prostitute in Juarez, no small achievement considering sheer number of competitors. She was both local hero and legend, and that should tell you something.

Tony left me at a corner table with a Carta Blanca and went off to "arrange things."

Leaning my chair back against the wall, I sipped the beer from the bottle — you could start a whole new civilization from the stuff on the grimy glasses — and watched the show. For me, the show wasn't so much the strippers as the audience.

The band was lurching into a greasy rendition of "Harlem Nocturne," with a breathy tenor sax whispering over the less important parts of the melody, when I saw her. She was standing at the top of the stairs, head held high, surveying the scene like Cleopatra, queen of her domain.

She had skin the color and texture of melted chocolate ice cream. Her eyes were beckoning bottomless pits of black fire. She had a strong, not quite aquiline nose, and high proud cheekbones that gave her a lean and hungry look. Her crown was a loose mane of shimmering blue-black hair that cascaded like an ebony waterfall to the backs of her knees.

The sparkling blue gown she wore clung to her like skin, enhancing every ripple and sway of her as she slowly descended the staircase to mingle with mere mortals, to do her noblesse oblige. Her taut breasts jutted out like the figurehead at the prow of a Yankee clipper, nipples protesting against the constraints of fabric. Her gait was unhurried, a soft, suggestive samba.

At that moment neither fire, rain, or wild monkeys could have forced me to avert my eyes. Like every other man in the room, I was completely captivated by the primal force of her presence. The naked dancers commanded as much of our attention now as Salvation Army sergeants beating tambourines for temperance. She was all that existed in the room, in the world, in any world, and I knew instinctively that this could only be Rosa.

My heart seemed to have sunk to my loins and a feverish pulse pounded there, spreading waves of heat through me like ripples on a pond. I had no other thought — if it could be called a "thought" — but to consume her and be consumed by her.

Halfway down the stairs she paused and her regal gaze swept toward me until her eyes met mine, and she was peering directly into my soul. It was a look that knew me better than I knew myself. I felt naked, vulnerable, with no place to hide, no way to get there, and no will to try.

Then she smiled.

Smiled right at me.

And spat a sluice of tobacco over the banister through the remains of black-stained teeth.

Somewhere along the way, Antonio had rejoined me, though I had been too mesmerized to notice. Now, as if reading my mind, he leaned in close to my ear and whispered with warm beer-breath, "Hey amigo. You don't have to *kiss* her."

It was true. In fact, I didn't.

The episode brought home the truth of an old adage: Never look a gift whore in the mouth.

One night, after the club was closed, Estrella and I were sitting on the corner of the stage unwinding with a bottle of tequila. I strummed, riffing off of Jose Feliciano's version of "Light My Fire." She crooned along throwing in some Spanish scat, and I hummed a little harmony and counterpoint, too. She wasn't just singing with me, she was singing *to* me. Her melody was an invitation, and I sang an acceptance. I often wish we'd recorded that little jam session. I still hear parts of it in my better dreams.

She led me to a spot behind the empty club. There under the full moon, she pressed my back against the rough, cold bricks, and wrapped her arms around my neck, and her legs around my waist. I cradled her hips in my arms to keep her from falling. Her kisses were ravenous and her mouth tasted of salt and lime. She pounded against me so hard, I could barely remain standing, but I did so for long enough. She called me "querido" in a soft, soft whisper right into my ear, and she trembled hard, breathing in short, sharp gasps, before falling limp against my shoulder. A breeze tickled across my thighs, wet with sweat and juices, and our mixed scents wafted up into my nostrils like the salty smell of the sea. My butt smarted where it had scraped against the brick. Reluctantly, I at last let her slip away until her feet found the asphalt. We leaned against that wall together a long, long time, feeling the cool night breeze, watching the moon. Riding the wave. Silent.

A couple of days later, at a rehearsal, it was Antonio who mentioned just in passing, something about a real bad scene involving a biker gang and a dope deal double-cross and a "priest's daughter."

The bottom lurched out of my stomach.

I set a new record for ignoring speed limits. When I arrived at the church I knew *something* was wrong because there was no one around and there was ALWAYS someone around. Not sure what else to do, I approached the nearest neighbors and made inquiries. It took me a couple of tries to find someone at home, and a couple more to find someone at home who knew anything. Finally, I learned that Amy had been in some kind of "accident."

Accident, my ass.

According to Stede, this is what happened:

He and Amy are waiting at a secluded spot to meet a biker named Preacher, a member of the Aryan Knights gang. Shaved head. Swastika tattoo on the back of it. Stede had done business with him a number of time before. Preacher is late and Stede is just about ready to bag it when five bikers come roaring up, and stop in a circle surrounding Stede's bike. Stede had bumped into these guys at before at the Harley shop.

"Hey, how's it goin', Preacher?" Stede waves.

Preacher grabs a backpack from his bike, walks slowly over, tosses it to Stede.

"How they hangin', Kid?" Preacher said.

One biker, known as Bad Larry, hangs back with his ride. Huge guy. Short hair; full red beard. The others flank out, surrounding Stede and Amy. A baby-faced guy called Duce

*hovers very close to Amy. Weasel, scrawny as the name
implies, with an equally scrawny mustache and thinning
straggly hair, takes a place beside Stede and mimics Stede's
arms-folded stance. Stitch saunters over, walks around Stede's
bike, looking it over. Short and stocky with a scar on the right
side of his face, running from his temple, down along his jaw
to the point of his chin.*

*"Nice wheels," says Stitch. "I mean, you know, for a
pussy."*

*Stede hands Preacher an envelope full of cash. Preacher
snorts, shaking his head, skins the cash, tosses the envelope
over his shoulder.*

"That's fuckin' littering, man," says Bad Larry.

"Call a fuckin' cop," says Preacher.

Duce strokes Amy's hair with a finger.

"Who's this?" he asks, breathing on her ear.

"That's my girl," says Stede.

"Yeah?" says Duce like he doesn't quite believe it.

*"Hi," Amy says in her let's-all-be-friends way. "I'm Amy."
Amy offers a hand to shake. Duce ignores it.*

*"Got to tell you, kid," says Preacher, "that's REALLY
good shit this time. Like extra good. I oughta charge you more.
Seriously."*

"We had a deal, man..." says Stede.

Preacher shrugs. "I'm just sayin'."

Stede shrugs back. "That's all I've got, brother," he says.

*"Hey," says Duce, " if he don't got more cash, maybe he
can throw in somethin' else. Like barter, you know?"*

*Suddenly, a fist slams into Stede's stomach. He never saw
it coming and he's not sure who hit him. Maybe Stitch. He
collapses to his knees retching for breath. Behind him, Duce
tears Amy's shirt away from her.*

"No! Don't!" Amy protests.

*Bad Larry leaves his post by the bikes, to join in the fun.
He casually kicks Stede in the head as he passes by him. And
Stede's got one foot in La-La Land after that. But Bad Larry*

stands over Stede, puts a boot on his neck, just in case he gets any ideas. The other bikers pin Amy down. She struggles desperately to escape, but they are too many, too big and too strong. They laugh at her efforts. Preacher and Duce pull off her jeans and tear away her panties. She kicks wildly at them. Duce grabs one of her legs.

"No! Oh, God! No!" she whimpers "Please! Please don't! Please don't!"

But begging throws gasoline on their fire.

They take her down. Duce grabs her arms, holds them over her head. Stitch and Weasel each grab a leg and spread her open. Then Preacher rapes her. Amy screams. Preacher gives her a mean punch in the face that breaks her cheekbone.

"Shut the fuck up, Cunt," he tells her. And punches her again, this time knocking out a tooth. He finishes using her, zips up and then takes Duce's place. They all rotate around in the line-up, each taking a turn on top of her.

By the time Weasel finishes grunting over her, her naked body jolting with every thrust, Amy lies limp, only semi-conscious, one eye swollen shut, mouth and nose bloody. After a moment he gets off of her.

"Hey, Larry," somebody says. "You want a piece of this?"

Bad Larry gives Stede another kick that almost knocks him all the way out. And one in the ribs for good measure. "Flip her over," Bad Larry says.

Stede hears her screaming, but it sounds far away.

Stede must have passed out. Didn't know for how long. Next thing he knows, it's raining and someone is saying, "Hey, kid, are you ok? Speak to me, kid, speak to me…" And there's laughter.

It's Preacher. He's standing over Stede pissing on his face.

Amy is unconscious, lies sprawled out awkwardly, like a broken doll. Stitch is standing over her, zipping up his jeans. He hawks up something foul and spits it on her. Weasel comes over and unzips, too. Preacher gives him a shot in the arm.

34

"Hey! Go find your own," Preacher corrects him. "Rude mother-fucker."

Weasel waddles over to Amy and urinates on her. "Ahhhh... We got any more beer?" He flicks the butt of his cigarette onto her.

It's the last thing Stede remembers.

"You took her WITH you?" I asked, incredulous that Stede could be so stupid. "To make a dope deal with an outlaw biker? You took her with you? What the fuck?"

Stede didn't say anything. Not much he could have said.

"Did you I.D. these mother-fuckers to the cops?" I asked him.

"Are you crazy?" he hissed through his wired-shut jaw. "They'll come back and kill us, man."

"If you don't, they'll fuckin' walk," I told him. "And you know it."

"They'll *kill* us, man."

I went to look in on Amy.

Seeing Stede in his hospital room in a body cast, with his jaw wired up was bad enough. But when I saw that poor, little girl lying there... Her face was so swollen and bruised you couldn't even recognize her. She had all kinds of tubes hooked up to her, an IV, a catheter. Head all bandaged up, with some kind of metal contraption around it. Seeing her like that, this sweet young girl, who never harmed anybody, never even spoke a bad word about anybody... seeing her so abused and so degraded, I felt something happen inside me.

It was as if a cold, dark shadow crept across my heart like an eclipse. It completely blocked out whatever light there was in me, and all that was left was a kind of black, seething rage, like rattlesnakes twisting around in my gut. It was a rage bone-hard and alligator-mean, and utterly without mercy. The "me" I knew disappeared. Only the rage remained.

I had never felt anything quite like that before.

I didn't know it then, but it wouldn't be the last time.

From that moment on, I was like a robot. I couldn't feel anything, couldn't feel the usual connection with my own body. It was almost like watching myself on T.V. Yet, paradoxically, I experienced a sense of clarity as acute as a pinpoint, as if my senses were all heightened fueled by crystalline fury.

A shrink once told me that's called "dissociation."

Whatever it's called, there was only one thing on my mind now. And I think you know what it was.

Visiting hours were limited and Amy was doped up enough to be unresponsive anyway. I felt awkward being there with the Reverend and family members, though his wife hugged me real hard and thanked me for coming. Her eyes were red and raw from tears; her body trembled. They ushered us all out at the end of the appointed time, and I parted company with the Rev and family, with them asking me to pray for their daughter.

I don't pray.

But I didn't tell them that.

I went out, got some fresh air. Waited until everyone else left. Then I went back and slipped into her room. I sat in a chair by Amy's bed, watching her sleep until the night nurse came in.

"I'm sorry, Sir, visiting hours are over, you'll have to go now."

"Ten minutes?" I asked her.

"Sir, I'm sorry, I can't..."

"Five minutes," I begged her. "C'mon, just five minutes. Then I'm gone. Please."

I took her hand and palmed a C-note into it. "Please," I said again.

"Five minutes" she said. "Don't get me in trouble."

"Five minutes," I agreed.

The nurse left and I sat back down beside Amy.

"I can't stay long," I whispered to her as if she could hear me. I remembered her favorite song and I started singing to her, real soft, the way you'd sing a lullabye:

Hey Jude, don't make it bad
Take a sad song and make it better
Remember to let her into your heart
Then you can start to make it better...

I was gone before the night nurse came back.

It was, in a demented sort of way, merciful that the first punch to the face had rendered Amy only semiconscious, and she had not been fully aware of the worst of what happened after that.

Unfortunately, it also meant that she made a lousy prosecution witness because she was unable to describe in precise and convincing detail who had done what to her and when. Any of the assailants could claim he only watched. Or that none of them had attacked her and it had been her boyfriend who had done it. Something could be gleaned by any salvaged semen samples, if they'd salvaged any, but unless someone had a rare blood type, it wasn't exactly incontrovertible evidence. Nowadays, of course, DNA testing would slam the green door on the guilty parties, but in 1968 DNA testing was just science fiction.

Besides that, the other dozen or so members of the Aryan Knights would give their pals an alibi, putting them somewhere else at the time of the assault. Probably having a wholesome glass of milk while at a Bible study session. So the case against Amy's attackers would rapidly wither on the prosecutorial vine, even if Stede did decide to finger them. Which he wasn't about to do. I suppose I couldn't blame him. Unfortunately, the same law that's intended to protect the innocent, sometimes also protects the guilty.

In short, I already knew that these scumbags were going to walk.

And I already knew what I was going to do about it.

Just had to fill in the details.

Stede felt so guilty that he'd gotten Amy involved in the first place, and then that he'd been unable to protect her, that it was easy to convince him that my plan was actually *his* plan, and that I was just backing *him* up instead of the other way around. But that was bullshit. I was going to do this whether Stede was into it or not.

I went to see my man, Tony Garcia. I could hear a baby crying inside when I knocked on his door.

"Hijo de puta," he was muttering as he opened it. He squinted like he was trying to read me from too far away.

"Lo siento mucho to bug you, amigo," I said.

"Manito? Que pasa, man?"

"I need a favor," I said.

Less than an hour later, we were at a café, sitting in a booth under the picture window sipping coffee that was like expresso. I like strong coffee.

Tony's got a copy of Downbeat Magazine on the table in front of him. He put the last forkful of cherry pie in his mouth and pushed the plate away.

"You sure you don't want no pie, man? It's goooooood."

"I'm all right."

"You sure you want to do this?" he asked me under his breath. "These guys don't fuck around. If you're not 200 hundred per cent sure…"

"I'm sure," I said.

"I don't like it," he said, wiping his mouth with a napkin. "You need somebody to watch your back."

"I'll be ok."

In a little while, a guy pulled up in a dark green Chevy, parked next to my car. He got out, took a large gymbag out of his trunk. Red, white and blue. Put it in my back seat. Then he came inside.

I got up so he could sit next to the window. I would be leaving first.

He ordered coffee and Tony introduced us. The guy's name was Miguel. He had the scrawny look and furtive air of a coyote, and an acne-ravaged face. Tony slid the magazine over to him, no way you could see what was hidden between the pages.

"You seen this issue?" Tony said.

Miguel folded it and stuck it inside his jacket.

"I gotta get going," I said nodding good-bye to Miguel. I still had to buy a telescope. "Tell Estrella I said hi."

"You better come by and tell her, yourself." Tony said.

As I left, I heard him say to Miguel, "Try this pie, man. It's goooood."

You know the difference between predators and prey?
Predators know the patterns of the prey.

The Aryan Knights had a "clubhouse," a derelict honky-tonk way off the beaten desert path out on Old Route 59. It had once been a gas station, but the new Route 59 had taken an unanticipated swing some miles to the west. The gang had picked up the long-abandoned premises for back taxes, according to the county clerk.

I set up my telescope about a mile and a half away on some low hills to stake the place out. White paint was mostly peeled from the concrete blocks now. To one the side of the building there was a rusty "Sinclair" sign that featured a brontosaurus and advertised "regular" at 29 cents a gallon and "ethyl" at 39.

I kept my eye glued to the lens for several days — it could've been a couple weeks, even. I don't really remember. But it was a long time. Watching and noting their activities in a small notebook, mostly at night. I lived on coffee and Lucky Strikes and the occasional burger, re-supplied at irregular intervals by Stede. He still had his cast on and I knew it was hard as hell for him to drive way around and approach on foot so as not to be spotted by the gang. But, unfair as it might seem, I still held him responsible for what had happened to

Amy, and I was in no mood to show him much sympathy. Or maybe it was because I felt responsible, too. I'd figured out that Amy was getting worked over just about the time Estrella and I were enjoying the night and each other, and I hated that I'd been experiencing so much pleasure while Amy had been experiencing so much pain. I felt that I'd let her down, that somehow I should have known, should have been there. Should have protected her, myself. God damn it.

It was like bird-watching. I quickly learned the comings and goings of the gang. The telescope was easily strong enough that I could identify individual gang members. I picked out Preacher, Stitch, Duce, Weasel and Bad Larry. There were about 10 others whose names I didn't know.

Didn't care.

Didn't matter.

Before long, I knew their habits as well as I knew my own name. Their routine was actually very regular. Not much happened during the day. But most of the gang was there every night, going by a hog count, from about nine PM until what would have been closing time if the joint had ever closed. Because it was a "private club" and not a "public house" normal restrictions didn't apply.

Preacher and company must've been the real nucleus of the gang. They were there every night, and often crashed there. Often there during the day, or part of the day, too. The other gang members were more irregular. They were pretty easy targets. It's funny how predators never imagine that they, too, can be prey.

Crossing the flat, open desert to get to them was out of the question during the daytime. We'd do it at night. Saturday night. When most all of the gang would be there. Only five them had actually assaulted Amy. But the rest had provided her assailants with an alibi, aid and comfort, and wore the same colors, so fuck 'em, As far as I was concerned they were all equally guilty and could all chip in to pay the piper.

Stede and I huddled in our jackets — the desert gets cold fast once the sun goes down — and waited for the din to subside, which it started to do about 1a.m. By 2 a.m. it was relatively quiet.

We went to my car, hidden between hills, and I popped the trunk. I reached in and pulled out that red, white and blue gym bag I'd gotten from Miguel. Inside was a Colt .45 and two extra magazines. I stuck the pistol in my waistband and the extra mags in my jacket pocket. I pulled out a Smith and Wesson .38 police special, handed it to Stede. He stared at it like it was a dead bird. Some extra rounds for that one, too. Then I brought out the two sticks of dynamite.

"Jesus Christ," Stede said through clenched teeth.

I checked the mag of the .45, slammed it back in like a real badass pistolero. You'd think I'd done this a hundred times before.

"What if they see us?" he asked.

"They won't," I said. "We circle around to the north side, and approach from there. No windows on that side. Just that little one, up high. Probably the john. Let's go."

We approached on our bellies. Stede had a hard time of it due to his injuries. The cast was awkward, his jaw hadn't fully heeled, and I knew everything he had must have hurt like an old, unrequited love.

We paused about 25 yards away, just to get set. I could hear the crack of billiard balls, muffled conversation. Cream on the jukebox playing "Born Under a Bad Sign." Clapton cranking up a guitar solo.

"Sounds like they're having a good time," I whispered. "Ready?"

Stede took a moment, then rolled over on his back like a whale going belly up.

"Fuck," he said. I waited for him to finish it. I knew it was painful for him to talk around his broken jaw. "I don't think I can make this scene, man. I'm sorry."

I wasn't sure whether he meant that he was in too much pain to carry out the plan, or that he was having second thoughts about the plan itself. I suspected it was the latter, cloaked in the former — he was doing enough Darvon to manage the pain. Stede's problem was that he was basically a decent guy who just wanted to smoke reefer, listen to music and get laid. Reasonable ambitions for a young man in his circumstances. He was slipping and sliding with his local draft board so he wouldn't have to kill strangers in Vietnam. I think he didn't have it in him to kill *any*one.

"OK. Fuck it," I said. "Wait here," I checked his .38 to be sure it was loaded to the gills, safety off, and handed it back to him. "Don't let anybody shoot me in the back if you can help it," I told him.

"What are you going to do?"

But I was already crawling the last 25 yards to the clubhouse.

There were about a dozen bikes out front, and an old Ford truck with no plates parked around the back. All the windows were open. No screens. I stood up, crept along the wall, peeked in a window.

Inside, the good times were rolling.

Stitch and a couple other guys shooting pool. Preacher, with that unmistakable swastika on the back of his shaved head, was sitting at the bar where some biker chick way past her prime was playing bartender for him. Bad Larry was sitting at table with a bunch of guys and one other woman. He was comically pantomiming fucking, and his admirers roared with laughter.

"No, shit." Bad Larry shouted to be heard over their chuckles and guffaws. "I swear to god she loved it in the ass! I might ask the little bitch to marry me."

At the pool table, Stitch was sucking from a bottle of beer as Weasel broke, sinking nothing. Duce came out from the john, shaking a leg like he'd dribbled down his pants.

I took a couple of breaths like a weight-lifter getting ready for a world record. My zippo started on the first try. I lit the fuse on a stick of dynamite, starting counting to myself, *one-one thousand, two-one thousand…*and tossed it through the window.

Almost.

The damn dynamite hit the fucking window jamb and bounced to the ground at my feet. *Fuck. One thousand, four-one-thousand…*

"What the fuck was that?" I head someone inside say.

"What the fuck was *what?*" somebody else said.

I pounced on that dynamite, reached in through the window and tossed it. As soon as it left my hand I was sprinting like mad for the other side, lighting the fuse on the second stick — or *trying* to light it while running in sand, counting and cursing. I had cut the second fuse a lot shorter than the first one. Shorter even than the one I was born with.

I reached the other side, this time pitched the dynamite right in through the window next to the front door. I figured I had about five seconds to run.

Figured wrong.

No sooner had I turned my back, and heard someone yell "What the f…" but that dynamite went off, and I pitched face first into the dirt, while debris sailed past me. A piece of something cut the back of my head, but I didn't feel it until later. I wasn't feeling much of anything. The CR-BOOM-CR-BOOM of it made my ears ring.

It's amazing what a little dynamite can do.

There wasn't a lot left of the clubhouse. Walls blown out, roof mostly collapsed. Flames dancing inside. Bikes knocked over like dominoes. I clambered to my feet, digging out the Colt. Tried to clear my ears by opening my mouth as wide as I could, but no dice.

A figure staggered out from the wreckage. It was Duce.

I aimed the .45 and squeezed the trigger but nothing happened. I'd never cocked it. Yeah, a real badass pistolero, that's me.

I cocked the pistol, thumbed the safety off, and fired again. Missed. Wood splinters flew from an exposed stud. Fuck.

Duce turned and looked at me.

I fired twice more, using both hands, this time, and both of those .45 slugs pounded into Duce's chest, knocking him off his feet. One would have been enough.

I entered the smoldering ruins and picked my way through debris and bodies, pistol ready, scanning, searching. I still couldn't hear anything. The smoke made me cough. I turned one guy over and squinted at his face. He wasn't one of the guys who raped Amy, so I dropped him, and continued the search.

I stepped on a guy's leg, lost my balance, fell on my ass, scrambled to my feet. I pulled part of a wall off of him. It was Stitch. He was dazed and confused. I put the muzzle of the gun against Stitch's forehead and pulled the trigger.

I stalked through the ruins, still trying to restore my hearing by working my jaws again. Must've looked like a big fish. Little by little sounds started seeping in. Somewhere a man was grunting and gasping for breath. I followed the sound. Preacher. He was pinned to the remains of a wall impaled on a broken pool cue, but still alive.

I slapped his cheek a little to revive him "Hey, I yelled at him. "HEY!"

With some effort, he focused on me.

"Who the fuck are you?" he spat.

"I'm a friend of the girl you raped, I told him.

"Well, fuck you. And fuck her, too."

"I don't think so," I said, put the muzzle of that .45 between his legs and fired. That got his attention. He howled, and growled. "Fuck you," I said. And put a round between his eyes.

In retrospect, I kind of regret doing that. I should've left him to suffer.

My hearing seemed okay now. Could hear flames crackle. Something glass fell and broke. A roof timber creaking. The place was filling up with smoke and it made me cough some more. Then I heard another cough. From behind the bar, came a woman's voice, weak and trembling.

"Help me…" it said.

I made my way to the bar, past the capsized pool table.

She was lying on her back behind the bar. Hefty build. Short hair. Freckles. Wearing the gang's colors. One leg under her, knee bent at a completely alien angle.

I hoisted her up and she cried out, but I got a grip under her armpits and started dragging her toward fresh air. I noticed blood leaking out of one of her ears. I was concentrating on her and almost missed the grunt Bad Larry made as he swung the remains of a 2x4 stud at my head. Not sure I actually heard it as much as sensed it. I ducked down and the blow sailed past me with skull-crushing force. I dropped the woman on her butt and she screamed.

Then Bad Larry was behind me and I could appreciate how big he really was. And strong, too. He got that 2x4 around my neck and pulled.

Not good.

I back-pedaled as hard as I could, we bounced of a wall, two walls, like a pinball wizard, went spinning and sprawling into the dirt outside the club. I heard the muffled crunch as I rolled over a bunch of broken glass. Blown out window maybe. Before I could get to my feet, Bad Larry was on top of me, pressing that broken stud down against my throat. With his full beard and the whiskers of his mustache falling over his mouth, hiding his upper lip, and his eyes bulging, he looked ridiculously like a monstrous beaver. That's a pretty odd thought to have when somebody's trying to kill you, I guess. But again, I felt very distant from myself through all this. Like it wasn't really me. So I felt eerily calm and relaxed. I don't know. It just struck me funny.

I'd lost the Colt during the tussle. I reached around, groped for a shard of glass, found a good-sized one, and jabbed it repeatedly into the side of his neck until something began spurting. He started to weaken almost immediately, not too much, but enough that I could keep him from crushing my windpipe. In another moment, I was able to roll him off of me, and he lay in the dirt beside me, twitching, while I caught my breath. I noticed that the night was very clear. There were zillions of stars smeared across the black sky. Their distant twinkling reminded me of the sparkle of Estrella's almost-black eyes. "Estrella" means "star" in Spanish. But there weren't zillions of her. She was one of a kind. The thought made me smile. Somewhere nearby a bird warbled.

When I rolled to my feet, Stede was standing there, the .38 hanging at his side, useless as a limp dick. I went back into the clubhouse, where fire was starting to gnaw at anything that might be edible, and getting was stronger with every bite. I stopped by Preacher's remains and stripped off his colors, tucked them under my arm. I found Bikergirl and dragged her the rest of the way out, dropped her ass unceremoniously in the dirt, and stripped her colors off of her, too. I removed the gas caps from the capsized bikes, and sloshed as much gasoline around as I could. I dipped Bikergirl's colors into the gas tanks and painted the bikes with it. Then I tucked her colors into one of the tanks and lit it up with my trusty zippo.

Stede was still standing there like he was posing for a statue, mouth open, staring.

I dug out a smoke, offered him one, but he just stared at me. I lit up and took a drag.

"Time to split," I said.

I'd jogged a few steps in the direction of my car before I realized he was still standing there. I went back and took him by the arm.

"Time to go, daddy-o."

He snapped out of it then. Or at least, he collected himself enough to move. I could hear the gas tanks go up behind me as I jogged away.

A loud *whoosh*.

It was a pleasant sound.

Remembering it now, telling it, takes a long time. A lot longer, I think, than it took for it to actually happen. It's funny, what parts of it are fuzzy, and what parts are clear as high mountain air.

I recall that Stede was very quiet on the way back to town. When I dropped him off at the church, I noticed that he looked at me very oddly.

He thanked me and we shook hands and hugged each other. But there was something new in his eyes when he looked at me.

Fear.

Adam Adrian Crown

PART TWO

Adam Adrian Crown

I was raised by a toothless, bearded hag
I was schooled with a strap right across my back
But it's all right now, in fact, it's a gas!
But it's all right now, I'm Jumpin' Jack Flash
It's a gas! Gas! Gas!

("Jumpin' Jack Flash," The Rolling Stones)

CHAPTER THREE:
THE CHILD IS FATHER TO THE MAN

I don't believe any little kid sits down and says to himself, "Oh, boy, when I grow up I want to be a stone cold killer." I know *I* never did.

But I suppose the smart money would have bet on it.

For a time, I was seeing this therapist. A psychiatric social worker named Golda. She was a very gentle woman, getting a little matronly, but with an impish smile that made her seem like a kid. She loved cats and smoked too much. Winstons. She had a disarming manner, a strange admixture of warm friendliness and cool, professional objectivity.

I had been having recurring nightmares.

I dreamed that I was a child again. Back where I grew up. Back with my mother and father. Probably doesn't sound like much of a nightmare to you. No monsters, nothing Stephen King-ish. But it would leave me so depressed, I didn't want to go to sleep, and sleep deprivation can make you nuts. I was getting edgy. Golda was recommended by a friend of mine. An acquaintance, actually.

I don't have friends.

It took a long time for our chats to be therapeutic. In the first place, trust is not my strong suit. I had to make sure I could trust her and that took a lot of testing. Sometimes I spent

51

an hour telling her my favorite dirty jokes. Then one day she started telling *me* some, too — delightfully nasty ones, too. It was odd hearing it come from her, like watching a chimpanzee singing opera in the original Italian. But I started to feel better about her after that. I don't trust anyone who never uses the word "fuck."

At first I couldn't recall any of the details of my dreams to discuss with her. There didn't seem to be any particular plot to them. It was just re-living my childhood. So she started asking me about what actual memories I had of that.

It's hard to remember what you've tried hard to forget, and I had tried hard to forget by simply pretending that none of it had ever happened.

One day I had an unusually clear recollection of something that happened when I was around seven, and I was able to tell her about it in lurid detail. At the end, I was astonished to find that Golda was wiping her eyes with a kleenex. I felt terrible about that. She said that until I was able to cry for that poor child, she would lend me her own tears.

Turned out to be a long-term loan.

I was born on a mountain top in Tennessee and killed me a b'ar when I was only three.

No.

Wait a second.

That was Davey, Davey Crockett, king of the wild frontier.

Me, I was born in a slum in Chicago, Illinois. I was a fat, wheezy child. Weak and afraid, afraid of everyone and everything. I was quiet, a loner. No social skills, as they say. Didn't know how to make friends, and didn't have much opportunity to learn. But I was smart. Real smart. Maybe I didn't kill any b'ars, but I learned to read practically in the womb. Reading in the waiting womb, you might say.

It's easy to disappear into books when your actual life ain't that hot, and mine wasn't that hot.

Eclipse of the Heart

My first grade teacher was a puffy, dour woman, Mrs. Leeman. Pulled her graying mouse-brown hair into a bun so severely it made her look Chinese. Tiny red capillaries clutched at her cheeks like thin, skeletal fingers. From a distance it gave her a flushed appearance. I fantasized her in all kinds of erotic situations. But more about that later.

My classmates were well-scrubbed, well-combed, well-dressed little fuckers. I don't think I ever wore anything that hadn't been worn by at least one other person. Those threadbare, faded and patched clothes were a uniform that identified me as dirt poor, helped put me on the fringe of polite society as effectively as ringing a bell and hollering "Unclean, unclean..."

Nice kids didn't want to catch whatever it was I had.

One day, we were in the throes of excitement that can only be incited by the breath-taking adventures of derring-do undertaken by Dick and Jane. And of course, their trusty dog, Spot. I think maybe they had a cat, too. I forget.

I had a book of my own I was reading on the sneak and Dick and Jane weren't in it. Not even good old Spot. Naturally, Mrs. Leeman, instead of going around the room in row-by-row order to have kids take a turn reading like she generally did, on this occasion decided to call on a reader at random.

She called on me.

And I didn't have a clue what page we were supposed to be on. Worse than that, in trying to figure it out, I fumbled my sneak-book and dropped it. Hit the floor loud as a gunshot.

A .22, anyway.

"What's that?" Mrs Leeman demanded.

I exercised my right to remain silent.

With an imperious wave, she signaled me to bring my contraband forward.

Though I made the trip last as long as I could, I eventually arrived at her desk and she shushed the whispers and giggles of the other kids. She held out her hand and I put my book in it.

"What are you doing with this?" she asked. Yeah, I thought it was a pretty stupid question, too.

"Just reading," I told her.

She gave me a sly, sidelong gaze, pursing her lips, as if she'd caught me red-handed fondling myself in my pocket, and I was now trying to convince her that I'd been searching for a kleenex.

"Read some of it to me," she said, twisting the screws. "Quiet, class. Jack's going to read for us."

So I read a page, maybe two. She seemed bewildered. Like she'd walked in on me fucking the school nurse on her desk. When she pulled herself together she interrupted me with "Thank you, Jack. That's fine. Take your seat."

I thought she was going to have it in for me, after that, but she actually turned out to be ok. From then on, when Dick and Jane made the scene, she gave me a pass and sent me down to the library. So I got to read whatever I wanted.

That was pretty cool of her, don't you think?

You just never know.

Oh, yeah. The book was Ivanhoe, by Sir Walter Scott. If you haven't read it, you should. It's a good one.

Anyway, I didn't have much going for me, but I wasn't stupid .

My father — or the guy I always *think* of as my father — was a laborer. Truck driver. Mechanic. Pick and shovel man. Drove a snow plow in the winter time. Jack of all trades, as they say, master of only one: drunkard. When he was drinking he was violent, brutal and cruel. And he was almost always drinking. I later learned that he had been sexually molesting my half-sister, his step-daughter, from the time she was hardly more than an infant. He may even have done some time for it. I have a dim recollection of a train ride, the Black uniformed porter, wilted lettuce soaked with French dressing, my father in handcuffs. How footsteps echo in the marble hallways outside a courtroom.

My old man was an accomplished child-beater, too. I'll never forget what it was like to have his heavy belt crack across my legs, my back. If I was lucky it would be the strap and not the buckle-end.

I wasn't always lucky.

Sometimes he wouldn't have his belt handy, or maybe it was just too much bother. Then it would be a slap or a punch or a kick. Grab a handful of your hair so tight it felt like your scalp would rip off your skull, slam you into the wall, follow it up with a couple of good kicks.

Most of the time, I had no idea what these beatings were for.

Could have been anything.

Everything.

Nothing at all.

Worse maybe than the physical punishment itself was the look on his face while he was dishing it out: teeth bared, lips curled back, face twisted into a vicious snarl. I've only seen that look two other times in my life: once on a rabid timber wolf, and once when inadvertently catching a glimpse of myself in a mirror.

I would eventually heal up from the blows and later learned to avoid them.

But my dad wasn't just all muscle. He had mouth, too. He was an expert at ridicule, allowing no opportunity to humiliate or belittle to escape him. It didn't matter what I had accomplished, big or small. From getting A's in school, to Boy Scouts, to Little League. Sooner or later — usually sooner — he'd be launching into his standard harangue:

"Boy Scout, huh? You call yourself a goddam Boy Scout. Why, you wouldn't make a pimple on a real Boy Scout's ass..." This was, of course the opening aria that was followed by a beating.

Pretty soon I quit doing things like getting A's, Boy Scouts, Little League.

It just wasn't worth the extra attention.

My mother was a waitress.

One of my first jobs was as a busboy at Inga's Restaurant, where she was working. It was interesting to watch her hustle around, quick on her feet despite her obesity, smiling, laughing and joking with the customers, fawning over them, anticipating their every wish — and seeing her smile vanish as soon as she left the floor to go into the kitchen. Then — *presto!* — she's beaming again as she hits the floor with their orders, all sweetness and light.

On and off like a light switch.

I guess that should have told me something.

As I said, my mother was obese. Not sideshow obese, but way past pleasingly plump. For her, time had stopped in the mid-1940's as evidenced by her Andrews Sisters pompadours and make-up that would be excessive in any conservative Kabuki theatre. I suppose she had been attractive as a teen, and now she mourned for her lost looks as for a dead child.

One of my filial duties was to help her get ready for work.

In addition to polishing her shoes and dousing the inside with powder, I helped her dress. My part was to assist in getting her into her girdle, though what visible difference the garment made, I could not detect. I performed this task by grasping the elastic waistband and pulling it outward with both hands as she hurriedly tucked herself into it.

A collateral duty was to fasten her bra behind her once she had wrestled her huge breasts into the confines of the cups. Sometimes she would have me fasten the hook first. Then, as she pulled each cup forward, I would lift her breast and set it inside, settling it according to her instructions, making sure the nipples lay just right.

Her cleavage and tops of her breasts were badly scarred, a swirling molten-looking scar. A childhood accident, she said, involving a pan of boiling water.

I wonder what the truth was.

My mother never turned to full-blown prostitution, though she would give the occasional hand-job. I once glimpsed her at work, in the walk-in cooler jacking off the cook — but I don't know whether that was for love or money.

Perhaps this is what allowed her to maintain such an inflated sense of her station. She saw herself in the role of the tragic heroine, deserving of far, far better than she'd been served, and she laid the blame for her fall from grace squarely at the feet of her husband and children. Her favorite moments came when she could roll her eyes heavenward, spreading her arms in supplication, and wail about how unjustly God had saddled her with such rotten, lazy, good-for-nothing children. With operatic melodrama she beseeched the Almighty that we in turn would be similarly cursed as punishment.

Absolutely Wagnerian, daddy-o.

A pathological liar, my mother never told the truth where a lie would do as well, and I suspect she had lied about so much for so long that she herself no longer knew what the truth about anything really was. She would sometimes "remember" things that never were and would be irritated to no end when we failed to recall them exactly as she did.

While my father beat us for nothing, my mother took the strap to us for everything, always had a good excuse, and it was always "for our own good."

She had strict rules regarding precisely how t-shirts and undershorts and socks were to be folded, and exactly where in which dresser drawers they belonged, and woe be unto him who forgot. One time, I re-arranged my drawers the way I liked. Don't know what made me do that. I didn't make *that* mistake again.

Things had to be clean.

Beyond clean.

And it was never possible for them to be clean enough for her satisfaction. No amount of sweeping, vacuuming, mopping and dusting was ever sufficient to the task. She would always find some dirt I had missed and point it out to me. I learned to pretend that I saw it, too. Naturally, the entire room had to be cleaned all over again while she stood over me with a belt, just in case I missed a spot.

Doing the dishes was another one of the chores that fell to me. I spent a lot of time scrubbing the bottoms of pans that had been permanently blackened since before I was born. I learned to tolerate extremely hot water without any outward sign of pain.

By the time I was nine or ten it was my job to do the shopping. I'd get dropped off at the A&P with a list and a coin purse holding *exactly* the right amount. Sometimes it wouldn't be enough and I'd have to put something back. No matter what I chose, it was the wrong thing. The strap would help me make better choices in the future. And sometimes I got the wrong item, too. The strap would teach me better judgment. Afterward would be my responsibility to walk back and return that wrong item.

But worst of all was the waiting.

I did the shopping on Saturday. My father would drop me off there early, maybe 10 a.m. — important to get there early to get the "on sale" items, you see. Then I'd wait with a basketful of groceries until he remembered to pick me up. Often this wouldn't be until he ran out of beer money — or beer credit. Sometimes I'd wait there all day, until the store closed. In winter, they'd let me wait inside until it was time to lock up.

One time, the store manager got a cab for me, paid for it himself. Nice guy. Thought he was doing me a favor. When my father finally got there and found that I wasn't where he'd told me to be — I'd already been home a couple hours by then

— he went berserk. I think I couldn't sit down comfortably or lean my back against anything for a week.

Another time I wrangled a shopping cart all the way home, at night, along the highway. I don't know how far it was. I'd guess maybe five miles, but I could be off on that. Seems farther when you're little. Got most of the stuff home, though. Paid for stuff lost along the way with the strap, of course.

Doing the laundry was the same deal. Drop the kid off, pick him up, whenever. For some reason laundry was done Sunday night. Slept in that laundromat a few times. It wasn't so bad. Warmer than our house. Quieter, too.

I was smart enough to catch on to this routine after a few times, and whenever I could, I would sneak along a book to read. I read a lot of books between the Speedy Wash and the A&P.

My mother's favorite rant was about penises.

"Oh, the trouble men cause with that thing between their legs," she would soliloquize in grand Shakespearean fashion. She went on to enumerate all the world's troubles that would not be, were it not for The Penis. This, you might surmise, is not the best message to be giving a young boy about himself. Particularly when coupled with "You're just like your father," spoken venomously, with wrinkled nose, as if maleness itself was unbearably foul-smelling.

"Just like your father."

Worst insult imaginable.

It was ironic that these anti-male monologues came from a woman who was apparently not completely unacquainted with The Penis, herself. She'd had five children — at least, five that I know of — each with a different father.

The oldest was George, whom I never met. He was living with relatives somewhere in the great northwest and the question of why he did not remain in the custody of his natural mother is one that begs to be asked. I'll bet it's a juicy tale. I don't recall her ever getting a letter or even a card from him, either. Nevertheless, my mother kept a picture of him in a gold-plated frame, as a holy altar to the Perfect Child. He looked to have been about five when the portrait was done. Blue eyes and long curly blonde hair, and one ringlet curl right in the middle of his forehead, just like the little girl who was very good when she was good.

Next in line was Ellen. Ellen was a sister I never knew I had until I was about 30.

One day, out of the blue I get a phone call from some woman.

"Are you so-and-so?" the woman asks.

"Yes," I said.

"Was your mother so-and-so from such-and-such?"

"Yes."

"Well, you don't know me but I'm your sister."

Bang. Just like that. She was passing through, so we met for dinner and some drinks. She was redskin dark, like me. She had been raised by foster parents and had made out all right, bless her heart. Lived on a big farm now out in South Dakota.

Next came Kay, with her red hair and green eyes.

Then me. Dark brown eyes, straight brown, almost black, hair.

Last, the caboose papoose, my little brother, Danny. He's almost five years younger than me. Good looking kid. Dark. Kinky black hair. Big grin. Reminds me a little of the young Muhammad Ali.

So five kids, none of whom looked much like each other and none of whom resembled the husband of the mother, either. Perhaps you can imagine how this came up when my parents fought, which was, if not nightly, at least five nights a week, with matinees on Saturday and Sunday just like at the Sahara.

My dad would do his "niggers and redskins" bit, a real crowd-pleaser: "Niggers and redskins. Niggers and redskins. If you like 'em so much why don't you go live with 'em? Niggers and redskins. Where the fuck are they now? Why ain't they paying the bills? No, I'm payin' the fuckin' bills. That's what good your niggers and redskins are..."

My mother countered with, "Big man. You can't even pay your liquor bill with the money you make. Look at this shack. Look at the kids' clothes. Every time you get a little money you drink it up. I'm the one paying the bills. What kind of a man is that?"

This duet would crescendo with my dad shattering some dishes against the wall — often with dinner still on them — or smashing his fist through a wall and storming out, presumably for a drink.

Applause.

Curtain.

Don't miss the midnight show featuring, "Quiet, you drunkard, the kids are asleep."

Vaudeville in hell.

My parents were a strong argument for sterilization. Or at least for requiring some kind of a license before you can go around popping out children. They had as much business raising kids as Charles Manson. Two wretched human slugs. They deserved each other. But kids deserve better parents than that.

The one pleasant memory I have from my childhood is about me and my sister, Kay.

I couldn't have been seven years old yet.

I recall having my seventh birthday at the cottage on Fox Bay, a suburb about 45 minutes from the Chicago Loop. I remember that birthday because my mother, going all out for that Good Mother Oscar Nomination, baked a cake. To be fair, she was a good cook, when she felt like it. It had cherry-flavored icing and real cherries on top. And this thing with

Kay happened before that, when we were still living on Tippincott Avenue. So I had to be younger than seven. Kay was six years older than I. So if I was, let's say six, then she would have been twelve. I'm guessing I was five or six.

My mother worked nights and steadfastly refused to learn how to drive so that her carefully calculated helplessness could allow her to control others by making them feel obligated to help her. Maybe you know the type.

My father would take her to work and pick her up after. The low sputter of the Packard's engine would rouse me from sleep a little. The headlights washed across our room like a search beacon sweeping the prison yard as the car rolled away, crunching on the gravel drive.

Kay and I shared a lumpy bed with oak leaves and acorns carved into the headboard. Every time you rolled over, the springs squealed like Maynard Ferguson going for that high F.

On one particular night — in Spring, if I recall correctly the fragrance of lilacs on the warm breeze, I awakened to find Kay watching out the window as the Packard grumbled off into the distance. The moonlight gave the world a bluish cast, but made it seem like high noon.

I wish I could remember more of the details, more clearly, exactly how it got started, exactly what happened and in what order, but I really can't and I must cautiously resist filling in the blank spots from my imagination. What I *do* remember is that Kay got back on the bed with me and took notice of my transient night-time little-boy erection.

"That's called a cock," she informed me. I liked the sound of that better than my mother's simpering references to it as a "pee-pee" or "wee-wee" or, at her most sophisticated, "peter" or "thing."

"You should see Dad's sometime," she added. "It's huge."

I couldn't recall having seen my father's penis and it didn't dawn on me to wonder under what circumstances she had done so. My attention was on her hand, which she now had wrapped around my little cock — well, a couple fingers of her hand, anyway. She had begun to massage it up and down in a very pleasant fashion.

It created sensations that were not completely unfamiliar. When my mother bathed me, she would be very judicious about washing my penis, making sure that it was very, very, very clean. And toweling me afterwards, she always made certain it was very, very, very dry.

"This is what you call 'jerking off'," Kay instructed me. "Now you do it."

I did as she bade me, happy to comply. It took a bit of fumbling before I found a grip that mimicked the feeling of hers, but I was soon enthusiastically tugging away. Almost at once I realized that, while it had felt good for her to do it, I was really much better at it myself. Meanwhile, Kay slipped off the bottoms of her flannel pajamas and was rubbing between her legs. I could see a dark patch of sparse hair, but, alas, no cock.

"This is my cunt," she told me. "Girls have cunts and boys have cocks. Want to touch it?"

I gave her the predictable reply.

If I was curious about why this cock vis-à-vis cunt arrangement existed, I was willing to accept it at face value for the moment.

"C'm'ere," she said, waving me toward her. I strained my eyes to see better in the moonlit room. Just enough light to reveal and conceal at the same time.

"Touch it if you want."

I touched it.

I was surprised at the coarseness of her pubic curls — I, of course, had no pubic hair yet. She took my hand and gave it a guided tour, initiating it to the soft dampness of her lips, the tiny bump of her clitoris. Slick warmth inside. Like a mouth. But no teeth that I could find.

"Kiss it," she whispered.

I drew close and set my lips lightly on her, the scent of her sweet young musk searing its way forever into my brain.

"Harder," she said.

I kissed her harder and felt her hips begin to rock, the hair around her vagina rough against my face.

"Lick it. Put your tongue in it."

I did just as she asked, enjoying the salty, fleshy taste of her. After a while, she changed her position, pulling away from my mouth, and reached for my penis.

"This is what you call 'cock-sucking', she said and began to suit the action to the word better than the Bard ever imagined. I had heard my father use the term "cocksucker" on numerous occasions, in a very derogatory way. I was certain now that he must be referring to something else. I couldn't find anything negative about the activity nor conjure up uncomplimentary thoughts regarding the person engaging in it.

The heat of her mouth was overwhelming and seemed to spread warmth throughout my entire body. My cheeks felt flushed with fever. My eyes, hot. It was difficult to breathe.

It was wonderful.

Then at some point, Kay climbed on top of me, supporting most of her weight on her arms, nuzzling her legs between mine so that her pubis was above my own.

"This is called fucking," she explained as she reached around and made some attempts to insert my fledgling cock into her inexpert cunt. For a moment, I think, she succeeded. There was another rush of heat through me as what felt like another mouth engulfed me. But I simply could not sustain the intromission myself and she was not skillful enough to do it all on her own. Even without it, she continued to rub against me with increasing intensity until I felt her shudder, a soft moan escaping on her breath.

She rolled off of me then and, spreading her knees wide, began to rub her cunt furiously, digging her fingers inside it. Instincts awakened, I re-gripped my penis, still wet from her, and began stroking again. Shortly, I seemed to lose track of Kay as a fierce tsunami of pleasure racked its way through me, surging forth from the penile epicenter to explode out from the tips of my fingers and toes. I let myself be pulled down by the undertow, unafraid of drowning, and then floated lazily back toward the surface, in no particular hurry. When I bobbed up to catch a breath of air, I found Kay watching me, not exactly giggling, but pretty close.

"You like it?" she asked.

You know the answer to that one.

"Just don't tell anybody," she admonished. "We'll get in trouble."

Who would I possibly tell? And what words could I use to describe it? But I agreed to keep it a secret, and keep it a secret I did for all these years.

Until now.

Now if the shame-crippled Puritans have their way, we'll all have to cluck our teeth and shake our heads because I was sexually "abused" by my sister. Golda tried to convince me of it, too, even though she was an intelligent person otherwise. I never suffered any injury from that episode with Kay. It was one of the only moments of tenderness and joy that I can recall from that awful time, and I love her for it, and wouldn't trade it for anything.

True, I became immediately fascinated with sex and that had its complications — such as casting Mrs. Leeman — and many others — in starring roles in my masturbation fantasies. I realized that every girl and woman I saw must have a cunt, and I wondered what they were like, was each one different, or what? I did extensive research on that topic for decades to come.

But Kay had given me something of a life-jacket. If I couldn't rely on my parents for nurturing, at least I could provide myself with some measure of comforting and pleasure. And often during the long, soul-aching oppression that was childhood, a bout of masturbation was the only moment of sunshine on a dismal day. And rarely a day went by that I didn't find time to engage in it — or that I didn't need it. Most often at night, just before going to sleep — rocking my own cradle, I suppose you could say. On a good day, I'd have other opportunities. I'd have been content to spend every waking moment doing it over and over.

So there's no way I can consider my sister's tutelage "abuse."

Maybe that's because I know what real abuse feels like.

One part is the beatings and strappings; one part is ridicule and humiliation. And one part is the spirit-crushing power of "love" used as a carrot-and-stick. Affection or abandonment. Do what I want you to do and you're a good boy and I'll love you. Don't do it and you're a bad boy and I won't love you.

My mother was the virtuoso on this one. If I had been bad — let's say because I hadn't folded my t-shirts just right, or hadn't put my socks in the drawer where she wanted them to be, or hadn't dusted the furniture well enough to suit an eye that could detect "filth" where there was absolutely none — she would push me away from her, saying nobody loves a bad boy. At times she threatened to put me in a "home" which I later began to view as a rather hopeful prospect, all things considered.

I should perhaps be grateful for this early exposure to emotional blackmail, since it seemed to immunize me against similar extortion later in my life. So I never fell into the marry-me-and-provide-for-me-and-I'll-let-you-fuck-me trap that has been the ruin of many more poor boys than the House of the Rising Sun. Why more people don't see marriage as state-sponsored prostitution, I'll never understand.

The only thing I regret about my secret encounter with Kay is that the occasion was never repeated. I liked my sister and would love to have had sex with her again, especially after I had gained some practical experience. I hoped that she would initiate another session, but she never did, and I was too shy about it. Often, I wanted to talk with her about it, but the time never seemed right for it. Though I often returned in masturbation fantasies, to our time together, all I could do was wait and hope, contenting myself to catch a glimpse of her in the bath, or getting undressed for bed,

Keeping our secret.

I frequently tried other ways to recapture the pleasure I experienced with Kay.

With Raggedy Ann, for example.

Ann was a life-sized (kid-sized) doll complete with blushing plastic cheeks, a mop of straw-yellow hair and elastic bands on her feet. The idea was to attach these bands to your own feet so you could "dance" with her.

We did more than dance.

Under her red-and-white checkered skirt (which looked a lot like the tablecloths at Inga's Restaurant), I was disappointed to find no trace of the succulent vagina that Kay had shown me. There was, however, a seam between her legs, and with a scissors and my imagination I created a sufficient orifice there. Practicing cunnilingus on Annie's red-cotton crotch was less than awe-inspiring, but by mounting her in the same way that Kay had lain on top of me, I could rub my penis against her with not unpleasant results.

Her plastic mouth had been molded to render her lips slightly parted, but not sufficiently for me to insert my penis. Probably just as well.

In the days since my rendezvous with Annie, I've seen a number of inflatable "love" dolls, some fashioned with very realistic labia and orifices. Lately there are some that you can have custom crafted with relatively "life-like" materials. But they aren't cheap. I don't quite understand why you'd put all that energy and money into humping a toy woman when you could be fucking a real one.

I suppose some people just can't tolerate small talk.

Sometime before my seventh birthday, one other significant event took place. I'm not exactly sure whether it happened before or after my single, sweet interlude with Kay.

When I was about five or six, I discovered electricity.

I was on the floor, looking over the "funny pages" from the Sunday Newspaper — though I'm not sure whether I could read them yet. At the same time I was eating a piece of cake. Chocolate cake. With white coconut frosting. Damn good cake.

I apparently decided that the lamp cord might go well with chocolate cake, and started chewing on it, too.

As it turned out, it wasn't such a good idea at all.

I can remember absently putting it into my mouth, the texture of the plastic against my tongue and teeth. I don't recall much after that.

I have a vague recollection of pain, searing white-hot pain. And blinding white light. Peoples' voices around me talking very fast, though I couldn't make out the words. I'm told I was in the hospital quite a while. I can remember a lot of people doing a lot of head-shaking and tongue clucking, and saying things like "It's just a miracle he's alive," when they thought I was asleep and couldn't hear.

There was a nurse there whom I remember, too. Not details. Just that she was dark, and young and very pretty. And that she would spend extra time sitting by my bed, reading to me. Her voice was soft as rabbit fur and felt good on my ears. She wore a perfume that was sultry and musky and suited her perfectly. I've tried to identify it over the years, but have never been able to find it. Maybe it was her own personal scent. I can believe that.

There followed a long bed-ridden convalescence, during which time I was swathed in more bandages than Boris Karloff in The Mummy. I'll never forget the greasy, gooey feeling of Unguentine burn ointment all over me, or the smell of it. I ate everything through a straw, my lips cracked open and bled so easily. Liquefied baby food. Now there's the devil's milkshake.

It was during that time that I first had The Dream.

I dreamt it over and over while I was recovering. Little by little, as I got stronger, it recurred less frequently. But it never left me completely. Every once in a while, over the years, I'd have it again for no apparent reason.

The Dream went like this:

There was an elderly Indian, his features nearly lost among the wrinkles. A Hawk nose. Deep dark eyes, like mine. Wispy white hair, thinning on top, stirred gently by the wind. Straggly braids wrapped in blood-red cloth. He wore some kind of robe wrapped around his shoulders, the fur nearly as white as his own hair. His weathered skin stretched across stringy muscle and I could just glimpse a pair of ragged scars, one on each half of his chest, like a pair of exclamation points. He had the dignified manner of a chief.

Beside the Dream Chief walked a magnificent white horse with a luxurious mane and eyes like quiet fire. He shook his head, and snorted, and his breath made little clouds of steam in the chilly air.

Dream Chief was singing to himself in a high, scratchy voice, not words, really, just an Indian version of scat. He turned toward me and fell silent, gave me a dead-serious look. When he spoke, he didn't speak English, but a language I didn't recognize — even though I understood it. He pointed a boney finger at me and said:

"Go where the arrow points to the rainbow."

He indicated the direction with his hand. Then smile-wrinkles ate his face and, with a phlegmy chuckle he went back to his song. I had a feeling he was laughing at me. Not in a mean way, just teasing a little...

When I woke up, not quite re-oriented from dreamtime, I fully expected him to be sitting there beside my bed. I could still hear those words, his gulch-dry voice still in my ears. ***"Go where the arrow points to the rainbow."***

It wasn't the only odd dream I ever had. Even when I'd have the dream again, I wrote it off as insignificant, forgetting about it between times.

I didn't know what it meant, so I told myself it didn't mean anything.

I was wrong.

It was also before my seventh birthday, that we were evicted from the Tippincott house. I remember the cops putting us out. We had no place else to go, so we lived in our car for a time, my parents, Kay, baby Danny and me. I don't know how long this lasted.

Once, we "moved in" to an abandoned house on Rollins Road, but the Sheriff came and we were obliged to "move out" again. I don't believe I've ever had an encounter with a law enforcement officer that was substantially more endearing than this.

Eventually, we found the place on Fox Bay.

The Fox Bay Hotel had been a favorite hang-out of Al Capone in his glory days, and was a majestic four story affair in the Greek revival style. By the time we discovered it, it was quite run-down. Only the first floor, with the bar and restaurant, and the second floor rooms were still in use. It overlooked Fox Bay and was not more than twenty-five yards from the water's edge. A pair of long piers accommodated a couple of dozen boats, mostly cabin cruisers, and one of the piers had a fuel pump. In the summer, there were speedboat races on the lake.

The grounds, at that time, were beautiful. All meadow and forest. Naturally, the owners eventually bulldozed it all away for a boat-house and a parking lot.

There were three summer cottages along the shore on the north side of the hotel, also in sad disrepair at the time we arrived. They still had signs bearing their names: Bay View. Shady Rest. Oak something-or-other. Two of the three proved so dilapidated as to be uninhabitable except by squirrels and the odd skunk or raccoon. The third cottage, the biggest, was salvageable. Kitchen, living room and bath downstairs, two bedrooms upstairs.

My father struck a deal with the Jacksons, who owned the whole kit and kaboodle, to fix up the house and do other work for them in exchange for rent. As a "benefit" they allowed my father to run a tab at the bar. He did his drinking "on account" between paydays when rent and booze would be deducted from his wages. They paid him so low an hourly wage — much less than they would have had to pay anyone with the same skills and not so desperately in need of a job — and charged so much for rent for a place that, in a just universe would long since have been condemned and demolished, that frequently he wound up owing them money after the payday accounts were balanced. He would then have to borrow money for things like food, which they were happy to lend him at the going interest rate. It doesn't take too many laps on that Merry-go-Round before you find yourself deeply in debt. He couldn't afford to quit working for them because he would then have to pay up what he owed, which he couldn't, and would have to pay rent, too, which he couldn't, or move into a new place, which he couldn't afford.

To make matters worse, he'd signed no contract with these folks; he'd given his word. And he believed that a deal with the devil is still a deal.

It would be a long time before I'd read Karl Marx's Das Kapital, but when I did I would immediately recognized the Jacksons as the very sort of exploitive blood-sucking pricks he was referring to.

Them that's got shall get.

And they get it by fucking them that's not.

And that's still the news.

Winters were tough.

These houses were intended to be summer cottages, not year-around dwellings. They had no insulation. No storm windows. No heat. So we stuffed rags in the larger cracks in the walls, nailed heavy plastic over the windows and wore a lot of clothes. Later my dad found an old oil stove at the junk yard and made it work. It heated about half the living room. We spent a lot of time huddled around it.

But in the summer, the livin' was a little easier.

Danny and I shared a bedroom fitted out with a pair of bunkbeds, navy surplus. Mine was the top one. When it was just right, I could lay with my head at the foot of my bed (official "head" and foot" were designated by my mother, of course) and see the moon reflecting on the water, in countless dancing diamonds. The breeze would carry on it the rustle of oak leaves, the chuckle of waves lapping at the hulls of boats, the shush of other waves licking the shore. The creak of dock timbers and ropes. The squeak of a boat's gunnels, nudging against the old tires that were hung on the dock posts for fenders. I would try to get as close to the breeze as I could, get that wind in my face. It would take me somewhere else, somewhere I could be as free as the moon, the wind, the water.

Naturally, if I fell asleep that way, head at the "wrong" end of the bed, it would mean a strapping. But it was worth it. Anyway, I learned to wake myself up early, before my mother got up, and turn back around so she'd never be the wiser.

We had a well for water, but the pump was very temperamental. When it would go down, it was my task to carry empty plastic jugs up to the Hotel and ask to have them filled from their tap, which they did, though it clearly put them out to do it.

If you've never done any actual begging, you should give it a try.

Does wonders for your self-esteem, I can tell you. Today, I wouldn't ask you to piss on me if I was on fire.

I spent as much time as possible out of the house, away from my parents.

My mother worked nights, so she slept days. My dad worked from early until late. Most of the day I could spend by the lakeshore. Though I loved the water I was afraid of it, too.

Even now, I can swim a couple of miles if I have to, but it isn't really my idea of a good time. Danny swam like a fish though, inspired by Lloyd Bridges' "Sea Hunt" on TV.

Ah yes, TV.
We had one.
A second-hand set that only got one channel, WGN, channel 9 from Chicago. Fortunately for me, they ran a lot of movies. My favorites were "Beau Geste" and "The Mark of Zorro" and anything with Errol Flynn. I must have watched "Captain Blood" a hundred times.

That story really touched me.
Peter Blood, having once been a soldier, had become a doctor, "a healer now and not a slayer." He is called out in the middle of the night to administer to a gentleman who had been wounded in a battle against King James' troops, part of a catastrophic attempt at rebellion. Though he had no part in the rebellion, he had given "aid and comfort" to a rebel and was adjudged as guilty as the rebels themselves. Blood gives the judge a few pointed words before being sentenced to the slave colony in Jamaica.

Looks pretty bad for Doctor Blood.
But he uses his wits and courage and with luck and pluck, he escapes slavery, becomes a successful pirate and eventually is appointed to be the new governor of Jamaica.

And he gets the girl, too.
Not bad.
These days an ex-con usually can't even get much of a job.
I suppose what I saw in that story was my own story. Born under a bad sign. The situation wasn't one of my making. The world was fucked up when I got here. But maybe if I used my wits, had enough courage — and enough luck — I could escape my slavery, be successful and even get the girl. I didn't really care much about being governor of Jamaica.

Anyway, Captain Blood became my ideal. Errol Flynn, my model.

So far so good.
I'm not a slave anymore.
I've been a successful "pirate."
And I've gotten the girl a few times.
I don't know how it's going to turn out yet.
Who knows? Maybe that governor gig in Jamaica will open up.

When I was about 8 or 9, I discovered drawing, not the color-inside-the-lines stuff, but pencil sketching. I drew on every piece of paper I could find and when the Hotel people threw away a file drawer full of old papers, I thought I stumbled across El Dorado.

I concentrated most on drawing some of the things Kay and I had done together, but I also drew things I couldn't possibly have seen: couplings of men and women entwined in acrobatic orgies; women with dogs and horses; men with impossibly huge cocks spraying fountains of semen; hermaphrodites engaging women and men simultaneously, and so on. It would be a while before I discovered my first Playboy Magazine, or, even better, more explicit pornography of which I became and remain rather a fan. Until then I made do with my own custom-made porn for those quiet moments alone with my cock. And, even if I do say so myself, you'd have to go a long way to exceed — or even match — my imagination.

Though I never again shared a sexual feast with my sister, I was always on the watch for crumbs.

My mother kept birds — Australian Cockatiels. Half a dozen or so of them in a couple of cages that set on the tops of the dressers in my sister's bedroom. These birds loved to peck at the sheet rock walls and by happy coincidence had pecked a hole all the way through the wall that separated my room from Kay's. The hole was not quite as high as my mattress and so was hidden from view. With a little effort, I enlarged the hole enough so that I could peek into Kay's room. I'd try to stay awake until she came to bed, then squeeze down to press my face against that hole. Most of the time, I couldn't see much of anything. But on occasion, the light was just right, and she happened to stand in just the right place at just the right moment for me to glimpse her breast or the curve of her ass. The sight would fuel my masturbation engine for days.

When Kay was old enough, she followed in my mother's footsteps and got a waitressing job. It was at a Chinese place and I remember she tried to make up her eyes in an exotic oriental fashion and wore a black uniform with a mandarin collar. I thought she looked irresistible.

One evening, after she had left for work, I was so caught up in her that I slipped into her room and went into her dresser drawers. I quickly found the one that held her lingerie. It was breath-taking. To think that I was touching these things that had touched her breasts, her cunt, that still even smelled of her. I wanted so badly to touch her again. I tried to imagine it. I went so far as to put on one of her bras and a pair of her panties and look in her mirror, imagining it was her. It was an illusion that was difficult to sustain for very long. For one thing, wadded-up socks don't act or feel much like breasts and for another, it's quite challenging to tuck an erection out of sight.

So this experiment proved less than satisfying. En finale, I contented myself to wrap one of her satin-crotched panties around my cock and masturbate — then I realized I'd have to conceal the embarrassing evidence. But I couldn't bring myself to throw her panties away. Though I knew it would be my ruin if they were found, I kept them for a long time, until they were too semen-caked to be serviceable any longer. I hoped she would assume they'd been lost in the laundry.

Some people believe dreams are as real as the waking world. Some believe a dream is a wish your heart makes.

Some believe it's the sub-conscious sorting and filing. Some believe they are the result of an undigested bit of cheese. I have no opinion on the matter, but I have had dreams that are certainly out of the ordinary.

When I was 9 or 10 I dreamed that I was in the living room of our dilapidated cottage. My father was sitting on the worn green sofa having a cigarette. He had a guilty, hang-dog look. My mother seemed unspecifically anxious, wringing her hands, pacing.

Down the stairs from the bedrooms came Kay. She was naked. Both my parents refused to look at her. I knew something was very wrong. It was then that I realized that Kay had managed to sprout a penis — a hefty one, too. It hung, thickly-veined and swollen in that post-coital way, lolling from side to side with each step she took, reminding me of an elephant's trunk. She reached the bottom stairs and looked expectantly at my parents, who continued to ignore her. She seemed embarrassed and I thought she was about to cry. So I rushed over to her, threw my arms around her and hugged her as tightly as I could.

"Don't worry, Kay," I told her. "I still love you."

As is so often the case with gloomy dreams, I awoke then, but the image stayed with me and I never forgot it. Many years later, Kay confided in me that she was a lesbian.

I had another dream, an occasionally recurring one, which, as it turns out, was also somewhat prophetic. It went like this:

I was bathing in our scarred, white claw-footed tub, filled almost to the brim, but with clean, not soapy water. Ranged around the tub were women, many women. All colors, sizes and descriptions. One was black and switchblade lean. Another was Asian, with long blue-black hair reaching almost to the floor. Another a big-boned Greco-Roman type with forests of coarse dark hair under her arms and on her pubis. There was a Scandinavian-looking blonde with pendulous breasts. A petite red-haired Celtic lass with green eyes, freckles and the smile of a mischievous leprechaun. And every variation beyond and between.

All these lovelies were clearly doting on the child in the bathtub, smiling and cooing, the way women are inclined to do when confronted with something inexpressibly cute. Then one or another of them would toss an item of lingerie into the tub and I would plunge after it, splashing around to their delighted squeals, making a great show of retrieving it. Returning the item would get me a hug and a kiss on the cheek from the owner and approving applause from the rest.

Like I said, prophetic.

As the song goes, "I wish I didn't know now what I didn't know then."

My father had substantial physical courage, got to give him that. Once, while clearing some land for the hotel's new parking lot, he was struck on the top of the head by a falling tree. It split his scalp open in a huge cruciform wound, to the very bone. The rest of the crew had to refuse to go back to work before he would consent to be taken to the hospital. Everyone was quite amazed that it did him no apparent serious harm and the event was good for a lot of free drinks until the bandage finally came off.

My mother was quite the opposite, never over-looking any chance for sympathy. Every ache and pain became the death scene from Madame Butterfly. This was magnified a thousand-fold during her menstrual period. I don't want to seem insensitive. I know that some women have serious cramps at that time, and I don't want to be one who jests at scars, never having felt the wound. Nevertheless, knowing my mother as I did, I could not help but suspect some degree of exaggeration. I have seen women give birth with less distress. My mother's displays were no doubt compounded by the injustice of even having a period, something that was certainly the fault of The Penis. But she did not bear her righteous martyrdom silently. It was a wonderful opportunity to use her helplessness to control those around her.

Not infrequently, I was dispatched by bicycle to Boyce's Pharmacy to obtain sanitary napkins for her. At that time, high-fashion models were not advertising a variety of designer pads in a sort of menstrual-chic debate of which shape was most comfortable. "Feminine hygiene" was among the many things not discussed in polite society, like blowjobs and crooked politicians.

Don Boyce was the pharmacist of choice because he was willing to put things "on account," though I don't know why. If he were ever actually paid in full for all the pills and potions my mother craved, he could have retired to the Caribbean. Periodic partial payments seemed, if not to satisfy him, at least to sustain the status quo.

While Mr. Boyce was filling prescriptions and such, I was free to lounge near the magazine rack and skim through the latest comic books. Superman. Batman. Green Lantern. The dime store version of the Greek pantheon. But my favorites were "Classics Illustrated."

One such occasion was on a bitter cold winter Sunday. There was little enough snow that peddling my bike wasn't impossible, but I remember the wind gusting right through my clothes. I was so glad to reach the drugstore and get inside where it was warm. Mr. Boyce praised me lavishly for braving the cold for my mom, and fixed me a mug of hot cocoa at the fountain. He suggested I stay a while and warm up, which I considered a superb idea.

As I sipped the rich chocolate (made with milk, not water) Mr. Boyce inquired in a friendly way if I had a telescope. I didn't, of course. He then invited me to have a look at his, which he had set up downstairs. It didn't occur to me that a telescope would be of very limited utility in a basement. Mr. Boyce paused to lock the front door and turn the sign to "closed."

The basement was mostly a storage room, stuffed to the gills with merchandise. But there was a small desk and beside it a roll-away bed, and, true to Mr. Boyce's word, a telescope. There was also a stack of magazines nearby.

"I'll be right back," Mr. Boyce said. "Look at some magazines if you want."

I looked at some.

I was amazed by what I saw.

These mags were full of pictures of men, and *what* men! Lean, powerfully muscled, skin shiny, glowing. Some wore posing straps, others were entirely nude. I had never seen such beautiful physiques — except in comic books. It was like seeing a snapshot of god and realizing you really were made in his image. In some of the magazines the men posed together, sometimes handling each other's cocks. Or sucking them. Or they lay on top of each other like spoons.

When Mr. Boyce returned, he asked me if I'd found any photos I liked and pointed out some of his favorites to me. Indeed, I liked some of them, too. He offered me my choice of magazines to keep and I selected one that had a lot of photos of the great Steve Reeves. I considered taking one of the more explicit issues, and I think he would have liked that. But by then, I knew better that to reveal anything I actually thought, felt or wanted to anyone, since it would only be used against me later. "You still look cold," he said. "Let me rub your back. It'll warm you up."

In fact, I was still chilled and, though it was a bit awkward, I didn't see any harm in it. I lay down on the bed on my stomach and Mr. Boyce loosened my clothes and slipped his hand under my shirt. It felt warm and soft against me. I was surprised by how soft it was. Not rough and calloused like my dad's hands. It was not at all unpleasant.

Mr. Boyce asked me more about which photos I liked best. Did I like the ones where the men were playing with each other? Had I ever done things like that with any of the other boys? Did I think I might enjoy doing some of those things? The combination of his hand on my back (now more at the top of my buttocks) and talking about the men in the photos quickly gave me an erection, which was uncomfortable to lie on.

"Here," he said softly, "why don't you turn over?"

I turned over.

For a while, Mr. Boyce caressed my belly and chest. Very gently. When it finally dawned on me that I'd been there quite some time, I became alarmed about the predictable repercussions of being gone so long, and I began to cry. Mr. Boyce must have thought I was upset about his behavior. Immediately, he withdrew, pulled himself together and assumed a soothing air.

"Don't cry," he said. "I didn't hurt you in any way did I? There's nothing to be afraid of. I would never, ever hurt you."

I believed him.

His concern seemed very real. Whether it was for me or for himself, I couldn't say.

No, I assured him, he hadn't hurt me. But it was getting late and I had to go. I didn't tell him I was sure to get a strapping if I took too long — and no matter how long it took, it would be too long.

When I had re-arranged my clothes, we went back upstairs. Mr. Boyce had my mother's things bagged up in a split second. He placated me with candy, and some money and my choice of any of the comics I wanted. I chose a Classics Illustrated edition of The Three Musketeers.

The wind had picked up and was blowing against me and I pedaled hard through miniature cyclones of snow. The wind-chill seared me as if I were naked and I was freezing again by the time I got home. Naturally, I got a strapping. But I had hidden my magazines under my clothes so it wasn't so bad, plus I got to keep the magazines.

A couple years after that incident, Mr. Boyce was arrested on "morals" charges, accused of fondling some of the local boys. Had a hard time of it, and I regretted that because I liked him. I wouldn't have minded another time with him.

My mother immediately sprang to the defense of this wonderful man, insisting that these kids — as all kids — were rotten liars and good-for-nothing trouble-makers. Never in my wildest fantasies did I ever consider telling her — or anyone

— about my own experience with him. She wouldn't have believed me and I wasn't about to go *begging* for a strapping.

The truth is a dangerous thing and you have to be very careful with it. Grip it tightly and control it, like the head of a rattlesnake.

Somebody once said the truth will set you free.

Maybe.

But it's far more likely to get you killed.

There are times when death looks like freedom.

In summary, class, I grew up in an environment that was volatile and unpredictable, arbitrarily violent and unnecessarily cruel, seething with dark, forbidden and perverse sexuality. Thus my parents prepared me perfectly to survive in a world that was volatile and unpredictable, arbitrarily violent and unnecessarily cruel, seething with dark, forbidden and perverse sexuality. Thanks to mom and dad, I'd feel right at home.

I suppose I should be grateful.

Well he's bad, bad, Leroy Brown
Baddest man in the whole damn town

("Leroy Brown," Jim Croce)

CHAPTER FOUR: COOL

I was cool, man.

I was slick. I was bad. Cruising the streets like a great white shark. Never sleeping. Always hungry. Always moving.

I would swagger into Mr. Katz's deli, resplendent in my handed-down black leather jacket — still a little too big for me — a "Dago" t-shirt, skin-tight jeans, Cuban-heeled boots. My hair was coerced into an elegant d.a. through the violent application of Old Spice brilliantine. With a matching splash of after shave — though I didn't yet practice the shave for it to come after — my scent, if not my reputation, was sure to precede me.

I was lured into the shop by the irresistible siren song of halvah, a sweet kosher treat made from sesame seeds and honey. I had been given some by Phyllis, the neighborhood heart-breaker, and now I was hooked. I needed my fix.

But in the land of the rat and the home of the cockroach, there was no bread for that kind of luxury. There was only money for absolute necessities.

Like booze.

Anything I needed, I had to find a way to get on my own. And I did. I got pretty good at it, too.

With a little bit of subtle timing, casual misdirection and nimbleness of hand, I regularly scored a bar — sometimes two

83

— of the world's most savory candy. Right under Old Man Katz's nose.

I was bad.

I was cool.

Too cool to be a fool.

So on the day I went to pick up my hit of ambrosia and saw the Old Man talking very seriously to Fat Ernie, the cop, I just meandered up and down a couple of aisles, playing the discerning, window-shopping patron, and then headed for the door.

No hurry.

Real casual.

Real cool.

The jingle of the bell above the door as I pulled it open was suddenly drowned out by Mr. Katz's basso profundo, laced with a heavy Polish accent.

"Hey, Kid," he called over to me, and I turned around to look him in the eye. "Aren't you going to take your candy today?"

Eyes hot, ears awash with an awful prickly rush, heart pounding its fists on the bars of my chest, I just stood there a second. Then, out. I backed out the door.

Walked away fast.

Faster.

Fuck it, run.

By the time I stopped under the el tracks to catch my breath, I was pretty sure that even if Fat Ernie was after me, he'd have dropped dead of a heart attack by now. So I was safe. I pulled myself together and started walking. No place in particular — just anyplace but home.

Gradually, it sunk in that Old man Katz had just taught me an extremely valuable lesson, something I didn't ever want to forget:

A man's only as big as what he steals.

So never steal anything small.

Folks say Papa never was much on thinking
Spent most of his time chasing women and drinking

("Papa Was a Rollin' Stone," The Temptations)

CHAPTER FIVE:
AL THE CARPENTER

Usually, when I remember my father, my chief regret is
that he had a stroke and was confined to a wheelchair before I
ever had a chance to beat the shit out of him, fair and square,
just one time. When he wasn't kicking me around out of some
spontaneously combusted drunken rage or molesting my older
sister, Kay, he was gone with the wind.

But lately, if I try real hard, sometimes I can squeeze past
the cold pizza leftovers of anger and pain and recall a few
fleeting moments when, I realize now, I may have gotten a
glimpse of the man he might once have been, but would never
be again.

Al the Carpenter was as hillbilly as a backwoods West
Virginia hillbilly can get.

Until he went into the Army, he'd never seen a flush toilet,
according to my dad. I'm not sure why he was always referred
to as "Al the Carpenter," as if it were a title of nobility like
"Alexander the Great," or "The Duke of Earl." I don't know if
he really was a carpenter, for that matter. And it wasn't like
we knew a bunch of guys named "Al" and had to use such
modifiers to distinguish between them. But that's what my dad
always called him. "Al the Carpenter."

They had met in the Army and served in the 99th Infantry together. At the tail end of the war they had been in on the final assault on the crumbling Thousand-Year Reich — you know, the one that fell about 987 years short?

They had been in a Veterans' Hospital together awhile, too. Al the Carpenter had had one leg pretty badly maimed. Mortar, I think. I'm not sure why my dad was there. He never discussed the war.

Ever.

Guys from the American Legion used to bring poor families — especially families of veterans — food baskets on Christmas with some cheap-shit hand-me-down toys for the kids.

Toy soldiers mostly.

Red tin fire trucks.

Candy cigarettes.

They were all beams and smiles, enjoying what good guys they were, giving to the less fortunate, and they were happy to do it, too, providing the less fortunate were suitably self-deprecating and lavish with their thanks. They were always ready and waiting for a chance to launch into stories about the war, "The Big One," they liked to call it, and listening to their tall tales was the price you had to pay for a "free" Christmas turkey or ham.

Once they came to our house, and my dad very abruptly, unceremoniously, and quite literally, threw them out, and whipped the contents of their gift package after them as they tried to scramble out of the way, ducking cans of Campbell soup and boxes of Ritz crackers and such. My dad picked them off like Sandy Koufax taking out that runner on first. The yard was icy and they fell on their asses a number of times while making their getaway. It was quite a spectacle to behold. Good thing the "krauts" hadn't had cans of Campbell soup laying around or we'd all be speaking German.

"Son," my dad said to me, "when some asshole wants to yak about all the brave shit he did in the war, you can bet a dollar against a hole in a donut he was a mudderfuckin' cook.

Or a typist. Or some brass hat's pet fuckin' poodle. You understand me?"

I didn't, of course.

At least, not then. But I knew enough to nod my head "yes," anyway. A couple of wars later, I found his observations had been more or less accurate.

"And we don't take any of their mudderfuckin' charity, either," he pronounced.

Long after my dad died, I learned from his sister, Bonnie, that he'd once been the happy-go-lucky "scamp" of the family. I remember that so vividly because it was the only time I've ever heard the term "scamp" actually used in conversation.

Aunt Bonnie recounted how, no matter how bad things were — and things could get pretty bad on a Minnesota farm during the Depression — they could always count on my dad to cheer them up with his antics. I also learned that he'd lied about his age to join the Army so that he could send money home to the family, and had hardly kept out enough of his pay for an extra pair of socks for himself.

His outfit had been one of the first to penetrate deep into German-held territory and had liberated prisoners at a concentration camp called Muldorf, very near to a place called Dachau. It was apparently right after that that he'd quit laughing and started serious drinking.

Al the Carpenter was one of my dad's best drinking buddies.

They were both collecting disability payments from Uncle Sam and on the day the monthly checks arrived, you could easily predict the course of human events. So I did my best to make myself invisible.

Al the Carpenter's bum leg gave him this weird, rolling gait, a bobbing and weaving, shucking and jiving, sauntering danse macabre, as if he were listening to his own private be-bop and really digging it. It was impossible for the neutral observer to tell whether he was drunk or sober. Maybe that's why the cops picked on him.

Or maybe they didn't need a reason.

Maybe they just did it because they knew they could get away with it.

I didn't see all of what happened. When I came around the corner by Bernie's Five Star Deli, all I saw for sure was that fat fuck Ernie the Cop — swing a kick into a guy curled up on the ground, like he was trying for a 99 yard punt to save the game for the home team. Rah-rah.

Another cop was already getting into the blue-and-white. As he slipped behind the wheel he paused to look back and shake his head, laughing. He yelled something to Fat Ernie that I couldn't make out except for the word "gimp."

There were two other cops standing there with their arms folded but their nightsticks were in their hands.

I didn't know at first who it was who was twisted into a bloody fetal coil in the gutter. Then I recognized the cap laying on the sidewalk.

It belonged to Al the Carpenter.

"Hey, kid, what the fuck're you lookin' at?" It was one of the cops. He slapped his stick against his palm meaningfully. "You wanna move along or you wanna go to juvie?"

I moved along.

In fact, I moved along about as fast as I could. When I got home, I countered the threat in my dad's "Where the fuck have you been?" by telling him what I had witnessed.

"Dad," I blurted out. "They beat up Al the Carpenter."

"What? *Who* did?"

The effect was profound. My dad was instantly reduced to straight razor-sharp sobriety. He had me take him back to where Al the Carpenter had lain, but he was gone by then and so were the cops. There were some smears of blood on the pavement and someone told us that somebody had taken Al the Carpenter to the hospital.

I went along to the hospital. It was grim. Al the Carpenter's jaw was wired shut, face all black and blue. He looked like The Mummy, all bandaged up like that. He smiled at us when we came in but I could tell it hurt him to do it. He didn't want to tell us what had happened.

"Shoot, cuz," Al croaked. "I been whupped wors'n this here a time 'r two. Jes let it go, cuz. Jes let it go..."

But my dad wasn't one to let things go.

He finally got Al the Carpenter to fill us in.

"Them boys musta already been mad about sompin. Asked me where was I goin' and I told 'em down to Ely's to get good 'n' drunk if it was still a free country, and *pow*, jes like that, one of 'em got me with his stick. Then the rest jes kinda joined in fer fun, I figger.

"Weren't like I was a-fightin' though. Didn't git a lick in. Don't believe I even tried. Jes covered up, y'know. Tried to cover my teeth and my nuts, but I didn't do so good, huh?" He tried to grin. I noticed he had even fewer teeth than before.

Al the Carpenter refused to identify the cops.

"Shoot, cuz, if they done this here fer no reason why, no how, I don't figure I want to be a-givin' 'em one..."

My dad didn't push it.

But once we were out in the hall, he knelt down and looked me in the eye, real hard.

"Did you see the sons of bitches who did this?"

I told him I had.

"Think you can point them out to me?"

I told him I was pretty sure I could.

"Okay, son," he said, rustling my hair. "You and I have got some work to do."

He rarely ever called me "son" unless it was followed by a blow. Can't recall another time that he ever rustled my hair that way, either.

As it turned out, I had no trouble recognizing the cops who had done the knuckle tango on Al the Carpenter. They more or less all hung out together at the Diamond Bar and Grill, which was kind of a cops' bar, I guess, owned by an ex-cop who gave the boys in blue plenty of free drinks and credit. We went by there one night and I pointed them out while I sipped a coke and listened to "Green Door" on the jukebox: *"Midnight, one more night without sleepin'; watching til the morning comes creepin'; Green Door, what's that secret you're keepin'...?"*

The only one I actually knew by name was Fat Ernie, who spent a lot of time foot-patrolling our neighborhood. In Chicago-ese "patrolling" means stuffing yourself with free deli sandwiches, collecting "insurance" money from the shop-keepers, and popping into an alley now and then for a quick complimentary blow-job from a hooker.

I made the other cops on sight, though, no doubt about it. Even in their civvies.

Over the next week or so my dad paid a call on each of those cops, one at a time, when they were all alone, when there were no witnesses. I didn't witness any of these encounters, or know any of the details, but I strongly suspect it was something they did not enjoy, would not care to repeat and would never forget. Fat Ernie was the only one of them I remember seeing again, and at that time he still bore some signs of my father's fists on his face.

No charges were ever brought against my dad, and there was no retaliation in kind. That was very odd, to say the least. Cops in general, and the Chicago cops in particular, are infamous for getting payback. As far as I saw, Fat Ernie never spoke a word to my dad or looked him in the eye, ever again.

In a couple of weeks, Al the Carpenter was out of the hospital and able to bend his drinking arm again. Naturally, my dad volunteered to tip a few with him, just to celebrate the occasion. On his way out of our apartment, he abruptly stopped at the door, as if he'd just remembered he'd forgotten his car keys.

He came back, sat down next to me on the couch and got real serious. The look in his eyes was distant, as if his body was here and now, but his soul was someplace else far away at another time, and he was trying to catch sight of it.

His eyes welled up — not drunkard's tears, this time, but real ones.

"One of these days, Buddy-boy," he said softly, "you're going to be a man. You remember this: just because some cocksucker is wearing a fancy-ass uniform or has a badge on his chest, or some fucking band around his arm, that don't give him no right to go around fucking up anybody he goddam pleases. If you ever see that kind of shit happening, you step in, you step right the fuck in there right in there and you kick some fuckin' ass or die trying, you understand me?"

I didn't, of course.

At least, not then. But I knew enough to nod my head "yes," anyway.

Satisfied, he headed for the door. But then he paused once more.

"Don't forget what I told you now, son."

I said I wouldn't.

"Promise me," he said.

He looked so choked up, it made me choked up, too, and I didn't even know why.

"I promise," I said past the knot in my throat.

He looked at me a long time, looked at me hard like he was trying to memorize the details of my face. I thought for a moment that he was going to smile. Then he nodded his head a couple of times and was gone.

That was the only promise I ever made to my father.

But when I make a promise, I keep it.

Adam Adrian Crown

He's a rebel and he'll never be any good
He's a rebel because he never does what he should

("He's a Rebel," The Crystals)

CHAPTER SIX:
CHICK & THE PADDLE

If Zeus had been a beatnik, he would have taken earthly form as Chick Davis, from his butch-waxed crew cut, to his fine blonde goatee, to his golden earring. Garbed in the sacred raiments of beatdom — cut-off sweatshirt, chinos and sandals — he cut an impressive figure with his powerful physique, part body-builder, part stone-mason and sculptor. Yet, in movement, he appeared to be more or less weightless, as befitting a cat who could wail some very cool licks on the tenor sax. I first heard Monk and Bird and Coltrane on his living room stereo, while hanging out with Chick's son Tommy, who was a year older than me. I was also introduced to the husky voice of Astrud Gilberto, the definitive girl from Ipanema, who immediately became the star of a thousand boyhood fantasies, temporarily edging out my perpetual favorite, Sophia Loren.

If I learned about music in the living room, I got my first real lesson on the exquisite art of the female form in his workshop, where he conjured taut-breasted, full-hipped torsos from blocks of marble, chiseling in the tiniest details of nipple, navel and pubis with loving and expert care. He seldom spoke, and when he did it was soft, short and to the point. The older I get, the more I listen to people who don't say much.

I spent a fair amount of time wishing Chick was *my* dad.

I guess one of the reasons I hung out with Tommy was that he didn't quite fit in with the White Bread baby boomer crowd, either. He just didn't look the part; he was half Japanese.

Tommy's mom, born Alice Yamamura, was a Nisei, Japanese-American. Though her parents were both originally from a place destined to become famous — Nagasaki — Alice, herself, was born and raised in the US of A, as baseball and apple pie as anybody. She scarcely even spoke Japanese.

The day after the Japanese skunked the American fleet at Pearl Harbor, Chick and his then-fiancee's five brothers were at the Army recruiting office swearing to protect and defend the Constitution from all enemies, foreign and domestic, and so on. Chick and Alice quickly got married, had a one night honeymoon and then he was off. He served in the Pacific for the duration, where he was wounded twice and earned a bronze star for heroism.

All five of Alice's brothers saw action with the 442nd Regimental Combat Team, a unit made up entirely of Nisei, except of course for the officers. They fought in seven major campaigns in Europe, including the rescue of the "Lost Battalion," 300 Texans of the 36th Infantry Division who had been cut off and surrounded by the Germans for five weeks. It took the 442nd 35 minutes to do what other Allied forces couldn't accomplish in more than a month. They routed the Nazis in no uncertain fashion, suffering about 60 per cent casualties to do it. Three of Alice's brothers were among those killed in action. A few years after the war, the Governor of the Lone Star State signed a proclamation that made all the men of the 442nd honorary Texans. To really understand the import of that, you kind of have to know Texas, but that's another story.

During the time they were members of the most highly decorated unit in the entire history of the United States Army, each of Alice Yamamura-Davis's brothers was wounded at least once, two were awarded silver stars, one was recommended for the Congressional Medal of Honor, but was given a Distinguished Service Cross.

Posthumously.

It's customary for the parents of dead heroes to go to Washington to accept the honors in their son's stead. Or at least be given the red-carpet treatment at the nearest major base. But not so with Mr. and Mrs. Yamamura.

They were unavailable.

While their sons were distinguishing themselves in Europe, "fighting for freedom" so people wouldn't get put into Nazi concentration camps, the Yamamuras, themselves, had been put into in one — albeit one much less severe — right here at home.

No charges. No trial. No due process involved.

So much for "liberty and justice for all."

Along with 110,000 other innocent Issei and Nisei, including Chick's wife, the parents of P.F.C. Joshua Yamamura were herded up and put in "Wartime Relocation Centers."

The government didn't call them "concentration camps." Or "prisons."

But there were tar-paper barracks, surrounded by barbed wire, with searchlight watch towers and guys with machine guns who would be glad to shoot you if you tried to leave.

Sounds like prison to me. I know. I've been there.

Now, to be fair, there were no ovens in the relocation centers, either. But Oklahoma Congressman Jed Johnson did apparently suggest that Congress make an appropriation to have the entire relocated population sterilized. Kind of makes you wonder who was on which side.

The excuse for the establishment of these "relocation centers" was, allegedly, to counter a threat of espionage — although no Nisei was ever charged, much less convicted, of any such crime. In contrast, there was, among German-

Americans and even non-German-Americans, a very strong
Nazi sympathy, at least early on.

There was a big "German American Bund" to solidify
Uncle Adolf's rep as a nice guy. There were, in fact, a few
instances of espionage, possibly involving German-
Americans. But there were no "relocation centers" for
German-Americans. Nobody even suggested such a thing.
Even though many of them lived on the east coast where
submarine bases and defense installations were more
numerous and the "threat" of espionage and sabotage appeared
to have been greater.

The whole thing was like that old joke :

This guy is crawling around on his hands and knees late at
night at the corner of State & Randolph, like he's looking for
something.
A cop asks him what he's doing.
"I lost my wallet on Green Street," the guy answers.
"Green Street?" says the Cop. "This is State and
Randolph. Why're you looking here?"
"Well," shrugs the guy, "the light is better here."

Japanese people may not have been *guilty* of anything, but
they were easier to see. And that beat goes on.

Unfortunately, this "relocation" scam wasn't just an
innocent or ignorant mistake. Follow the money. The net
result was that a lot of valuable property that had belonged to
Japanese-Americans wound up in the hands of a few Anglo-
Americans.

Interestingly, the camps were set up and run by a guy
whose previous experience had been with the Bureau of Indian
Affairs. That ought to tell you something.

So, no way was Alice Yamamura-Davis a fucking spy.
Although, frankly, I'd have told her anything she wanted to
know. Chick always called her "Kumi," short for "Kumiko,"

which means something like "always beautiful." And she was, too. First time I saw her, at a little league baseball game (I met Tommy when he and I wound up on the same team), I noticed that right away. I noticed that Chick — the man with the cannonball biceps — did not stand for the national anthem. Today, a lot of years later, that's one of the things I don't stand for.

It happened, on one particular occasion, that Tommy Davis fell afoul of The Law According to Mr. Hopkins, who was our school principal. Like most kids, I didn't so much dislike going to school, per se; it was just the principal of the thing. Hopkins was a puffy, balding little man with tiny glasses and an ego big enough — and twisted enough — to comb his remaining four strands of hair, from one ear to the other across his sweaty pate.

Tommy's alleged spit-balling and related subversive activities won him a date with THE PADDLE, a mephistophelian device that resembled a ping pong paddle on steroids. It was engraved "board of education," which was, presumably, supposed to be funny. Mr. Hopkins kept it in his office and used it to educate the buttocks of "trouble-makers," a practice with which I was well acquainted, and to the futility of which I was living testament. Ten whacks later, Tommy was sent home with a note to his parents in a sealed envelope.

Sealed.

The note requested that Chick set up an appointment to discuss his son's "disruptive deportment."

What followed, I have on information and belief from unnamed but reliable sources close to the President. Here's the deal:

Chick showed up at the school that afternoon. He walked into the front office. Smiled at blue-haired Miss Deering, the secretary. Headed directly into Mr. Hopkins' office. Right past Miss Deering's sputtering protests.

No appointment. Just went right in.

And closed the door.

Mr. Hopkins stood, ready to glad-hand Tommy's dad. Chick kept his hands in his pockets.

"I'm Tommy Davis' father," Chick announced, looking casually around at Mr. Hopkins' various diplomas.

"Thank you for coming by, Mr. Davis. I'm afraid I'm a little tied up at the moment but if you'd care to set up a time when...."

"You went to Northwestern, man?"

"Pardon me?"

"Like, *I* went to Northwestern, man. On the GI Bill, dig?"

"Uh... really... that's...."

"You got a master's in elementary ed — and what's this? A doctorate in education?"

"Yes. That's right."

"Boss, man. Very boss. Is that it?"

"Pardon me?"

"Is that like the famous paddle?"

Chick picked up the paddle from principal's desk and hefted it.

"You know, my old man didn't know anything about raising kids. He didn't have, like, a degree in education, dig. Never got past 8th grade himself. All he had was a big, nasty old belt. He just, like, improvised. Can you dig that scene?"

"Well, I think I..."

"You must've worked like a dog, daddy-o. How long'd it take you to cop your Ph.D?"

"Eight years."

"Eight years? Heavy, man," Chick nodded. "Heavy."

Mr. Hopkins beamed as Chick copped a casual squat beside the desk. He settled back in his high-backed leather chair like Kirk on the Enterprise. The man with a plan in command.

"So, like, elucidate something for me, man," Chick went on. "How come you got all these degrees, and really, like, wail on the education scene, and my old man was a ignorant chump. But when it comes down to it, you both decide to make the scene with violence?"

"I beg your pardon?"

"I mean, like, you can paddle a kid cause you're bigger than he is. And you got the righteous wrath of the law on your side. But after all those years digging it, the best you can do is the same as my old man did and he like never went to school at all, you dig?"

"Well, it's the policy of the school board that when..."

"That's cool, that's cool. I can dig it. But let me, like, tell you *my* policy, man. My policy is like, anybody lays a hand on my kid goes to the boneyard. You don't smack my son. Or paddle him. Not no way, not no how. Not ever. Can you dig that?"

"Mr. Davis, your son has been very disruptive in class and..."

Chick stood and leaned on the desk, looming over Mr. Hopkins like a thunderhead. "Well, just between you and me, I don't give a fuck if he burns this place to the fucking ground. You keep your hands to yourself. He's *my* son; I will take care of it *my* way. Now can you dig *that*?"

By now Hopkins was sweating through his cheap suit.

"Why, yes, Mr. Davis. I think I can."

"I *knew* that you could," Chick grinned. "Then we're cool, man. Right?"

"Yes, I believe we are."

"Crazy. Then there's just one more thing, man."

"What would that be?"

"Drop your pants."

A long pause ensued.

"I beg your pardon?"

"Drop your pants, daddy-o."

Hopkins tried to laugh, but it came out more like a cough. This was a joke, right?

Wrong.

"Now, wait a minute..."

Chick whacked the desktop with the paddle, scattering a few items, here and there. It sounded like a gunshot in such close confines.

"You got to pay your dues, man. Pay to play. Ten whacks you gave, ten whacks you get, dig?"

"You can't be serious."

"Sure I can. Now do it."

"Absolutely not."

"No? That's cool. Then you and I will get together in some private place, dig, and we will dance *mano a mano*. But I got to tell you, daddy-o, you just don't look like you're in good enough shape to make that scene. So, like, you choose. Which way you want to blow this tune?"

Slowly Mr. Hopkins stood, like a man in a trance, acting in spite of himself, completely apart from his own will. His cheeks were red, jaw tight to keep his undershot chin from quivering.

And he dropped his pants.

Ten whacks later, Chick left Mr. Hopkins' office.

He took the paddle with him.

I'm a girl, and by me that's only great!
I am proud that my silhouette is curvy,
That I walk with a sweet and girlish gait
With my hips kind of swivelly and swervy.

("I Enjoy Being a Girl," Doris Day)

CHAPTER SEVEN:
SANDY'S GRAND SLAM

Sandy Borella was a cute little girl.

Hair the color of late summer honey. Slight overbite. Huge dimples. Green pixie eyes. Like me, she was an early reader and a good student. But what made her stand out most was her athletic ability.

You name it, she could play it: baseball, basketball, touch football, running, jumping — Sandy could do it all *and* do it better than most of the boys, including me. In playground athletics, I always tried to be on her team; I liked to win.

I don't know exactly why we became friends, but we did.

I was still a fat, wheezy child. Not much of an athlete, though I tried my best. For some reason, Sandy chose me to hang around with — me and a scrawny kid named Danny Jenkins. Between Danny and I, we were the alpha and the omega of nonathletic ability. She was our hero. We were like her sidekicks — though she never treated us as underlings. For someone of such physical prowess, Sandy didn't think it was that important. Maybe she took her ability for granted because it came to her naturally. But for her, it seemed like just fun, nothing to take too seriously.

One summer — I was maybe 8 or 9 years old — we all decided it would be cool to play Little League baseball, as long as we could all be on the same team. The American Legion more or less ran the Little League. They fielded about a dozen teams and organized the whole thing. Some other businessmen sponsored teams, too. Mostly they sprang for caps and jerseys with their name and logo on them. A few bats and balls. Catcher's gear and batters' helmets. You had to have your own glove. I had one I stole from Sears. A Don Drysdale model. To be honest, I had no idea who Don Drysdale was.

Sign-up day was on a Saturday, the week before Memorial Day. They wanted everyone signed up by then so the teams could march in the next weekend's parade, though I never quite understood the connection between Memorial Day and baseball.

It was chaos at the Legion Hall that Saturday with parents and kids and Legion guys all talking at once, trying to figure out who was going to be on what team. We had no idea how to go about signing up. There were some beefy-looking guys wearing overseas caps at the main table. They looked to me like they were in charge — hey, they had special hats — so I screwed up my resolve and went up to them. I told them that we wanted to be on the same team and pointed out Danny and Sandy.

They gave each other an odd look, and one of them, a guy with a whiskey nose, shook his head and said, "She can't play."

"Yes, she can," I assured him. "She's really good. We want to be on the same team."

"Sorry, son," he said again. "She can't play."

"No really, she *can*," I insisted. "You should see her hit. She's better than me."

That last part was faint praise, I guess. I was a lousy hitter, but Sandy had been coaching me and I was getting a little better.

"Look, kid," Whiskey Nose's pal piped in. "Girls can't play."

Eclipse of the Heart

"But she *can*," I insisted again. Boy, were these guys *thick*! "We play all the time. Just come watch her."

This went on for a while until one of the guys finally spelled it out for me.

Of course, they weren't saying Sandy wasn't *able* to play baseball; they were saying she wasn't *allowed* to play, whether she was *able* to or not. Girls weren't allowed to play Little League baseball.

I didn't know what to say.

There was something going on here I just didn't understand. It didn't make sense. They'd let a lousy player like me sign up, but they wouldn't let a really good player like Sandy in? Because I was a boy and she was a girl? What possible difference did that make? I wasn't going to hit the ball with my *dick*, for godsake. I had to be missing something here. That just *couldn't* be it. *Could* it?

I'll never forget the feeling I got in the pit of my stomach when it finally dawned on me what these assholes were saying. I got a sour taste in my mouth. Like bile. This just wasn't right, wasn't fair. It hit me really hard and I felt like my head was spinning. Sucker-punched by reality. I didn't know what to do; there was really nothing I could do.

Sandy cocked her head at me and squinted one eye as if she were looking into the sun, but it wasn't the sun that made her eyes start to water.

"It's okay," she said. "You guys can still play. See ya later." She turned away and started to leave.

"But...but...but that's..." I was searching for the right word. I found it. "That's BULLSHIT!" I said. I said it really loud, too, and just as there was one of those odd lulls in the general noise level, so everyone could hear it, even in the cheap seats.

The two Legion guys glowered at me. But they didn't scare me. They didn't look as strong as my dad, and I was already pretty used to him beating on me. And I was mad.

Trapped in a red haze that made my ears hot, I looked Whiskey Nose right in the eye.

"This is bullshit!" I told him defiantly. It was easier to be defiant with that registration table between us.

But then he looked like he might just leap over the table to grab me, so I grabbed the edge of that table and flipped it up, sending all kinds of paper and pencil shrapnel all over the place.

And I took off.

No point in pushing my luck by sticking around. I guess I spent a lot of time as a kid making fast getaways. Sometimes it worked, sometimes it didn't.

Danny looked like he was listening for sounds only dogs can hear. He didn't have a clue what was going on. Sandy did, though. She grabbed him by the arm and the three of us ran like hell.

We didn't so much as look at a baseball all summer.

We spent most of our time hanging out by the lake instead. We never said much about it, but the whole stinking thing continued to eat at me for a long time. I guess it still does. But heaven hath a hand in these events, to whose high will must we bind our calm content, or so says Big Willie. And heaven's hand showed up just after school started again in the fall.

One day we wound up on a neutral playground after school, just in time for a pick-up game of ball. The field was mostly gravel, in an old, somewhat cleaned-up lot that was between neighborhoods and kids from a couple of different schools congregated there. I guess it was a kind of DMZ.

One of the team captains was a kid who had been a winning pitcher on a Legion team during the summer — coincidentally, his dad was the coach. Owned a big used car business. The other captain was Gil Sanchez who lived just down from me and went to our school, too. Teams were almost decided when we got there. The Pitcher was glad we showed up because he was having a hard time choosing between two of his pals, the last two to be picked.

"Wanna play?" he asked us. He was referring to Danny and me, naturally, not Sandy.

So we conferred.

We'd play but only if Sandy could play, too and if we could be on Gil's team. The Pitcher got both his pals, and the opposition got a fat kid, a scarecrow and a girl.

Easiest deal ever struck.

As for Gil, he just smiled and didn't say a word.

We didn't have enough kids for a whole team. We each had a pitcher and a catcher, a guy on first. Another guy covered third and second, another took short center field and the last covered almost the whole outfield. We agreed that left field would be "out." We lost the toss and the Pitcher's team chose to bat last.

At Sandy's first time up there were two men on. She drove in all three runs. Her second time, she hit a line drive that just missed beheading the pitcher and made a double. She then stole both third and home.

When we took the field, Sandy pretty much played the infield and the rest of us stood around watching. At one point she pretended to throw the ball back to Gil who was pitching, and suckered the runner leading off second base. She covered home plate while our catcher scrambled for a ground ball, caught the toss from him and tagged out the Pitcher trying to slide home.

And that's pretty much the way it went, inning after inning.

With Sandy hitting, running, throwing and catching, we incinerated them. She got a nice workout. The rest of us worked on our tans.

The crowning touch was in what turned out to be the last inning. Sandy hit a grand slam. That ball went so high and so far into center field that John Glenn couldn't have caught it. When Sandy trotted home, the bewildered catcher was standing in her way, gazing waaaaay out to where his outfielder had gone.

"Hey, kid," Sandy said. "Move it or lose it."

He moved it.

He watched with open mouth as Sandy jogged past him and stamped hard on the flattened cardboard six-pack container that was home plate.

This experience proved, shall we say, jarring, for the Pitcher and his hotshot American Legion chums. But I'll say this for him. He did have the balls to shake hands with Sandy and say "Nice game."

That was a real good day.

I don't know what became of my friend, Sandy. But I sure hope wherever she is, whatever she's doing, she's still knocking them out of the park.

Sweet dreams 'til sunbeams find you
Sweet dreams that leave all worries behind you
But in your dreams whatever they be
Dream a little dream of me

("Dream a Little Dream of Me," Mama Cass Elliot)

CHAPTER EIGHT: ELSA GREY

Until I was about nine or ten, my old man used to take me fishing with him, like it or not. After a few cracks on the head, I learned not to object. Sometimes it was just off the pier of the Minola Hotel; sometimes from a row-boat on Fox Bay; sometimes under the overpass in Big Hollow, where the remains of the Fox River trickled past. The ritual often occurred on a Saturday and commonly began with an early morning visit to Grey's Bait Shop, out on old route 12, just over the railroad tracks and almost directly across from Inga's Restaurant, where my mother worked as a waitress.

Bob Grey was an old army buddy of my dad's. They had met in the VA hospital shortly after the end World War II. He had a jarhead haircut, waxed up sharp and square in the front, almost skin-close everywhere else. It was the kind of haircut my dad thought I should have. Figured it would make a man out of me or something. I don't know. Maybe it was just to piss my mother off. She wanted to cutsie-fy me into being her little Elvis. Had a thing for hair. So that was one more thing they could go around and around about. My fucking haircut. Like two dogs playing tug of war with an old rag. If the rag gets torn to pieces in the process, they don't really care. Maybe they don't even notice. But it was rough on the rag.

Bob Grey had married well, which is to say, he'd married a Cuban bombshell named Elsa. Elsa had a voluptuous figure that made Jane Russell seem like a cardboard cut-out. She had copper-colored skin, deep black eyes that sparkled like wet hunks of coal in the moonlight and shoulder-length hair of that most peculiar orange-red color sometimes found on Spanish or Black women and nowhere else in nature. She had several gold fillings and a gold cap on one prominent front tooth that were all visible when she laughed — and she laughed a lot, a throaty chuckle, leading to a high pitched squeal that went up so many octaves that every dog for miles around started barking.

She had a heavy accent that sounded like sipping margaritas on the beach. Her voice could be as brassy as a cheap trumpet when she was cussing out her husband in staccato, machine-gun Spanish, but could be as hoarse and husky as warm brandy when she spoke to me.

If you had to describe her in one word, that word would have to be "earthy." No matter what anyone said, if it were possible to construe some sexual meaning out of it, she'd find it, and respond with that brazen chuckle-squeal, chuckle.

Sometimes she'd find a double entendre even if it *wasn't* possible.

She made Charo look like the Flying Nun.

The front of the bait shop was a little bar and grill. Nothing fancy: Burgers. Fries. Soda. Beer. About six stools at the counter and maybe three tables out on the floor. Out back was the bait area: a variety of worms, minnows and devices designed to ambush the wild and elusive Blue gill, perch or crappie. The choice of the day's bait required military precision and thus the planning required extensive reflection, facilitated by a few beers. Or more than a few, though Grey, himself, was a vodka drinker.

While Grey and my dad made death plans for perch, I remained perched on a stool out front, sipping Coke from one of those classic phallic bottles. I think for every Coke we bought, Elsa gave me two on the house while we chatted. She didn't seem to mind entertaining me and I liked her.

One midsummer day, the bait brain trust was in full swizzle, and I was on my customary stool, the lone customer in the bar and grill. There were sinks under the counter and Elsa chatted amiably with me while she leaned down to do the few dishes that had accumulated during the morning rush. If you can call a half-dozen fishermen a rush.

It was a particularly hot day and sweat had made enormous dark circles on the light cotton wrap-around dress she was wearing.

Blue, if I recall.

With little flowers.

Where the dress wrapped over itself in front, Elsa's breasts swung forward, protesting against the puny fabric the way waves lap up against a seawall, swung in a way that exaggerated cleavage that needed no exaggeration

It was mesmerizing to watch her rock and sway.

Comforting as the swell and roll of the sea itself.

Reassuring.

Soothing.

She was asking me about my little girlfriends — she always asked me about my little girlfriends, even though I always told her I didn't have any.

"No?" she'd say. "You just wait until the girls get a good look at you, honey. You'll have more girlfriends than you can shake your stick at." At the time I thought she meant to say "*a* stick" not "*your* stick" and chalked it up to the language barrier.

Now, I'm not so sure. I think maybe she meant exactly what she said.

Suddenly I became aware that she'd stopped speaking.

About that same time I became aware that I'd really been staring at her breasts. I mean *really* staring.

And about that same time, *she* became aware of it.

And I became aware that she had become aware of it.

And she... well, you get the idea.

She drew a sharp breath as if utterly scandalized. "You," she almost whispered. "What are you looking at?"

The day suddenly got a lot hotter. My cheeks felt like they might actually burst into flame.

"What are you looking at?" she asked again.

The answer was so plain, it had to be a rhetorical question. Didn't require an answer.

Didn't have one.

I waited a beat, preparing myself for what would happen after she sounded the alarm. I didn't wonder if my dad would give me a beating. He never needed a reason. I did speculate as to whether Bob Grey would join in.

But no alarm came.

Instead, Elsa leaned down close to me and whispered "Don't be shy, honey. You can tell me." Her breath smelled like cinnamon and cloves.

But I still couldn't manage any words.

Then, with the practiced ease of a matador, she stood, pulled loose the bow that had held her dress closed, and let her enormous bronze breasts spill out. My mother's breasts were as large, but hung heavily down toward her waist under the weight. Elsa's jutted forward like the prow of an ice-breaker. And while my mother's nipples and aureolae resembled fried eggs, Elsa's nipples were like large red grapes surrounded by a puffy purple life-ring.

I don't know how long she displayed herself to me. It seemed like eternity and not nearly long enough, both at once. Then she re-wrapped her dress.

"You like to look at me, honey?"

"I think you're beautiful," I squeaked.

That was enough to bring on her hoarse chuckle-squeal-chuckle. I think maybe I laughed too, don't ask me why.

"You're such a sweet boy," she said in that sacred tone women reserve for puppies and small children. She laid her hand on my cheek; it felt cool as a coke bottle. "You just wait until the girls discover you, honey," she winked at me. "You just wait."

The rest of the summer, when no one was looking, quite often she'd give me that wink and one day, I winked back at her and she roared with laughter that filled the place like a five piece horn section. We continued to trade winks like that, furtively, privately, our secret handshake.

And it was wonderful.

Adam Adrian Crown

Promise me, son, not to do the things I've done.
Walk away from trouble if you can.
It don't mean you're weak if you turn the other cheek.
I hope you're old enough to understand:
Son, you don't have to fight to be a man.

("Coward of the County," Kenny Rogers)

CHAPTER NINE:
THEO VON REMPLE

Theo von Remple was a bully.

He'd been held back so many times he was older than some of the teachers and was easily twice or even three times the size of the other 4th graders. Within a short time of his arrival, he became the terror of the playground. If he wanted to play basketball, for example, he'd just step in, tell someone else to step out, announce who was on whose side, and proclaim what the rules were. Not surprisingly, he always won. If you were lucky, he gave you your ball back. If you complained to the teacher, he promised you a beating that he seemed easily big enough, mean enough and quite anxious enough to deliver. The best thing you could do was try to avoid him. Make as small a target as possible. That's what most of the kids did.

That's what I did, too.

It was an unreliable strategy.

With his appetite for power and his confidence unchallenged, Theo grew ever bolder. He began extorting lunch money from the kids. Helping himself to their new notebooks, pens and so on. No one resisted him, but he would on occasion punch someone in the arm, or shove them to the ground just to demonstrate his strength, just to put the fear of Theo into the rest.

One balmy day in May, just before school let out for the summer, a scrawny blonde kid named Alan Nelson got a new baseball glove (Mickey Mantle model) for his birthday. In a lapse of judgment, he brought it to school so that he could use it.

Theo was on it like JAWS on a tuna boat.

"Nice glove," said Theo. "Let's see it."

Alan grudgingly handed it over.

"Really nice," repeated Theo. "Mind if I use it?" He didn't wait for an answer. Just tucked it under his arm and started to walk off with it.

Alan's eyes filled with tears as he demanded the glove back.

Theo smacked him with it a couple times, pushed Alan down. Alan skinned up his palms and knees as he fell. His glasses popped off his head and one of the lenses cracked on the asphalt. In spite of his efforts not to do so, Alan let a few tears escape. He got incredibly red in the face — all the more remarkable because he was so fair, his fine blonde hair almost white.

It was then that the most amazing thing happened.

Alan Nelson got to his feet, ran after Theo, grabbed him by the shoulder, spun him around and smacked him right square in the nose.

The rest of us stood by, mouths agape, frozen in stunned silence, waiting for the world to come to an end.

But it didn't.

Theo dropped the glove.

He grabbed his nose.

With both hands.

Then his legs went out from under him and he landed heavily on his fat butt. And then he began to blubber like an infant.

I almost felt sorry for him.

Almost.

Alan grabbed up his glove and ran away. But he needn't have run.

The fight was finished.

And so was Theo.

Naturally, Theo ran right inside and told the teacher that Alan had punched him "…and I wasn't doin' *nothin'* …"

It might have gone badly for Alan, but at that point some of us finally spilled the beans about what Theo the Terrible had been doing. So many kids reported so many grievances that the teacher was aghast — and probably embarrassed that she hadn't picked up on what had been going on all this time.

Faced with his victims' denouncements Theo didn't try to deny his crimes. He just kept saying, "But he *hit* me…"

Theo finished out the remains of the year in sullen silence. And we pretty much ignored his presence.

It was nice to have money to eat lunch again, though.

Bullies always select victims whom they perceive to be helpless, defenseless, powerless. Someone they can victimize with impunity. You can't negotiate with a bully, you can't reason with them, or change them by showing them the error of their ways. There's only one way to deal with them effectively: the Alan Nelson method.

Scratch a bully and not far beneath the surface you'll find a coward.

You want to remember that.

Adam Adrian Crown

JFK blown away
What else do I have to say?

("We Didn't Start the Fire," Billy Joel)

CHAPTER TEN: JFK

Former President and former head of the CIA, George H.W. Bush, says he can't recall where he was or what he was doing when President John Fitzgerald Kennedy was murdered. That would make Mr. Bush just about the only human being who can't. On November 22, 1963, if you were at least five years old at the time and not in a vegetative state, I'll bet YOU remember exactly where you were and what you were doing. I know I certainly do.

My impressions of that day are probably a little different from most people's. I was 12 years old and at school when word came that classes were cancelled for the rest of the day because someone had shot the President. For a heartbeat, I was swept with elation — no math class today, and I hated math. Then it sunk in.

By the time I got to the bar, where I knew my old man would be, the regulars had already assembled. These guys were, like my dad, working class stiffs. Construction guys. Truck drivers. Carpenters. Plumbers. Regular guys. A lot of them were WWII or Korean War veterans.

There was Big Johnny, the owner and bartender. Big Johnny had a guilt-thing going on because he hadn't served in the Big War with the rest of the boys. 4F, I heard. He certainly was a soft, tubby little man. Parted his thinning locks up the middle, like an old-time, wild west bar-keep. To make up for missing the party, Big Johnny offered up his eldest son, unmistakable as his offspring because of the identical bulbous nose. Little Johnny was a sergeant with the military police, stationed in Berlin. The German one. He was home on leave for the holidays, and seemed to be trying to break the potato chip consumption record.

Randy Ross, a local cop, was there, too. At one time he had been a notable "tough cop" with the Chicago P.D. rubber-hose brigade. Don't know why he left the city to take up small-town policing. Story is he got kicked off the Chicago force. I can't even begin to imagine what you'd have to get caught doing to get shit-canned from the Chicago PD. Usually the worst abuses won you a promotion. Shortly after taking a job in the sticks, Ross had caught a bullet in the head making a routine traffic stop out on Route 12 one lonely night, and hadn't been quite right, mentally, ever since. Some say it improved his personality considerably. He was still a cop, but "temporarily" assigned to the school cross-walks while the days ticked away until his retirement. He liked us kids to call him "Officer Randy." We got along well with him because he seemed to be doing his thinking on a child-like level these days. No sense of subtlety or guile. Couldn't understand irony or puns. Just took everything literally.

If you said, sarcastically, "Real good move, Officer Randy," he'd blush a little and say "Gee, thanks." Couldn't understand the sarcasm, see?

He also sometimes got words confused. Once he mentioned that he was going to an optimist to get some reading glasses. That brought out some general mirth. "Don't laugh," Randy said. "You might need glasses yourself, someday."

Chuck, of Chuck's Trucking fame, was there. He was a round, ruddy-complexioned guy with eyes, nose, and mouth continually at war for control of his face. The family business included two sons and a grandson about to graduate high school. They worked together, drank together, stuck together. I wondered what that was like.

Also on hand was Nora, who got both blonde hair and an inflated sense of desirability from out of a bottle. She drank Jack Daniels, measured in fists, not fingers, chain-smoked Camels and had the baritone voice to prove it. She would laugh at a dirty joke as easily as anyone else, and could generally top it with a dirtier one. I guess I always thought of her as "one of the guys."

Stanley was another regular. An accountant of some kind. On the oily side, a smidge too polite, committed to a losing battle to look dapper. Combed his remaining strands of hair from just above his left ear, across the top of his head to the right ear, held it in place with a pound of brilliantine and some nails. He tried for a dashing mustache, but he clipped it too short, making it look like a coal miner's runny nose. Stanley was a "confirmed bachelor," as gay men were called back then. He was mostly quiet.

Then there was my dad.

Everybody said hello to him when he sauntered in with me in tow. They were sometimes a little too cheerful, I thought. A little bit too "hail and well met" with smiles that looked like they were pumped up. It was the way you might say, "gooood boooy" to a dog you were afraid might bite you. I guess they all knew my dad was a little bit nuts.

No business as usual today. All bets were off. The watering hole was the logical place to gather, and the assassination was the only topic of conversation. The discussion went well into the night, as more news reports came in.

I perched on a stool next to my dad and sipped a coke, as the group watched the TV in stony silence. Walter Cronkite went over the known details once more, top to bottom, no new news, and then went to a station break. Hardly anyone stirred. What was there to say?

"Oh-oh," said Randy Ross. "Somebody fucked up." Spoken with the expression and tone of a man whose keen olfactory wit had detected a rude and silent fart.

"More like *everybody* fucked up," coughed Nora. "Who was guarding him, the fucking Cub Scouts?"

"No, I don't think so," said Officer Randy. "Secret Service, I think. Isn't it?"

JFK was shot at around 12:30 PM. By 2:00PM, the Dallas cops already had a suspect in custody, guy named Lee Harvey Oswald. Oswald denied shooting the President or anyone else.

"Well, all I know is, Oswald is one hell of a marksman," said Sergeant Little Johnny. "They're saying he hit a moving target — moving AWAY from him with that shitty Manlicher-Carcanno from 6 floors up. What'd they say, two hits out of three shots in, six, seven seconds? Not sure *I* could do that?" Little Johnny was an expert marksman as far as the Army was concerned, and he wasn't modest about it. He'd won a bunch of trophies for his shooting abilities, too, which Big Johnny kept on display behind the bar.

Several heads nodded sagely.

"You guys remember when the mob got Vincelli in that barbershop?" Chuck asked no one in particular. "Where was his bodyguard? Out taking a piss or something, am I right? It was a double-cross. The body-guard was the inside man, am I right? And this guy Oswalt. It's like right away they knew it was him. How? How come the cops made him for it so fast? And found him so fast? That's some fancy damn police work, am I right?"

"Yeah," said Randy Ross. "Jeese, those Dallas cops must be REALLY good, huh?"

Chuck went on. "If he was some kind of lone nut fanatic, wouldn't he be proud? Take the credit? Am I right? He says he's just a patsy."

"I don't know," intoned Randy, scratching his ear. "Something ain't right. Something about this stinks."

The group stared at Randy as if he'd started to sing Ave Maria in Mandarin Chinese.

A day later, Randy began to seem as much savant as idiot.

The Dallas cops were transporting the suspect, Lee Harvey Oswald, and in waltzes mafia underling Jack Ruby, like he owns the place, and shoots Oswald dead, right in front of the cops, the TV cameras, God and everybody.

The usual suspects were on hand in the bar to watch that live on TV. Chuck had his sons with him. For a moment, everyone was stunned speechless.

"What the fuck?" said Chuck, finally breaking the silence.

"What the fuck?" echoed the sons of Chuck like a Greek chorus.

"This is bullshit," Said Sergeant Little Johnny. "BullSHIT!"

"Bullshit," agreed the others, desperately looking to each other for a reasonable explanation.

"Oh-oh," said Randy. "Somebody fucked up."

My dad stared grimly into his beer.

"Mother-fuckers," he said, as if reminding the group of the operant natural law which governed all such phenomena, the way "gravity," would suffice to explain a man's fall from a great height.

The Kennedy Murder — these guys never called it "assassination" — would be the leading topic of conversation for many days to come, if, indeed, mumbling, grumbling and head-shaking and swearing can be considered conversation.

When the Warren Commission report came out the following year, the official verdict was that Lee Harvey Oswald, acting alone, shot JFK .

And Oswald was dead.

So, like, case closed, daddy-o.

The regulars at the bar didn't buy the Warren Report.

For one thing, a lot of these guys, like my dad, were combat veterans, and Arlen Specter's ridiculous fairy tale about a zig-zagging "magic bullet" held as much water as a soup strainer. For another, as Sergeant Little Johnny so immediately pointed out, it was an impressive feat of marksmanship that Oswald had carried off. A feat that, to this day, has not been replicated by any of the numerous expert shooters who have tried it. And Oswald himself, it turns out from his Marine Corps records, was only a mediocre shot at best.

There's an old African proverb that says, "Even a jackal will insult a dead lion," which, in this case, roughly translates as, "Blame the dead guy." Oswald never made it to trial, never got his day in court. We never got to hear the evidence against him or hear his defense — indeed, the alleged evidence and records have been sealed for the last 50 years. Why do you suppose that is? Some people still think Oswald did the crime, and that's still the "official story."

Many years later, I happened to assist in an investigation (I was hardly more than a gofer for the detective on the case). A series of rapes had been committed against young women, all of a similar physical description, in a medium-sized mid-western city. The assaults were increasing in brutality — characteristic of an assailant who would be killing his victims before long.

The local cops were on the case.

They picked up a vagrant (these days called "homeless") they liked for the crime. He attempted to escape and was shot dead by the cops. After that, the rapes stopped and everyone was happy that the law had got their man. And it was a very good year for the undertaker.

Case closed.

Except that the family of one of the victims thought there was just something fishy about it.

Enter, my boss, retained by the family to sniff out the source of that tuna odor. He said the case gave him an itchy feeling in the back of his neck. What my mentor found out was that the rapes had *not* stopped. They were still happening, but they were happening near Phoenix, Arizona. The rapist, as it turned out, was a relative of one of the local cops and pals with a few others. The hapless homeless gentleman was just a patsy. He took the heat for the crime while the cops hustled the real rapist out of town.

The homeless man never made it to trial, never got his day in court. We never heard the evidence against him or heard his defense. Some people still think he did the crimes.

These two case, unfortunately, are not two isolated and unique cases. I personally know of two others:

A small town rape-murder suspect allegedly hangs himself in his cell "with his shoelaces." Case closed.

Another murder suspect dies in a hail of police gunfire. Case closed. Even when it turns out later that the most incriminating evidence against him had been planted on the scene by one of the officers, the case is still closed.

I guess the point is that, what I learned from the JFK murder is that whenever a suspect, prime or otherwise, gets shot resisting, or "escaping," or hangs himself in his cell "by his shoelaces," or dies of "an overdose," or accidentally falls down and hits his head, or has a heart attack, or gets struck by fucking lightning, I start getting an itchy feeling in the back of my neck, too.

It's my bullshit detector going off.

If you really want to know who killed JFK, all the evidence you need is right in front of you and all the main players are readily identifiable. Just takes a little legwork, but if you really want to know what happened, take a good hard look at unanswered questions and unquestioned answers. Start with the basics: motive, means and opportunity. Ask yourself: Who benefitted from the crime? Who can you catch in a lie?

What's physically impossible? Who suddenly disappeared?
Connect all the dots.

I figured it out, and I'm not exactly a genius.

You can, too.

If you really want to know the answer.

Pussycat, pussycat
You're delicious
And if my wishes can all come true
I'll soon be kissing your sweet little pussycat lips

("What's New Pussycat?" Tom Jones)

CHAPTER ELEVEN:
GETTING A BOOT OUT OF PUSS

Mr. Z's Carousel Theatre was set up in the parking lot of a shopping mall near Waukegan, Illinois. Summer stock. In-the-round. A huge circus tent and lots of folding chairs. This particular season, they were doing West Side Story and I figured I was a natural for any show about juvenile delinquents. I got a part as one of the Sharks, the Puerto Rican gang. It was, as Jumpin' Jack Flash says, a gas, gas, gas.

I had an immediate crush on about five or six of the dancers, including the dark, smoldering beauty Sarah Wolf, who played "Anita," and a copper-haired, powerfully built girl named Dale. Chief among them, though, a baby-faced, blue-eyed blonde named Skye. I was smitten by her unpretentious laugh, and a crooked smile that made her nose wrinkle.

I loved to watch these dancers and better yet, I got to dance with them. Unfortunately, I wasn't exactly Gene Kelly. But I did all right. Had to do some spins, some lifts. It was hard work. Don't let anybody kid you. Dancers are in great shape.

My partner for some of these numbers was a bouncy Jewish girl who was a little buxom for a dancer and once, while twirling her way toward a lift onto my shoulder, she spun her breast right into my face. *Smack!*

Almost knocked me over.

We were both pretty embarrassed, and she apologized all over the place, but it wasn't her fault. Centrifugal force, you know? Good thing it was in rehearsal.

About four weeks into the six week run of West Side Story, the cast got laid low by a flu bug. I had it, myself, for a day. Some people had it for a week or more. It was miserable. Trouble was, there were some "crowd" scenes in that show. The dance at the gym. The rumble. Try staging a convincing rumble with only seven guys.

But the show must go on, daddy-o. Find a way to make it happen, make it work. So about half the chorus members would go out, do The Jets Song, quick race back and get in P.R. make-up, come out and do America. We were practically pulling people out of their seats to join us for the dance in the gym, and for the rumble...you guessed it. The girls were slicking their hair back and dressing in drag to fill out the gangs.

It was nuts.

But it was fun.

Thanks to the flu, I got a big promotion and played "Chino." I got a couple of lines and I was the guy who shoots "Tony" at the end. We had this funky starter pistol, borrowed from a local track coach. We never knew if it would fire or not. So taking no chances, instead of one dramatic shot ringing out from the back of the theatre, I strode down the aisle like a man on a mission, firing away. "Tony" had to listen carefully to know how many times he was getting shot, so he could react well. I was tempted to try to trip him up, just to be mischievous, but I resisted the impulse.

All in all, it was a great time and I was sad when it was over.

I learned a lot that summer.

I learned that not all male dancers are gay, but enough are so that if you're not, you're real popular with the female dancers.

And I learned how easy it is to be someone else and make people believe it.

That would come in handy.

Another girl I had a big crush on was Ellie.

She was directing a couple of plays for the Saturday morning Children's Theatre. Owing to an injury practicing gymnastics, she had a cast on one foot but hobbled around fairly well in an exaggerated Walter Brennan kind of way. She recruited me to star as Puss of Puss-in-Boots fame. The costume we put together for it combined some old Cowardly Lion stuff and some threadbare Cyrano de Bergerac pieces. Voila! A swashbuckling feline.

Actually, the script had a lot of pretty risque material in it — kind of a kiddie play for adults. So it was fun to do, and I got some great hugs from the director.

I guess I worked cheap.

We did two shows on Saturday, morning and noon. Then, at two, the matinee of West Side Story. Another show at 7pm. Between the Puss shows, we sent a stagehand down the street to a deli to pick up some lunch for us. I enjoyed those huge sandwiches.

One Saturday, there was no stagehand to do the lunch run for us, and it was a cinch that Ellie couldn't hobble down to get it on her cast, so it was up to me.

Fuck it.

Off I went, in Puss-in-Boots drag, lion face, plumed hat, bucket-top boots and all.

I entered the deli during the pre-lunch lull, gave the guy my order.

He was as utterly unphased as if a caped Mouse-Cat-Ear walked into his place every day of the week. Didn't so much as bat an eye, let alone crack a smile.

It took no time at all for them to rustle up our sandwiches and as I approached the register, the counterman asked me absolutely deadpan, "So. You want a saucer of milk with that or...?"

I left him a big tip.

I was born lonely
Down by the riverside
Learned to spin fortune wheels
And throw dice

("Ramblin' Gamblin' Man," Bob Seger)

CHAPTER TWELVE: CHILL CON CARNIE

Like most of the fire departments in Small Town, USA, the Wolf Lake F.D. was a volunteer company. They operated on a shoestring budget and when they wanted to buy something, like a new pumper, they had to fund-raise to get it. They held raffles and pancake breakfasts, bingo nights and chicken bar-b-q's. But it was in the summer that they really made their money for the rest of the year by sponsoring a carnival.

Now, it was called the Wolf Lake Fireman's Carnival, but the carnival was a traveling package, complete with rickety rides, cotton candy and games of chance and skill. They closed off a couple of streets in town to spread it out. The carnival took a percentage and the fire department took a percentage. People had a good time and the community was a little safer with their new pumper or whatever.

The Firemen got into the act on Saturday at high noon with dueling hoses. Very Freudian. Two hose teams would square off in the street with an empty beer keg set between them. When the whistle blew, they each tried to push the barrel past the other team using the stream from their hose. Needless to say, they all got drenched as did everyone in the crowd — some of whom even brought umbrellas. Not a bad way to spend a hot July day.

We lived within walking distance of the carnival. Actually, since we generally walked everywhere, we were within walking distance of everyplace we wanted to go, if we wanted badly enough to go there. My father would be well past drunk by summer sundown. When I was littler, I didn't understand what was what, so I went there with my old man. He did some drinking and some gambling. I rode the rides and played the games.

The summer I was about eleven or so I went there by myself. I didn't have much money — just what had fallen from the old man's pockets while he was passed out on the couch. A couple of bucks in change.

I was naturally quite conservative with my poke and gave every game a close eye before I decided it was worth the try. No point in spending a buck to win a fifty-cent prize. There were some games that had some pretty nice prizes: TV's, phonographs, radios. But I couldn't remember anyone ever winning one of them.

I decided on the milk-bottle throw. One of the prizes was a transistor radio. Another was a guitar. I was pretty sure I could throw a baseball hard enough to knock down some milk bottles. And you got three tries besides. But I decided to watch awhile. Leaning against a tent post, I sipped a coke and watched guys pitch away.

Now some of these guys were big guys. I couldn't believe they couldn't do it. Then when the scrawny little carnie tossed, he took them down with one shot, and I knew there was something odd about it. That just didn't make sense. The Carnie tried to be helpful to the customers, gave them advice, what kind of spin to put on the ball, like that. But all to no avail. I must have watched two dozen guys whip baseballs at those damn bottles. They all won something, some cheap trinket then made in Japan. But no one got the radio. Or the guitar.

An hour, I must have stood there. A couple of times the carnie asked me if I wanted to play. He even offered me a free play if I didn't win big on my first one. I smiled and shrugged him off. But I think I made him a little uneasy. Just standing, watching, watching.

You watch close enough for long enough you can't help noticing something, and I noticed something.

I noticed the way the carnie set the bottles up on the shelf, placing them quickly, but very precisely. There were three of them. Two shoulder to shoulder in front, one behind and between them.

It was so simple.

So obvious.

I just had to be sure. I waited until a couple of guys — big guys — with their dates stepped up and one of them decided to try to win that giant fluffy panda bear for his girlfriend. He took a couple of turns. Got frustrated. Took a couple more. Man, that guy could throw, too. Hate to have to catch one of those pitches. Spent a fair chunk of change going after that bear. No dice. When I thought the right moment had come, I finally stepped up to the plate and asked the guy if I could have a turn.

"I think I can do it," I told him.

"Sure, Pal," the guy said. Good luck."

"If I win that bear," I said, "you can have it. I don't have a girlfriend." Yeah, real innocent. That's me.

"Isn't he sweet, Mike" his date cooed.

"Thanks, kid," her boyfriend chucked me in a big brotherly way. "How about that guitar?"

"I'm kinda hoping to win that for myself."

They all chuckled. And just as I'd hoped they all stuck around to watch. I told the carnie I wanted to play. But I wanted to see him do it first. Was that okay?

Sure, kid. Anybody can do it. Everybody's a winner.

He set the bottles up and knocked them down easy as pie. Then he started to set them up for me. Meanwhile, a couple more of Mike's friends with their dates showed up. That was good.

The carnie handed me my three baseballs and I hefted them. Then I gave him a come hither waggle of my finger, got him to come close, got him to lean down so I could whisper in his ear.

"I know how you're cheating, " I whispered. "Want me to tell these those guys?"

The carnie's smile froze on his face but it had definitely turned sour.

"You looking for trouble, kid?" he threatened me behind his smiling teeth.

"Are *you*?" I replied. "Set them up for me the same way you do for you. Touching."

I did a casual one ball juggle while he decided.

With a furtive look at the guys behind me, he adjusted the set up. When the two bottles out front weren't touching the one behind and were spaced just right, they blocked for the rear bottle. No matter how strong you were, or how hard you threw, you'd NEVER get through to the rear one. Physics, man.

The carnie grudgingly set me up fair and square, and down went those milk bottles.

That guitar was going home with me.

"Hey, everybody's a winner!" the carnie barked. "Look at that, folks! Even a kid can do it! C'mon up!"

"No way," laughed Mike. "I don't believe it..."

"Sorry about the bear," I told him. "You might win it though. Why don't you give it one more try?"

And I shot the carnie a wicked glance. He was sweating a lot, even for July. Never saw anybody glower and smile at the same time. Thought his head might just pop.

As I was walking away from that game, I heard some bottles scatter and Mike's girl squealed "Yay, Mike, he's our man. If he can't do it, Nobody can…! " I think that bear got a new home, too.

Hadn't gotten far with my guitar when I noticed a surly-featured man in a straw fedora stroll over and whisper to the carnie. The carnie nodded in my direction and the straw fedora started my way.

Fuck.

I picked up my pace, nudging through the crowd.

Weaving my way for the exit.

I didn't make it.

The straw fedora cut me off at the pass.

"Hey, Elvis," he said to me. "You just win that?"

I nodded.

"You know how to play it?"

"Not yet."

He pecked a smoke out of a pack of Luckies and offered me one. Naturally, I took it. He lit us up.

"Your daddy a policeman, Elvis?"

"No," I said. "But he spends a lot of time with them."

That's how you lie with the truth, daddy-o.

"Can I ask you something?" Only he said "axe," not "ask." "Just between you and me, right?"

"Okay."

He axed me to tell him what happened at the milk bottle game.

"What made you think that he was trying to cheat you, Elvis?"

I explained it.

"Is that right? I'm gonna have to have a talk with him. Enjoy your guitar."

Relieved beyond belief — and in no mood to push my luck — I started to make tracks. Then I heard Straw Fedora call after me, "Hey, Elvis…"

I froze. No such thing as an easy getaway.

But he surprised me.

"How'd you like to make a little money?" he axed.

You've heard the expression "running away to join the circus"? Well, this was a carnival, and I didn't have to run very far. If 1969 was the summer of love, I'll always think of that summer as the summer of larceny. What an education I got.

I spent the rest of July and August — right up until Labor Day — working at the carnival. If my parents even noticed, they certainly didn't care. I told them I had a job and that was explanation enough to please them. I suppose my old man missed me at those times when he needed something to beat on and I wasn't within easy reach.

I taught myself to play the guitar that summer, too.

Spoils of war.

The show jumped from town to town with a play of one or two weekends in each. The closer to home a carnival is, the more of a Sunday School show it becomes, the more honestly the games are run. But these rural towns were a long way from home. About half to two thirds of the games were gaffed.

One of my first lessons in larceny was location. Though the overall effect may seem like chaos to the marks, every location on the lot is as carefully calculated as Caesar's placement of his cohorts.

The flash is at the front end. Merry-go-round. Ferris wheel. Cotton candy. Souvenirs. All the things to entice customers in. The best locations are on the right side because people tend to go there first and spend their money there first. The game agents at these locations paid a bigger cut for the privilege. In the back, all the way back, was the freak show, the girlie show and the most serious gambling. Adults only. Except for me. I enjoyed watching the belly dancers.

The Amazing Martino did his magic act back there. He wasn't all that amazing, but his assistant was worth seeing. Hard to take your eyes off of her. Which was why she was his assistant. You watch *her*, you don't notice what the magician is doing. Men watch her because they love her, women watch her because they hate her. Of course, a lot of times it's actually the assistant who does the trick, but probably not with the parts of her body under closest scrutiny. "Illusion," they say in the magic biz. That's a secret. Don't tell anybody. But no matter who does what, it's all about misdirection. And assumptions. And appearances. It's about making you think you see something you're not really seeing. Your eye sees it, but your brain makes sense of it, gives it meaning. A Magician knows the way your brain naturally works, and uses it against you.

Along the left side of the lot, which would be on your way out, are more games. In the center is the midway with four-ways — attractions that can be accessed from all four sides. No waiting.

One of my jobs was as "outside man." An outside man is a shill. I'd go up, play a game, win a nice prize, show everybody how easy it was, how honest it was. I must've heard "Even a kid can do it!" barked about 3.2 zillion times. Later, I'd put the prize back into the stock. The first inside man I worked with was Mel, the milk bottle impresario from whom I'd won my guitar on the square. He didn't hold a grudge though. I also shilled for the Amazing Martino, a couple of times. Later on I worked for the guy who ran the basketball throw game.

I was pretty good at that one.

These high school heroes would bring their dates by and take a crack at winning a teddy bear. Just sink three in a row. Lesser prizes for two out of three. Something smaller for one out of three. For zero, you got a free play at another game. Hey, everybody's a winner.

Ever borrow someone else's car?

Remember how it jarred you the first time you hit the brake?

That's because you are very highly skilled at driving *your* car in particular. These basketball lettermen were very skillful, too — at putting a ball of a *particular* size, weight and shape through a hoop of a *particular* size hung at a *particular* height. What happens if that ball is smaller and heavier and not perfectly round? What happens if the hoop isn't quite round, is hung at a lower height, set at an odd angle?

What happens is I take their money.

I wasn't a basketball player. Seemed like a pretty stupid game to me. So I didn't have any skill at shooting a regulation ball at a regulation basket. But I got plenty of practice with *our* ball and *our* basket. I looked like Wilt the Stilt with it. Tossed it in from all angles. Emptied out lots of pockets.

There are ways to gaff the game, too, but that seemed like overkill in this case. In an honest game of skill, a mark can win a prize if he has the skill — a prize worth a lot less than the price of a play. Most of these games can be straight or gaffed.

Since outright gambling is illegal in most places — though exceptions can be made if you grease the right palms — usually there's some kind of a skill element that gets the game agent off the hook.

Funny thing is, skill games are easy to gaff.

Gambling games are a lot harder. You've got a better shot at winning in an honest game of chance than with a gaffed game of skill. Can't tell you much more about that. Most of what I learned about the gaffed games I promised to keep to myself and I never break a promise.

Never.

I learned a little about playing a short con, too. Most of that I can't tell you about either. It'd be like revealing the secret to a magic trick. In fact, the only difference between a magician and a con man is the larcenous intent. But I'll tell you about one easy con, just as an example. It's called the ticket switch and it's well-known enough that it's not much of a secret anymore, and I don't feel like I'm breaking my word with that one. It goes like this:

You and your partner go into a restaurant to eat. One of you has a meal; the other just orders coffee. You get separate checks. When you're finished, you switch tickets. The guy who ate the meal takes the coffee ticket up to the register to pay — the waiter assumes he's paying for the meal. The guy who just had coffee, tells the waiter "It's on the table."

Out you go.

Next place you find, it's the other guy's turn to eat.

The only problem with this con is that the waiter or waitress will probably wind up having to cover the till and they don't make much money to start with — and I remembered how my mother worked her ass off for chump change. It's one thing to do it at a big chain restaurant, or when the waitress is snooty or lazy. But a couple of times I'd start out to work this con and change my mind, because the waitress or waiter treated me right or gave really good service. I'd wind up paying — plus leaving a nice tip.

Some con artist I turned out to be.

But I couldn't help feeling for the waiter/waitress. I couldn't help putting myself in their shoes, feeling what they would feel, and I just couldn't do it.

Seems I had a conscience.

My fatal flaw.

Adam Adrian Crown

I never looked for trouble, but I never ran.
I don't take no orders, from no kind of man.
I'm only made out of flesh, blood, and bone
But if you want to start a rumble,
don't you try it all alone

("Trouble," Elvis Presley)

CHAPTER THIRTEEN: THIRTEEN

Thirteen's an evil number.

Lots of bad juju attached. Ask anybody.

Back in the way-back-when, back in Viking country, twelve of the Aesir, the gods, were having a little soiree in Valhalla. The god Loki, known to be cunning, mischievous and a general asshole, wasn't invited. Who needs a wet blanket? But Loki crashed the party anyway, making him the thirteenth guest. Before you could say "Who invited you?" Loki had hustled Hoder, the blind god of darkness, into shooting Balder the Beautiful, god of joy and happiness, with an arrow tipped with deadly mistletoe. Balder died and the entire world fell dark in mourning.

You can see why the Norse would consider thirteen an unlucky number.

Of course, the hex might go back farther than that.

In ancient Rome, it was believed that witches met in groups of 12 — the devil was the 13th participant. Christians will tell that there were thirteen at the last supper table, Judas being the thirteenth. He's the one that dropped a dime on Jesus. The ancient Hebrews considered thirteen unlucky because the thirteenth letter of the Hebrew alphabet is "M" which is the first letter in the word "mavet" which means "death." In 1307, Philip IV of France, double-crossed the Knights Templar.

139

Seems he owed them a lot of bread from the Crusades. So he had them arrested on charges known to be false, tortured them into confessions, and had them burned at the stake. That was on Friday, October 13th.

About 80% of high-rises have no floor numbered thirteen; it goes from twelve to fourteen, something which pisses off the fire department if they have to respond to an alarm on the "fourteenth" floor. A lot of airports have no gate 13 or flight 13. Hotels and hospitals skip room thirteen. In some places, a street address that would be number 13 becomes number 12A instead.

But maybe the most ominous and chilling thirteen of all, in most people's experience, is the thirteen that marks the transition from child to "teenager," making them an official resident of hell. The no-man's-land between childhood and adulthood is a demographic that didn't exist before WWII. Too old to keep saying, "Yes, sir," but too young to say "fuck you." An unenviable situation.

For me, it's different. I'm kind of a heyoka. So I consider thirteen my lucky number.

It was the day after my thirteenth birthday.

Or maybe the day after that. My father was doing his usual thing, slapping me around the room. At one point, he back-handed me so hard with those rough knuckles that I went down, my head spinning. Maybe he finally knocked the last bit of sense out of me, because I don't know what made me do what I did next. Up until now, if he knocked me down, I'd stay down, cry it out, hoping he'd be satisfied with that. Appealing to the pity factor, I guess. Begging the gods for mercy.

But gods are fickle.

Arbitrary and capricious.

Sometimes it worked. Sometimes it didn't.

But *this* time, I don't know why, but I snuffled back my tears and I got back up. I got up and walked up to him and looked him right in the eye. And stuck my face out at him. Like, *Thank you, sir, may I have another?*

His face screwed all up as he gathered his anger for another whack at me, but this time, for the first time, I wasn't afraid. I just didn't care anymore. Fuck you, you mother-fucker, I was thinking. *Go ahead and fucking kill me, why don't you?*

Go ahead.

Do it.

The worst that could happen was that he would kill me and if he did, at least the whole miserable mess would be all over. I knew I couldn't just keep on going the way things were. If I did, I'd be as good as dead, anyway. Might as well go all the way.

Fuck it.

Yeah.

He hit me so hard my jaw popped and my ears rang, and I went down again, cracking my head against the wall for good measure. The room was spinning at odd angles, like a Hitchcock movie. My legs were wobbly and it was hard to get up.

But I got up.

I walked up to him again. My face throbbed and I could feel it swelling up. Then I did something really strange. I could feel the wetness of blood on my nose and mouth. Without taking my eyes off his, I wiped some blood off my lip with my fingertip and then licked it off. Mmmmm. Good. I think I may have smiled at him.

Then I offered up my face for another one.

That's when the miracle happened: he didn't hit me.

He got this confused look on his face and his fist wavered, then lowered. I took a step closer to him, daring him to clobber me; and he stepped *back*. I stuck my face out even further, literally turning him my other cheek as an invitation. And he took another step back.

I couldn't fucking believe it.

Something changed right then, in that very moment.
Something went out of him.
And something filled me up.
He looked at me for a second, trying to figure out what was happening, I suppose. Then he wheeled away, kicked a side table across the room, shattering a lamp, and stormed out. I could hear him slam the front door when he left. Slammed it so hard that the windows trembled.
But *I* didn't.

As soon as he was gone, my legs went completely rubbery and wouldn't support my weight. I slumped down on the floor. I was dizzy for a while, but I came out of it all right.

That was the last time he ever made me shed a tear. It was the last time he ever hit me. I'd learned something very important that night, though I didn't then completely understand what it was.
I wasn't afraid of him anymore. And since fear had been his only hold over me, I was, suddenly, free.
Free.
Only someone who's been deprived of freedom, been a slave or a prisoner, can understand what that word really means. I was my own person now. I would be who I wanted to be, do what I wanted to do, and do it my own way. I would make my own choices for myself from here on out and if anybody didn't like it, fuck 'em. At least, that's what I thought at the time.

One of my first choices was to sign up for karate at the Y. That would turn out to be a huge decision. I was pretty dedicated. I went to class four or five times a week and I practiced every day.
There are lots of reasons people say they enroll in martial arts courses: to have fun, to get fit, to meet people and make friends, to improve self-discipline...
Bullshit.

Karate might result in all those things, of course. I enjoyed it. I got in better shape. I met some people. I learned something about self-discipline and focus. But if you just want to have fun, get fit, meet people and improve self-discipline, daddy-o, then you should study ballet. Ballet will do it all. Dancers are probably some of the fittest athletes on the planet.

Karate is about fighting.

Period.

Fighting is its sine qua non, its reason for being. You can geld it if you like, water it down, lay all kinds of pseudo-spiritual crap on top of it, make it politically correct. But if it isn't fighting, it isn't karate; it's dancing. Might as well just be honest and dance. It's really stupid to carry around a toy gun and act as if it were a real one.

Over the years I would study karate, ju jitsu, aikido, kung-fu, hapkido, moo goo gai pan, and good old western-style boxing. I would learn a million variations of "fuck-'em-up waza." Probably not the best choice I ever made. But it started with a relatively innocent desire not to be anybody's victim ever again. Ever.

I bought some pretty good fake ID's that made me 16 instead of 13. With those, I could get a job. A driver's license. God bless the child that's got his own. I technically still lived in my parents' house, still went to school. But I came and went as I pleased. If I stayed out late, even overnight, I wasn't about to put up with any shit about it. My old man looked surly, but basically, didn't give me any. And that was weird, too.

One of the earth-shattering events that occurred in 1964 was the first appearance of The Beatles on the Ed Sullivan Show. I was still working as a busboy where my mother waitressed, at that time. It was a Sunday night, as I recall. Manny, the bartender, called over to me as I was taking the relish tray to the kitchen for a refill.

"Hey, Jackie," he said, "You play guitar doncha? You gotta see this."

He had the TV on and I leaned against the bar to watch. I'd never seen anything like it. The Fab Four were there in all their rag-mopped splendor with their Cuban-heeled boots and cardigan jackets. They did their big hit "I Want to Hold Your Hand," and you'd have a hard time finding four guys who looked like they were having more damn fun. And why not? There were dozens, maybe hundreds of girls in the audience experiencing a condition that psychiatrists refer to, clinically, as "completely fucking nuts." They applauded, they screamed, they cried, they tore their clothes, they swooned in their adoration. And there was something contagious about that frenzy. The pop press started calling it "Beatlemania."

Today, I guess, they'd give kids a drug for it.

It was madness, all right. But madness of a rare kind. Sinatra had provoked it. And Elvis. The music was like magic madness that set people free.

The Beatles came back and repeated their performance on Ed's "really big shoe" the next two Sundays. It wasn't a band, it was a Phenomenon. The Liverpool lads became the first pop stars to have their likenesses in wax at Madame Tussaud's Museum in London. They cornered about 60% of the singles market and at one time held all five of the Billboard top five spots and fourteen out of the top one hundred, breaking Elvis' record of 9, set back in 1956. Their second album took the number one spot in just over a week. And everywhere the Beatles went, throngs of adoring teens — mostly, but not exclusively, girls — were sure to go, wanting nothing but to worship them.

As Manny the bartender mused, "Jeeze, those guys must have to throw away pussy like it was cold pizza."

Man. How do you *get* a job like that?

It was all the convincing I needed.

Maybe it wasn't the very next day, but probably by the day after that, I went out and got myself an electric guitar — not a very good one — and the Beatles first album, "Meet the Beatles." I couldn't afford an amp so I practiced without it. I listened to those tunes over and over, played along again and again, learning each one, lick by lick. By the time I could afford an amp, I had some of those tunes down cold. When I wasn't practicing karate, I was playing and singing along with the Beatles.

But it wasn't just the Beatles, of course. I did what I guess most people were doing: I went out and got as many of the top 10 of the Billboard top 40 as I could buy or steal, and learned them. I swear I played some of those records so many times you could hear both sides at once. My first "set list" which, like everybody else, I wrote down and scotch taped to my guitar, included not only the Beatles' "Can't Buy Me Love," "Twist and Shout," "I Feel Fine" and "She's a Woman," but also Roy Orbison's "Pretty Woman" (which became the fastest selling single in recording history), "You Really Got Me" by the Kinks, "She's Not There" by the Zombies, and an up-dated "House of the Rising Sun" by the Animals.

I was a star, man. Just waiting for my chance to shine.

All the leaves are brown and the sky is grey
I went for a walk on a winter's day
I'd be safe and warm if I was in L.A.
California dreamin' on such a winter's day

("California Dreamin'," The Mamas and the Papas)

CHAPTER FOURTEEN:
ELVIS AND THE VAMPIRES

As a kid, school was always pretty easy for me. I used to hide my report cards, not because I got poor grades, but because I got mostly A's, something that would have been used against me. How I did it, I can't imagine. I was never able to study at home where there was a constant chaotic state of alarm. Whatever I was able to learn was limited to what I could absorb in class, or do during school hours, at least.

I can remember my 8th grade graduation, partly because people asked me where my parents were and I had to make up something plausible, and partly because no one bothered to invite me to the party. But that was all right. One less time I had to put up a normal front.

Just before graduation, I had a chance to meet the principal of Abraham Lincoln Community High School, in what was euphemistically referred to as a "counseling session." It made a huge impression on me. I was pretty excited about high school. I don't know why. I thought everything was going to be different now. High school was just four years away from college. And college was the ticket to the future. I was practically an adult. The prospect made me giddy with optimism.

The principal turned out to be a small, beady-eyed man wearing a sour expression and a cheap suit. Mr. Milner, by name. I entered his office as if I were approaching the great and powerful Oz, and stood before him, too timid to clear my throat. I stood there and waited while he shuffled some papers. When he finally squinted up at me, his face got even more pinched, which was quite a feat.

"Get a haircut," he ordered me.

First thing he said to me.

Just like that.

Not "Hello." Not "Welcome to Lincoln High School." Not "I'm afraid I'll have to ask you to get a haircut because we have a certain dress code here that we feel is very important because..."

Nope.

Just "Get a haircut."

And, you know, more than what he said was how he said it. His tone was utterly dismissive. As if I were no one. As if I were nothing. Less than nothing. As if he had some inalienable God-given right to dictate my every action, my every thought, right down to personal grooming. Hell, I could have stayed home for that kind of treatment.

"Get a haircut." That pompous little weasel. Just who the fuck did he think he was? It made my heart sink and my jaw tighten. Took all the wind out of my academic sails. I guess I knew right then that all the good possibilities I'd imagined for myself were never going to be. I don't think I heard a word he said after that. I was already someplace else.

As it turned out, there were two kinds of teachers at Lincoln H.S.: the humanitarians and the disciplinarians, more or less coinciding with the adherents of theory y and theory x, respectively. The humanitarians believed that every student had a desire to achieve excellence, to fulfill his or her unique individual dreams, and was capable of accomplishing great things, given a little encouragement and guidance. The disciplinarians believed that every student was a lazy, surly hooligan interested in nothing but sex, drugs and rock 'n' roll, and would be responsible for the demise of our great nation and the entire free world unless someone cracked the whip over them every second of the day.

The two camps had settled into what amounted to an academic cold war, each side hunkered down in its own fallout shelter. Unfortunately, there were fewer humanitarians than there were disciplinarians, and the disciplinarians were in greater positions of power, which forced the humanitarians more and more underground, like maquisards.

I had six classes.

I got three A's and three F's.

Nothing in between.

That says a whole lot more about the teachers than about the student, wouldn't you say?

Mr. Thomas, for example, was a pom-pom boy in the disciplinarian camp. He was a stocky bear of a man with short legs, a crew cut and a pronounced underbite. I'm not sure whether he was a good wrestling coach who was a lousy history teacher, or a lousy history teacher who was a good wrestling coach. But he was one of those staff members who made it his business every day to tell me to get a haircut. It didn't end there, either.

On one occasion he gave the class a test on ancient history — on which he'd misspelled the word "Thermopylae." I knew that battle so well I could put it to music.

In 480 BCE Xerxes demanded "earth and water" — meaning submission — from the Greek city-states. When they told him to take a leap, he took a force of at least 200,000 men (some say it was a lot more) into Greece through Thrace and Macedonia. The Greek army, led by Leonidas, of Sparta, met them at a place called Thermopylae. Against overwhelming odds, they held the pass — until a Greek turncoat named Ephialtes led a detachment of Persians along a side route that enabled them to attack the Greek position from the rear (a tactic still widely known as "Greek"). Caught in a pincer type action, most of the Greeks decided to split. But Leonidas with

300 of his own men and 700 Thespian allies, refused to retreat and were slaughtered to the last man.

The legend has it that, as he lay dying, Leonides wrote on a rock in his own blood "When you find our bodies lying here, return to Athens and tell them we kept our word." If it isn't true, it ought to be. Unfortunately, the Persians destroyed Athens. Maybe the Athenians and the rest should have been more stand-up.

At least, they might've gone down swinging instead of running.

To hear Mr. Thomas tell it, the pass at Thermopylae was a hole in a wall where the Spartans killed the Persians one at a time as they tried to get through. Actually, the pass at Thermopylae was more than a mile wide.

Suffice it to say that I finished Mr. Thomas' little test with lots of time to spare and I was the first one to walk the long green mile up to his desk to hand it in. He gave it a quick once-over and gave me a cold stare with his piggy blue eyes, as he opened his fingers daintily and let my test slip through them and into the wastepaper basket below. "Get a haircut," he ordered me, and wrote and big red "F" in his ledger next to my name.

So that's the way it was going to be.

They didn't care what was in my head, only what was on it.

I suppose my response would be predictable to anyone who knows anything about kids. Or about self-respect. There was no way I could buckle under to this and not feel like the worthless piece of shit these clowns so obviously thought I was.

Might as well hang for a goat as for a sheep, the saying goes.

So this was WAR.

I resolved NEVER to get a haircut. So, my hair was not to touch my shirt collar in back or over my ears in front? Fuck that. I'd grow my hair down to my ass, now. Fact is, I didn't really like it that long, myself. But I was just about finished allowing other people to do my thinking for me. I was still too inexperienced to understand that reacting against someone can be giving them control, too. Mindless rebellion is just as stupid as mindless obedience. Somebody else is still pulling your strings.

On the humanitarian side, there was one teacher, Mrs. Roper, who became my friend. A *real* friend, too. I want to tell you about her.

She taught English. She was a mousy woman with a large round nose, and the merriest hazel eyes you could imagine. She had awful bouts of bronchitis and asthma but she toughed it out and I both felt sorry for her and admired her tenacity. I don't know how it happened exactly, but at one point, it became clear that she enjoyed puns — and I always had enjoyed them, too. So I began to collect them and stay after class to share them with her.

Puns led to jokes. Jokes led to questions. Questions led to discussions. Before long I was staying after class all through my entire lunch period, just talking with her. We talked about a lot of things. Everything. She was the only adult in my entire kidhood I could trust to give me a straight answer.

I could tell she was being honest with me because she'd often lower her voice and glance around to see who might be within earshot. Sometimes we'd close the door. I told her about my various romantic escapades — I was at that stage where I was falling in love twice a day on average — she told me about how she and her husband Mark (who taught science) were trying to "start a family." That was a polite way to say they were fucking a lot, and I sometimes tried to imagine her in the act. With her, there was something wholesome about it, something sweet. Like cuddling a kitten.

We talked about music, about our favorite books — she even brought me one as a gift. One of her favorites, she said. A poetry collection heavy on John Dunn and Kit Marlowe. I still have that book, though it's a little tattered now. Loose pages. Cover taped together.

She sometimes gave me a special pass to a later lunch period so that I could woo the mysterious Finnish Linnah Knudsen, or whoever my flame du jour was. It was at Linnah's birthday (which I'd kind of crashed) that I first sat in with the guys who would be my first rock and roll band, practicing, true to stereotype, in Mr. Knudsen's garage.

The Sinners, we called ourselves. We thought that was racy as hell. We did a melange of Beatles hits and Presley standards, with a dash of Roy Orbison, and soon, songs I wrote myself. Nothing very original. Teen-age angst with a good back beat. But, pretty soon, people were requesting my songs whenever we played. That felt incredibly good. It was one of the few times I felt like anyone was listening to anything I had to say. It later helped me exact my petty revenge against the Lincoln H.S. fascist regime.

I manage to last out my freshman year, more or less. But when I left, I went out with style.

In the spring, you see, Three Momentous Events converged like Venus rising in Mercury, or driving a Mercury, or something. The first was that Mrs. Roper confided in me after class one day that she was pregnant. She just beamed when she said it, like all her most wonderful wishes had been rolled into one and granted. She was so happy she cried. I was so happy for her I almost cried.

All right, fuck you. I *did* cry.

I even hugged her, and I'm not a big hugger. It was a warm, soft hug, sweet as the Ivory Soap scent on her skin. Something in me wanted to keep holding onto her, and it took some resolve to let go. Sometimes I still wish I hadn't.

Now the last thing we need is high school students seeing one of their teachers pregnant. Then we'd have to admit that nice people fuck, and, gee whiz, we can't do that. Why it would open all the moral floodgates and the kids would just run wild in the streets and pretty soon there'd be a Russian flag flying over the capitol building. So naturally, a pregnant teacher was forced to go out "on leave" before she started advertising her delicate condition. As a result of this stupid policy, Camille (she asked me to use her first name when we spoke in private) had to ask me to promise to keep it a secret.

I don't often make many promises. When I do, I keep them. So I promised.

Then she asked if I would consider doing her a big favor. Well, for her, I'd have done *anything.* I'd have crawled across crushed glass. I'd have crawled across crushed glass backwards singing "Mary Had a Little Lamb," in French. Hell, I'd have gotten a damn haircut for her if she'd asked me to.

I told her to name it.

And so we came to the second of the Momentous Events: the senior class play.

They called it the "senior class play" even though a lot of other students worked on it, too. But the seniors, or at least certain seniors, were the stars. You know who: the sport team captains and the cheer-leaders, of course. Certainly not social lepers like Doc, the nerdy A.V. man with the plastic pocket protector, or like Colin "The Rat" Ratkovich the Elvis Worshipper, or like one-eyed Tico Sanchez, whom everyone suspected of knowing some of the white girls far too well.

Or me.

This year, some committee of the School Board in unholy alliance with the PTA had decided that the kids should to do an adaptation of Stephan Vincent Benet's, "This is My Country." This decision was a departure from the tradition of having the kids themselves choose what play they were going to do, usually a Shakespeare or a musical.

It was a big mistake.

The script that the committee had frankensteined together was a shamelessly jingoistic piece of crap, long on sound and fury, but signifying nothing even distantly approximating historical fact, leaving aside the issue of plagiarism.

Mrs. Roper had been put in charge of the project, having been unable to think of an acceptable excuse as quickly as her colleagues had, and now she had to select a "student-director" to work with her on it. She asked me if I would take the job. I might as well have been offered a Socrates cocktail, no chaser. No matter what, as a freshman from the wrong side of the tracks taking on a potentially important role in the senior play, I was going to be on the spot. If anything screwed up, it would be my fault. And if I did a good job, no one was going to be very pleased about that, either.

Camille understood all that. She knew what she was asking me to do.

"Sounds like fun," I said.

Morituri te salutant.

It *was* fun, too, using the word "fun" in the broadest possible sense. The super-patriotic diatribe that the committee had come up with made Adolf Hitler's nationalistic chest-pounding seem almost self-deprecating. The play was full of smug pronouncements that the Good Old U S of A was the greatest country on earth, probably the greatest in the history of Mankind, was ordained by God to carry the torch of freedom and justice...

You get the idea.

It was enough to gag a maggot.

There was no mention of enslaving the blacks, slaughtering the Indians, exploiting the Chinese, or oppressing women; no mention of child labor sweatshops, nothing at all about murdering union organizers, or about executing political scapegoats like Sacco and Vanzetti or the Rosenburgs on evidence so thin Brother Ray could see through it. Hey, why be a party-pooper?

The irony of this sanctimonious crowing about "democracy," contrasted against the utterly un-democratic way in which the play had been selected, was not lost on the brighter kids, and even the least rebellious among them was a little resentful about it. For those already on the fringe, it was a slap in the face to which a suitable response was a moral imperative.

So when Mrs. Roper and I suggested to the cast that the play might be improved with just a teeny bit of re-writing, they were all ready to embrace the idea.

We spent the first rehearsal brain-storming. What to put in, what to cut out, how to do what. Then it was up to Camille and me to take those ideas and whip them into a script.

As we set to work revising this piece of putrid propaganda, I witnessed a completely different aspect of Mrs. Roper come to light, a character change to remain unsurpassed in my mind until Linda Blair was projectile-vomiting pea soup. My mousey Camille got a devil in her eye and by the time we were finished, we had red-penned so much it looked like we'd bled all over the pages. We tried to use all the cast members' ideas as much as possible. The original script had a lot of quotes from George Washington, Thomas Jefferson and other members of the 3F's (founding fucking fathers). We kept a few of those. But we interposed quotes from other people, too: Frederick Douglass, Susan B. Anthony, Mother Jones and Sitting Bull. We made it a study in contrasts between American Mythology and American History.

And we ended it with an appeal to the audience to make America actually become what it had always pretended to be. As Martin Luther King had not yet said, to "rise up and live out the true meaning of its creed." When we showed the new script to the cast, we got a lot of nods and smiles. Everyone was on board – and knew that we had to keep these changes more or less secret.

Unfortunately, Camille's pregnancy was taking a heavy toll on her. She was sick quite a lot and as it turned out, it fell to me to keep the ball rolling. She felt bad about shifting so much of the load onto my shoulders. I told her it was cool. I was having a good time with it.

Okay, that was a bit of a stretch.

But I was doing it for Camille and that felt great. I was doing it for truth and justice, and that felt pretty good, too. And I was also doing it to give a big single-digit salute to the Mr. Milners of this world. I think you know how *that* felt.

Besides, once we started working on it together, the cast — even the tech crew — came up with good ideas and worked incredibly hard. It was a group effort; I really didn't do all that much. Just tried to keep things on course, more or less. Just a nudge here and there.

I'll admit that I was pretty nervous the night of the play. A Saturday night. Full house in the auditorium. It was a little late to have any second thoughts but I remembered something the great Cherokee humorist Will Rogers had said: "If you're going to tell people the truth, tell it to them in a way that makes them laugh. Otherwise they'll kill you." I began to feel ill at ease, and wished we had thrown in a few fart jokes.

The kids did a passionate job. I was surprised as hell. Even Tony Tobani, a senior whose head had about the same size, shape and intelligence as a basketball, rose to the occasion and spoke his lines with a diction no one had suspected he was capable of.

When the final curtain came down, there was a long silence, and I waited to hear a voice cry out "Somebody get a rope!"

Then there was some scattered applause, not very enthusiastic, just polite. The curtain came up for the cast to take their bows to find the audience clearly polarized. Most people applauded perfunctorily — these were their kids, after all; they had to applaud. But a few people really dug it and were standing, clapping very loudly. And a few people were already walking out in a patriotic huff. My pals, Tico and The Rat, were in the balcony whistling and cheering and when I got called out for my bow, they went into an orgiastic frenzy.

If it wasn't a complete success, at least we didn't get tarred and feathered, either.

That night, there was a pizza party for cast and crew, and I put in a brief obligatory appearance — long enough to connect with a lovely be-freckled blonde with cat-green eyes, named Leni. She'd played one of the anti-war demonstrator/beatnicks. We were both dressed in black and she had a "peace" medal around her neck — the first such medal I ever saw. I thought it was just a costume thing, for the play. It turned out to be hers. Her older brother had been killed in a distant and little known place called Vietnam. She took off her amulet and put it around my neck like a lei.

"I thought it was pretty good," she said. "Anyway, it took real balls, you know it?"

Turned out Leni really liked guys with balls.

Sometimes I lead a charmed life.

The most interesting thing about all this, for me personally, came afterward. There were certain people — the football players, the cheerleaders, that group — who had never acknowledged my presence — or even existence — in the course of the daily school grind. Suddenly, I found that people who had always looked through me were now looking at me.

I got waves.

I got smiles.

I got "hi."

I got a little uncomfortable.

It doesn't take much for people to love you or hate you. And they can switch-hit with ease.

The third Momentous Event that came to pass was the Lincoln High Talent Show.

This annual event featured everything from poetry readings by black-garbed pseudo beatniks to bird calls by scrawny Eagle Scouts; from lip-synch'ers to tuba solos; from folk singers to joke flingers doing everyone else's material. This year, it looked like several bands would also be in the line-up, each in its way representing a particular faction of teen society.

First, there was "The Malibus," named for the beach and not an evil mass transit vehicle even though that's the way they spelled it on the bass drum. Four blonde guys in rainbow-striped shirts, white Levi's and penny loafers. No socks, please. They sang primarily about hot-rods and surfing — though I doubt any of them had any actual experience with either.

Then came the Shantells, kind of a doo-wop group with instruments. Their main asset was a doe-eyed heart-throb named Gordy Bianchi on "lead" guitar. These were "greasers" in black leather jackets, skin tight blue jeans and engineer boots, preferably with a dog chain around one ankle. In their free time, they enjoyed going out to a deserted stretch called "The Skids" to swig beers and play chicken in souped-up Chevy's and Fords that rode like tanks, shades of "Rebel Without a Cause."

The other group was Larry and the Vampires. The Larry of Vampire fame wasn't a great musician, but his father owned a music store so they had the latest and the best in guitars, amplifiers, p.a. systems, and lighting, to say nothing of hand-trucks and vehicles to transport it all. They dressed in vampire drag complete with phony fangs and capes, and no, I'm NOT kidding. Their big number was a version of "Wipe Out" with about an hour-long drum solo. You guessed right: Larry was the drummer. He was the hero of every rich little dweeb, dork and geek in the school.

My band, the Sinners, was an odd duck. The guys all affected black turtle-necks and those English fisherman's caps that were a hot ticket after John Lennon was photographed wearing one. I, on the other hand, always wanted to be either Frank Sinatra or Elvis Presley, but both jobs were taken. So

I'd usually step out in a tux or a white dinner jacket, something uptown like that.

Understandably, the other members of the Sinners — all of whom were seniors — were pretty keen on having a crack at that big talent show trophy and having their names added to the plaque in the little display case near the library. Their last hurrah, and all that. I could hardly have refused them, even if I hadn't had my own private agenda. It wasn't long before the impending "battle of the bands" was the meat of conversation and speculation. When it came down to it, I graciously volunteered us to go on last.

It was a long, and winding show.

The Shantell's opened with Little Latin Lupe Lu and finished up with Louie, Louie. They were big on "L's." Not too big on tuning up, though.

Two brothers, dressed like clowns, did some tumbling, sort of. Maybe more like stumbling.

A chick in a fright-wig lip synched George Carlin's bit, Al Sleet, The Hippy-dippy Weatherman doing the Hippy-dippy weather, man.

The Malibus came on with I Get Around and Little Surfer Girl. Not too bad, really, if you were into that castrati scene.

Then came more stuff putrid enough to make you squirm in your seat. A trumpet quartet. A flutist stumbling through Flight of the Bumble Bee in which the bee had to make an emergency landing. A kid telling really bad, really old jokes with no particular theme. A baton twirler prancing to Stars and Stripes Forever, her red, white and blue panties slowing creeping up her hefty nether cheeks — up to that point, the highlight of the show.

Next came a brooding young girl reading sepulchral poetry so depressing she made Sylvia Plath seem like the Three Stooges.

If there was a cliche that we missed, it couldn't have been for lack of trying.

Sometime during this interminable march of mediocrity, Larry and the Vampires came on. It was almost a relief. They did their big tune, Wipe Out. Larry out-did himself, this time. His drum solo was so long even the other Vampires looked embarrassed. The M.C. (Mr. Blake, the music teacher) gave him the "wrap it up" sign about four times. Finally, they started closing the curtain on him and he got the idea.

Finally climbed down off his high-hat. Very cymbolic.

I laughed so hard I thought I'd have a kitten.

What came right before us, as we set up backstage, I have no idea.

Finally, Mr. Blake told us we were running late, so we'd only have time for one tune. That was ok.

I cued Ritchie the Drummer to crank it up and he set down the steady rock beat that would be the spine of our 12-bar rhythm and blues. Then Alan the Bassist joined in, as if it were a spontaneous thing. Derek, known as The Cicero Kid, bent out some guitar licks and took the stage doing a few steps of the Chuck Berry Shuffle. It got some applause. The curtains then opened fully to reveal Albert the piano player — the best musician of us all — as he chipped in some boogie-woogie. Then I stepped out, grabbed the mic and off we went.

There are only about a million 12-bar blues tunes that follow that classic I-IV-V progression. Roll Over Beethoven, Jailhouse Rock, Travelin' Band, Boys, Hard-Headed Woman, Big Hunk o' Love — you probably could add a dozen more to that list, easily, just off the top of your head. It's a standard thing that people jam to when they get together, a common language every musician knows.

Our song, penned especially for this show, was a medley of a dozen of the most familiar such tunes, leading up to our own original verses — each verse about a particular school personage.

For example, one verse celebrated the school principle:

160

You all know Mr. Milner;
You all know Mr. Milner's The Man.
You all know Mr. Milner,
 You all know Mr. Milner's The Man.
He knows how to fake it
'cause he never really had a plan.

See, on stage, you can just about get away with murder.

We sang more verses, most very uncharitable, roasting each member of the disciplinarian gestapo in turn. Then we did a couple more about the good guys. About Miss LaPlante, who taught Latin, Mr. Durwood (known as The Mouse) who taught math. And it was my very special pleasure to sing a verse about my sweet friend, Mrs. Roper.

If you know Mrs Roper
 I know you'll know what I mean
If you know Mrs. Roper
I know you'll know what I mean
When the play's the thing
she knows how to make the scene.

As you can imagine, the kids really got into this. Every succeeding verse got more applause. Hoots. Whistles. Shouts. Cheers. And Mrs. Roper's verse brought down the house. Apparently, I wasn't the only one who loved her.

I dug that.

Ritchie did a few bars of a solo, heavy on the tom-toms, just a little pun on Larry the V's epic Wipeout solo. Just a teaser. Then we launched into the second half of our medley, the old Presley tune called "Big Hunk o' Love."

I played this one directly to every chick in the auditorium, of course. I walked way out on the apron, made a lot of individual eye contact, pointed to a couple of girls in particular, all the tricks of the trade. Through it all I rocked and rolled, bumped and ground, using my hips like a weapon in such a suggestive manner that I made Elvis the Pelvis look like the bass player from the Kingston Trio. See, when Elvis first appeared on TV, they wouldn't show him from the waist down, because they thought his hip action was immoral or in poor taste or some kind of crap. But that moment, there was nothing they could do to censor ME. So I got a little payback for Elvis on that one.

The effect was profound.

And a little scary.

People went nuts.

They started clapping along. They got up and danced. The girls screamed and wrung their hands. And they started to move toward the stage like the oncoming tide, with one burning thought...

Okay. Screaming and tearing your hair and swooning and all that kind of hysteria was very much in fashion at that time. "Beatlemania" had set the standard several years earlier. So now adolescent girls screamed instead of clapping their hands. In retrospect, not that big a deal. Somewhere between silly and adorable.

But when you're just a kid yourself, and you get that kind of adulation, it can be overwhelmingly heady stuff. And, the first time, yes, a little scary.

We could hardly hear ourselves play.

We looked around at each other; the guys were way out on cloud nine.

So we played an encore.

And another.

And another.

As we were winding down that last tune, Mr. Blake came out with that big old trophy and set it down in front of us. That made everybody go extra crispy.

We bowed. We waved. I blew kisses. We stepped back and the curtain closed one last time.

Out front we could hear Mr. Blake on the microphone trying to get control, talking about hoping the kids had a good time and wasn't that a great show and would you PLEASE

GO THE FUCK HOME NOW! I think he may have put that last part a little differently, but the spirit was there.

Backstage, we listened as we broke down our gear. We were all packed up before the din began to dim.

Albert looked like he was in shock, shaking his head in disbelief, or maybe trying to wake himself up.

"Holy shit," was all he could manage.

The Cicero Kid bopped over to me, pecked a Lucky Strike out of a pack, flipped open his lighter and by snapping his fingers, put it into action. He took a long drag. The tobacco tasted much better when smoking it was breaking a rule.

"Hey, daddy-o," he said softly. "Did you see the fucking look on fucking Milner's fucking face?"

I feigned bewilderment. "Who?" I asked innocently.

The Kid blew a perfect smoke ring high into the sky.

"How sweet it is," he said.

No doubt about it.

Victory is sweet.

But short-lived.

A couple of decades later, I decided to do something I had been promising myself I'd do for a long time: track down Mrs. Roper. I wanted to thank her for all the kindness she'd shown me, for being decent and caring when I desperately needed it. I wanted to tell her how much that meant to me, how much *she* meant to me. And I wanted to see how her daughter had turned out. I had imagined a lot of different scenarios, in several of which I made tender love with that sweet woman, even though she was still married and many years my elder. It would be a separate, private, one-time moment between us that we would cherish forever, and would nurture and enrich us both.

That's fantasy for you.

It wasn't hard to trace her. I'd learned how in the interim and I was good at finding people who didn't want to be found. And it's not like she was hiding.

But I wasn't ready for what I found out.

Camille had died shortly after giving birth to her daughter. All those years I'd thought about her, wondered about her, wanted to find her, she was already gone.

I spoke with Mark, who'd re-married to a woman who'd been a close friend of them both. They'd raised Cam's daughter, Camille Marie, and had had several other children together besides. Camille Marie, who'd never known her mother, was all grown up and married with kids of her own. By the sheerest coincidence, she happened to be visiting when I called and I had a chance to tell her what I knew about her mom. How decent she had been. How gentle. How strong. I told her all about the senior class play and made her laugh a couple of times. Her laugh sounded just like her mother's.

When I ran out of recollections, Camille Marie was clearly choked-up. And I guess I was, too. She thanked me for telling her about her mom, and invited me to come for a visit sometime. Said she'd like to meet me. I told her I'd like that, and that I'd see about it.

But I knew I never would.

I didn't promise.

Two wheels a-turnin',
One girl a-yearnin'
Big motor burnin' the road
I'll ride the highway
I'm going my way
I'll leave a story untold

("Ride Away," Roy Orbison)

CHAPTER FIFTEEN:
THE LEGEND OF JAKE YAMADA

When I was a kid, I spent a little time in McNulty County Jail. No need to go into the details, too much. I'd gotten into it with a local cop, kind of a Barney Fife on steroids.

He was a pimply-faced little wretch who used to be that kid who reminded teacher that she hadn't collected the homework. He had his lips super-glued to Authority's ass, and like most of his ilk, while he was a mincing sycophant to those above him, he was a cruel sadist to those under him.

He made the assumption that I was one of those under him, and that where he made his mistake. He naturally thought I gave a fuck.

But I didn't.

I was leaning against, almost sitting on, the bumper of my car, enjoying a smoke on a hot summer night, waiting for a certain young lady to get off work when Barney came waddling down the sidewalk like his dick was bigger than his leg. He ordered me to move along, and I tried to explain to him that it was my own car that I was leaning on, so it was cool.

Like most cops, he got all aggressive, regardless of whether he was legally right or wrong. It brought my hackles right up.

But, hey, fuck it.

I was in too good a mood, what with the romantic prospects before me, and I was determined not to let this schmuck with a badge ruin it. I could drive around the block for the next ten minutes and pick up my sweetie on the fly.

Without another word, I turned away, started to get in my car.

I felt a searing hot pain and felt the impact as he cracked me across the ear with his nightstick. And then I kind of lost control of myself.

I don't remember much detail. The drift of it is, I took that stick away from him and did everything except literally shove it up his ass — and I considered that. I remember dragging the moaning dickhead by his belt, down the hill to the police station, right across from the McNulty Bijou Theatre. I got the door open, dropped him unceremoniously in the lobby. I said something cocky — don't remember what it was — then turned on my heel and strode righteously for the door.

I didn't make it.

Now I was waiting for trial on charges of assaulting a police officer, resisting arrest, disturbing the peace, and possession of a bad attitude. I didn't have the bail money handy so I was in for about thirty days. During that time, I had approximately one visitor.

One.

And he was somebody I hardly even knew.

"Heard what you did, kid," he said, instead of "hello." "Kind of stupid, wasn't it?"

"Yeah," I said. "Kind of."

"Still. Took balls."

"I was just mad," I said shrugging it off.

He brought me a whole carton of smokes. Lucky Strikes, too.

166

Eclipse of the Heart

His name was Jake Yamada. Not to be confused with heavy-weight champ Jake LaMotta, though, like the champ, not a bull you'd particularly want to be in the way of when he started raging.

Yamada was older than me by a good chunk. I once, long before, had watched him play in a homecoming football game. He had much the same effect on guys who tried to tackle him as a windshield traveling at 60 miles an hour has on bugs. He jogged downfield with the ball while tacklers ricocheted off of him like .22 rounds off of 1-inch thick steel plate. As he approached the goal line, two, three, then *four* guys jumped on him and he just kept going, carrying or dragging them along. A few yards away from scoring, he shook himself free of defenders the way a dog shakes off water, and calmly strolled across the goal line.

Since that time I'd seen him around, here and there, now and then, and always said hello to him, the way kids do to someone they admire.

Yamada was Japanese and Cherokee, the fruit of two groups that had been treated less than decently by Uncle Sam. He had a powerful physique from many years of construction work and recreational weight-lifting. Had boxed some, too. Reminded me of a Great Dane — deep chest, broad, powerful back and shoulders, tiny waist, massive thighs. He had a reputation for having a short fuse and being tougher than a cheap steak. Judging from his gridiron performance, I figured it was probably true.

But I had no idea.

Yamada had two loves in his life. His Wanda and his Harley. Some would say not necessarily in that order. Wanda was a cute black pixie with a button nose who stood about four feet nine inches tall and weighed a little less than one of Yamada's legs. They were the odd couple's odd couple and plenty of guys cracked wise about how Yamada liked Wanda because she stood at perfect blow-job height. Or how Yamada didn't actually fuck her, he'd just stick her on the end of his penis and spin her like a propeller. Stuff like that. And never when Yamada was within earshot, of course.

Wanda's only competition for Yamada's affection was that motorcycle. He'd raised it from a pup, rebuilt it, tuned it up, finished it all himself. He spent every possible moment tooling around on that chopper, usually with Wanda riding behind him, her arms wrapped tightly around his waist. That was his bliss, daddy-o. He just loved to ride.

I can remember once coming out of a Woolworth's with a coffee-to-go, on a gray morning in early November, with pellets of freezing rain tapping into my cheeks like little needles. Yamada cruised slowly by wearing just his ragged Levis and a dago t-shirt. No helmet, no jacket. I guess my mouth must have dropped open because he kind of smiled at me. I nodded and he nodded back.

Bad as he was, Yamada wasn't a real hell-raiser. Not a big boozer or doper or anything like that. He'd been in a couple of scrapes, but he'd ended them in each case with exactly one punch — all that was needed to send the antagonist to never-never land for a while. Doesn't take long for word to get around about that kind of thing. He became known unofficially as "the F.B.I." — "Fuckin' Bad Indian." Hell, maybe *officially,* too. Most everyone came to leave him alone — which was perfectly fine with him.

Unfortunately, "most everyone" did not include the McNulty County Sheriff. It came to pass that Yamada was pulled over and cited for a loud muffler. He apparently told the deputy what he thought of that, and the deputy cited him for a bunch of other stuff, too — everything from reckless driving to sinking the Lusitania. The deputy had — very wisely — called for back-up and once Yamada was safely in handcuffs, the officer grew quite bold. Somehow, while in custody, Yamada grew a split lip, and a black eye, and bruises the shape of a nightstick on his back and belly. Somehow, while impounded in the Sheriff's parking lot, his bike also got busted up, if not completely demolished. When Yamada's case got to court, the judge felt no need to inquire how Jake had sustained his injuries, let alone ask about the bike. Jake copped to the loud muffler and disturbing the peace and paid the maximum fine in exchange for which, the rest of the charges were dropped.

And I'm pretty certain the smug deputy figured he'd gotten over on Yamada and that was the end of the story.

He'd have been wrong about that.

It was 4th of July weekend and one of the hottest summers on record in McNulty, Illinois. People flocked to McNulty Dam State Park in search of a little breeze. It's a lovely place and one of the things it's locally famous for is a long set of hills where the bolder set would take their toboggans in the wintertime. You go downhill a long ways, great for getting up speed, then the hill suddenly curves up, like a giant speed bump, then another long descent and another speed bump. There were three, maybe four of these. It was known as "Suicide Hills." Not very original, but apt.

Around mid-afternoon, the hue and cry came to the Sheriff's office that some naked wild man was terrifying people picnicking at the park. Two of the County's Finest were immediately dispatched. As they entered the park, they spied the aforementioned wild man — who was, indeed, naked, and whose physique, they knew, could only have belonged to one man. He acknowledged them with a rude hand gesture and sprinted away.

The cops went after him in hot pursuit. Lots of heat but no light.

As they flew over the second of Suicide Hills' giant bumps they abruptly discovered to their chagrin that Yamada had dug a small trench across the road. It wasn't as wide as a church door nor deep as a well, but was more than enough to bring the squad car to a lurching halt with a broken axle. Fortunately for the gendarmes, they were wearing their seatbelts As the dust cleared, Yamada appeared, taunting the cops with vivid descriptions of both their ancestry and their mating habits, and the cops got out and took after him on foot.

Silly boys.

He led them into the woods and while they were in there chasing their tails, he circled back around to their cruiser. He took the shotgun out of the car and emptied the magazine at it, taking out radiator, windshield, windows and radio. He then set the vehicle on fire.

Not burdened with puny appetites of any kind, Yamada used the payphone at the entrance of the park to call the Sheriff's office and apprise them of the situation. The two remaining squad cars were dispatched to the scene. In the time it took them to get there, Yamada had lain a home-made chain of calthrops with four inch spines across the road.

When the officers arrived on the scene, they saw the dense black smoke from the burning squad car drifting up over the hill, and sped toward the site. The calthrops eviscerated all four tires on the first car, which impeded its progress sufficiently that the second car — losing two tires of its own — rammed into it from behind. One of the officers sustained a fractured wrist, but otherwise they were unhurt. When Yamada appeared again and made some uncomfortable sounding suggestions as to where they might stick their badges, they took off after him as fast as their little donut-powered legs could carry them.

Yamada led them on another merry chase through the woods. Giving them the slip, he then returned to the road and gave the two recently arrived squad cars precisely the same treatment that he'd given the first one.

Carrying the three shotguns he'd now collected over one shoulder, like a major leaguer warming up to bat, he ambled over to the McNulty River, calmly exchanging pleasantries with folks he happened to pass along the way. He broke down the weapons and tossed them into the river. Then he prepared to enter it himself and effect what, in the trade, is known as a quick get-away.

A woman's hysterical shriek stopped him.

"Tammy! Tammy!" she screamed as she ran stumbling along the riverbank The lady's daughter, maybe 5 or 6 years old, had apparently been wading and had been swept up by the deceptively swift undercurrent. You could just see a bit of her yellow dress wafting on the surface, heading downstream.

While other bystanders were too stunned to move, or hadn't yet figured out what was wrong, Yamada was already in the water. He overtook the girl in just a few powerful strokes, retrieved her and quickly carried her to shore where a crowd had gathered. For a moment it didn't look good for her. She was limp and not breathing.

Yamada set her down and gave her mouth-to-mouth. It took only a few breaths, but it seemed like forever. Then she puked up a lot of McNulty River water began to cry for her mommy.

You can probably imagine how mommy grabbed her up and held her tight. There was a good bit of back-slapping, then. Oddly enough, no one even seemed to notice that Yamada was still stark naked, or if they noticed, they just didn't care. At that moment, it just wasn't important. He withdrew shyly and slipped away like the Lone Ranger, before anybody saw him go. He hit the water just as sirens began to approach from the direction of the entrance. Emerging two miles upstream, for good measure, he managed to sink a Sheriff's Water Patrol boat while the skipper was ashore grabbing a sandwich.

And with that, Yamada made his way home.

I have no idea how long those six cops chased each other through the woods after Yamada split. I suppose it was just lucky they didn't wind up shooting each other.

Whether that was good luck or bad luck, I'll let *you* decide.

I was playing a gig at Harrigan's Roaring 20's Marina Bar and Grill, where Yamada sometimes worked as a dishwasher, cook, bartender, bouncer, and/or general roustabout. We covered the Billboard Top 40, more or less. Rock standards. Did an original when it was late enough and people were drunk enough. One of the big hits at the time was a song that a particular lady at the bar kept requesting. The lyrics went like this:

Baby, let me bang your box.
Baby, let me bang your box
Baby, let me bang it; Baby, let me bang it.
Baby, let me bang your box.

Come to think of it, maybe that was the title, too.
Not exactly Cole Porter.
But, as they say on American Bandstand, it had a good beat and people could dance to it, so we covered it. They didn't make enough booze to enable me to sell that stupid song convincingly. There was, however, that lady at the bar, a regular patron, a green-eyed girl with long straight brown hair, whose curves could inspire much better lyrics. She came in alone, didn't drink all that much, but she loved to dance. She usually wore out several partners in the course of an evening, just the kind of endurance I find delightful.

She not only danced with complete abandon to the Bang Your Box song, she sang along, for god's sake. Sang along and looked me right in the eye all the while.
You don't suppose...?

We had just finished banging the box for the umpteenth time that night and I was announcing our "short break," a "pause for the cause" just long enough for a boozin' transfusion and for the cats to scratch in the sand box. With all the windows open to catch a breeze, I could hear a car crunch to a sudden stop on the gravel outside.
Several cars.

172

Hell, a *lot* of cars.

Then cops started pouring into the place like we had a free all-you-can-eat donut special going on. There were all kinds of cops: local, county and state. And they were in a surly mood. I decided to stay up on the bandstand.

Then it happened.

Some sort of explosion.

No, not an explosion, a tornado.

No, not a tornado.

An earthquake.

No, not an earthquake.

Yamada.

The cops had come to arrest him for his indiscretions at McNulty Park and Yamada had decided that he didn't care to be arrested again, thank you. And now cops were flying in every direction, most of them quite perturbed at the way this was presently going.

I don't know how many cops there were.

But there were a lot.

I don't know how many Yamada sent to the emergency room.

But there were a lot.

No matter how tough you are, though, if enough guys armed with clubs and saps and guns want to take you down, you're going down, brother.

And Yamada went down.

But even when they finally walked him out, with four guys on him, it wasn't clear who was taking whom where. Nevertheless a whole bunch of cops inadvertently earned their pay that night and a fair number would carry reminders of it for some time.

Sometimes, that's as good as it gets.

There's a postscript to this saga.

Not too long ago, I got a note from a guy who knows a guy who knows a guy I know. Sent me a newspaper article about some social worker who was being recognized by the

173

community for his many years of service as a juvenile officer. Had a lot of quotes from kids whom he'd helped out along the way, stuck up for them when it was a bum rap. Went to bat for them in a hundred different ways. Not your typical juvie officer, trust me on that one.

Yeah.

You guessed it.

Jake Yamada.

Hell, you just never know.

I'm on my way,
I don't know where I'm goin',
I'm on my way,
I'm takin my time, but I don't know where.
Goodbye to Rosie, the Queen of Corona
See you, me and Julio down by the schoolyard

("Me and Julio Down by the Schoolyard,"
Simon and Garfunkel)

CHAPTER SIXTEEN: MITSUYOSHI

When I was a little kid, I was not only the fat, wheezy kid, but I was often the new kid and, thanks to my scholastic achievements, sometimes "teacher's pet," besides. Perhaps you can imagine what a winning combination that was. More than that, I had no idea that I was good for anything but to be a punching bag. My parents taught me how to take a beating. Never taught me how to give one. I saw everyone — every male anyway — as bigger, stronger and more powerful than me.

Resistance was futile and was going to hurt a lot.

So I was the favorite target of every punk and playground bully within pushing distance. I gave up my seat on the bus, my pen, my crayons, my lunch money, whatever. Once a couple of older kids almost made me give up my pants.

Later on, I learned how to adopt tough-guy camouflage and, as long as I was careful not to be in the wrong place at the wrong time, I could get by with it. Slicked back my hair. Black leather jacket. Switchblade in my pocket. Straight razor in my boot. But that was all bluff. And I was just savvy enough to know that the first rule of bluffing is that sooner or later your bluff gets called. I lived in day to day terror that it might be today.

175

But I made it into my teens without being found out. That's when I met Lori Ohashi. She was the most exotic-looking girl I had ever seen up close, and being close, close enough to catch the scent of her hair, made me almost dizzy, presumably from all my blood leaving my brain to flood into my dick.

She had dark, almond-shaped eyes, set at an oblique angle; long, very straight, very black hair. Subsequent to my emergence as a petty local rock star, I'd been getting a reputation as a make-out artist and decided to shine my light on her at the Christmas Dance.

She was very sweet to me. Danced with me. Went for a little walk with me. As far as I knew that was the international signal for "Let's make out." So I kissed her on the side of the mouth. Then lightly on the mouth and she kissed me back. Then I kissed her adding some tongue, too, and she even answered with the tip of hers.

I thought I had been transported directly to heaven. Do not pass go. Fuck the 200 dollars.

Then I slipped my hand up to her breast; she gently moved it down to her waist. More kissing. Then back went my hand; and she moved it back to her waist and shook her head "no." More kissing. And my hand, all by itself, drifted up to her breast again. She let the kiss end, looked into my eyes, and put her hand lightly on mine.

In the next instant, a white-hot pain seared its way through my wrist, up my forearm and into my elbow. Instinctively, I turned away from the pain and went down on my knees to try to escape it. As it subsided a little, I realized that I had not been struck by lightning. Or hit in the elbow with a baseball bat. Lori had done something to my hand, had turned my wrist in a direction god had never intended the joint to go. Backwards, upside-down and inside-out.

She was holding me completely at her mercy — using one hand. Not *even* one hand. Two or three fingers.

No words can ever convey the shock and dismay that swirled through my adolescent brain. Somewhere in the distance I heard her say, so softly, "I like you. But I'm not like all your other girls. Okay?"

"Okay," I said. "I'm sorry. I like you, too."

What the hell else could I say?

That was the first moment that I began to question the standard mating dance I'd learned. For some insane reason, even though girls liked sex as much as boys did, they had a social obligation to decline the first offer, for fear of being considered too "easy." The proper thing for a gentleman to do was to offer a second time, possibly a third. Even the absolute "easiest" girls I'd ever met, felt compelled to do this dance the first time you were with them. I thought it was stupid. But it was the way things were done.

That was also my first introduction to "martial arts," in this case, ju jitsu. which Lori's father had been teaching her since before she could walk. He knew all that stuff — ju jitsu, karate, kendo. I asked her about it later that night, much later and very casually, too, so I wouldn't seem too un-cool. Just idle curiosity, see? Say, honey, I was just wondering what was that incredibly painful fucking thing you did with my hand?

Something like that.

The next day, Saturday, I went to the YMCA to join Mr. Ohashi's beginners' class for two of the wrongest possible reasons. First, I figured, here was the secret weapon I needed to become the Invincible Lord of the Neighborhood. Bullies beware. Second, I was pretty sure that I was taking the shortest road to Lori Ohashi's panties.

Wrong on both counts.

That first day, Mr. Ohashi showed me — along with some other newbies — how to practice falling so you don't get hurt, or at least not hurt as badly as if you fell any other way. That's all I did, besides watching. But what I saw amazed me. Sensei (as I came to call Mr. Ohashi) would invite three, four, even five of his black belt students up at one time to spar with him. He tossed them around like rag dolls, and none of them ever even came close to tagging the old man. While he did it, he smiled and gave them pointers, compliments, encouragement. This went on until the point of exhaustion — not his.

The students'.

There was something going on here I didn't understand and I was determined to find out just what the hell it was.

So I started going to the dojo every day, even days when I knew Lori wouldn't be there. Two or three hours a night. An added benefit was that it gave me someplace to go other than home or the street, and the street gets fucking cold in the wintertime. On a good roll, I wouldn't have to see either of my parents for more than a couple of minutes a day, or every couple of days, even better. They didn't care much for my comings and goings, but I did it anyway. There was nothing they could threaten me with that they hadn't already done to me, anyway, and I was past the point where I was afraid of them.

The intriguing thing about ju jitsu is the degree to which you use your opponent's own strength and energy against him. It's almost as if he hurts himself. The tough part is that it takes calm precision to do effectively and that takes practice and practice takes time. And I was far too impatient.

Karate appealed more to my immature spirit. Not as subtle as ju jitsu, but just as effective, in its way. Block, punch, kick. I could understand that. Ego problem.

The word "karate" is something of a pun. It can mean "China-fist," that is, Chinese pugilism, or it can mean "empty hand." Unarmed combat. Mr Ohashi's style of karate was called goju-ryu, which is also kind of a pun. "Goju" means hard/soft, which aptly describes the combination of hard blocks, soft parries, hard strikes and soft locks and throws. Goju also means fifty. There are fifty basic techniques in the system. And in training, we practiced each technique fifty times.

I visited quite a few other martial art schools in my days as a singer/songwriter-errant. I sampled shoto-kan, uechi-ryu, aikido, t'ai chi, tae kwon do, kung pau, and a few odds and ends. Each of them had some value. Each one had a bit of the truth, and none had a monopoly on it. Before long, I had learned dozens of ways to inflict harm on another human being virtually — and literally — at my fingertips.

Lucky me.

In the process, I also learned about some weapons: the jo, or short staff; the bo, or long staff, the sword, the tonfa, in happier days a rice grinder; nunchaku, a flail for beating the chaff from the grain, a sai, sort of a trident for fishing. I was fascinated by how the Okinawan people of that time, having been forbidden swords or other weapons, had devised ways to use everyday farming implements as weapons every bit as effective as the samurai's katana.

Truth is, practically any ordinary object, from a drinking straw to a pencil to a credit card, can be put to deadly purpose.

Anything can kill in the hands of a killer.

That's because a fighter's effectiveness has nothing to do with his fighting "style" or school, or the weapons he does or doesn't carry. The fighter's real weapon is commitment. Commitment is the result of cultivating a superior will.

In my experience, the one who wins a fight isn't always the biggest or strongest or fastest. It isn't always the man who's in the best shape, or has had the most training or most experience. It isn't always the man with the best gear, or most high-tech weapons. But it is always and invariably the one who, at the critical moment, has the superior will.

There are many ways to cultivate that will. Just like you build bigger, stronger biceps by subjecting those muscles to a greater workload than they've ever done before, you cultivate the will through challenging it. The keenest blade is forged in the hottest fire.

You might, for example, decide to throw a thousand short front kicks. Now it is highly unlikely that you will ever actually be in a situation where you have to throw a thousand short front kicks for some tactical reason, and you don't need that kind of muscular endurance in a fight, either. Fights don't last that long.

So why throw a thousand kicks?

Because by doing it you become the kind of person who's willing to throw a thousand kicks. And most people aren't.

A man with a superior will is more dangerous half asleep, hung-over and stark naked than most men are well-rested, sober and armed to the teeth.

Took me a long time to figure that one out.

I should mention Mitsuyoshi.

He was a year or so older than I was but we were about the same size and picked things up at about the same pace, and often wound up practicing together. When the time came that I was invited to take the test for shodan, first degree black belt, Mitsuyoshi was ready for his, too.

A black belt isn't a big deal. It does *not* mean you're some kind of "expert," no matter what you see in the movies. But it is your first real rite of passage. Even though it only means you know the basics well enough that you can practice without hurting yourself, it also means that now, you really belong. Lots of people — maybe most people — quit before they get that far, which is like being satisfied with learning most of the letters of the alphabet.

The test was pretty tough.

The first part included a collection of pre-arranged movement exercises called "kata." There were fifteen in all. We had to do three — but we didn't know which three. We chose one of them. Sensei chose the others. So we had to know all of them well.

180

The second part was kumite, sparring. Each of us had to spar with every other member of the dojo, starting with the lowest ranked students and working our way up to the four higher ranking black belts who helped Mr. Ohashi run the dojo. There were 35 or 40 members in the dojo. I sparred three minutes with each of them, one right after another, with no more rest in between than it took for one of them to leave the mat and another to take his or her place. Do the math. By the time I got to the black belts who could pretty easily kick my ass, anyway, I could hardly hold my hands up.

But the toughest opponent was Mitsuyoshi.

We were very well matched. Partly because we had practiced together so much that we could read each other's intentions, and we liked similar moves. We pounded each other, with neither able to score a clear point. Drew some blood though. It recalled to my mind something from Shakespeare: *"...who today shall shed his blood with me shall be my brother."*

After Mitsuyoshi, I had nothing left for the black belts. I stayed on my feet but I have no idea what I did. Nevertheless, Ohashi-sensei looked pretty pleased. Mitsuyoshi and I both passed.

After we had showered and changed, we joined sensei for what amounted to a marathon drinking session. It's impolite to pour yourself a drink, so you pour one for someone else, then he responds in kind, pours you one of whatever you just poured for him. Nothing like hot sake to soothe sore muscles from the inside out.

Before long we began taking turns telling very crude jokes. Some of them were hilarious. Some were just crude. They got worse — and funnier as the night wore on. I was surprised to hear Lori tell one or two.

By the wee hours, I had drunk so much sake, I couldn't remember where I'd parked my legs. My lips and tongue did unfamiliar things when I tried to speak. With supreme effort I could make the room stand still.

And I wasn't the only one. By two in the morning, most of the students had folded and excused themselves to stagger back to their sleeping bags. Mitsuyoshi and I were among the last few who still hadn't succumbed.

Mr. Ohashi, himself, showed no signs of inebriation. No sleepy eyelids. No slurred speech. No inaccurate hand. He appeared to be ice cold sober — right up to the moment he passed out. The senior black belts then ushered the remaining students out, and Mitsuyoshi and I began the challenging task of making our way back to the room we were sharing, leaving Mr. Ohashi to his slumber, snoring so loudly we thought he might swallow his face.

It took an incredibly long time to travel the hundred feet to the converted-garage apartment, stopping every few steps to brace against each other until the seas calmed down a bit, then lurching into the trough once more. When we finally arrived, the other two guys sharing the space — the other two black belt candidates — were asleep more or less where they had fallen. We cat-footed around and whispered, but a platoon of buglers wouldn't have awakened them.

It was hot and sticky as the devil's armpit that night and I opted for a refreshing shower. But I couldn't recall the correct order for removing my clothes and wound up on my ass from trying to pull my pants off over my shoes. Mitsuyoshi came to my rescue — he could afford to be magnanimous since he was wearing shorts. He tugged my trousers until they came free, taking shoes with them and then helped me peel off my shirt without taking the skin along. He aimed me at the shower and cast me off in that direction.

The spray was ice cold and felt glorious. I let it sting my face, fill my mouth and over-run it.

"How is it?" he whispered loudly.

"Mglempff," I said.

"Move over," he said.

In the next instant, he had stepped out of his shorts and shirt and was standing under the cold spray beside me. The shower wasn't really big enough for two, but we shared it anyway, half in, half out. It was easy to do if we sort of put an arm around each other's shoulders — which also helped us remain standing. I remember that his body was all but completely hairless, smooth as marble. Just a small black patch of fine hair around the base of his penis.

I turned around to let the spray pinprick the back of my neck and felt my leg brush against Mitsuyoshi's cock. I glanced down and was somewhat surprised to see that he was erect.

And so was I.

Well, what do you know?

He made a sound close to a chuckle and started stroking his cock. Great minds think alike, of course, so I did likewise. We stood close together, looking down at each other's work. His cock was classically sculptured, the skin of it slightly darker than the rest of him. We pressed closer then, letting our hands, then our cocks brush against each other. We placed them side by side. I remember how warm his felt against mine and I wondered if he was feeling the same thing from me. Then we each put a hand down to encircle both penises together and wound up naturally intertwining our fingers to keep them in place.

As if we shared one hand and one cock, we began stroking them in tandem, together.

I don't know how long this went on. If felt like a very long time — and a very short time. Eventually, we both reached orgasm, roughly at the same moment, because as I saw that he was getting closer, it brought me closer too and vice versa. We shot warm semen at each other, all over our clasped hands, all over each other's cocks. I remember how some of his clung to my thigh, to be swept away by the shower spray.

We used up a lot of water, I guess.

That must have been the only part of us that hadn't been exhausted during our test, and now we were completely spent. I collapsed on my tatami, not very well dried off, and watched as Mitsuyoshi lowered himself down slowly, until he fell the rest of the way. Then he sprawled out, part of the soft, white cotton sheet draping his thigh.

I couldn't remember ever feeling so completely content.

As I was drifting off to sleep, I spied a mosquito landing on my out-flung forearm. I was too weak to move, and frankly, hadn't much of an inclination to do so, either.

"Knock yourself out, pal," I mumbled to him as he drank his fill.

Then, the most remarkable thing happened, and I swear this is true. There he was, engorged with my blood, and when he tried to take off he couldn't do it. Now, whether he had made too much of a pig of himself, or whether there was so much alcohol in my blood that he'd become a second-hand drunk, I didn't know. But he ran along the runway of my arm trying to get airborne, bouncing along my skin like the Wright Brothers in the fucking Kittyhawk. I could almost hear his little engine sputter and cough. It was so poignant and so ridiculous that it made me laugh. I laughed so hard I cried.

And I couldn't stop. I believe I laughed myself to sleep.

Blood brother to a bug.

PART THREE

Adam Adrian Crown

Old woman, old woman, oh you treat me so mean
You're the meanest old woman that I ever have seen
Well I guess if you say so
I'll have to pack my things and go
Hit the road Jack and don'tcha come back
No more, no more, no more, no more
Hit the road Jack and don'tcha come back no more

("Hit the Road Jack," Ray Charles)

CHAPTER SEVENTEEN:
THE JUDGE

After dropping Stede off, I found myself driving around aimlessly for a while, on automatic pilot, and was surprised to find myself at the apartment of Estrella Garcia. She opened the door still mostly asleep. One look at me and her sleepy face was replaced with a grimace.

"Gato," she gasped. "Baby. Are you all right?"

"Not exactly," I said.

"Jesus, you got blood all over…"

"It's not mine."

Well, *some* of it was. But not a lot. Had a gash on the back of my head that maybe could use a couple of stitches. Otherwise I was good to go. That wasn't my main concern at the moment.

At the moment, I was starving.

I asked if she'd like to go out for breakfast. She said she'd rather make us some. Smart girl. Couldn't very well go skipping into Denny's looking like a slasher-movie stunt man.

"You get out of those clothes," she said, and led me to the bathroom.

I was feeling giddy and uncoordinated. Hands were shaky. Couldn't unbutton my shirt. She helped me get undressed. Clothes were getting crusty. Dried blood. She put them into a green plastic garbage bag.

She got me into the shower, which was in a white clawfoot tub. Kept asking me if I was okay. I kept nodding that I was.

I don't know how long I stood under that spray of water. Long enough for her to make breakfast. At one point, I turned the handle from hot to cold. Could hardly feel the difference. Maybe there wasn't any.

Orange juice.

She gave me orange juice and it spread its magic through me like sweet, liquid sunlight. I drank some more. A lot more. Maybe a quart. Thirsty.

Steak and eggs, God bless her. Toast. Lots of toast. And butter. And jam, do you have any jam? Grape? Perfect.

I ate.

She watched. Sipping coffee. Our Lady of the Furrowed Brow.

When I couldn't eat anymore, I leaned back in the chair and sighed. I was still wrapped in towels.

"More, Baby?"

"No. Thank you," I said. "That was…" I sat there nodding, unable to find the right word. "Could you get me some clothes, you think?"

"Sure," she said.

"If I could just stretch out for a little bit…"

"Mi sofa, su sofa," she said.

She helped me over to it. I felt like Samson, post-haircut. She found me a pillow, too, and I lay down, nestling into the bosom of that wonderfully soft couch, like being hugged by a big teddy bear.

"I just need a few winks," I said.

I slept for two days.

I awoke in her bed.

I didn't know how I'd gotten there. She was sitting beside me, fully dressed, propped up on pillows, reading The Moon is a Harsh Mistress, by Robert Heinlein. She was about halfway through it.

"TANSTAAFL," I said.

"You're awake," she replied.

"What time is it?"

"Tuesday," she said.

"Wow."

"You had bad dreams," she said.

She had gotten me some clothes. Jeans. A white t-shirt. Sneakers. Hat. I got dressed.

"Where's my other stuff?"

"Burned it," she said. Very smart girl. "Are you in trouble?"

"I don't know. Maybe."

It was about noon. She made us sandwiches and coffee.

What I'd done was too huge to wrap my mind around. People were dead. And I had killed them. It didn't seem real.

I remembered the look on Preacher's face when I shot him, that moment of terror in his eyes when he understood that his time was up. I couldn't help wondering about him. How did he come to be who he was? Did he like Chinese food? Did he like to dance? Did he *turn* mean, or was he born that way? Yesterday he was alive and now he was dead, and that was absolutely, one hundred per cent on me. I felt a loss, somehow. There was something sad about it. I felt sorry for his death, not because it was *him*, but because it was death. Every death is sad. Blessed be the merciful for they shall obtain mercy. I guess I was fucked, mercy-wise.

Then I remembered what that sonovabitch had done to Amy.

So fuck him.

But it still scared me. No, not scared. Disturbed. Nevertheless, I was astounded by what I'd done, especially at my capacity to do it so well. It was an awe-inspiring thing.

189

Like the first time you ejaculate, or better, the first time you reduce some lady to a shivering, senseless jello of ecstasy. Wow. Did *I* do that?

And you know that this is some serious fire you're playing with.

And if you're not careful you're going to get burned but good.

Probably even if you *are* careful.

Maybe Bikergirl gave the cops my description.

Or maybe the cops put the pressure on Stede.

Maybe I should've stayed in Mexico.

It took the cops a little less than two weeks to pick me up. I was arraigned on charges including arson, multiple counts of murder, and felony murder, and a whole laundry list of other stuff. Each of those murder charges could mean twenty years to life in prison, or even the death penalty. If sentences ran consecutively, there would be no point making plans for what you were going to do when you got out.

I pleaded not guilty on all counts, and was remanded without bail, pending a preliminary hearing. I didn't have bail money, anyway.

When Stede came by to visit me he told me that one of the cops who arrested me, and had led the boys in giving me the requisite beating for "resisting" — a guy named Parker — had been present for at least two of the drug deals with the bikers. I made a mental note of that.

The Reverend came by, too. He offered to help me with an attorney, a member of his congregation. In Texas, as in most places, if you're represented by a public defender, you might as well play Russian roulette with an automatic. Besides which, the public defender who'd represented me at the arraignment looked like he was about 12 years old and bore a disturbing resemblance to Howdy Doody. I knew if he represented me at trial I would be in Howdy Dog Doody. So I accepted the Rev's kind offer. Past that, I was glad to hear that Amy was home now, recovering as well as could be expected. Physically, anyway.

Sometimes the physical healing is fast and easy compared to the emotional healing.

My advice is never to go on trial for any crime in Texas. They love to fry people down there. If they could get away with it, they'd have the death penalty for jaywalking. And this was even without a psychopath like George Bush as governor. It isn't just that there's a presumption of guilt. They really don't care if you're innocent, as long as you're convicted according to the rules, and they're not particularly worried about the rules, either. They don't exactly have a portable gallows right out back, but they might as well.

They'd rather kill ten innocent people than let one guilty person slip through their fingers.

And, of course, I wasn't innocent.

A charge of capital murder required that either a grand jury or a preliminary hearing be convened to determine whether or not there was sufficient evidence to warrant a trial. The rules vary wildly from jurisdiction to jurisdiction and I don't know how they decided which one they were going to do, but there's a big difference. At a grand jury, it's just the prosecutor and the jurors. There's no judge, no defense attorney, no nothing. You might not even know you're the subject of a grand jury until the cops come knocking with a warrant for your arrest. It's the prosecutor's show, and he'll only present the incriminating evidence no matter how much exculpatory evidence he knows about. Thus the maxim: "A prosecutor can indict a ham sandwich."

At a preliminary hearing, there *is* a judge, there *is* a defense, and all the rules of evidence attach. The judge decides whether a crime has been committed in the jurisdiction, and if so, whether there is probable cause to believe that the accused committed the crime.

The cops had nothing on me, but in Texas, they convict people on *less* than nothing. They claimed to have acted on an anonymous tip. I wondered if that was Stede.

Stede certainly would have been the first suspect — boyfriend of the girl these bastards had violated. If they leaned on him hard, threatened him with a dope beef, some hard time, maybe, I couldn't blame him for folding. He'd have lasted in prison until the first lifer tried to recruit him for the drop-the-soap championships.

For most people, being in a prison environment is beyond their experience. They can't begin to imagine the casual cruelty and the arbitrary violence. It sucker punches them and they never get over it. It's the shock of it that gets to them. But it didn't take me by surprise me at all. I had grown up in hell.

While I was awaiting my hearing, I had a bachelor pad at the El Paso County Jail for a week. My roomie was a hillbilly named Ronnie Lee, going down for a jewelry store smash-and-grab. We mostly kept to ourselves.

While I was there, I witnessed a guy die because the guards withheld his insulin. I know for certain that they murdered another inmate, making it look like he hanged himself with his shoelaces.

Shoelaces.

That's a knee-slapper. Not many legit coroners will buy that one, but it seems to be a favorite when the cops know nobody's going to ask any questions.

Another guy, next cell over, sliced his arteries up with half of a double-edged razor blade he'd palmed on shaving day. Did the deed right after "breakfast" which was an egg, half an orange, a slice of white bread, and the world's shittiest coffee. We yelled for the bulls all morning. By the time the Sheriff's goons came lollying in, he'd been cold for a couple hours.

The presiding judge at my hearing was a woman. A female judge was a rarity anywhere in those days, and in the wild west, it was unheard of. So she must have been really something. I'd later learn that she was, indeed, something, and even at her tender age — I guessed late 30's or early 40's — there was talk of her running for governor.

She had blonde hair, with a dash of silver in it, and cool green eyes, quick and sharp, eyes that could so suddenly dart in your direction like a cat pouncing on a field mouse, that it could take your breath away. She had the kind of beauty that no make-up could enhance, and maybe that's why she didn't bother to wear any. She had a tendency to lower her head, and peer up from under her brow, like a boxer. Her high cheekbones made it look like she was always on the verge of smiling. But when her full, puffy lips, stretched across those broad teeth, it was an expression without humor. I had the uneasy feeling that I was appearing before the Cheshire Cat, and those broad teeth would be the last thing I would see before she sent me to perdition.

When she spoke in her languid Texas drawl, her voice was steady and sure, completely in command, and at ease with her authority. I knew that I was shipwrecked in the land of no bullshit, where she reigned as Queen. If I displeased her she could order me hanged as easily as she could swat one of the flies that she ignored buzzing around the courtroom.

I could scarcely take my eyes off of her.

At the very start of the hearing, before the prosecutor could even get a good head of steam up, the judge interrupted him.

"How did the accused come by those injuries, Mr. Graham?"

"Resisting arrest, your honor."

Her cat eyes pounced on me.

"Is that correct, Mr. Flynn? Did you resist arrest?"

"No, Ma'am," I said, standing up. "But I sure would have if I'd known I was going to get a beating, anyway."

193

"You may sit down, Mr. Flynn. Go on, Mr. Graham."
I was beginning to like this judge.

On with the show.
The prosecution had that "tip from an anonymous informant," and not much else. Bikergirl was unable to pick me out of a line up. The best she could do was narrow it down to me or one other guy, and that's not something you can get a conviction with, not even in Texas. I had broken down both guns — even though the .38 was never used — into their component parts and ditched the pieces in different places. So they didn't have any ballistics evidence, and there was no way to tie me to the guns. Every stitch of clothing I'd worn, Estrella had burned, including my boots. I miss those boots.
I suppose it was possible that they might find a fingerprint, but it didn't seem likely.

Technically, when you're the defendant, it's not your job to prove you're innocent, it's the state's job to prove you're guilty. If they can't do that, you're under no obligation to say a word in your defense.
But this was Texas.
So it's good to hedge your bets.

It seems that the day after the incident at the roadhouse, a reporter from the El Paso Herald-Post got a phone call from someone who called himself "Primo." According to Primo, the Aryan Knights were put down by his gang, Los Lobos, as a warning to all gringo gangs to "keep their shit North of the border." Primo provided the reporter with proof. A trophy he'd taken. It was Preacher's blood-stained colors.
When someone else confesses to the crime you've been charged with, and there's evidence to back it up, that takes a big bite out of probable cause. Even in Texas.
But I had a better defense than I thought I had, because the Reverend did something I wish he hadn't done. He perjured himself. He testified that Stede and I had been at the church all

194

night on the evening in question. We had attended a prayer-vigil for Amy, and had crashed there afterward. There were affidavits from a half-dozen other witness willing to testify to the same thing. I wondered who these people were.

The Reverend's testimony got it on the record — and reminded the judge — what had happened to Amy, too. The testimony of a man of the cloth is not without some clout. And the gang-rape of a sweet young girl doesn't go over well in very many places. But the main thing was that I had an alibi. And that someone else was credibly claiming responsibility for the crime.

The defense rested.

The judge turned toward the prosecutor.

"Anything else to offer, Mr. Graham? Do you have any other witnesses?"

"Uh, not at this time, Your Honor."

"Do you have any physical evidence connecting the defendant to the crime?"

"Not at this time your honor. The People are confidant that we can develop further…"

"When you do, Mr. Graham, you're free to re-file. Charges are dismissed without prejudice. You're free to go, Mr. Flynn."

She looked me right in the eye when she said it.

She wasn't smiling.

Later, when I signed for my meager personal belongings, there was an item I didn't recognize in amongst my wallet, keys, sunglasses, ring, watch and change: a note, neatly folded and tucked into my wallet, sticking out at the top like a bookmark.

I opened it up and read it: *2155 El Dorado Drive 7 p.m.*

"Are you stayin' or goin' ?" the surly cop asked me.

"I'd love to stay," I beamed back at him, "but I really have to split. Thanks for everything. Give my love to the rest of the guys."

He didn't think it was very funny, either.

I drove out to El Dorado Drive at the appointed hour; found the address easily. It was in an upscale residential neighborhood. Big houses on big lots. I recognized her name on the mailbox.

She answered the door herself. She had a highball glass in one hand and it struck me that she hadn't waited for me before getting started.

"Thank you for coming," she said.

"It's my pleasure," I replied.

She offered me a drink and I accepted, but we didn't haggle about what it would be. She brought me a scotch, neat. The place was furnished in a mix of wild west and ultramodern chrome and glass and leather. Original oil paintings of horses on the walls.

I wondered if she had painted them.

I perched on the edge of a cream-colored leather sofa and she sank back deeply into the matching chair opposite me. I waited for her to talk.

"Tomorrow's my birthday, Mr. Flynn."

"Happy birthday, Your Honor," I said, and raised my glass to salute her. I was out-classed and trying my damnedest to be suave, but I was only seventeen. At seventeen you think a hard-on is suave.

"Perhaps you'd like to give me a present?"

My mind went slightly loopy. This was like one of those stories in the tits-and-ass magazines. "How I fucked My Girlfriend's Grandma," or some such drek. I was not yet over my near fatal case of testosterone poisoning, and my imagination and my cock shared a direct hot-line, just in case of emergency. I wondered what it would be like to kiss her, what her body looked like, what it would be like to fuck her. I wondered if I should move closer, say something more...

"Do you have a dollar, Mr. Flynn?"

"Yes, I think I do."

"Wonderful. Give it to me and sign this."

She handed me a two-page agreement retaining her as my legal counsel. She'd already signed and dated it.

I didn't get it.

She handed me a pen. It was a Montblanc.

"Once you retain me as your legal counsel, anything you tell me is privileged, and I cannot be compelled to reveal it to anyone. You sign right there."

I signed.

"Good." She took a deep swallow of her drink and set the glass down lightly on the mirror-topped table. "Tell me about that roadhouse massacre."

"I don't know anything about..."

"Mr. Flynn," she cut me off. "Please don't insult my intelligence." Her voice had all the chill of the grave in it when she said that. I immediately knew two things in my gut. One: This was a person not to be fucked with. Two: This was a person whose word could be trusted.

"In confidence," I said. "Just between you and me.

"Attorney and client," she said.

So I told her.

When I was finished, we sat in silence for a long time. As if she were meticulously parsing what I'd said. Tasting it in every part of her mind, the way you swirl good wine around your palate. She asked me a few questions. Why did I do this or that? How did I feel about this and the other. She took her time, digesting it all.

"You don't plan on staying in this area, do you, Mr. Flynn?"

"I don't have any particular plans one way or the other."

" Good. Then would I earnestly advise you to seek out opportunities elsewhere. That is, I assure you, friendly advice. I do hope you take it."

"I appreciate that, Your Honor."

Abruptly, she stood up and extended her hand to me. "Thank you for coming," she said again by way of dismissal.

"You're welcome."

"Good luck to you, Mr. Flynn.

And that was that.

I decided to take the Judge's advice and git outa Dodge while the gittin' was good. I had wanted to say good-bye to Parker before I split, but that didn't work out. I still kind of regret that. I owed him a split lip. But, alas.

I did stop by to say good-bye to Amy.

She was up and around, healing up pretty good. On the outside, anyway.

"I don't understand," she said. "Why do you have to split?"

"I just have to."

"Are you coming back?"

"I don't know," I said. "Maybe."

"I love you, you know." And she brushed my cheek with the back of her fingers.

"I know," I told her. "Thank you." And I kissed her on the cheek.

Outside, I paused for a breath and slipped on my shades, taking one last look around before shoving off. I heard the Reverend calling my name. I waited while he jogged across the lawn to catch up to me. When he had, he stuttered around, like he'd forgotten something just on the tip of his tongue

"You sold your car, I heard."

"Traded it in," I said.

"On what?"

I pointed put the VW bug parked across the street. White. Convertible. My guitar case sticking up in the back seat.

"How are you fixed for gas money?" He started to reach for his wallet.

"I'm all set," I told him.

Finally, he just offered me his hand to shake, and I shook it.

"You take care now, son. Take real good care. And God bless you."

And then I got out of Texas as fast as I could get there. That lady judge was quite a remarkable person, and she left a real impression on me. She would pop into my mind unbidden from time to time, and I wondered about her, what her story was. What it might be like to — well, you know how that part goes.

I never expected to see her again. And I certainly never suspected that seeing her again would change my life forever.

Just goes to show you how wrong you can be.

Adam Adrian Crown

I've been a puppet, a pauper, a pirate,
A poet, a pawn and a king
I've been up and down and over and out
And I know one thing
Each time I find myself flat on my face
I pick myself up and get back in the race

("That's Life," Frank Sinatra)

CHAPTER EIGHTEEN: ODD JOBS

I left Texas so fast I was in Missouri before you could say "Hi-yo, Silver!" For the next couple of years I kicked around here and there, working odd jobs, sometimes literally singing for my supper. I started doing more folk type things that lent themselves well to a singer-songwriter, one-man band. Did a lot of Dylan, Joan Baez, Judy Collins, Woody Guthrie. Simon and Garfunkel. Folk music was once described as "hard-hitting songs by hard hit people." Seems to fit. Seemed to fit me, too.

During that time, three weeks in one place was a long time. Being a gypsy is a real education. You do a lot of different kinds of work. Meet a lot of different kinds of people.

One of the first real jobs I had when I was a kid, right after I dropped out of school, was at James Menswear on State Street in Chicago. Stockboy, first. Then salesman. I got the job through no fault of my own. It was the result of the good offices of my karate teacher's father.

Let me back up a second.

Jake Renway was only a couple years older than me but already a black belt. His Sensei, Mr. Mosby, gave him permission to start up a little dojo in his basement. Kind of a satellite of the main dojo which was in Evanston. Maybe Mosby-Sensei had other young black belts doing that, too. I don't know. Here in the States everybody thinks that a first degree black belt, shodan, is a big deal. They think it means you're an "expert." I suppose that's relative.

But shodan really just means you're not a beginner anymore and you can get down to the real work now. In Japan you're not any kind of a teacher until you're a fourth degree (Shidan) at least. Sixth degree (rokyudan) before you think about having your own school.

Shodan? It's kindergarten.

But here in the States? It's impressive to people who don't know any better. Or for people who are marketing karate like Dunkin' Donuts. A black belt in one year for one thousand dollars? Fat fucking chance. You'll deserve that belt about as much as George W. Bush deserved to be President.

Anyway, Jake had permission from his sensei, so everything was square business. And when Mr. Ohashi split for the coast, I needed a new place to practice. We worked out in Jake's cold, damp basement on that hard concrete floor every night. About a half-dozen hardcore kids. A bunch more tourists. But it was the fanatics that comprised the nucleus of the dojo. Besides Jake there would be Merle, Scott, and me. Merle eventually became a real martial artist. Mastered karate, ju jitsu, hapkido, and a few other side dishes, too. Got drafted. Went into Special Forces with all kinds of honors. Made it through combat with all kinds of medals and a few serious scars. He was tough. But not tough enough. Nothing he'd learned proved an effective defense against Agent Orange. A few years after the war he dried up and blew away. Leukemia, I think was the official cause. Naturally, the government refused to consider that his illness was service-related, and left him on his own.

Scott was pretty cool. Rode a motorbike. Gave me a lift on it from time to time. Got into the Easy Rider thing with my pal,

Stede. Stede made out okay. Scott didn't. Got knifed in the joint.

I think Jake became an engineer. Married the girl next door. Had 2.3 children. I don't know if he kept up with his karate practice.

Then there's me.

And you know how I turned out.

Jake's dad worked at the 1st National Bank of Chicago. Head Teller, Senior Head Teller, Grand Exalted Senior Head Teller For Life. Something like that. Basically he counted other people's money all day. That had to be a drag. Finally got to him, I guess, because he suffered a massive heart attack that almost killed him, and a second one sneaked up on him in the hospital and tried to finish the job. I went with Jake to visit him once. The man did not look at all well.

But he made it.

He started reading some of Jake's books while he was laid up. He was so weak that reading qualified as physical therapy. Went through a lot of books on yoga, zen and aikido. And you know what? He rehabilitated himself from that heart attack, lowered his blood pressure, lost some weight, quit smoking and started looking pink instead of gunmetal grey.

It was an impressive transformation.

His whole outlook changed, too. He was full of energy, full of drive. He became so extroverted, he'd start a conversation with a complete stranger and end up showing him some aikido, getting him started on the path. He made the Jehovah's Witnesses look like Shakers.

When Mr. Renway suggested I get a square job to hold me over just until I became a rich rock star, there was no way I could get "no" past his ears. He went off on the idea like a dervish and before I could say much of anything to protest, he was on the phone and had set me up with a job downtown.

Now, he knew I was under-age — legally speaking, you were supposed to be at least 16 to be working a regular job. But I had a pretty good starter set of false I.D's — social security card, driver's license, and a bunch of other junk — and he was willing to let me keep my private business private.

I like that.

Respect.

So, before I knew it, there I was, on the train from the near north suburb of Wolf Lake to Union Station 30 or 40 minutes every morning and back again in the evening. It was a nice chance to do some extra reading. Driving down and back is strictly for suckers. Takes you longer and you have to curse your way through a 20 minute back-up at Lincoln and Touhy every morning. Then you have to find a place to park all day, which costs you a pretty buck. There's no place you can drive to downtown that you can't walk to faster, or grab a taxi, if you're really feeling immortal. Then you get to fight the logjam of outbound traffic for another hour, the perfect end to a perfect day.

What's the point?

James Menswear was, at that time, one of the uppermost of the upscale men's shops in the Loop. Just a few blocks from Union Station, across the Jackson Street Bridge, make a right down State Street. It was well within splurging distance of the Palmer House (and occasionally we would make a delivery there), across an alley from the Berghoff, where they served better food than most people deserve. We carried only the best lines of the day, Arrow, Botany, Pierre Cardin. Had custom tailors on premises, too. You could have coffee, shoot some pool, read the latest Playboy or the Tribune or the Sun-Times, listen to the stock reports, and get a haircut and manicure while you were waiting for your new trousers to be hemmed.

The first day I reported for work, I was introduced to a Mr. Etienne, a dapper, balding little man with a pencil thin mustache on his lip, and a fresh flower on his lapel every day without fail. He was a walking textbook on how to dress with class. I forget his actual title, but he was the ranch foreman, pardner. Kept things going smoothly, assisted the salesmen so they could maximize their sales. Maybe write up a sale for you so you could move on to another "client," or he would give an opinion on a tie, tell a quick joke, compliment the wife's taste — whatever the situation demanded. He was a 40 regular menswear commando.

Each morning before opening the doors, he held inspection to be sure every salesman was a quiet statement of impeccable taste. He might have you change your tie, or stockings — even get a different shirt. Had to fit the James image. Look like a James man.

That day, my first day, it had been raining, so I wore a topcoat, a tan London Fog trenchcoat, over what I considered my best threads. But then I had to line up for inspection with the other seven or eight guys on my floor, and with my raincoat off.

I'll never forget that one.

Mr. Etienne walked down the line like a Regimental Sergeant Major, looked each man over from haircut to heels. Better be smartly dressed, starched and pressed, shoes shined. Here and there he made a comment, just a suggestion — which had the force of law.

When he stopped in front of me, he gazed at me as if he didn't actually see me. Or as if he were trying to see me through a heavy fog. Unable to make out my shape he gave up and moved on.

Then he stopped, turned back and gave me a twice-over.

What he saw was a kid with long, long hair, brushed back greaser-style, wearing a fuchsia jacket with a black velvet collar, a white pleated-front shirt, a white satin tie, skin-tight black trousers that flared at the bottoms to accommodate Beatles-inspired demi-boots with a 2 1/2 inch Cuban heel. I imagine I looked, to him, like the unholy love child of Roy Orbison and Paul McCartney.

"Do you," he asked me with sly suspicion, "belong to some sort of *singing* group?" From the sound of it, you'd have thought he was asking me if I belonged to a notorious Pig-Fucking Fraternity.

Dismissing the rest of his troops, he took me in tow and we went on a tour of the store during which he showed me where everything was, and dressed me from the skin out, remaking me in his own image.

"Do you have anything like this?" he'd say, pointing out a suit or a shirt or a tie. The answer, of course, was always "no." By the time we were done I had wardrobe enough for the job, and way more than I could afford. He waved it away. No problem. Just take a little each week out of my commissions until it was paid off. No interest. I had mixed feelings about the episode. The new clothes were definitely power clothes. Not the latest fashion — which would be gone in favor of the next fad in a matter of weeks. But traditional. Classic. Old money, classic. They'd been in style for decades and would be for decades to come. White on white shirts with French cuffs. Navy blue blazer, double breasted. Charcoal grey pinstripe vested suit. Subtle patterned tie, silk of course.

On the other hand, I felt like I'd been scolded for being childish.

The truth always hurts.

When were we finished and I was in uniform to his satisfaction, he gave me a nod and said, "Splendid. Now *that's* the look of a James man." Then, over his shoulder he added, "By the way, your topcoat? London Fog. Very nice. I have one just like it, myself."

No higher praise from him was possible.

There's a haiku that goes something like this, though it's better in Japanese:

Eclipse of the Heart

On an outlaw boy
A suit of fine clothing
Makes him more the rogue.

I guess I was living proof. I went so far as to go out and
get a bit of a haircut.

But I kept the boots.

I worked as a glorified stockboy first, even in my new suit.
Doing that, I got completely familiar with every item in the
place, where it was, how much it cost. The gig only paid
minimum wage, though, and that was scarcely enough to pay
for my room, a meal or two each day, and train fare — let
alone what I owed for my new wardrobe. After about a month,
Mr. Etienne gave me a salesbook and turned me loose on the
unsuspecting public.

I didn't do too badly. We got different commissions on
different items, depending on what the management really
wanted to move. My commission checks started to plump up
nicely. Selling was easy for me. Since I was a chameleon with
no real color of my own, I found I could get in synch with a
customer immediately, get a rapport going. It was like acting a
part in a little play.

But I was nothing compared to the two top salesmen on
the floor, each of whom easily took down double or triple my
commissions every week.

One was a gruff Jewish guy named Al Ruloff who
reminded me of Art Carney on a steroid rage. The other was a
demure milquetoast fellow named Hans, who barely spoke
above a whisper. Two completely opposite personalities,
which made for two completely opposite sales approaches, but
both made out like kings.

The competition was fierce, however, especially since the
top salesman each week got a nice bonus. They were always
accusing each other of "stealing customers" or "queering a

sale." When Al went into a rant against Hans, he put an exclamation point on it with, "You fucking *nazi*, you."

Whereupon Hans would spread his arms in supplication and insisted, "But I'm Swiss. I'm *Swiss*..."

"Oh, excuse me. You're the fucking Nazis' fucking banker. You schmuck with ears."

Only Mr. Etienne had the knack for cooling Al off and getting them to make nice again. Should've sent him to the Middle East.

With my earnings I bought a car, a '59 Chevy ragtop, don't ask me why. I didn't drive it that much. I don't even like cars. Found a better place to live, too, a furnished studio apartment. Some more clothes. Books. Lots of books. Read Yukio Mishima. Hemingway. Ian Fleming. Practiced martial arts after work during the week. Played music gigs on the weekends. Bought some better phony I.D.'s.

Shortly after I started working at James, one of my best regular customers, a very chic dresser named Mel, asked me if I had ever considered being a model. He gave me his card and said if I'd like to come by sometime, he'd shoot a couple of rolls, no charge, just to see what we would see. Naturally, I was flattered and gave him a call.

His studio was in an old warehouse loft on the west side. Big open room with rolls of colored backdrop paper on stands at one end, lights set up all around. A few pieces of furniture, a darkroom, a bathroom and a couch that opened out into a bed off in one corner.

He had a lot of his work up on the walls, and it looked pretty good. Had a portfolio on a coffee table. Portraits, weddings, nudes. The nudes were mostly men and boys. A few women. A few couples. Two or three family groupings, parents and children. All very tasteful and they were well done, too. Looked like golden-age Greek sculpture and brought to mind European physique magazines I'd seen as a little kid.

He started by doing some portrait shots of me, but in no time I was naked, and from there it was just a hop, skip and a jump to being sprawled out on an easy chair, jacking off for him. He buzzed around me, snapping away, all the time telling me what a great body I had, what a beautiful cock. When somebody — anybody — is telling you things like that — it's tough not to like them. And, frankly, I enjoyed flaunting myself for him. It's nice to be appreciated. And it isn't like he was asking me to do something I wasn't going to do anyway. Coming isn't exactly against my religion. More like it *is* my religion.

He asked if I'd be interested in making some extra money, and of course the answer was yes. So I signed a model release for him and he shot about a billion rolls of me for which he paid me an hourly rate that made my James money seem like a cheapskate's tip. A lot of it was just me, all or partly nude in different outfits, my cock always the featured player. Then he invited me to do some shoots with other guys. We'd start out getting undressed, lying naked together, jacking off together and so on.

Sometimes, if we felt like it, we sucked each other's cocks, too. It reminded me of the kind of playing around I had done with my little brother. It all seemed very innocent and was great fun.

The other young men I met modeling got to be almost like a family. Or so I guessed. One fellow, a rather scrawny blonde, was able to do an impressive trick: he could suck his own cock. That was something I'd never seen and never considered before. His penis was long enough and he was flexible enough that he could give himself a pretty good blowjob. He could do this standing up, just by bending over, but for the deepest mouthful, he'd lay out and roll into something like the yoga "plow posture."

It was awe-inspiring to behold. It's probably just as well that I couldn't manage that myself. I've often wondered what it would be like, though.

As good a reason as any to take up yoga.

On one occasion, Mel shot some 16mm film of a bunch of us and we took turns getting on camera and masturbating, while the others watched and cheered us on. If you ever come across on old film called "Jack-off Boys: Number 11," you'll see a dark, brooding lad doing some karate moves naked then milking the bull for the camera.

That would be me.

We also once shot a 17-man daisy chain, all laid out on the floor, one guy sucking another guy while he was sucking a third guy and that guy sucked a fourth and so on around in a circle. I wouldn't be surprised if that was some kind of record or something.

Should have called the Guiness people.

None of this homo-erotic play put a dent in my interest in girls. It was a very separate thing. Steak and eggs versus ice cream. Women were always my favorite flavor and still are. I had no romantic interest in men, just having some sexual fun together. I couldn't see any down side to that. I never felt like I was "gay," though I knew some of the other models were.

In all that time, Mel never made a move to hit on me — or any of the other guys, as far as I knew. I'm not sure what I would have said. I suspect it might have been "Sure, why not?" He was a handsome gent and I liked him.

About this time I became fascinated with spies and private eyes. I read crime fiction by the ton. Ian Fleming, Mickey Spillane, Raymond Chandler, Richard S. Prather and lots of others. I bought some textbooks, with titles like Practical Criminal Investigation, Crime and Science, The Detection of Murder, The Private Investigator's Manual.

I picked up a cheap TV and watched Bill Cosby and Robert Culp I Spy their way around the world. I loved those guys.

Overall, I was accumulating an enormous store of knowledge that was largely fictional, tainted with just enough actual fact to make the fictional part seem more believable.

I don't recommend it.

I got friendly with the store dick at James Menswear. He was a silky smooth black cop named Vic, who did a little moonlighting for the extra cash. Had a paranoia about bad breath and was always sneaking hits of Binaca mouth freshener, like a drunk copping swigs of vodka from a bottle hidden in the toaster. I guess he liked me though. We got to talking about police work. He gave me his card and referred me to a detective agency across town. They could always use a good operative, he advised me. So I gave them a call.

Harlowe Secret Services. "We Cover the World."

The agency had been founded by a husband and wife criminology team back in the late 1800's, contemporaries of and competitors with Alan J. Pinkerton, and the business had been passed down until it was now in the hands of George Harlowe IV, who, regrettably, shared none of his ancestors' acumen for investigation.

But he didn't realize that.

And apparently, no one would tell him.

Recently, on a "domestic" case, he'd barged into a motel room to snap some handsome 8x10 glossies of the errant spouse in flagrante delicto. Got some good photos, too.

Only one problem: wrong room.

And *these* folks weren't married to each other *either*.

Welcome to Lawsuit City.

So when I came aboard, most everyone was already swimming for shore, but I didn't know that. Besides George IV, there was John Willington Grey, vice-president of the company, who was also an attorney. He was paying himself so well, he was gradually sapping away the agency's resources like Nosferatu on a lily-white neck. All just this side of actual embezzlement.

Ever notice the similarity between the words "lawyer" and "liar?"

The Chief Investigator was Ray Coleman, a former FBI agent, who had his own dick license besides working for George IV. He was a bantam rooster of a guy with reddish brown hair, quick, clever eyes, an easy manner, and a voice that went down two octaves when he answered the phone ("Eight- Nine Hundred."). He didn't believe for one moment that I was 18 years old and asked to see my I.D. I showed him my new ones, for which I'd paid a couple of hundred bucks. The thing about these was that they weren't forgeries. They were real I.D.'s with false information on them and that's a whole 'nother level of sophistication. Coleman looked them over and smiled at me.

"These are pretty good, lad," he said. But that was that.

Coleman took me under his wing. I accompanied him on cases and he showed me the ropes. I don't know why he did that, but he did. I learned a lot from him.

I learned how to find out almost anything about almost anyone, and without doing anything even remotely sneaky, either. Just drawing from the public records. I got to know the public library and the county clerk's office as well as I knew the neck of my guitar. I learned how get information from the IRS, the Army, the Social Security Administration; how to get a handle on somebody's net worth, what did they own, who did they do business with, what corporations were they officers of, did they ever do time and what for — anything and everything you can think of and a lot more that you never would.

Not exactly exciting work, though. No gun needed. No sexy babes throwing themselves at me by the bunch. I was roundly disappointed.

But it did have its moments.

On a cold and grey Chicago morning, Ray and I drove
down to the south side to pick up a retainer check from a client
who wanted us to find her philandering husband so she could
serve him with divorce papers. Or so she said. We found the
place easily enough and Ray pulled up to the curb in front of
the house, scanned the horizon in all directions for enemy
action.

"Think you can handle this, lad?"

Knock on the door. Smile and say hello. Get the check.
Say goodbye. Where's the challenge?

"Sure," I said.

"Okay. Watch yourself. I'll be right here. Take your time."

I knocked on the door.

It opened.

I smiled and said "Mgwftmpthjjj..." Or something close to
that.

Standing in the doorway was an unspeakably beautiful
black woman, wearing an unspeakably transparent teddy, the
most negligible negligee I'd ever seen. And she was so black,
so dark, deep black she was almost blue. She had high
cheekbones and a small flat nose with flared nostrils like a fine
Arabian mare. When she let a smile suggest itself on her thick,
full, lips, her teeth showed brilliantly white.

She was a goddess.

Hey, I thought. This is more like it. So what if she's old
enough to be my mother?

She invited me in.

There were about a dozen guys in the living room manning
a dozen phones, scribbling down bets on small slips of paper.
None of them took much notice of me. I followed Afrodite
into her office. She sat down behind her desk and pulled out
her cash-box, started shuffling green.

"Was that five hundred dollars?" she asked, knowing
damn well how much it was.

"Yes, Ma'am," I squeaked.

213

She furrowed her brow as if deep in financial analysis and lounged way back in her chair. Waaaay back. And let her thighs part. Predictably, my eyes went to the bright pink bull's-eye visible between the thick purple lips pouting out of her dense rainforest of curls, like I was a major league pitcher focusing in on the catcher's mitt.

Steee-rike one.

"Is there any way I could give you just *four* hundred dollars?" she inquired coquettishly.

You bet your ass there was.

I did just what Ray told me to do: I took my time.

If I close my eyes and concentrate just right, I can still conjure up the taste of her, the scent of her, the way her coarse hair wire-brushed my chin. The power of her thighs locked around my waist.

When I finally came out, I turned over five hundred in cash to Ray.

"Good job, lad," he smiled as we pulled away. "If you don't mind my asking, how much of this came out of your *own* pocket?"

On another occasion, Ray recruited me, along with three other agents, for some black-tie body-guarding at the Playboy Club. Sounds exciting, I know. Lots of celebrities there, whose names I can't mention, but they included a blue-eyed big band singer, a black one-eyed song and dance man and a crooner with an exaggerated reputation for booze and broads. It was like working security on Mount Olympus.

I remember that time because I stood close enough to Blue-Eyes to spill a drink on him and I almost did. Also, I got to fuck a centerfold-perfect Playboy Bunny. Unfortunately, she had the IQ of a real bunny.

In late Autumn, Ray sent me to do undercover work at the big Sears store downtown. They needed extra part-time security for the holiday season. Needed plainclothes store dicks who could blend in with the shoppers.

I was a good blender. Being a kid, I looked like one, and I wore my own clothes to work, too. Leather jacket and jeans. No suits on this one. Nobody ever made me for a store dick — and on my first day, one of the dicks spent the whole morning following me. He was surprised as hell when we met in the lunchroom. This gave me an opportunity to do something I had never done before, and had come to believe was not possible: meet an honest cop.

Only an honest cop would bust his or her hump for the few extra bucks they could make on the side hours at Sears. You could make a lot more doing other things, easier, and put less time in. But he didn't go that way. If I'd found a gay brontosaurus operating a soup kitchen for the homeless in the basement, I couldn't have been more surprised.

Often, I worked with an older detective who would play the part of my mother. It was a perfect cover. We made a good team.

Most of the criminals we tackled were boosters, or shop-lifters. If you think this is some lady pocketing a free lipstick once in a while, I've got a surprise for you. That's the level of boosting I did myself as a young kid. Mostly food. And I got good at it, too. But these boosters worked in gangs, were well-organized and very slick.

The villain of the piece was an uptown hustler we called "Ali Babba," so-called because he had about forty kids working for him. He himself was the boosters' booster.

The law said you had to see the guy approach the merchandise, you had to see him conceal it, and you had to see him leave the store with it without paying. Chain of evidence kind of thing. So you had to keep your eyes on the guy every second.

Ali Babba drove us nuts.

Some of us'd go up to the observation windows — you didn't think those were really ventilation grates, did you? —

and others would cover him on the floor. He'd hover around a few expensive items, like a hummingbird sampling one flower or another looking for just the right one. Then he'd peer up at us in our "secret" spot, crack a big grin, wave to us, and head for the door. The dicks would go berserk.

"Dammit!"

"He's got it!"

"Did he get it?"

"What did he get?"

"Where'd he put it?

"Did you see it?"

"How'd he get it?"

"I don't know."

"Fuck!"

Ali Babba's hands were so good, he should have been a magician. I suppose in his way he was. I was almost sorry to bust him.

My "mom" and I were shopping, see. Trying topcoats on me. Right next to him. We watched him do an "over and under" — one cashmere coat on top of another — and remove the tags with a wave of his magic wand. We followed him toward the registers. We got in line; he sauntered out the door. My mom raced after him. I vaulted over a counter and headed him off by going out a side door.

Busted, daddy-o.

Not one, but *two* cashmere coats.

When he realized that my "mom" and I were store dicks, he was more outraged than chagrinned.

"Now that just ain't fair," he complained, shaking his head dejectedly. "I mean that just ain't fair..."

The other dicks took us to Pizzeria Uno's to celebrate.

Another common crime was "till-tapping." Not a very sophisticated gig. You watch for a salesperson to be busy, run behind the counter, hit "no sale" on the cash register, grab all the money you can, and run like hell. It's a desperation crime. Last chance for the painfully strung out.

If you're smart, you hit counters with the most expensive merchandise so there's at least some decent cash in the kitty. If you're real smart, you get a sideman to distract the salesperson for you and keep them occupied.

The till-tapper I remember wasn't very smart. He was working alone and selected about the worst counter in the store to hit, and at the worst possible time. It was the cosmetics counter where many expensive perfumes were sold. And it was about lunchtime. And what this poor dummy didn't know was that the lovely Hispanic girl working that counter was being hit on by every male detective in the store, me included — maybe the female ones too, for all I know.

We all found lame excuses to float around that department just to trade a word with her, catch her smile, get a whiff of her hair. And casually pass by at lunchtime, just to see if she happened to be going to the same place where we were going. So when this hapless clown taps the register and grabs a fistful of dollars, before he can take a single step toward the door, not one, not two, not three, but four store dicks tackle him like it's the last play of the Superbowl and they're protecting a one point lead on the one-yard line.

He had just a fraction of a second to glimpse these guys flying in his direction and the look on his face was vintage Wile E. Coyote.

It was closing in on Christmas Eve, during the last mad dash to buy presents. The Windy City was earning its nickname with sub-zero gusts pelting pedestrians outside with horizontal snow. We got a security call from the shoe department — they piped it over the muzak system when a clerk thought he spotted a booster.

When I got there, a dick named Gary B., a grizzly bear of a man with no discernable sense of humor, had already arrived on the scene. I found him kneeling down talking to a kid 6, maybe 7 years old. The kid was dressed in layers of tattered clothes, had a runny nose and a permanently angry look already in his eyes. On his feet were ragged sneakers and no socks. He might as well have been barefoot. He had a huge shopping bag he was dragging along with both hands. It was full of shoes.

"I'll take him," Gary said. But I tagged along.

We started walking the kid toward the security office, which was hidden way in the back near a side door, camouflaged by racks of ladies' dresses. A short way down the aisle, Gary stopped the kid.

"Wait a second," he said. Then he opened the Randolph Street door. "Beat it, kid," he growled.

The little boy started to creep toward the door, pretty sure it was some kind of a trap.

"Take the fuckin' bag, for Crissakes," said Gary.

The kid snatched up the bag and bolted away for all he was worth.

When the kid was gone Gary said to me "You didn't see a fucking thing, did you?"

"Me?" I replied. "Hey, I'm upstairs having coffee."

It was just after New Year's Day that Harlowe went down the toilet, owing lots of people lots of money, Ray and me included. When I got to the office that morning, the doors were locked and there was no one around, no cars in the small adjacent lot. I was wondering what the hell to do, when Ray pulled up to the curb in his black Barracuda, motioned for me to get in, and we swung into the parking lot. He'd already hit the office and gone down the street for coffee. He'd brought an extra coffee, too, figuring I might be around. That's the kind of guy he was.

He filled me in on the dirt with Harlowe. He'd seen it coming but hadn't thought it would happen quite this soon.

"Have you been paid?" he asked.

"Nope, " I said.

"Don't worry, lad," he assured me, "I'll cover it."

"Did *you* get paid?" I asked him back.

"No, not really."

"Then why should *you* cover it? They stiffed you, too, right?"

We were in the same boat all right. We paddled it over to a greasy spoon on Clark Street near Ray's apartment and tossed around our plans. Personally, I didn't have any.

Ray already had plans to marry money. His girlfriend was a Vogue-beautiful socialite named Magda who was filthy rich and filthy minded, which sounded like a pretty good combination to me. Unfortunately, she was filthy spoiled too, a rich princess brat who'd never heard the word "no" in her life and was completely convinced that the whole world existed just to make her every whim convenient. She was an uncontrite bitch and was always summarily rendering her final word on an issue with, "Well, I just have to lay down the law on this, I'm afraid..." Bang. End of discussion.

Ray was no fool. He knew what she was like. Her spoiled attitude and the "laws" that she laid down he collectively referred to as the "Magda Cunta." But he was willing to put up with it for the trade off. For Magda, Ray represented something wild and dangerous, like having a pet leopard on a leash.

To Ray, Magda's money represented, well, money.

It happened fast. So fast that Ray had almost 10 months left on his apartment lease when they headed off for a honeymoon that went around-the-world in every sense. He left me his keys, he left me his car, and he gave me a glowing letter of recommendation.

His apartment was on the 7th floor of the La Salle Arms Apartment Hotel, number 711, which sounded like a gambler's hangout. It was a nice one-bedroom place, with nondescript furnishings and private parking to boot. I'd never be able to afford to pick up the lease, but I lived there and let my money pile up until I absolutely had to find another place.

I went to the three detective agencies Ray had recommended. The last one was the Benjamin K. Barrens International Detective Agency, Inc. They were huge, handling everything from night-watchmen to bodyguards — executive protection, they called it.

Good pay, benefits package. It was almost like having a square job.

I filled out an application and left it with the receptionist and was about to leave when she called to me to wait a moment: Mr. McLean would like to speak with me.

McLean was a handsome black guy with perfectly manicured nails who rolled a cigar pensively around in his pursed lips without lighting it. He *never* lit it. For all I know, he only bought one cigar in his whole life. He looked over my application, looked over my identification and apparently over-looked anything he didn't like.

"Are you available to relocate?" he asked.

"Yes."

"How soon could you be ready to do that?"

"I'm packed," I told him.

I got the job.

That night I was riding on the train they called the City of New Orleans on my way to Madison, Wisconsin. Barrens was taking an awful gamble. They certainly hadn't had time to check me out. I could've been Jack the Ripper. But they needed someone RFN. I got a crash course in their administrative procedures that afternoon, filled out some more papers, got the details of the assignment. Didn't have any loose ends to tie up. No plants to water, cats to feed, people to notify.

I was a free man.

Just like Bobby McGee.

It was a case of industrial espionage, a term used to cover everything from stealing the secret to the secret formula to taking too long a coffee break.

This one involved a warehouse that was losing a lot of merchandise, and a lot of that merchandise was firearms. I was to go in undercover as a warehouse order-filler, which gave me access to all areas, and complete freedom of movement. I would file a report every day by phone. I was paid by the warehouse, like a regular employee, and the agency paid me the difference between that and my actual salary which amounted to something like $80 a day at a time when minimum wage was about a buck and a quarter an hour. I also got a subsistence allowance for relocating, not a lot, but it was enough to get a decent room with a murphy bed and hot and cold running cockroaches, the kind of place I needed for my cover.

The only guy who knew who I was and what I was doing was the warehouse foreman, an older fellow named Johannson, as in Yo, Handsome! The CEO knew he had someone on the case, but he didn't know who, didn't know my name or face.

So there I was doing the I SPY number. I could hear that jazzy soundtrack in my head, which I was in way over. Johannson introduced me to the dock foreman, a chubby, very amiable retired army sergeant called, what else? "Sarge." As Sarge and I left Johannson at the office, and I followed him deep into the warehouse, the first thing he said to me was, "Just keep your eyes open and your mouth shut and you'll do okay. We all make out all right around here, know what I mean?"

Yeah, I knew exactly what he meant.

That was it.

Busted.

It was over before it started

Damn fool.

I had been on the case about thirty seconds. Boy, was I brilliant or what? I couldn't believe that Sarge was so stupid as to introduce himself to a complete stranger by basically saying, "Hello. Nice to meet you. We're stealing the place blind."

But he did.

To him, I was just a kid. Hey, I *was* just a kid.

For the next month all I did was hang out with the Sarge and his guys and compile lists of who stole what, when and who they sold it to, with special attention to shotguns, rifles and pistols. At the end of the month, some guys got fired (I was also "fired"), some guys got arrested, and a couple of local cops lost their badges and were facing possible criminal charges.

Sounds easy, right?

Wrong.

In a month, working with these guys everyday, eating together, telling jokes, hearing about their families and their girl friends, their ex-wives, their kids, their favorite baseball teams and so on, you get to know them. You get to like some of them. You may start out *pretending* to be friends, but you can end up *actually* being friends. So at the end it's like you're turning in your friends.

I hated it.

But the agency loved it.

I was a rock star. My boss' snap judgment was vindicated. I met the Chief Investigator of the Chicago office, a fellow named Reagan, who told me what a good job I'd done. And they had another one for me right away. I took it, but I let it be known I'd be interested in executive protection if there was any room for me. I did a few more undercover gigs. I worked on some surveillance teams. Even some internal investigations, checking up on our own security people to make sure they were playing it straight, sometimes just seeing if I could get past our security system. All in all, I liked the job, I liked the people I worked with, and I liked my boss, McLean, a lot.

It was through McLean that I met a very interesting and scary guy named Andretti, known to those who know as "The Sausage." If this was a Hollywood screenplay, he'd be called "The Sausage" because he had a huge cock. But in reality it was because, in his youth, he'd once killed a guy by cramming

222

Italian sausage down the guy's throat until he choked to death. At least, that was the story.

Andretti was a mechanic, sometimes called a fixer. Nowadays sometimes called a "liabilities management consultant." No matter what you called him, when you called him, somebody died. But he wasn't some gun-toting goon, or "cowboy." He was an artist. His specialty was making murder look like anything except murder. He was clean as the upholstery on a new Lincoln, too. Never so much as a parking ticket. The night I met him, he spent most of the time bitching about how high taxes were and how shitty the schools were getting. Just another regular citizen, if you didn't know any better. He considered himself a soldier, except — unlike most soldiers — he never killed a "civilian" and he would never have worked for the chump change that Uncle Sam paid his own hired killers

Interesting point of view. I thought about it a lot.

I finally got my chance at a big money job: "executive protection." I went to a special training course called "Threat Recognition, Evaluation and Management." It included things like setting up security, evasive driving, weapons selection and use, bomb detection, assessing behavior, unarmed combat, improvised weapons — a lot to cover in three weeks, even putting in 24-hour days. But I got the basic principles down. After finishing the course, I worked on assignments with more experienced operatives calling the shots. I did high-risk stuff like making the coffee. But little by little I got to be a regular team member.

The most dangerous thing you deal with doing executive protection is complacency. And it's terrifyingly easy to fuck up, because that's the way the brain works — sorting out new things from old things, unknown things from known things, new information from old news, threats from non-threats.

MOST of the time, nothing happened, and it was the world's most boring occupation. And that lulls your brain, suffocates your awareness, lengthens your lag time. You start thinking it's a "routine" moment, a "routine" occurrence, a "routine" job.

But there's no such thing as "routine."

"Routine" thinking can get you killed.

Because when the fecal matter does hit the air conditioning unit, it can happen fast, faster than you can blink, let alone think. When it happens you don't have time to get ready, you have to be ready already. So you're always the most vulnerable when you think you're perfectly safe.

You want to remember that.

The last job I did for the Barrens Agency was a bodyguard assignment.

There's an old saying: A secret is a secret when only two people know it, and one of them is dead. As an operative, I didn't get all the fine-print details, just what I needed to know to do the job. And all I needed to know was that the "risk assessment" was "highest." That meant that the client was known to be or very likely to be the target of professional killers. My team's task was to keep her alive, and have her back on such and such a day and time to hand her over to the federales so she could sing her aria for the grand jury. What she would be testifying to, I had no idea. It didn't matter. But I figured it had to be something substantial to warrant all the fuss.

Guarding witnesses was a job for the cops; I had no idea how or why the Barrens Agency got involved. It was only later I learned that the lady in question didn't trust the cops and had told the prosecutor that she wanted to pick her own security guys or her testimony was no go. Pretty unusual arrangement. I'm surprised the DA went for it. Especially since the state was picking up the tab. I don't know if she picked Barrens out of the phone book at random, or what.

But I do remember getting the assignment.

Right across the hall from the conference room, was the pantry where the coffee-maker was. I had just finished typing up a report and was grabbing some java. The conference room door was closed, but as I turned around, there she was looking at me through the glass. She had bottle-blonde hair ratted up high in front. Black leather jacket. Mini-skirt. White "go-go" boots. Hazel eyes. Chewing a wad of gum like it was her only source of oxygen. Juicy Fruit. She was with some suit from the DA's office, and my boss. I caught her eye a moment, gave her a nod, and she said something over her shoulder to the boys. I was heading down the hall, when my boss called after me, asked me to step in for a minute.

I stepped in.

She gave me a quick once-over.

"You a cop?" she asked.

"Nope."

"Ever *been* a cop?"

"Nope."

"Wanna *be* a cop?"

"HELL, no."

"I want *him*," she said pointing at me like she was picking out a lobster for dinner.

After I got filled in — as much as they were *going* to fill me in — I requested a word alone with the client. Her name was Chantelle. Like the singing group. I figure she made that up. Didn't matter.

"Look," I said. "If somebody wants to get to you, they're going to have to go through me. Sounds like you've stepped in some very serious shit. That means whoever wants to kill you won't think twice about killing me first. So I'm looking out for my own life here as well as yours. If I agree to protect you, you have to agree to do whatever I say, do it immediately, no arguments, no explanations, no hits, no runs, no errors. Otherwise, I'm out."

She stopped snapping her gum and looked me in the eye. "Deal," she said. And stuck out her hand to shake.

Motive, means and opportunity.

There's a truism in body-guarding: You can't protect a client from a killer if the killer is willing to trade his life for your client's life. If somebody wants badly enough to kill your principal, and is willing to pay the price, there's nothing you can do to stop him. All you can do is die along with your client. Fortunately, most people aren't that highly motivated. Assuming the killer does have the requisite motive, your job is to deprive him of either the means or the opportunity.

To deprive the killer of the means depends on your defensive measures being superior to the killer's offensive means. Some people call this "turtling" or "sheltering in place." You make no mystery about where the client is, but you implement measures sufficient to defeat any offensive attempt. In other words, you hunker down in a "safe house," and keep your back to the wall.

First, the bad guys have to locate you, then they have to assess your security measures. Third, they have to devise a way around them. Fourth, they have to assemble the men and materials to do the job. You're betting that your defensive measures will trump the bad guy's offensive capabilities.

The Barrens Agency had several safe-houses at their disposal. One was referred to as the "castle." It was situated on a 5-acre lot on the north shore. It was complete with an 8 foot high stone wall topped with barbed wire around the perimeter and had cameras cross-covering the 25 yards of close-clipped grass that an intruder would have to transnavigate without being seen. There were two entrances in that wall, each with a heavy reinforced steel gate that was controlled from inside. Just inside the gate was a set of calthrops that could take out your tires if you crashed the gate with a vehicle. The calthrops only retracted when the gate was properly opened with the correct daily code, from the inside.

When the castle was in use, there was a roving guard consisting of two protection-trained German Shepherds at liberty wandering the grounds — dogs so well disciplined that they would not accept food from anyone but their handler.

All the windows in the house were bullet-proof glass with plate steel shutters. All the doors and door-frames were reinforced steel. Multiple locks, of course. There was an independent air filtration system and an independent generator in the basement that ran everything and switched on automatically if the power went down for more than 3 seconds.

Inside the safe house there was a safe room. The safe room is where you make your "last stand" in case of a breach. It was like a live-in bank vault with a separate phone line, citizen band radio, and a 7-day cache of food and water for 4, medical supplies, bullet-proof vests, weapons and ammunition.

But there was no moat.

I was a little disappointed.

This may not seem very elaborate in the computer age, but in the '60's it was cutting edge James Bond. I have no idea who built this place or why, what he'd been hiding from, or how Barrens acquired it. But unless you had a couple of Sherman tanks and a company of suicide rangers, you weren't going to get at anyone inside.

Trouble is, some people can get Sherman tanks and suicide rangers.

Personally, I wouldn't want to stake my life on the outcome of a pissing contest between the immovable object and the irresistible force.

That brings me to option number two: depriving the killer of "opportunity." Action always beats re-action and it's harder to hit a moving target than it is to hit one standing still. There's no time to make a plan, get your team together, etc. The faster and more unpredictable the movement is, the harder it is to hit the target.

If I had my choice of super-powers, I'd choose Unpredictability.

I discussed my plan with my boss and got the nod.

The first thing I did, with the help of Margie the secretary, was to cut off all that blonde hair that Chantelle was so proud of. Gave her a short pixie-cut and dyed it dark brown. My principal didn't say a word, but I could see the "fuck you" in her eyes. No problem. Not my job to be liked.

I was more concerned with body armor. Barrens had all the latest stuff. Would stop a .44 magnum at close range and you'd suffer nothing more than a monster hematoma and maybe some cracked ribs. Steel plates covered vital areas, the center chest and the spine. I wasn't completely happy with that. I consider all my areas pretty vital. But it was a lot better than nothing. The worst part is that these fabrics didn't exactly breathe and were very uncomfortable to wear. There's better stuff now, but at the time, it was top of the line.

Margie mentioned in passing that one of the other secretaries was pregnant, and that gave me an idea. I got a donation of a maternity dress from her, and belted a pillow to Chantelle's stomach. Also sent Margie out for some blue contact lenses and horn-rimmed windowpane glasses to boot. And no make-up or jewelry allowed. She did get to keep her own underwear. By the time we were done you'd have to go to fingerprints or dental records to know that this was the same girl.

When we were finished with Chantelle's make-over, she looked at herself in the bathroom mirror.

"Fuck," she said snapping her gum loudly. "I look like a pregnant dyke."

"Starting now," I said, "your name is Bobby. And lose the chewing gum."

"Seriously?"

"Seriously."

"It's so I don't smoke instead."

"Smoke instead."

"Anyone ever tell you you're kind of an asshole?" She smiled sweetly.

"All the time," I told her.

I had to assume that she'd been followed and that her present whereabouts were known. I had Margie reserve plane tickets in Chantelle's name for three different places, on three different airlines — none of which we used. Booked accommodations at hotels in each place, too.

We did use the castle, though — as a decoy. Margie volunteered to stand in for Chantelle and be escorted to the safe house under guard. She was close enough to Chantelle's size that Chantelle's clothes fit her, more or less. Add a wig, a scarf and dark glasses and it was convincing enough.

Meanwhile, Chantelle — now "Bobby" — and I hit the street as boyfriend and pregnant girlfriend.

I got us Greyhound bus tickets to another galaxy, far, far away. Halfway there, we got off, took another bus someplace else. Before we got to that place, we ditched the second bus, caught a train. We didn't stay in any one place for longer than about six hours. I backtracked and doubled back purely at random, sometimes literally flipping a coin. During the days, we stayed where there were crowds of people. At night we stayed in low-rent no-tell motels, sharing one room, paid cash, and often left in the middle of the night.

"I hope you don't think I'm going to fuck you," Bobby said when we landed the first night.

"I got dibs on the chair," I told her. "Stay away from the windows." Then I moved the chair so it blocked the door. Wound up sleeping on the floor.

And that's how it went.

Bobby didn't exactly enjoy it.

229

But, as the Tao says, it gave the tiger no place to put his claws, nor the rhinoceros a place to put his horn. The main difference between predator and prey is that the predator knows the patterns of the prey. But we had no patterns. There was no way anyone could anticipate where we would be going next — because *I* didn't know where we were going next. It was like a life-sized pinball game. But it worked.

The entire time was without incident.
Almost.

At the appointed hour of the appointed day we met at the appointed place.

The Barrens Offices were right downtown, just behind the State and Randolph baseline, on Wicker Drive, taking up two entire floors of the LaSalle-Wicker Building. We arrived a little ahead of schedule and found the federales already there in force.

The DA's guys plus a couple of FBI men — who were apparently old pals with Mr. Reagan, our chief investigator. They were having coffee and chuckling over old times when we arrived and turned Chantelle over to them.

Bravo. Job well-done and all that shit.

I rode down in the elevator with Chantelle and her new friends.

"I guess I should thank you," she said.

"Not necessary," I told her. "They pay me."

She looked like she might smile.

Then the elevator doors opened.

Gunfire is ear-splittingly loud in an enclosed area, like an elevator or even the lobby of an office building. It makes your ears ring so you can't hear anything at all, not even more gunfire. I'm not sure what exactly happened in all the details. Most of it, I didn't see. I remember spotting this guy just as the doors were opening, and he just didn't look "right." He didn't look like a guy innocently waiting for an elevator. Expression, body language, I don't know.

Later, they told me that I grabbed Chantelle by the shoulder and threw her down onto the elevator floor faster than she could say "Hey! What the f---!" and threw myself on top of her.

Then there was gunfire.

Quite a lot of it.

Lots of running, shoving and screaming, too

I do kind of remember lying on top of Chantelle on the floor of the elevator, not knowing what else to do. I'm not really sure whether I actually pulled her down and threw myself on top of her to protect her, or whether she just got in my way as I was instinctively trying to take cover. Part of me wanted to jump up heroically, pull out my (illegal) gun and blast away, smiting evil with a mighty and righteous wrath.

But I didn't.

Happened way too fast for me. I managed not to wet my pants, and I think that's heroic enough under the circumstances.

Most professionals wouldn't try to hit someone in the lobby of the LaSalle-Wicker Building just before noon on a Wednesday with the lobby and the street outside full of witnesses.

There's no future in it.

There were apparently three guys. Two were killed in the lobby. The third man ran out and was shot by a traffic cop who saw him waving his gun around instead of freezing when he was told to freeze. One of the Feds got shot in the thigh and was rushed to the hospital. Another cop took one in the shoulder, through and through. Two bystanders suffered slight wounds.

The whole thing took about 15 seconds.

Up to this point I SPY was just a game. I was just pretending.

But these guys were serious. They played for keeps.

It was company policy that agents involved in a high risk confrontation — and I think this qualifies — take a little time off afterward to recuperate mentally. I took some time. I never went back. Officially, I guess, I'm still on a leave of absence.

I wonder if they owe me any money. They may have a check collecting dust, waiting for me to return.

One footnote to this story.

This was during the long reign of Mayor Richard Daley, who ruled Chicago like his own private fiefdom. According to the papers, a Vietnam Vet had brought some kind of war souvenir home, had been showing it off to a pal and it had accidentally discharged, slightly wounding one bystander. That was the cover story for the downtown carnage. I often wonder why they put that out instead of the truth? Who were they protecting?

And that led me to another question: how did they set this up? Who knew where the witness was going to be and when?

I knew.

My boss knew.

The DA knew.

I sure as hell didn't leak it. I doubt that my boss leaked it. That leaves the DA's office.

You do the math.

Remember what I told you about secrets?

That experience was too much for me to handle at that time. Way too real. Didn't sleep well for a while after that. Always kept a gun on me or near me.

Even in the shower.

I needed a change.

I found a place in the distant suburbs again, laid back, found what may be the best square job I ever had: garbageman. Garbageman is not an exalted profession, I know, but I really enjoyed it.

I was up every morning before 4 and was riding around hanging onto the back of the truck by 4 am, rain, sleet, snow or shine. I felt invincible. To be up, out, and around while everyone else was still snuggled warm in their beds. To be on the watch, to take care of the mess they created, in a quiet, professional — and invisible — way.

Come to think of it, it was a lot like being a bodyguard.

The guy I worked for was a self-made man, built up his business over a lifetime. Now he had a fleet of trucks. He also black-topped driveways and put in septic systems. He had three sons and a grandson in the biz with him. He was also probably the fairest boss I ever heard of.

I'll give you an example.

We got a new contract to do the pick-up for a recently created subdivision. So the Boss takes a truck out and does the whole thing himself the first time. It took him around two hours. Afterwards if a crew did it in one hour, he'd still pay them for two, plus maybe sending them on to another job, like getting paid to be in two places at once.

On sweltering summer Fridays, he often showed up at the garage where we did our vehicle clean-up and maintenance at the end of the day. He'd have a six-pack of cold beer with him. Sometimes he'd meet us at lunchtime and pick up the tab. He gave little bonuses on birthdays. And on guys' kids' birthdays, too. He was always doing something unexpected for the crew. If all bosses were like that, there'd be no need for unions.

I didn't drive the truck much. I was the "helper," which means I did most of the actual calorie-burning. Sometimes I rode with Tommy, one of the Boss's sons, but I generally rode with Big George, who reminded me of Wallace Beery in

233

Treasure Island. He had a soft, round face, crooked eyes, one with an occasional tic that looked like he was winking at you.

No doubt about it, George was the best garbageman around. He could pick up four cans at a time, two with each hand, grabbing them by the lip, and empty them into the hopper with a single smooth toss. More than that, the cans were never damaged, always went back where they belonged, upside down with the lid on top, and never, never any spillage left behind. It was amazing to watch him. It was like t'ai chi. He was a black belt in garbage can-do.

There were several places where he returned the cans not to the roadside as required, but carried them all the way back to the house. "This old lady lives here," he would explain. "It's kind of hard for her to get around. Her son puts the cans out. I put them back for her."

At another stop on one route there was often a shopping bag or stationery box full of porno magazines tied up in a neat bundle — and put in a plastic bag on rainy days. There were a few Playboys in the bunch but this was mostly very hardcore stuff. If I'd never seen a vagina before, by the end of my time on this job I could easily have written a dissertation on the variety of sizes, colors and shapes.

As soon as I had the hang of the gig, George just did the driving and I did the loading while he thumbed through his latest literary acquisitions.

Mondays were an interesting day because there was a giant subdivision which two crews split up pretty evenly to pick up. Naturally, we made a race out of it, loser buys lunch. It probably would have been alarming to the residents if they'd seen us, but who's going to get up that early if they don't have to? George would put the truck in low, low gear so that it would just creep forward on the slight downgrade. Then he would jump out and we would both jog down the street, one on each side, grabbing cans, loading, tossing cans back to each other to replace, while the truck rolled merrily along driverless. It was the refuse disposal version of the Harlem Globetrotters.

Of course, George's standards were still high. Things had to be just so. You still had to do the job *right*, not just *fast*.

The part of the truck you toss the garbage into is called the hopper. A big rotating shovel then scoops the stuff from the hopper to the inside of the tank. Then a plate connected to a rod compresses the stuff forward until it's all packed in tight. At the dump, you open up the back of the truck and the whole tank tilts up to dump the load out. It's against the law to have anything exposed in the hopper while you're on the highway. A hazard from flying debris I suppose.

But you know, when it's your last stop on a Friday, and you can get off an hour early if you can avoid going all the way to the dump and back out again for just one more stop, you might leave stuff in the hopper. You might even stick some scrap cardboard in the hopper to build it up a little so you can carry a bit more. You might weave a little twine across the back of it to keep it from falling out all over the road. You might even have the helper — that would be me — ride on the back all the way to the dump, hanging on with one hand, and with the other support the makeshift monster hopper to prevent a whole mountain of guerilla garbage from spilling out all over the road.

And you might get pulled over by a State Trooper.

When he pulled us over, we were just about to make the turn from Route 12 onto the county road that went to the dump. It was the equivalent of rounding third base and heading home. He must have known that. He pulled up close behind us and as he got out of his car pointed a finger at me and ordered me to get down off the back of the truck, using his best Jack Webb voice.

Now, the thing is, he was pulled up real close to us. *Real* close. I was pretty sure if I let go of that twine the dam was going to burst. I started to explain that to him, but he cut me off, barked at me to do what he told me and get down off that truck, and he waved his fucking finger at me again, too.

I hate that.

"Yes, Sir," I said. And I leaped down off the truck and out of the way. When I did, the twine went limp, the cardboard which had soaked through with garbage juice collapsed, and maybe twenty or thirty gallons' worth of stinking swill washed over the hood of the trooper's car, like Neptune throwing up. Even though the cop tried to hop back out of the way, a fair amount of that splashed on him. It was unspeakably disgusting.

It took a lot of effort for me to keep a straight face.

Probably didn't do it very well.

Of course, I was the one who had to clean the cop's car off, as best I could. And we got a ticket, too. But it was mightily satisfying to know in my heart how that pompous mini nazi asshole would be driving around in that god-awful stench for the remainder of his tour — which, by our calculations, had just started.

As for the Boss, when we told him the story, he laughed until he cried. "That's one ticket I'll enjoy paying," he said.

See? That's the kind of boss he was.

Sometime during the winter of my discontent, we made a stop and found a dead Irish Setter that had been put out with the garbage, and was now frozen stiff. I didn't like it much, myself, but a very dark mood came over Big George that I'd never seen before, and it made me feel very uneasy. George went up to the guy's door and roused him — this is about 5:15 in the morning.

The guy comes to the door, opens it a crack, and they talk through the screen door and George tells him he really ought to bury the dog, not throw it away like garbage. I couldn't make the guy's response, but I could imagine from the tone what it was, and probably you can, too.

At some point, George decided he wasn't quite getting his point across, I guess.

So he reached in — *through* the screen on the door — grabbed the guy by the collar and pulled his ass out — *through* the screen door — onto the frost-crispy lawn. Then he picked the guy up by his bathrobe belt and carried him out to the truck. With this fellow scrambling and cursing. George took the shovel from the truck, dragged the guy's ass back to his yard and stood over him while he dug a hole under an oak tree and buried that dog.

When it was done, he then replaced the shovel, got in and off we went, leaving the guy shivering, fuming and cursing on his lawn. We headed back to the garage to see the Boss. George was white as a Klansman's chapeau and silent as we drove.

By the time we got there, the guy had already called and the boss was on the phone with him. Gertie, the boss' black lab, lay snoozing at his feet. Turned out the angry client was a lawyer. Somehow, that figured.

"They just came in, Mr. Smith," the Boss said. "Let me call you back in a few minutes." He hung up and turned to George. "What the fuck?" he asked.

"First," said George, "The kid here didn't do nothin'. It was just me."

Then he told the tale.

The boss, listened, staring down at his desk, and shook his head a lot. Then he dialed up the dissatisfied customer.

"Yeah, Mr. Smith? Hi. Yes, Sir. I just talked with them. No, Sir, I'm not going to do that. Uh-huh. Well, I guess you better go ahead and sue me then, sir. Then it will be public knowledge that you abused and neglected that dog. Think there might be any dog-lovers on a jury? I'll take my chances. Yes, Sir. Fuck you, too." Then he hung up.

We waited for him to read us the riot act or something but he just raised his bushy brows and said, "Was there something else?"

That's the kind of man he was,

I don't believe it ever went to court.

I learned to drive that garbage truck and a dump-truck, too. Learned how to operate a back-hoe and a bulldozer. I black-topped a few driveways — now there's a miserable job. Especially in the summer, with the acrid stink of that tar biting your nostrils, getting that stuff on your skin, on your clothes. Very tough work and you can't get clean again or get the smell of it out of your nose for days.

Nevertheless, I might have stayed with that job a bit longer if I hadn't gotten a call from a bass player I knew who was putting a band together and, did I want to play? He already had a job lined up, now he just needed a band! With the band rehearsing and playing nights, and the disposal crew gig starting before dawn, something had to give. I decided to go with the band, parted company with the Boss's crew without rancor. I left a big box of pastries for the guys when I left.

Just before I went into the service, I had a job as a line cook, at a Ted Garvey's Restaurant. Ted Garvey's was a chain that had little places at the oases along the Illinois Tollway. Nowadays you stop at an oasis and there's a Burger King, a McDonald's and every other franchise you can think of. But at that time there was just a Ted Garvey's and a gas station. I worked there a couple of months, just killing time until I had to report for duty.

Fucked several of the waitresses who were mostly high school or college kids doing the summer job to save up some tuition. Back then you could make enough money over the summer to pay your tuition, unless you were going to Harvard. Can't do that anymore, and that shit's got to change.

One girl I got together with was an aloof hostess, a swarthy Italian girl. Next day, we were strangers again. But that was cool.

Another was a girl with mouth so foul she made the average truck driver seem like a Lutheran choir director. I liked her a lot.

Most of the "cooking" was pretty easy stuff. Putting sandwiches together, frying eggs, deep-frying chicken, shrimp, french fries. It was all pre-measured, pre-packaged.

A monkey could do it. The cooks didn't make anything up from scratch; that was up to our "chef," a black guy named Sylvester. Syl was a recruiting poster boy for the Flaming Queen Brigade. He had a narrow build, a mincing walk, pursed lips and always wore a little scarf, knotted on the side. I never saw the same scarf twice. He was apparently committed to living out every gay cliche there was.

The regional manager was a young guy named Domano. As far as I could tell, he got the job because he was somebody's son or nephew. He certainly didn't have any particular expertise in the food biz or in management. He thought that being a boss meant to come in and give everybody grief.

In particular, he didn't like Syl. Domano was all over him. The kitchen wasn't clean enough, the portions were too big, the big batches of things like spaghetti sauce and pancake batter were all wrong.

It was all bullshit.

And after all this, after Domano bitches at Syl all morning, he takes a seat at a booth and asks Syl what the soup of the day is.

"New England Clam Chowder," Syl lisped petulantly.

"I'll have some," pronounced Domano. "And it better be good."

So Syl goes back to make it up and serve it to Domano, personally. After a bit, Domano called over to me, told me to see what was taking so long with the soup. I told him I'd check on it. I found Syl off in a relatively private corner of the kitchen, by the walk-in coolers. The chowder was all made up, and he had a bowl of it set on a tray. He was standing over it, jacking off.

Let's say I was a little surprised.

"Domano wants to know where his chowder is," I said dumbly, as Syl wanked away.

"Tell him it's almost ready, hon."

I did.

Syl brought out the soup and set it before Mr. Domano, beaming with pride.

"I hope you like it," Syl told him. "It's my own special recipe."

Domano finished every bit of that soup. When he was done, he called Syl over.

"I got to hand it to you," Domano told him. "That was pretty good. How about some more?"

Syl grinned so big I thought his face would break apart. "Well," he warbled "I'll see what I can do..."

As he strutted back into the kitchen, he gave me a big wink.

So look, at one time or another, I've been a menswear salesman, a musician, a garbageman, an investigator, a truck driver, a cook, a model, a seaman, a cop, a stable-hand, a punch-press operator, an actor, and a fork-lift driver, to name a few.

I'll tell you something I've learned from that. No matter what the job is, the people who do that job have a notion of what it means to do the job right. They also have an idea of who "the best" is at doing it. It's the Paul Bunyan/John Henry thing. There is an ideal. There's pride in a job done well. Doesn't matter whether you're slinging hash, counting cash, shoveling shit or making a hit.

A lot of people under-appreciate this because they're on their way to being somebody else. This guy's going to be a lawyer, but he's working at a gas station for now. That guy's going to be a movie star, but right now he's a waiter. He only cares about what he's *going* to be, doesn't care much about what he is *now*.

So there's no pride.

Guy doesn't care if he's a lousy waiter because it isn't really him, it's just temporary. But suppose he's on his way home one night and gets hit by a bus.

Nobody knows about the terrific movie star he was *going* to be.

All he leaves behind is the shitty waiter that he was.

I believe every job, done with integrity, has dignity. Whatever you do, do it the best you can. No matter what the job is, *how* you do it isn't about the job, it's about *you*. It's more noble to be a superb shit-shoveler than it is to be a mediocre brain surgeon.

Just my opinion.

Adam Adrian Crown

Brandy, You're a fine girl
What a good wife you would be
But my life, my lover, my lady is the sea.

("Brandy," The Looking Glass)

CHAPTER NINETEEN: CQD

You can always tell a sea story is coming when the guy starts out by saying, "Hey, this is no shit..."

So I won't say that.

I'll just say that something happened that I can't explain, something that still raises gooseflesh on the backs of my arms if I think about it too much, even all these years later. And I *know* this happened, because I was there.

After that thing in El Paso, I floated around, worked a few odd jobs, and finally wound up back in Chicago and went to college by taking my high school GED exam. I finished in the 98th percentile. I had an urge to send a copy of that to the assholes masquerading as teachers at my old high school, but I didn't.

I enrolled in a community college taking whatever struck my fancy. Psychology. Sociology. History. Political Science.

Disturbed by the glimpse of myself I'd gotten in Texas, I decided I was going to be a pacifist in the tradition of Ghandi and the Rev. Dr. King. I tried hard to convince myself, make it work, change those spots, out, damn spot. I treated that darkness in my heart like a monster hiding in my closet — pulled the covers over my head and pretended it wasn't there. It worked for a little while. Sort of.

243

I enjoyed college. Eventually, I ran out of money and lost my student draft deferment.

Vietnam. Prison. Canada.

Those were my choices.

It's very fashionable today for former flower children, now in their later years, to disown the anti-war movement, as if it were no more than a late adolescent rite of passage, like goldfish-swallowing, with President But-I-Didn't-Inhale, leading the charge. All that remains of the late 60's in the official record is long hair, pot, and psychedelic tie-dyed t-shirts and bell-bottomed jeans. Occasionally someone in the media will imply that Charles Manson and his murderous "family" were typical "hippies." Yeah. I'm sure "Peace and love" was his motto.

They'll also try to tell you that some people wore love beads but other people wore dog tags. The truth is, lots of people wore both.

I was absolutely certain by then that America's war in Vietnam was absolutely wrong, both in intention and in execution. Decades later, I'm even more certain. Some people will accuse me of "dishonoring" the memory of the Americans who died there.

That's bullshit.

The dishonor falls on them who betrayed and exploited the most noble (even if naive) inclinations of those young Americans, sending them to squander their lives in a most ignoble crusade, murdering several million innocent people.

What's dishonorable is to pretend that our guys died for something important, that they were "serving their country," instead of oiling the gears of what Ike called "the military industrial complex;" or that they died fighting for freedom and democracy, or some such puerile crap. It's dishonorable to lie about it, keep lying about it, rewrite it, edit it, so it'll be easy to trick the next batch of suckers into making the same stupid mistake.

Okay, it's certainly true that some joined the "revolution" just to smoke dope, some joined just to get laid, some joined just because they didn't know what else to do with themselves. There was a time when that was me. Some never really joined the revolution; while young people of conscience were engaged in just revolt, others were just revolting.

But what is too often and too conveniently forgotten is the critical detail that the fundamental energy behind the hippification of so many American kids was a despair-driven determination to keep from being maimed or killed and to avoid having to maim or kill Vietnamese kids.

That seems perfectly reasonable to me.

I think somebody ought to mention that once in a while.

Vietnam. Prison. Canada.

Now, I'm not a pacifist. As much as I tried, or as much as I pretended, or as much as I pretended to try, that's not me. I sincerely admire men like King and Ghandi, but I've never been able to find that kind of compassion and strength in myself. Never been all that big on "forgiveness."

See, I don't think a rapist, and a woman who kills the rapist, are committing morally equivalent acts. I don't think Nazis murdering Jews, and Jews shooting Nazis in self-defense are morally equivalent acts, either.

I think that's a scam that the wolves sell to the sheep.

So when it comes down to it, if you punch me, Pal, I'm going to punch you right back. Only you're not getting back up. I don't mind fighting at all. In fact, in some ugly part of me, I know I enjoy it. I know that's not a good thing. But there's no point in denying it.

I do, however, reserve the absolute right to do my own thinking, and to choose my own friends and my own enemies, to please myself and no one else. If I'm going to fight, I choose for myself who, when and why, and nobody else chooses for me.

I found inspiration in the greatest-of-all-time heavyweight champion, Muhammad Ali, who refused induction into the Army, even though it cost him everything he'd ever worked for to do it. "No Vietnamese ever called me nigger," he said.

That made sense.

I'd never met a Vietnamese person. No Vietnamese had ever done anything to hurt me. They weren't any kind of a threat to me or anyone or anything I loved. If some Vietnamese paratroopers landed on my lawn, that might be different. You call me in that case, and I'll come a runnin' with my musket. But there was no way in hell I was going over there to kill people I didn't hate for reasons I didn't believe on the order of people I didn't know or trust. That much I knew for certain.

Vietnam was not an option.

I had seen enough of jail to know that I didn't care to do a stretch in prison, either. Maybe if I'd had the courage, I'd have gone that way. But I just didn't have it. I'm not martyr material.

Going to Canada didn't appeal to me much either, nothing against Canada, you understand. Nice place. Beautiful country. Good people. But it isn't home. The good, old US of A is my home. Why should *I* be the one to leave? If everyone who dissented left the country, who'd be left? Just the jingoistic assholes. Imagine a whole country full of Newt Gingrich's and Jesse Helms's and George Bush Junior's. Man, if that doesn't make your patriotic scrotum shrivel up, nothing will. Besides, I'm not comfortable running from a fight, if it's the right fight to fight.

Anyway, that's how I wound up in the United States Coast Guard.

The recruiter was as oily as Jack Nicholson in The Last Detail. But he said something that reeled me in like a suicidal marlin: "We *save* lives," he said. "We don't *take* lives."

Yeah. He had me right there.
All the rest was hand puppets.
He told me that the Coast Guard was light on the military crap. "We're not fucking Marines," he said.
The Coast Guard didn't take just anybody, he told me. They were a small outfit, and selection was highly competitive. My having two years of college and a 4.0 average was helpful. After I took the "military aptitude test," he told me I scored high enough that I could write my own ticket.
Oh, Boy! I made the team! Hot diggety-dog.

It would be easy to blame him for hustling me, but the truth is I was easy to hustle. I was desperate to believe that there was good in the world, maybe even good in me. The prospect of joining an elite team of courageous, highly skilled men and women dedicated to saving lives on the treacherous seas, was irresistible. I wanted to believe it. Hell, I *needed* to believe it. So believe it, I did. I could do Search and Rescue. I could learn to fly a chopper. I could use my super-powers for good and not for evil.

The first step to my heroic Coast Guard career was basic training. After that, I'd go to officer candidate school. After that, flight school. Maybe do twenty years, retire young *and* with a pension. PLUS I'd have the GI Bill if I wanted to go back to school. I could still play music in my off-duty time. Had it all planned out. But I had not the daintiness of ear to hear the gods laughing. It wasn't until I stepped off the bus at the Coast Guard Training Center at Cape May, New Jersey, that I began to suspect I may have made a great big stupid fucking mistake.

"Listen up, you faggot pukes! In-fucking-credible. What a sorry bunch of limp dicks! You girls got just about 10 seconds to gather up your pathetic shit and get your sweet little asses out on parade! Move it, Ass-wipes! Move it, move it, move it...!"

This warm welcome was from a pig-faced petty officer whose jumper was far too snug for his beer belly.

For a moment, I was sure I'd somehow gotten on the wrong bus.

No such luck.

This was my introduction to the dedicated, highly skilled elite.

And it didn't get any better.

Experience is what you get when you don't get what you wanted. I got a lot of experience in the Coast Guard

It wasn't the rough language. Where I grew up you use the word "fuck" as a noun, verb, adjective, adverb and period. In fact, a sentence is not considered a complete sentence without *some* form of "fuck" included.

It wasn't that the training was challenging, either — it wasn't. Except, of course, as a challenge to your capacity to tolerate boredom.

What bothered me was that I had volunteered to do an allegedly vital job in the national interest; why should I be treated as if I were in prison? I suppose what really made me angry was that it was all such arbitrary abuse, completely unreasonable, petty, and, well, just like Mom and Dad used to make.

I seemed to have gotten myself into yet another dysfunctional family.

Somehow I was able to stomach the thirteen wasted weeks of so-called basic training, which was basically not much real training. During that time my recruit company spent a grand total of two hours on a boat (mastering the terms "port" and "starboard"), and an average of two hours per day marching around in a circle carrying rifles that had been obsolete for about 20 years, and where "left" was pronounced something like "layip" and rendered wondrously multisyllabic. On graduation day, I was pronounced salty enough to take a billet aboard ship, and was set loose upon the unsuspecting sea-going public.

My ship turned out to be a 180 foot buoy tender named the Juniper based in South Portland, Maine, as close to the bona fide edge of the earth as this city kid had ever actually been. When I arrived on a crisp December night, I was, I admit, a little impressed, and I temporarily convinced myself that, the perverse Disneyland of basic training notwithstanding, whoever was in command of a ship this big just *had* to know something.

Maybe I had not yet learned what a common fallacy it is to assume that authority has a rational basis. Maybe I was desperately looking for some kind of order in the world.

I was going to have to keep looking.

The commanding officer, known not-very-affectionately as "Captain Chaos" was arguably the most incompetent skipper ever to puke over the side of a Coast Guard vessel or hold the record for the most number of times ramming the dock at eight knots or more.

Before taking command of the Juniper, his previous responsibilities had been as the commissary officer aboard a larger ship — a "great white," as we referred to them.

Commissary officer.

That's the guy who buys the groceries.

A complete inventory of Captain Chaos's legendary fuck-ups would comprise a volume so weighty it would make Tolstoy's War and Peace look like Cliff Notes. It would include at least one misplacement of a channel buoy that resulted in an oil tanker running aground, engendering a mini-Valdez type disaster. It would include him comprehensively demolishing a fine boat while attempting to tow it in after it had developed engine trouble. It would include him sailing over our own lines (shades of Captain Queeg) while re-supplying a lighthouse with fresh water and fuel, the result of which fuck-up was our pumping a couple a thousand gallons of oil into the ocean. It would include countless occasions of taking two or three weeks to accomplish what the previous skipper had managed to do in two or three days. It would include taking a ship that had been rated in the top 5 in the entire Coast Guard fleet (highest performance marks, fewest AWOL's, fewest men "on report" and so on) and transforming it into one of the worst (lowest performance marks, highest AWOL's, etc.) in Coast Guard history, all in less than a year.

Let me give you one or two examples:

When a ship pulls in, the seamen attach clothesline-weight "heaving lines" to the heavy-duty "mooring lines," which are actually used to secure the ship in her berth. They "heave" the heaving lines to other men waiting ashore who then pull in the mooring lines to which they are attached, and loop the eye of the mooring lines around a post. Onboard, the mooring lines are turned around winches and by taking up the slack, the ship pulls herself in. It's a lot like reeling in a fish — or maybe a fish reeling itself in, if it had the pole and...

Well, you get the idea.

Heaving lines terminate in a huge knot, sometimes woven around a lead weight, which is known as a "monkey fist." These lines are a standard 50' in length, or are supposed to be, anyway. At least in the Coast Guard and, for all I know, the whole world over. Our heaving lines on the Juniper were all 50 feet long.

Now, picture this: Southwest Harbor, Maine. We're coming in to overnight at the base there after a grueling and frustrating 5 days out, during which time almost nothing of value had been accomplished. The rain is coming down in sheets so thick you can hardly breath, driven into us by a bone-chilling 35 knot headwind out of the Northeast. It feels like spikes being hammered into your face.

Some captains would over-shoot the dock and then let the wind do all the work, pushing us back into place so we could put our lines out easily.

Not Captain Chaos.

Not on your life.

I guess no one had ever told him about spitting into the wind.

His technique is to try to sail the ship into the wind, hold her in place long enough for us to throw the lines ashore and then use the winches to drag us the rest of the way. If this sounds to you like really doing things the hard way, you're already a better sailor than Captain Chaos was.

So there I am, on the foc's'l (salty talk for "forecastle" the forward-most part of the ship, where the crew lived in the olden days), soaked to the skin, shivering, probably turning blue as my reefer. Short on sleep (because we were sailing undermanned), urping from fried food, cruising on caffeine and tobacco. The wind is thundering in my ears so loudly that I can hardly hear a thing through the sound-powered headset that connects me to the bridge, where Captain Chaos is blathering orders.

I report our progress toward the dock in this fashion: "300 feet to the dock, Sir.....200 feet to the dock, Sir....100 feet to the dock, Sir....."

"Put out number one!" came the order.

Surely, he must not have heard me.

" I say again, 100 feet to the dock, Sir," I repeated as loudly and clearly as I could.

"Put out number one."

"Still 100 feet from the dock, Sir."

"Put out number one, dammit!" was the reply.

"Aye-aye, Sir," I said, and threw the heaving line into the water as ordered. "Number one's away, Sir," I reported.

Perhaps you can imagine how well this was received on the bridge.

While on the subject of heaving lines, I might mention that, when returning to our own home berth in Portland, our skipper rammed the dock at 8-12 knots so often that no one from the base there would come down to catch our lines. We had to lie to them, to radio ahead and tell them we were someone else. The uninitiated would be fooled — once, anyway — but they quickly learned to recognize us and sprint away for their lives, returning only after we had come to a dead stop.

If our skipper was a cross between Captain Bligh and Jerry Lewis, at least we had one real seaman aboard. Our first lieutenant, theoretically third in command of the ship, was a 30 year Warrant Officer from Kentucky, Mr. Hill, by name. He was as calm and soft-spoken as he was skillful and experienced, which naturally put him at loggerheads with Captain Chaos.

Closing fast on retirement, Mr. Hill's dream was to return to bluegrass country and raise thoroughbreds. It was, he explained around the ever-present pipe clenched between his teeth, as far inland as he could get.

Describing himself as "the most over-paid seaman in the Coast Guard," Mr. Hill was not only the advocate for the crew, but was also a seemingly inexhaustible storehouse of obscure nautical lore. In his leisure moments he plaited fancy ropework onto an impressive array of inanimate objects, boat-hooks and such, and I once observed him scan the night sky and detect from the stars that we had drifted off course.

He often delighted us with wild tales of "the *old* coast guard," back when it was known as "hooligan's navy," and he lamented its current sorry state. "No ballast," he would say sadly. "I was in the guard ten years before I ever even saw an officer; now they got 'em cleanin' the head."

252

I was actually fortunate enough to see the "old coast guard" style in action on one occasion. There was a matter of paint, gunmetal grey paint, in fact. We were required to paint our decks with it but there was none to be had, and apparently we couldn't just go to the local hardware store and buy some without compromising national security, even if it would have been simpler, cheaper and faster. It had to be *the* gunmetal grey paint. The official stuff. The stuff that cost about two and a half times what the identical but non-official paint cost. Your tax dollars at work.

It so happened we had an overnight at USCG Base Boston which is right next to a Navy base. And they have lots of official gunmetal grey paint. In short order, Mr. Hill organized a "special detail," of which I was a member, to pay a visit on the Navy. He wore his work khakis for the mission, but pinned all his ribbons over his pocket. He had earned enough decorations in 30 years to make a normal man walk crooked.

The kid on watch wasn't a day over eighteen, and had the wandering eyes of someone who wasn't really sure what he was doing. His uniform fit like it was made for his big brother, and he wore his Dixie cup the way it came out of the box. Mr. Hill strolled up to the watch shack, unlit pipe in hand, and asked the watch for a light, all the while patting his pockets to make the request convincing. The kid didn't have a light. Mr. Hill slipped smoothly into Plan B.

"Hey, I got one. What a dummy," he chided himself with homespun chagrin. "Y'all know Ensign Hopper?"

"No, Sir."

"Well, that's all right. I'll just wait. Where y'all from, son?"

Thus Mr. Hill engaged the watch in some personable salty chit-chat. Meanwhile, a pallet of gunmetal grey paint somehow found its way from the Navy's stores to our van. When it was loaded up, I went over to the watch shack and stood by Mr. Hill — the signal that we had finished our part of the mission.

There was no Ensign Hopper, of course. Mr. Hill used "hopper" to refer to the toilet bowl. So "Ensign Hopper" was his way of saying "Ensign Shithead."

Had it not been for Mr. Hill's presence, I'm sure my time aboard the Juniper would have been unendurable.

Scuttlebutt had it that I set the unofficial record for the most number of "Captain's Masts" in the district. You get a Captain's Mast when you've violated a regulation not serious enough to warrant a court-martial. You appear before the Skipper and his Executive Officer and your Division Officer (in my case, Mr. Hill) and they decide how much extra duty or loss of liberty time you get. My offenses were legion in the area known as "military courtesy." I repeatedly neglected to salute anyone (except Mr. Hill) or anything (such as the flag); I often wore items of "non-uniform" clothing (I had a white silk scarf I wore for luck) and failed to show our two dick-headed ensigns the respect they felt they deserved.

Incidentally, I believe "Dick-Headed Ensign" is the correct nautical term. Like Vice Admiral or Lieutenant Commander I never heard anyone call them anything else — and that "anyone" included full admiral.

On one occasion I fell afoul of the "old man" (as the captain of a vessel is generally called)) for organizing an informal soccer match. Although we were "off-duty" at the time, the other team was composed of crewmembers of a Japanese fishing boat we had impounded for violating U.S. waters. I, for one, was convinced that the violation was inadvertent — okay, Mr. Hill thought so, and I naturally agreed with the only guy on board I had any respect for. The Japanese crewmen — who had hoped to be heading home the next day, were now looking at another 3-6 weeks — at LEAST — stuck in Portland, Maine — and restricted to their ship and the dock.

I figured they could use some cheering up, and I was dead certain that we could. So I got some of the mates together, bought some beer and it was soccer and suds on the dock.

Funny, you put together a bunch of guys, some kind of a ball and a supply of booze and suddenly language isn't much of a barrier at all.

Unfortunately, a humorless Officer of the Day from the base showed up to inform us that our drinking buddies from the land of the rising sun were under arrest, and not there to be entertained. He followed that up with a hair-brained lecture on international relations, economics and the fishing supply with some other random threads thrown in, the gist of which I could neither follow then, nor repeat now.

You guessed it.

He was a Dick-Headed Ensign.

On the up side, it so happened that Japanese sailors wore the same kind of "Donald Duck" hats that we did — only theirs were blue. The hatbands were the same style. Ours said "US Coast Guard" and theirs said — well, whatever the hell the name of their ship was. The something-or-other maru. I swapped hatbands with a really good goalie named Yukio, and wore his band on my hat when I appeared for the Captain's Mast that inevitably followed the soccer game.

You know what?

Nobody even noticed.

No one noticed at the next three inspections, either. Except Mr. Hill. And he never said a word.

Inspections.

Now there was something Captain Chaos loved. In any organization, when you can't do the job you're *supposed* to do, you concentrate on things you *can* do— like making sure the guys' shoes are shined. In this regard, I enjoyed one of those small, tawdry victories I still recall with great relish.

Word came down that we were to be visited by an actual
four-stripe captain of some stature. Don't remember why, but
it was a big deal of some kind. Captain Chaos immediately put
Operation Sweat into action, and we prepared to stand
inspection on the dock in our dress whites.

Unfortunately, the regulation that determined the date on
which we would change from our winter wool blues to our
summer cotton whites did not take into account that we were
in Maine which gets 9 months of winter and three months of
cold. We resigned ourselves to the prospect of shivering our
balls off standing out on the dock while the Old Man kissed up
to this honcho from district headquarters.

But I decided not to take it lying down. So several of us
hustled into town to an Army-Navy surplus store which
boasted quite a collection of real and reproduction medals.

When the hour came, we stood proudly on the dock
wearing our service medals. An acute eye might have
wondered how so many of our crew — especially those so
young — had won, say the Croix de Guerre. Or the Blue Max.
Or the Order of the Rising Sun. But the only eye present that
was sufficiently acute was Mr. Hill's and he remained silent as
the sphinx, though from the way his jaw was working, I'd say
he did some teeth-clenching.

When the captain in question finally arrived, he pulled up
in a pick-up truck and was wearing a leather flight jacket,
rumpled khaki's, sneakers and a fishing cap. When our own
captain invited this dignitary to "inspect his crew" he
responded by giving us the briefest glance and the comment,
"They look fine, Captain — but don't you think it's a little
fucking cold out here for this?"

For my innumerable infractions I spent many weekends
chipping and painting, cleaning the heads (salty term for
"toilets"), inventorying and repairing equipment, and making

up lines. An unintended result was that I soon knew every inch of our ship better than most anyone.

You might ask, why didn't Captain Chaos just get rid of me?

He couldn't. At least, not right away.

First, we were under-manned as it was (thanks to the captain's effect on morale) and there weren't exactly crowds of sailors at the gangplank trying to beat their way on board.

Secondly, as a Seaman I was filling the billet — that is, doing the jobs — that normally required at least a 3rd Class Petty officer or higher. One of these was as coxswain of a lifeboat, in a worst case scenario. Another was boatswain's-mate of the watch. But the real reason I was so inconveniently vital was that I was one of only four men on board who could operate the ship's boom (crane), without which we were pretty much just an expensive bobber.

Mr. Hill could operate it, of course. So could Chief Lowe and Petty Officer "Frenchy" Brusseaux.

And me. I learned how from Mr. Hill.

While this ability often complicated my taking leave, or going on liberty, since I had to accommodate the other operators' schedules — and they all well out-ranked me — I'm sure it was also the thing that kept me away from an actual court-martial.

You might wonder what's so tricky about running the boom.

I'll tell you.

But you won't believe me.

The boom operator's shack is located above the buoy deck on more or less the same level as the main deck and right under the bridge. There are rotating four handles that you can crank to the left or right to either take up on or slack off on the cables. The handles farthest right and left are for the vangs attached to the boom itself and raise and lower it. By taking up on only the starboard vang the boom pulls up and to the right;

only the port vang, up and to the left; up on both together and it goes straight up.

The two middle handles operated the cables connected to the two hooks: the main hook and the short hook (or "number two") and it was often necessary to take up on one while slacking off on the other to keep the load (usually a buoy, sinker or chain) level and under control.

The man in charge of the buoy gang — usually the Chief or Mr. Hill — would direct the boom operator by means of hand signals. Or with a good boom operator he could just say, "Hey, Jack, put it over there," and leave the driving to you.

It may have occurred to you that the operation of the boom required the coordinated and simultaneous management of four handles, but that even a good boom operator only has two hands. Here's how the trick was done:

Believe it or not, to do this job, you perched on a stool and controlled the two middle handles with your hands. At the same time, you used your left elbow to move the handle on the far left; and you put your right foot up on the control panel to push or pull the handle on the farthest right with your toe. Your free leg was to help balance on the stool.

I never really appreciated how crazy this system was until I had to train a new guy to do it. He laughed so hard he cried and refused to believe that I wasn't simply fucking with him. Only when Mr. Hill confirmed what I had told him did the mate stop laughing.

When our ship was ordered to "underway training" at the Norfolk, Virginia Navy base, Frenchy wisely bailed out by taking leave and I was stuck going along. Captain Chaos didn't have the first clue what to do and spent most of the time pacing around, clucking like a chicken, and getting in the way (thus earning the new sobriquet "Commander Sweat-it").

Fortunately, we had Mr. Hill who knew exactly what to do. He made a list of things that had to be squared away by the time we reached Norfolk, and he explained to us that the

Captain was anticipating a dismal failure and had already begun to contemplate appropriate punishments for the crew. By this time, you see, Captain and crew were enjoying a clearly adversarial relationship, and the Old Man exercised his full wrathful genius on us. At least he was good at *something*.

It dawned on us — thanks to Mr. Hill — that the best way to shaft Captain Chaos was actually to do well. He also let it be known that District Command had set up certain unspecified rewards for the crew getting the best marks, and that he personally was good for some Kentucky sipping whiskey no matter how we did. Hell, the bucket was in bad shape and we were really undermanned. He couldn't really ask us to bust our nuts, all things considered.

So he didn't ask.

He didn't have to.

If the Juniper managed to receive passing marks on the week-long ordeal, it was because the crew spent every waking moment on the cruise south frantically preparing — with Mr. Hill getting just as dirty and paint-spattered as any of us.

For me, the highlight of our stay in Norfolk (called "No-fuck" by long-term residents) took place our first morning at the Navy base, parked next to some kind of ship — I have no idea what kind — about twice our size.

It was a study in contrasts.

I don't know what time they get up in the Navy, but they pipe their "reveille" bugle call over the P.A. system *real fucking loud*. Four guys turn out onto the fantail wearing their uptown uniforms, carrying the perfectly folded flag like a religious relic — which for some, I suppose it is. They march out in that board-up-your-ass posture that's completely unnatural to bipeds, hook up Old Gory, run it up and render a crisp salute while somebody pipes another bugle call — *real fucking loud*.

While these boys were looking very strike, cracked into their saluting pose, we had our own normal morning ceremony.

First of all, fuck the bos'n's pipe business. That shit would get you skinned alive on our tub. On our ship everybody slept as late as possible. 0745 gave you enough time to get up, get dressed, hit the head and report for role call at 0800. You made that 0730 if you wanted to grab a bite to eat. But 6 a.m.?

Un-fucking-civilized.

So the only guys actually awake when it's time to raise the colors in the morning are the two guys on watch. The engineman doesn't leave the engine-room. That leaves one seaman to attend to the flag ritual. So he goes out wearing t-shirt, dungarees and sneakers. Baseball cap. Cigarette dangling from his lips. Folded up Hustler Magazine sticking out of a back pocket, open to the centerfold so the lady's crotch is peeking back at you. Flag rolled up in a bundle under one arm. He shuffles across the fantail. Fumbles the lanyard free. Polishes a brass hook with one corner of the flag. Hooks up the flag. Raises it. Gazing up, he takes a beat to realize it's upside down. Scratches his ass. Lowers the flag and changes it around and ties off the lanyard. Takes a last drag from his smoke and flicks it overboard as he turns and heads back toward the smell of coffee.

Maybe you find this offensive?

Maybe you think it's disrespectful?

Then fuck you.

And I'll tell you why.

Never let a symbol become more important than the thing it stands for. If you're not going to have the liberty and justice that the flag is supposed to represent, don't worry about the flag itself. It's just a flag. And flags are like hemorrhoids: every asshole has one. I have this theory that the more flags you see, the less actual freedom you have.

Take Nazi Germany for example. Flags all over the damn place.

Freedom?

Not so much.

Anyway, next to us, the Navy guys are stretching their eyeballs out of their sockets with disbelief. Can't begin to accept that we're so casual about this thing. But then they have lots of time to worry about flags and rituals, because they don't actually have to do anything much while they're waiting around for a chance to kill somebody.

We, on the other hand, have actual work to do, in theory anyway, and have precious little time to piss away on pomp and circumstance. Maybe that's why we out-scored a lot of Navy vessels on things like fire-fighting and man-overboard drills.

Different priorities, see?

Anyway, we headed back home, none too soon, having delivered a pretty nice feather into the Captain's undeserving cap. On the sneak, mates not actually on watch, got to taste that Kentucky whiskey, just as promised. And Mr. Hill smoked a joint with us, besides.

Two days from home, we got a weather warning. Low pressure area. Hurricane force winds. May or may not head for the coast. We secured everything we could and ran a "life line" from stem to stern. If we hit rough weather, anyone who had to go out on deck could clip a safety harness to the lifeline to keep from going overboard.

As the seas began to pick up, the wind shifted, and soon we were crawling along, making only a couple of knots, engaged in a danse macabre with the ocean. First she would roll. Side to side. Side to side. Side to side. If you're going to turn green easily, that usually does it. Some of our rolls were approaching 40 degrees.

But then she added pitching to her repertoire. Pitching is like a bucking bronco, raising up then plunging down, fore-and-aft. For those who rarely got seasick, pitching might do it.

Not least of all, she gave us swells. A swell is like the ocean taking a deep breath, filling out her lungs, with you riding on her chest. It feels like a madman's elevator ride. You go up and then there's a moment of weightlessness, like on a ferris wheel, and you fall, fall, fall and then uuuupppppp again...

Even if you never get seasick this three-step tango might make you regret you'd eaten anything in the last three or four years. After about six hours of this dance, we had a lot of guys down and out, in the rack or on bended knee praying at the porcelain altar.

Only two of us, a brother from Detroit named Nick, a.k.a Simba, and I, were spared the torment of unending dry heaves. Just the luck of the draw.

In a show of compassion for our mates, we broke out a few tins of sardines, which, by itself, will make a lot of people wretch. The effect on those already sick was both profound and entertaining — particularly since one of those wrestling desperately with his gag reflex was Captain Chaos, himself.

The sardines we brought up to the bridge were just the nudge to push him over the edge. Mr. Hill, recognizing the Captain's pallor, suggested that the Old Man let him have the con awhile.

"Can't sleep anyway, Captain," Mr. Hill said casually. "No sense both of us being up. I'll call you if it gets rough."

Though Mr. Hill said it in such a way as to allow the Old Man to save face, the Captain knew the situation for what it was. We all did. Still, I was embarrassed to over-hear the Captain's reply to Mr. Hill. There was a tremor in his voice not put there by the rough weather.

"But I'm the Captain, dammit," he whispered. "I'm the Captain..." But the question was decided for him by his stomach.

"Mr. Hill has the con!" he managed to croak out past rising vomit as he ducked out for his stateroom.

As it turned out, I somewhat regretted the sardine thing. I ended up standing double watches because everybody else was sick.

262

Eclipse of the Heart

You pay for your thrills. It's the TANSTAAFL principle.

On a ship, the day is broken up into 4-hour "watches." We generally called them the morning watch (8 a.m.-noon) the afternoon watch (noon-4 p.m.), the dog watch from 4-8 p.m., the night watch from 8 p.m.-midnight, the mid-watch from midnight to 4 a.m. and the dawn watch from 4 a.m. to 8 a.m.

Most everybody hates the mid-watch. Even though it's customary for the mid-watch to be allowed to sleep in until noon the following day, few can manage to sleep while the rest of the crew turns to, with little or no regard for your peace and quiet. As a result you really don't get any sleep, and you spend the next day with your ass dragging a little.

Me, I loved the mid-watch.

The entire crew is bedded down and everything is secured. It's like a ghost ship. Nothing but the engine, the creaks and squeaks of the ship herself, the deep breathing of the ocean, the soft gossip of the wind.

I almost feel like it's *my* ship.

As bo's'n's mate-of-the-watch (BMOW), you make rounds of the ship every half hour. You check that nothing's burning and nothing's flooding and that everything that should be secured is secured. You make sure that the officer-of-the-watch is supplied with coffee, that the helmsman is on course, and that the look-out is awake. Sometimes you relieve either one of them for a quick head break.

Between those duties, I would just wander the ship, feel the sea under my feet, listen to her snoring, knowing she could roll over at any time without warning and completely erase me and my little boat without even waking herself up in the process.

If you've never been on a ship, out at sea, a day or more from the nearest landfall, you owe it to yourself to try it, at least once. It's both exhilarating and terrifying and it's probably as close to real freedom as you'll ever get. You'll see the sun gloriously rise up out of the ocean in the morning, and marvel at indescribably beautiful sunsets of purple and red and gold, with the sea and the sky becoming indistinguishable on the horizon. The wind sings in a different key, and the moonlight dances feverishly on the wavelets, You'll see whales up close, and waves of dolphin, and the occasional shark.

Even being stuck in the Coast Guard couldn't ruin it.

It was about halfway through the midwatch when the message first came in.

Seas were rough; weather decks closed. No man aloft. Mr. Hill had the con. Seaman Apprentice Whelan on the helm. Quartermaster's Mate 2nd Class Tom Harding was hunched over his charts, mumbling. Suddenly, he perked up. "Mr. Hill," he said, "I'm getting some kind of traffic..."

"What kind of traffic?" Mr. Hill asked, wiping the steam from the windshield as if that would help us see farther than about twenty-feet through the sheets of rain.

"I don't know, Sir. It sounds like Morse Code. It's broken up. Real bad..."

"Morse Code?" snorted Mr. Hill. Not a lot of people used morse code. "Put that shit on the squawker, son."

Harding switched on the loudspeaker so we could all hear it. It was mostly static. Faint bleeps, like erratic heartbeats, faded in and out. It was all noise to me.

"Are you getting any of this, Harding?"

Harding was still listening in on his headphones squinting with the strain, translating it out loud as he scribbled on a note pad.

"We... fuck... This is... (burst of static) i-n-g. T-i something-something... dammit."

"Easy, son..." said Mr. Hill.

"There's something... it repeats. C...Q... doesn't make any sense. C... Q... D! It's a D! CQD. What the fuck is that?"

"Stay with it, now Harding." Mr. Hill had perked up.

"... r-e s-i -m... no, n — Oh, shit. It's 'We are sinking fast'. It says 'we are sinking,' Mr. Hill..."

"You're doing real good. Stay on it."

"There's no — Wait! I think he's sending his position."

"You get that position, son."

He got it.

Harding was able to decipher enough of the noise to get what might be a bearing toward what might be a vessel in distress, and Mr. Hill changed course to head for her. I informed the Captain and the old man joined us on the bridge, still a nice shade of ready-to-puke green.

I sounded "general quarters; this is not a drill," roused the crew, and started search and rescue preparations. We brought PO2 De Santos up to monitor radar, manned the searchlights, and put every other available man on lookout, both aloft and on the foc's'le, all clipped in with safety lines attached to their belts. Chief Lowe put two men in wetsuits, we broke out towing lines, the whole drill. Our medical corpsman, PO1 Geeson, started getting ready to treat hypothermia and whatever else.

We saw nothing but sea and rain for half an hour, during which time the distress message continued to fade in and out, with Harding picking up additional pieces of it here and there, not quite enough to confirm our course. Then the signal ceased and the radio was nothing but static.

"It's gone," Harding finally said.

The mood on the bridge was grim. The sinking of a ship, any ship, is a matter of profound grief for a seaman. And in this case, someone was calling for help and had gone down before we could reach them. Hell, we weren't even sure we were sailing in the right direction. I was, surprised at myself, a little choked up. I turned to Mr. Hill. "There might still be..." but I couldn't finish it.

And before he could reply, one of the foc's'le lookouts spotted something ahead and hailed the bridge.

She was a 45 foot motor-sailer, turtled in the water, just the keel showing, like a tiny iceberg. Clinging to it, mostly unconscious, were a man, a woman and a young girl. We came alongside, and our divers went in, wearing harnesses attached to lifelines, and we managed to pull the people in and get them all aboard in about five or ten minutes. The man's leg was fouled in some cable and it took some effort to free him. Only moments after getting him aboard, his boat (Titiana, named for the woman, his wife) disappeared under the boiling sea.

It was fortunate that hypothermia was their chief injury — though that's nothing to sneeze at and can easily prove fatal. We warmed them in the shower, wrapped them in blankets, gave them hot coffee to sip. The little girl (Rebecca was her name) had us worried. She remained unconscious for the time it took us to rendezvous with a chopper.

Only a Coast Guard pilot would fly in that kind of weather. For a moment I couldn't help thinking, goddam it, that's what *I'm* supposed to be doing. If he hadn't, it would have been another six hours to landfall. We sent her aloft in a stokes litter and the chopper carried her to the nearest hospital in Rockland. I won't say we prayed for her, though some of us probably did, but I bet we all thought about her, hoping for her real hard. By the time we made it to port, we had received a message that she was doing fine, and there was no small amount of cheering and shoulder slapping among the mates.

County Sheriff met the parents ashore and gave them transport to the hospital.

Mr. Hill broke out his personal store of Kentucky Bourbon and we drank a toast with it. "Shoot, son," he said to me. "This is almost like the *old* coast guard."

And that was that.

Or it would have been, if Mr. Hill hadn't invited me to his stateroom a few days later and shown me QM2 Harding's transcription of the distress message. It read: "CQD...CQD... THIS IS ....TIT..AN....WE ARE SINKING FAST...WE ARE

SINKING..." That part was followed by their position and then repeated.

I handed it back to Mr. Hill who was looking at me expectantly, as if waiting for me to get the joke.

"I don't get it," I said.

"Well, now the fellow says he had one of them automatic s-o-s signal devices, but he never got a chance to switch it on. Breaker hit 'em and over they went, bang. And he says he didn't send any other distress signal, either. Wouldn't know Morse Code if it bit him on the ass."

"But he did," I said lamely. "Maybe he just doesn't remember doing it. The stress of..."

"See this part here, this 'CQD?' Ever see that before?"

"Nope."

"Uh-huh. You know why not?"

"No, why not?"

"Because it hasn't been used in about sixty years. But it used to be a distress code. We use 'SOS' now. But it used to be 'CQD.'"

"Wait a minute," I said. "I'm confused."

"Join the fuckin' club, son."

Mr. Hill then handed me a book that was laying open on his desk. He pointed out a passage he wanted me to read. It was a distress message. I started reading : "CQD. CQD. We are sinking fast. This is..." I stopped reading. I was getting a very odd feeling in the pit of my stomach.

"Now look at the other message again," Mr. Hill told me.

I did.

There was a lot missing, but the parts of the distress call that *were* there were identical to parts of the distress call cited the book. Only the one in the book had been sent more than half a century earlier.

By the radioman of the ill-fated HMS Titanic.

And that's no shit.

Number forty-seven said to number three
You're the cutest jailbird I ever did see
I sure would be delighted with your company
Come on and do the jailhouse rock with me

("Jailhouse Rock," Elvis Presley)

CHAPTER TWENTY: HARD TIME

People talk about doing hard time as if there were such a thing as easy time.

There isn't.

There's just hard time and harder time.

Real hard time is when you're innocent. Of course, nobody believes you. Nobody. Especially not the other cons.

One kind of time harder than that: when you were a cop. Combine those two and you've got the hardest time it's possible for a man to do. And that's just the kind of time I was doing.

Ok. I better back up a little.

After getting out of the service, I was loose gear. No particular direction. I took some classes at the State University on the G.I. Bill. Majored in Nothin-in-Particular. Just studied whatever interested me, no special focus. Environmental science. Chinese history. International relations. Anthropology. Anatomy and physiology. Played a little music, visited this and that martial arts school. I thought about becoming a fireman. In retrospect, it would have been a good choice.

I never wanted to be a cop.

Ever.

269

Adam Adrian Crown

Hell, I *hated* cops.

As far as I can tell, there are only three reasons why anybody *would* want to be a cop.

Reason number one is you want to help people. You want to "serve and protect." You want to be one of those honest men and women who are willing to put themselves in harm's way if necessary, to defend those people who are unable to defend themselves. If anyone asks you why you're a cop, this is the answer you're supposed to give.

Trouble is, 99.999 percent of the time it's bullshit.

Honest cops don't last long on the job. They either get the Serpico treatment from other cops, are assigned to permanent cross-walk duty, or they quit in disgust. Other cops sometimes refer to these rare idealists as "boy scouts" or "eagle scouts." Those aren't compliments. When former-cop Joseph Wambaugh wrote the best-seller, The Blue Knight, some cops started using that title as a sarcastic term. Eagle Scouts tend to be very by-the-book when it comes to themselves and very lenient with the book when it comes to the unfortunate folks they deal with on the street every day — the exact opposite of what most cops do. About the only way an eagle scout can make it on the force is to go into the internal affairs division, if there is one, and try to take down bad cops.

Fat chance.

So. Reason number two: you're a worker bee and a job is a job.

Easy work, good pay with lots of opportunity for overtime. Regular hours, more or less. Not too much heavy lifting. Medical benefits. Decent retirement plan — and one you can use when you're still young enough to remember why you wanted it. Much of it is routine, but no two days are exactly the same. So to some extent it can be interesting. And for all the wailing and gnashing of teeth about how dangerous police work is, it's really not a very hazardous occupation. Logging, fishing, roofing, steel working, truck driving, farming and ranching are ALL more dangerous than being a cop.

Worker bees do the job, and they are loyal to the job and others who do it. They fit in. They follow orders. They don't ask questions. They leave the thinking to their "superiors." They do what they're told to do, whatever they're told to do, and pick up their paycheck with a smile. They go along to get along, and they won't hesitate to lie to cover up for other cops if called upon to do so. If the house is clean, they're clean. If it's dirty, they're dirty. Worker bees aren't psychopaths, they're sociopaths because they'll take orders from a psychopath. This is the kind of guy that would gas Jews, not because he's particularly anti-semitic, but just because it's his job.

That brings us to reason number three — the reason nobody wants to talk about, and, in my opinion, the most prevalent reason why any person would become a cop: you're a fucking bully.

No doubt about it, if you're a sadistic son of a bitch and you want to brutalize and terrorize other people, and do so with impunity, get thee to the police academy.

A badge is a combination hunting license and get-out-of-jail-free card. Maybe you're just a small, mean-spirited prick, and you love giving people unnecessary grief, you enjoy making them squirm, obliging them to kiss your ass with every citation you hand out. You love that power. There are a million laws out there, and you can always find some reason to fuck with somebody, and if you can't, you can just invent one. Anything you don't like is against the law because you SAY it's against the law, whether the law actually says that or not. By the time it goes to court — IF it ever goes to court — your victim has already been wrongly arrested, imprisoned, beaten, tortured or even killed. And dead men file no lawsuits. And the worst you'll get is a paid vacation called "administrative leave."

In nearly all cases, whatever the cop does is found to be "justified" or "consistent with departmental policy." Even when there are scores of witnesses, and video evidence that proves that the cop is lying. It's *extremely* rare to find a cop who takes a fall for *anything* — I mean it almost *never* happens. I can count the cases I know of on one hand and still have plenty of fingers left over to jack off with.

If you're a psychopath, you realize that a badge lets you do anything you want, to anybody you want, anytime you want. You want to steal? You want to rape? You want to murder? And you want to get away with it?

Just get yourself a badge.

These guys wouldn't just gas Jews, they'd invent amusing little ways to torment them and tell jokes about it later.

You think the psychopaths among the legions of cops are just "a few bad apples?"

Wake the fuck up.

It's possible to have more than one reason to be a cop. For most it's a combination of reasons. You could have reason number one supported by number two, or vice versa.

You could have reason number three re-enforced by number two or vice versa.

But you can't have number one and number three.

Those two are mutually exclusive.

If you think you have both these in you, I've got news for you: your reason is number three. Number one is just you bullshitting yourself.

If I had to guess, I'd guess about half of all cops are in category two and the other half are category three.

What happened to category number one?

Don't worry. There's a good cop for every unicorn you see out there.

Eclipse of the Heart

In my life, I'd never had an interaction with a police officer that I would call "positive." Where I grew up, on the South Side of Chicago, the only cops I ever saw were definitely in category three. They were bullies, thugs, drug dealers, bag men — even hit men. They brutalized the helpless — meaning the poor of any ethnicity, but especially non-whites — and protected the privileged rich — meaning politicians, business executives and mafia bosses — quietly cleaning up their messes and disposing of their garbage — that garbage often being inconvenient people. They enforced two completely different sets of laws, one for the rich and powerful, another for the poor and helpless.

Suppose my old man got pulled over in our dilapidated old Rambler on a drunk driving beef. They'd pull him out of the car, cuff him, thump him around, lock him up and impound the car. How we got home — my mother, my sister, my baby brother and I — that was our problem. You say it's 2am and home is forty blocks away through some very nasty neighborhoods? Tough break. Walk fast.

But suppose some rich white guy in a new Caddy is cutting through my home sweet turf, also drunk as a skunk behind the wheel, and clips a black kid on his bike. Suppose he's only prevented from leaving the scene entirely because he rear-ends a pick-up truck down the block, at the light. Now the boys in blue are all sugar and spice, it's all "please, Sir," and "Thank you, Sir," and "Let us make sure you're all right, Sir." Cuffs? No, not necessary.

The guy at the light who got rear-ended? Hispanic. He's got out-standing tickets. Take his ass in. Cuff him and frisk him and none too gently, either.

The black kid on the bike? Miraculously he's not hurt bad, skinned elbows and knees, though his bike will never play the piano again. They let him off with a warning. Didn't have a reflector on his bike, see?

Rich White drunk? Gets a ride home.

273

So, given my experience and attitude, what the fuck was I doing taking the civil service police officer exam?

I guess I blame that damned Adlou Zelman.

I met Adlou at the university.

It was lust at first sight.

Little did I know that her name was a contraction of "she'll addle you."

She was black, with skin the color of bittersweet chocolate. Her color exaggerated the sharp whiteness of tooth and eye, the soft pink of her mouth.

And some other parts.

Her hair, always shorn close to the skull, was thick and coarse as sheeps' wool, and I loved the feeling of it brushing against my skin. Her nose was broad and flat, with flaring nostrils that suggested to my imagination some mythic mare-beast eternally alert, sifting the air for any sign of danger to the herd. She was wirey and surprisingly strong for her size. Surprised me, anyway.

She was in several of my classes: sociology, constitutional law, Chinese history. She came to several gigs I played on campus. She liked folk and light jazz. When she listened to me play, she half-closed her eyes, and nodded along in rhythm. I liked that. I remember singing Buffy St. Marie's "Universal Soldier," and afterward catching her eye. She didn't applaud. She raised her fist in the "power to the people" salute.

Saw her in the student union the next day, and had to say hello.

I quickly discovered that she had the one quality I find almost irresistible: a keen mind. "Well-read" doesn't begin to describe her. She could wade into any political discussion with both fists, citing Madison or Mao with equal ease and flay both their philosophies along the weakest line with surgical precision. Having a real talent for languages, she was already fluent in French, Spanish, Italian and German, and was working on Russian and Swahili when I met her. Whatever she did, she went all out.

I dig that.

She went all out when it came to sex, too.

She preferred to be on top — which is fine with me — straddling me like a jockey, posting furiously in the saddle for long, long stretches, until we were both sweat-soaked and sweetly spent. Made me feel like Seabiscuit. After exhausting ourselves, our "pillow talk" included history, philosophy, and politics. We discussed everything that was wrong with the whole damned world and what needed to be done about it.

It was quite an extensive list.

And I have to admit, she had a pretty good fixit plan, too. It was a long-range, we-shall-overcome type plan that would take a couple of generations to bring to fruition. She emphasized education, self-reliance, community consciousness, and the subtle but steady integration of certain humanistic values into social institutions as people with her enlightened point of view moved into positions of increasing authority with the power to change what got done and how we done it.

I was particularly vulnerable to her vision of a better world as I lay in that utterly relaxed jelly-fish state of post-coital satori, and Adlou's passionate intellectual seed found a fertile reception in my imagination.

"BE the change you want to see in the world," she whispered sweet Ghandis in my ear.

Be the change you want to see in the world.

The gospel according to Adlou.

In my case, according to Adlou, that translated to: "if you don't like the cops, then you *become* the cops and do it differently."

It sounded good.

It made poetic sense.

It had a certain immediate appeal to me, the way a well-made-up hooker might look pretty good at first glance, until you get closer.

And see her Adam's apple.

But I wasn't in a position to look closer. I might not like what I saw. I wanted Adlou's vision of the world — and of me — to be real. To be true. Because, deep down, I knew it wasn't.

In El Paso, I'd gotten a glimpse of a side of myself I wasn't real comfortable with. And I was still trying to pretend it wasn't really me. Just a fluke, see. I did everything I could to convince myself that that part of me didn't exist. My therapist called that "denial."
I call it "lying."

Anyway, I wanted to be the good Dr. Jekyll, and I was afraid it might turn out that Mr. Hyde wasn't just a slice of Jekyll's id, but that Jekyll was just Hyde in denial.
I was terrified that, once that ugly djinni got out of the bottle, there'd be no getting him back in again; I wouldn't be able to stop and I'd do things that I didn't want to do. Or, more on point, I'd do things I didn't want to want to do.
Yeah. It's kind of a tangle.
It was like driving on black ice. You can do whatever you want with the steering wheel; it has no effect on what happens next, with inertia and lack of traction calling the shots.
I was terrified of what I might be capable of.
And I'll tell you why.

When I was just a little kid, I saw a film called "Night and Fog." It had lots of explicit footage of the horrors of the Nazi concentration camps at Auschwitz and Dachau. Piles of sad, limp emaciated corpses. Mountains of eyeglasses, and shoes — mountains big enough to tell you that there were a lot more bodies, too. Those scenes burned into my brain right down to my soul. I don't know about you, but for me, that's the stuff of nightmares. Sometimes those nightmares occurred during the day, as those images would intrude on my thoughts in random, unguarded moments.

The part I find most disturbing is that the Nazis weren't nuts. At least, not foaming-at-the-mouth, howling-at-the-moon, tin-foil-hat nuts. If only they had been raving lunatics listening to voices in their heads.

But they weren't.

Those atrocities would be a lot easier to bear if we could reassure ourselves that the Nazis were not regular people. Not like you and me.

Not like you, anyway.

But they were.

They weren't freaks. They didn't have brain tumors.

They were just assholes.

Assholes with power.

Hanna Arendt coined le mot juste in the phrase "the banality of evil." Adolf Eichmann was on trial for crimes he'd committed during the second world war, my father's war. Like so many other Aryan ex-supermen, he pled "only following orders" as his defense. The world wanted the monstrous things he'd done to have been done by a monster. But Eichmann turns out to be an insipid, little man, a petty bureaucrat whose biggest delusion of grandeur was to anticipate career advancement. He was just another unremarkable, merely competent, corporate ass-kisser, a "company man," who merged his own personality with "something greater than himself," and who believed it was his duty to do whatever was demanded of him by his "superiors."

Not a monster at all.

Just a mean little cog in a big monstrous wheel.

The Nazis weren't unique, either.

You'd have writers' cramp for a month if you tried to make an exhaustive list of all the nasty nazi-type sons of bitches who have polluted this planet with their presence over the course of human history – and still do.

That list would include a lot of Americans, too. The slaughter of innocent women and children at Sand Creek and Wounded Knee pre-date the Nazis by half a century or more. One generation after the Nuremburg Trials, rosy-cheeked American boys were murdering, raping, torturing and mutilating folks in Vietnam, at My Lai and a thousand other not-as-famous places just like it.

I'll spare you a litany of the times and places that the good old US of A went a-murdering. It would be enough make you weep.

Or puke.

But probably, it wouldn't be enough to make you do something about it.

That's not my point, anyway.

What *was* my point?

Oh, yeah.

My point is that as far as we know, Hitler didn't gas any Jews. Not personally.

Nope.

Somebody else did that.

Somebody "just following orders."

And the beat goes on.

I didn't want to be one of those guys.

For a while I had tried my damnedest to be a pacifist.

I was pretty good at faking it, too. Even fooled myself for a time. But then fate stepped in to show me up for the fraud I was. I don't want to go into the details too much. Been a lot of years and it still aches. Let me just put it this way: somebody got hurt and I could have prevented it. Hell, I *should* have prevented it. If I'd been true to my nature, it wouldn't have happened that way. I *knew* this guy was a wrong number. I should have put him down.

But, no, I had my head up my ass with this "pacifist" crap. So I didn't do what I damn well should have done. I fucked around instead. And somebody else paid the price for my bullshit. That's a debt I can never pay.

And that's a feeling I don't ever want to have again in my life.

By accident, I stumbled onto an interesting quote by Gandhi. He said something like this: "It is better for a man to be violent, if there is violence in his heart, than to put on the cloak of non-violence to cover his impotence. There is hope that a violent man may become non-violent; there is no such hope for the impotent."

That was the end of my "pacifist" period, see?

Back to Adlou Zelman.

Someone once said that the way to a man's heart is through his stomach. If that's true then the penis is one hell of a short-cut to a man's mind.

It's always a mistake to let someone else's theory trump your own actual experience. I know, because that's what I did.

At the time I had no real idea of how completely futile it is to try to change a system from within. Lots of people have tried it. Lots smarter people than me. Never heard of anybody able to pull it off. But I was young and stupid, and started visualizing myself as the New Blue Knight. I could take my capacity — my inclination — for mayhem and put it to constructive use. I could be a cop who took that "serve and protect" oath seriously. I could be the defender of the poor and powerless. I could stand up for all those things that need standing up for.

I could be like the Lone Fucking Ranger.

Like I said, I was young.

Sometimes I wonder what became of Adlou. I'm a little disappointed that she hasn't become our first Black female President.

I'd love to see her again.

I'd love to fuck her again.

I'd love to give her a good smack.
But deep down, I know she's not to blame.
It was my own damn fault.

I got the top score on that damn civil service test, even without the extra points for being a veteran. Police departments are, of necessity, organized along para-military lines, and I guess they figure an applicant is more likely to be successful if they already know that drill, unit discipline, chain of command, that kind of thing. They never asked me what I *thought* about any of that military shit, though. Probably a good thing they didn't.
Next stop: the state police academy in Springfield.
12 weeks.
480 hours.

I could've kicked myself when it dawned on me that I'd just let myself in for another three month long "boot camp" experience. But this one, I'd have to say wasn't quite as useless as the first one I'd done.

On the menu were courses entitled: State Vehicle Code, State Penal Code, Civil Rights and Civil Liability, Firearms and Weapons, Law Enforcement Driving, Control and Arrest Tactics, First Aid, and everyone's favorite: Physical Training.

Very little of actual police-work would be good material for a TV episode and the program pretty well reflected that. I'd say we spent 70 percent of our training time in the classroom getting assaulted and battered with chalk-and-talk lectures from instructors ranging from truly excellent to what-the-fuck-is-he-talking-about boring.

Most police manpower is committed to patrol operations, either on foot or in a car, more rarely on motorcycle or horseback. Patrol theory covers all of that stuff. Everything from how to use your radio, the ten-dash code and writing citations, to building searches and field interviews. Report writing is a big part of this one, too. As a cop, you spend a hell of a lot of time writing reports.

The most comprehensive course was probably criminal law and the state penal code. You learn when and how to make a lawful arrest, rules of search and seizure, rules of evidence, reasonable suspicion and probable cause, motor vehicle codes, juvenile law, personal and property crimes. This one was taught by a former police sergeant who was now an assistant district attorney. I think one time he even mentioned The Constitution.

Next came the court system and courtroom testimony.

Outside the classroom, we spent time on firearms training (I'd love to have a buck for every shot we fired on the practice range), including lectures on what was called "the judicious use of lethal force." We learned to handle the P-24 baton, which is based on an old Japanese improvised weapon called a "tonfa" or "rice-grinder." We worked on unarmed "control and compliance" techniques, pursuit driving skills. One instructor called it the "catch 'em, & cuff 'em curriculum." I'm sure there were a lot of other odds and ends thrown in, but those were the things I remember most.

After graduation from the academy we went into the field with a veteran Field Training Officer, to get the practical, day-to-day lowdown. That was another 6 months worth on "probation."

There's an old saying that at the Academy they teach you how to be a police officer; your FTO teaches you how to be a cop. That is, at the academy you learn how you're supposed to do things; under your FTO, you learn how things are actually done. The difference between those two was greater than I ever could have imagined.

Nearly all of what I did centered around traffic enforcement, motor vehicle accidents, domestic disturbances, drunken disorderly & disturbing the peace — not exactly Lone Ranger material. If I had to guess, I'd say medical emergencies outnumbered criminal ones about 3 to 1, so I'm glad for the emergency medical training. I'm not sure I ever helped anybody in any meaningful way.

Maybe once.

It was during the last week of my rookie year, partnered with a 15-year veteran patrolman named Leary. It had been his job to help me bridge the gap between the police academy and the real world, and he'd not relished the task. For a year it was "Stay here, kid" "Call it in, kid" and "Jesus, kid, didn't they teach you *anything*?"

We'd started out on the wrong foot, I guess.

Our first day together, we'd stopped in at a deli on 63rd Street to grab a sandwich and a coffee. I'd been keeping my eyes open and my mouth shut all day. But then I made the mistake of asking for the check.

Leary looked at me like I'd lost my mind. The waiter, an old Russian Jew named Yuri looked at me like I'd lost my mind.

"I'll take care of the check, kid," Leary told me shaking his head in wonder that anyone could be so stupid.

But I hadn't lost my mind.

I knew what was what. I hadn't just gotten here from Mars; I remembered the cops in my own neighborhood, not all that far from the area Leary and I were patrolling. Cops on the take. Free food. Free shoe repairs. Free blowjobs. A c-note to look the other way at the right time. Bagmen. Thumb-breakers for the bookies and loan sharks. I sometimes wondered if they had started out corrupt assholes, or had gotten that way, little by little over time. Maybe they started out to be good cops. Maybe it started with a free cup of coffee and a sandwich.

"Ok," I said to my mentor. "You get the check. I'll leave the tip."

I put a ten-spot down on the table. Nice tip. About 400%. But I had to make the point to both of them. Plus I was a little full of myself.

"Have it your way, kid," Leary sighed and shook his head in a way that made my integrity feel like infantile pomposity.

The waiter shrugged and tucked away the ten and wished us a good day.

As we left, I could see him jabbering to some of his pals at the counter, shrugging, pointing my way. I was hoping he was telling them that I was an honest cop. He was probably telling them I was an idiot.

I guess I was from Mars after all.

One late summer afternoon, just before the end of our shift, we responded to a call of a domestic disturbance at a residence on 51st and Halstead.

"It's the heat, kid," Leary explained. "It makes people crazy."

We arrived on the scene about three minutes after taking the call and proceeded to the apartment building in the middle of the block where the super was standing outside. He flagged us down, and directed us to an apartment on the third floor.

"They're at it again," he warned us.

We knocked on the door and identified ourselves.

The door was opened by a male caucasian, late 20's, brown and blue around six feet tall, maybe 175 or so. No visible scars or tattoos. He identified himself as Mr. Donald Petersen and admitted us to the premises.

I could smell his beer breath from across the room and he swayed on his legs like the seas were getting rough. He took on an amiable, ingratiating manner with us. Assuring us it was just a little argument. Nothing for us to get involved in.

Nowadays, many states have a mandatory arrest policy in cases of alleged domestic violence. But back then, a man's home was still his castle and nobody wanted to pry into family matters. Not until there was a dead body involved. It was a policy that resulted in a lot of dead bodies being involved.

Mrs. Peterson was locked in the bathroom with their son. There was broken china on the kitchen floor. Some kind of pasta and tomato sauce dish was splattered across the wall.

While Leary took Mr. Petersen into the living room to calm him down and get his side of it, I convinced Mrs. Petersen to come out of the bathroom. She had obviously been crying. Her nose had been bleeding — she had a bloody kleenex rolled up in one trembling hand — and one side of her mouth was swelling up. Her little boy had wrapped himself tightly around her waist, and was not very inclined to let go.

I took a close look at Mrs. Petersen's mouth and asked her how she was.

She shrugged.

"Does this happen a lot?"

She shrugged again. As was so often the case, the wife didn't want to press charges. He was basically a good guy, see. He works hard and everything. He's just got this temper...

Like talking to a wall. A very frightened wall.

I knelt down to talk with the boy.

"What's your name, pal?" I asked him.

"Alan," his mother said.

"Hi, Alan," I said. "My name's Jack. Are you okay, Alan?"

Very lightly, I put my hand on his arm and he winced. I noticed that, despite the heat, he was wearing a long-sleeved baseball jersey. White Sox. Maybe it was his favorite shirt. Maybe not.

It took some persuasion but I got him to let me look under his shirt. There were finger-shaped bruises on his arm so distinct I could practically lift prints from them. New bruises. There were older bruises on his ribs and back.

Leaving Mrs. Petersen and Alan where they were, I joined Leary in the living room where he was playing good cop with Mr. Petersen.

"Mr. Petersen," I addressed him as calmly as I could, "are you aware that your son has a lot of bruises? On his ribs and back. And on his arm."

"Ah, that shit. He was playin' and fell down the stairs. Looks worse than it is."

He was lying and I knew it. And he knew I knew it. He acted as if we were pals, all in on the charade together. I could feel a dark, cold shadow falling across my heart.

I took Leary aside and spoke very quietly to him.

"Do me a favor," I said. "I want to take the father's statement. Take the mother and kid down to that Dairy Queen and get him an ice cream, will you? Get some ice on her face, okay?"

There must've been something especially convincing in the way I said it because Leary agreed and the rookie never, and I mean *never* calls the shot, *any* shot.

When they had gone, the father and I had a little heart-to-heart chat.

Maybe fifteen minutes later, Leary came back in alone, having left the wife and child out on the stoop.

Mr. Petersen was sitting on the floor, back propped against the fridge. I had put some ice in a towel for him and he was holding it against his face, moving it from spot to spot. One eye was swollen almost shut. His lips were split and I was pretty sure his nose was broken. His ribs probably didn't feel that great either.

"What the hell, kid?" Leary whispered. "What did you do?"

"I didn't do anything," I lied.

"Then what the hell happened?"

"Mr. Petersen," I said "tell my partner what happened."

He looked at me, then at Leary, then at me. Looked at me hard. I looked right back.

"I fell down the fuckin' stairs," he said.

Leary pushed his cap back on his head and started to fish for his cigarettes.

"That stairway is real dangerous," I said. "Mr. Petersen is going to see to it that it gets fixed. So nobody has any more accidents. Ever. Right, Mr. Petersen?"

"That's right, officer. No more accidents."

"Great," I said. "I'll check back from time to time. Just to check on it. Make sure it's up to code."

I don't know if I really did any good. Before we left I took the boy aside and gave him my card and told him to call me anytime, day or night, if he needed help. I also promised Mr. Petersen, privately, that if I ever found out he was beating up his kid again, I would come back and find an excuse to blow his fucking brains out. I think he understood that I was being very sincere. I actually did stop back a couple of times, too, unexpectedly, just to say "hello," and it may be that I'd caused him to think twice. Punch a wall if you have to. But not your wife. And not your child.

I remember that when we went back to our cruiser, I paused to look back, thinking maybe I should do or say something more. But just then we got another call.

"C'mon, Jack," Leary said. "Time to go."

That was the first time he called me by name. And he never called me "kid" again.

At my sentencing, the judge gave me quite a sermon. He described the crime I had been convicted of with words like "ruthless," and "depraved" and "heinous." He went on about how, when a cop goes bad, it's the worst possible thing because he betrays the public trust. It isn't just a crime against the particular victims — though that would be bad enough — it was a crime against *all* the people. It disgraces every honest police officer and makes their job more difficult and more dangerous. He regretted that the state had no death penalty and he could only sentence me to prison time. It was clear that tearing me to pieces while still alive, and feeding the bits to the rats while I watched would have been far too lenient in his view.

Funny thing was, I more or less agreed with him. Only, since I was innocent, it didn't apply to me. He didn't care for it much when I told him so.

He sentenced me to four terms of 25 years to life to run consecutively, which meant I would only be eligible for parole after I served eighty-five years. Which meant I would die behind bars.

The crime for which I was convicted had indeed been ruthless, and depraved and heinous. It involved what appeared to have been a drug deal confounded by mistaken identity, and aggravated by the murders of five, possibly six people. That included a family of four: husband, wife, 12-year-old son and 7-year-old daughter. It included my one-time training officer and partner, Leary. And it included a possible witness.

The family had been done "execution style," tied up and shot in the back of the head with a small caliber weapon. The evidence indicated that probably several hours had elapsed between the death of the wife, who was killed first, and the death of the husband, shot last. Whoever did it took their time, and made the husband watch his whole family get murdered. My guess, they must have been looking for something and thought the husband knew where to find it.

Leary had been shot in the temple with the same weapon. Died with a mouthful of donut, something which a man of his demented sense of humor would have appreciated.

At first, the detectives liked a small time thief for the crime. He had the credit cards of the deceased and went on a spending spree that could have led Stevie Wonder to his door. Unfortunately, cops shot him to death in his mother's home "while resisting," so we'll never know his side of it. The fact that he had never used a weapon before or done any violent crime didn't seem to bother anybody. It didn't bother anybody that his girlfriend, a 15-year-old prostitute, was found dead of an overdose, virtually the next day.

But it bothered me.

Another thing that bothered me was that someone had set fire to the house — presumably to cover up the crime — had started the fire out in the garage, far enough from the bedrooms where the killings occurred, that when the fire department responded to the call and found the bodies, the crime scene was mostly undisturbed.

Now it might have been a drug deal hit. Or it might have been a bumbling thief biting off more than he could chew. But you couldn't have it both ways. The credit cards had been taken. But not the husband's rolex. Not the wedding rings. Not even the $367 in cash in the husband's wallet.

You didn't have to be Sherlock Holmes to get a sinking feeling about this one. But you had to be a detective to work on the case and I was still just a patrolman and still damp, if not actually wet, behind the ears. In fact, I was still innocent enough to make some unguarded comments to my partner. Not that Leary was a rat. As far as cops are concerned, whatever is said between partners in a patrol car is about eleven times more sacrosanct than private conversations between husband and wife, doctor and patient, and lawyer and client *combined*. Leary was stand-up all the way. But by running my mouth, I stupidly involved him and got him killed.

I started dogging the case on my own time. Poking around here and there. Just checking this, verifying that. Nothing special.

I'll cut to the chase. It hurts to talk about this, anyway.

Long story short: I made two detectives for the crime due to a time discrepancy in their reports. Something everyone overlooked. I wasn't brilliant; I tripped over it completely by accident. I was going to go to internal affairs with it, but I didn't think it was enough, by itself. I figured I'd be slick, get them saying something stupid on tape.

But stupid was my department.

Before I could say "fuck me," these guys were kicking in my door. It was like magic.

Presto! They "find" a stash of cocaine hidden in my apartment.

Allah-kazaam! They find 50 large in cash.

Abra-kadabra! They find the murder weapon in the trunk of my car.

It was magic, all right: now you see him, now you don't.

And all thanks to an "anonymous tip."

I should mention the ring.

At the time I was seeing this lady named Caroline. It had been getting pretty serious the last few months. We were spending more time together than alone and had even mentioned the "M" words: monogamy, marriage and mortgage. When my pals busted me they just happened to find an engagement ring in my desk drawer (they said) with a diamond big enough to choke a small dinosaur. Even hot, it was way more than a guy could afford on just a patrolman's salary. Or two patrolmen's salaries.

The ring was a nice touch.

Considering that getting one cop to testify against another is usually like pulling teeth — and with the dentist going through your rectum — these guys were way too happy to take me down and sing a merry song for the prosecutor. I went from arrest to conviction so fast I almost got whiplash. Jury broke the land speed record. Case closed.

Everybody seemed happy with it. Well, almost everybody. But there wasn't much I could do about it. Truth is, most people didn't even notice. Ronald Reagan had just become president, Mount St. Helens erupted and some asshole shot and killed former Beatle, John Lennon. I was hardly worth 2 column inches on the 4th page.

My lawyer told me not to give up; we'd appeal.

We did.

We lost.

I was transferred to the state penitentiary for the rest of my life.

I had been in jail briefly before, once or twice. But that was just county jail, waiting for my trial date. This was different. This wasn't jail; this was prison. You'll never be able to understand the feeling unless you've been there. Those massive green barred doors clang shut and your heart pounds, your palms get sweaty, you feel clammy all over. Your bowels churn. You struggle to breathe.

It's like being buried alive.

A decade earlier I'd been acquitted of some killings I had actually done; this time I'd been convicted of killings I hadn't done. The karmic irony of that wasn't lost on me, but I just wasn't in the mood for a laugh.

A former cop doesn't normally last long in the joint. Very often they don't put him in with the general population because they know he's fair game. But that's where they put me. Clerical error, no doubt.

Even a lowly patrolman like me, there were four or five guys in there doing time because I helped put them there. None of them would have hesitated to kill me, if they had a good chance, or to have me killed if they didn't want to wrinkle their own clothes with it. Probably cost them a couple of cigarettes. And a lot of guys would do it for free. As for the rest of the population, you're scum to them. A corrupt cop can't be trusted by anybody.

The guards don't care much for you either. Most of them have neither the brains nor the balls to cut it as real cops, so there they are. They're glad to see one of their "betters" on the inside. Schadenfreude, they call that in German.

Eclipse of the Heart

Imagine being a leper with a bull's-eye on your back and you've got the idea.
The only way to survive the situation was to assume nothing, expect nothing, trust no one. Sleep light, don't take too many showers and keep your back to a wall.
I felt right at home.

Not long into my stretch — a couple of weeks, maybe — an event took place that changed things. We were lined up to go to chow. Near the back of the line, way back on the tier, was a weasel named Victor, who belonged to the White Aryan Nation Circlejerk, or whatever those pathetic pea-brains were calling themselves that week. Shows you how desperate Victor was to belong, to be somebody.
Anyway, something happened, I don't know what, and the guards started cracking him with their sticks. Initially, I paid no attention. Eyes front. Just like everybody else.
First of all, it was none of my damn business.
Secondly, these neo-nazi, skin-head jerk-offs are not exactly my favorite people. This particular asshole had probably mouthed off or otherwise dallied with a guard and was now picking up the tab for that little indiscretion.
So maybe it was because the beating seemed to go on and on and on and on and on...
Or maybe it was the look on the guards' faces; they were enjoying this. They were practically coming.
Or maybe it was the way the scrawny little shit whimpered, like a small animal or a child, and tried to ward off blows with his hands as he squirmed around spastically on the cold concrete floor.
Or maybe it was something else.
Death wish, maybe.
But the guy next to me — a black guy whose name I didn't know — muttered under his breath, "Mother-fuckers." I assumed he meant the guards. So did they.
"Who said that?" one of the goons demanded.
That's when I went for the guards.

291

It surprised hell out of everybody, especially me. I sent them sprawling like bowling pins and twisted the stick out of the hand of the nearest goon. They recovered quickly and turned their attention on me. Victor, the Weasel, was completely forgotten.

They smiled — no, they grinned at me. They were happy as pigs in shit, because these pigs knew I was the one in the shit. They looked like kids on Christmas morning. They wet-dreamed about this kind of thing. They could beat me to death, if they wanted to, no questions asked. Hey, I had assaulted a guard. A bunch of guards. They caressed their sticks like big dicks they were going to fuck me with. Man, were they going to enjoy this. In fact, they were looking forward to it so much that they forgot a couple of very, very important things.

Number one, I had been a cop, myself.

Number two, I knew how to use a stick.

I sort of reminded them. They were, I'd say, quite chagrined.

Before re-enforcements could arrive, I had caught one guard in the nuts, cracked another in the mouth hard enough to put him on soup and strained bananas for a few weeks, and sent somebody's kneecap to kneecap heaven. It only took a few seconds.

Somewhere an alarm was going off.

Almost at once, two squads of goons jogged in, one from either side of the block. They were armored up like Star Wars troopers, carried clubs and shields. Some of the new goons went right to crowd control and the other inmates wisely put hands on heads and knelt down as ordered. The rest of the goons came after me.

I may have gotten one or two other licks in, I don't know. I kind of doubt it. No matter who you are, or how tough you are, no matter how many black belts you've got, no matter what you've been drinking or smoking, when half a dozen or more men are after your ass, they get it.

They got mine, but good.

I curled up and did my best to protect my head and my testicles, but I was finished. I don't really remember much of it.

Kind of glad I don't.

The thing that surprised me most about waking up in the infirmary was waking up in the infirmary. I more or less figured they'd kill me. To be fair, I think they gave it a shot. Sometimes being hard-headed pays off.

I spent about six weeks in there and then a long stretch in isolation. Most of that's a blur, too. I had cracked ribs, a concussion, a fractured collarbone, a few broken fingers and assorted unpleasantries. They thought I might lose a kidney, but I got lucky on that one. All in all, nothing that wouldn't eventually heal up.

And, all in all, the best thing that could have happened to me.

Suddenly, I had a halo behind my head. I was popularly declared a stand-up guy.

Some other lifer sent me a pack of smokes, which in the joint is like gold. The black guys thought I was covering a brother's ass. The Aryan fuckheads thought I had done it because I was on *their* side. I told them it was nothing personal, that if I'd known it was one of theirs I'd have interfered only to piss on him. But, alas.

The net result of all this was that most of the inmates decided they wouldn't fuck with me and wouldn't especially encourage others to do so. Doesn't sound like much, but it can make all the difference.

You could say the rest of my time was relatively uneventful.

But it was a real education. I learned a great many things, chief among them, what an idiot I had been. It's embarrassing to admit.

When you only get out of your cell an hour a day for exercise, half an hour three times a day for meals, and a shower twice a week, you have a lot of time on your hands. The challenge is to fill it with something other than going crazy. I rediscovered a childhood pleasure: reading. I read everything I could get my hands on. Everything: philosophy, how-to manuals, the Bible, Ladies Home Journal. I didn't care. I went through Webster's Dictionary and the Encyclopedia Britannica page by page.

Go ahead. Ask me something.

As you can imagine, I got to know the librarian really well. He became something of a mentor to me. His name had been Wilson Smalls, but was now known as Simba Ali, a born-again Muslim. A member of the Black Panther Party, he'd been convicted of murder in 1969 and was doing life without parole. No matter that a dozen witnesses (all black folks, unfortunately) put him a hundred miles away at the time of the killing. No matter that the chief prosecution witness was a paid FBI informant who later recanted. Word was that the FBI's own surveillance tapes proved him innocent. But those tapes never materialized in court because they were illegal, a routine part of a huge and glaringly unconstitutional campaign to disrupt, discredit, and destroy organizations that were "left wing." By left wing, they meant anything that didn't support status quo with smile and a patriotic song. They called it COINTELPRO.

The Feds just love acronyms.

Helps to muddy up the waters.

So the first thing I learned was that I wasn't the only innocent man in prison. Came as something of a shock. As I said, I'd been something of an idiot. It may well be that everybody inside claims to be innocent. It may well be that some of those guys are exactly where they belong and should never be released anywhere near society ever again. But it's a simple fact that prisons — no reason to suspect the one I was in was an exception — are full of people who are either innocent, or are being punished far more harshly than any decent human being would punish them for what they've done.

Simba Ali knew everybody's story. And the more he told me, the less sense things made. A lot of the population — almost a third — was in for some kind of drug-related offense. A non-violent drug offense. Mostly, simple possession. Never hurt anybody at all. Otherwise law-abiding citizens.

There was one kid — a good kid with an academic college scholarship — doing a mandatory ten years for possession of two lousy joints. There was another guy who had been giving away marijuana to assuage the pain of fellow cancer sufferers. He got ten years, too, though the smart money said the cancer would get him before the state did. Ironically, he was now in the one place where he could get all the marijuana he wanted.

There was another kid in for statutory rape. He'd had sex with his childhood sweetheart, to whom he was engaged. Her mom was sending out wedding invitations. But there wouldn't be a wedding. She became pregnant. And she was only 17 years old — wouldn't be eighteen for two months. Her betrothed was nineteen. Somebody reported something to somebody and the wheels started turning and before you could say, "You can't be serious," the boyfriend was on cellblock B, looking at ten years.

I kid you not.

There were a lot of stories like those.

Too damn many.

Then, after I'd been in a little over seven years, a serial rapist named Koch was released "early" more or less as part of a plan to make room for more casualties from the war on drugs. Less than a week after his release, he raped, sodomized and strangled an eleven-year-old girl in her own bedroom, while her parents were asleep down the hall. He then fixed himself a snack in the kitchen and watched a little TV before going back upstairs to kill both of them with a bread knife.

When I heard about it, it was like I tore a ligament in my heart. I felt such a heavy weight on my chest I could hardly breathe, and I wanted to just yell or scream, or cry but I was afraid if I did, I'd never be able to stop. I sat down on the edge of my rack and held my face in my hands, chanting a mantra in Chicago-ese: "Motherfuckers, motherfuckers, motherfuckers..."

They say you change every cell in your body every seven years, literally becoming a different person than you were before. I guess it was at this moment that I dusted off the last remaining cell of the old me. I was like a snake struggling to wriggle out of a skin that had become way too tight. When I was free of it, I seemed to see the world with a new kind of clarity. What had been complex had become simple. I had been viewing the world through Alice's looking glass and had gotten it all wrong, all backwards, upside down and inside out. What I had taken to be true had all been a lie. What I had thought false was true. Black was white, day was night, dark was light, wrong was right.

I thought someone should jump out at me and yell, "April Fool!"

I happened to be reading Shakespeare's sonnets at the time and the one I read that day seemed written for me, from me, and has been my favorite ever since. You know the one?

> *"...Past cure I am, now reason is past care,*
> *And frantic mad with evermore unrest;*
> *My thoughts and my discourse are as mad men's are,*
> *At random from the truth vainly expresse'd;*
> *For I have sworn thee fair, and thought thee bright,*
> *Who art as black as hell, as dark as night."*

In my ninth year inside, two things happened which may redefine the word synchronicity.

First, I had a visitor.

I hadn't had any visitors in about four years, not since the last time I'd seen Caroline. She had stuck with me longer than most women would, I think, making the three-hour drive to spend 20 minutes with me whenever she could. I don't know what it was like for her, but it became torture for me. I finally convinced her to cut me loose, reclaim her life. I told her that, if she were out there living, loving, being happy, then a little part of me that would always be with her would be free, too.

Or something sappy like that.

Anyway, it's easy to sell somebody what, in their heart, they already want to buy. I heard she got married and had a son. Good for her.

For a moment, when they told me I had company, I thought it might be Caroline, but I decided not to consider that possibility. Too romantic, I thought. And I was right.

In fact, my visitor was a petite young woman, dressed in a business suit, with red hair in a page boy cut and glasses way too big for her face. Made her look like she was wearing goggles. She had a great gift for conversation, though. The first thing she said to me was, "I've come here to see you because I believe you're innocent. I'd like your permission to work on your case."

No lawyer in her right mind would want to waste her time on me. As it turned out, Ms. Alice Burton was in her last year of law school. Figured.

"My case has been closed for quite a while, " I said. "Why the interest?"

"To be honest," she said, which told me she wasn't going to be, "I need something that will make a good project. Something I can publish afterward. Your case is one of several that might qualify."

I'll be damned, I thought. She *is* being honest. She was looking for a shortcut to a reputation.

"I don't know," I said. "I'm kind of busy."

"I understand. Sorry to bother you..."

"Hey," I stood up as she stood up and two guards leaning against the far wall braced to pounce on me if necessary. "Just kidding," I said. "Let's talk."

So we talked.

Actually, she didn't really need to talk to me. She had it all figured out already. It was a simple equation. If I was innocent, then the guys who testified against me were lying. If they were lying, then they were covering up something. Either they had done the crime themselves or knew who actually had.

See? Simple.

She already had a briefcase-full of material. Court transcripts, and such. She described my attorney as utterly incompetent. Pointed out things smacking of probable prosecutorial misconduct. I told her everything I knew, suspected, wondered. She listened, made notes on a yellow pad.

"So," I asked after our interview, "got a plan?"

"Yes. I plan to get you out of here."

It was cute.

Synchronicity.

You're thinking about someone you haven't thought of in years and bang, the phone rings and it's them. That kind of thing. Weird. Suggests some kind of invisible energy connecting things in ways we can't imagine. Some karmic sleight-of-hand.

It was a very short time after my initial chat with Ms. Alice Burton, soon-to-be Esquire, that now-sergeant of detectives Earl Neilson, working out of robbery/ homicide, left his wife and four children after a lazy Sunday brunch at home, to stroll the two blocks to Dario's Market to get some sweets and the Sunday paper.

Upon entering the store, Neilson was confronted by two youths armed with pistols who were engaged in sticking up the place. One of the perpetrators, Salvatore (Sally) Ciabattari, immediately made Neilson as a cop, having been busted by him previously, and without the slightest hesitation pumped three 9mm slugs into the dick's chest.

The thieves then fled the scene with a little over eighty dollars in cash and some candy bars.

ER doctors labored heroically to save Neilson, but it was a losing battle and he knew it. A good Catholic, Neilson began asking for a priest before the paramedics had even gotten him on a gurney. He was a tough guy and he fought death a long time, long enough to get last rites and to confess that he, along with two other officers, had framed an innocent man.

Me.

He confessed that his former partner had done the murders, that they'd been trafficking in cocaine, that they had manufactured and planted evidence, and lied to incriminate me. It had all been his partner's plan; he'd gotten sucked into it. Just before shuffling off this mortal coil, Neilson begged the priest to see if he could help me.

All this was witnessed by everyone in the ER: three doctors, five nurses and a couple of other cops. Word of it spread faster than the thighs of a ten-dollar hooker. Before you could say, "There goes your pension," the second officer involved in setting me up — a guy named Harris, who I don't think I ever even met — had the decency to eat his gun.

Sort of corroborative evidence, if you look at it right.

Neilson's other partner-in-crime had corroborated the dead man's story by disappearing with as many of his assets as he could pack quickly into a bag. Detective Pete Whaley vanished, leaving behind wife, kids and dog. Took only money. I think that says something about him, don't you?

All this made Ms. Alice Burton, soon-to-be-Esquire's job a whole lot easier. She was able to have some of the physical evidence tested for something new called "DNA."

It had been first used in '87, in a case in the UK and was just getting accepted as science fact instead of science fiction. The short version is this: it conclusively proved my innocence.

Less than two months after Neilson's untimely demise, I was out.

Completely out.

Free.

Exonerated.

Not pardoned, but conviction over-turned. The judge who heard the case ended his decision by ordering my "immediate release."

The assistant DA who had prosecuted me fell under quite a shadow, too. He lost his bid to become the lead singer in the band and left the DA's office for private practice.

I met with the police commissioner, who had previously always been too busy to bother with me, and had often re-confirmed his certainty that, in sending me up, they'd gotten a "bad apple" off the force. Suddenly, the commish had some free time, just for little ole me. He shook my hand. He offered to reinstate me. With back-pay plus interest. With my prison time counting as time on the job for benefits. With a detective's gold shield. With a commendation. With my own parking space. I asked him if the offer included him kissing my ass in Times Square on New Year's Eve. I loved the look on his face.

My attorney — she had passed her bar exam with ease — Ms. Alice Burton, now-actually-Esquire, filed a civil case against the police department, the DA, the city, the state and some other people I'd never even heard of. Civil rights violations. Wrongful imprisonment. All kinds of good stuff. Asked for about a billion dollars in damages.

Didn't get a billion.

But got quite a chunk.

More than I'll ever be able to spend unless I just dedicate the rest of my life to thinking up outrageously silly shit to buy.

Part of the settlement deal is, I can't tell anyone how much or any of the particulars. The down side of the deal is that none of them had to cop to any wrongdoing. Going after them to get that would have entailed a huge legal battle, would have taken years, and was less likely to be successful.

"Fuck it," I told Alice. "Let's take the money and run."

So I was a police officer for a little over five years, and in prison for almost ten.

As part of that settlement agreement I mentioned, I can't reveal *which* police department I was a member of. So I won't tell you that, not because I have any respect for them, or concern for them, but because I gave my word, and when I give my word, I don't break it.

Never.

It doesn't matter who I give my word to or why.

For that reason, I'm generally very careful about giving my word, but I was younger then, not as smart and not as careful. What I *can* tell you is that I was a cop in a major metropolitan area in the midwest, in a city that is nearly always in the top ten when it comes to homicides.

You can do the rest of the math yourself, if you're that interested.

Two of the three guys who sent me to prison were dead. To me, that seemed like one too few. I gave a lot of thought to tracking Whaley down. When you have a beef with somebody you can either kill him or forget about it. If you can't kill him, forget about it. If you can't forget about it, then kill him. Trouble is, I couldn't forget about it, but I'd have to find him before I could kill him. I knew how to find people, but so did Whaley. He'd be hell to find if he didn't want to be found.

I remembered something I'd read: "Wait long enough, and you'll see the bodies of your enemies floating down the river." That might have been Sun-tze. Could've been Sonny Bono.

For the time being, at least. I decided to be patient, and see what came floating down the river.

Adam Adrian Crown

I don't want your golden mansions
with a tear in every room
All I want is the love you promised
beneath the halo moon
But you think I should be happy
with your money and your name
And hide myself in sorrow while you play your cheating game

("Silver Threads and Golden Needles," Dolly Parton)

CHAPTER TWENTY-ONE:
SAINT JACK

At a few minutes after ten o'clock in the morning on Christmas Day I walked out those thick iron doors and into a winter storm that would be a record-breaker. It had already accumulated about a foot of snow at a rate of an inch an hour. Visibility was about to your elbow. I turned my face to the heavens and let snowflakes alight on my skin like icy little butterflies. The flakes melted and ran down my cheeks like tears.

Hell, maybe they were tears.

I came out the way I went in, with just the clothes on my back. All the meager possessions I'd accumulated, I'd given away. Plus cartons of cigarettes to a few of the guys, by way of celebration.

"I'll be seeing you," muttered the screw at the gate, a fat-assed prick named Grant. He apparently took it like a personal defeat whenever a prisoner was released. Like it came out of his salary or something. The fact that I was innocent, had been *proven* innocent, that didn't matter to Mr. Grant one little bit.

"Go fuck yourself," I advised him with a big smile, delighted by the mental image of him giving it a try. In drag.

My lawyer was waiting for me. Good thing she drove one of those new four-wheel drive soccer-mom pseudo-trucks, or I'd have been stuck out there until the spring thaw.

"Good morning, Mr. Flynn," she said, always formal and proper.

"It's a beautiful day in the neighborhood," I said, and meant every word.

I got in, fumbled with the seat belt. As she did a U-turn, I noticed something I hadn't seen on the way in: there was an enormous clock set in the stone above the gate. It had Roman numerals. A giant time-piece where guys were doing time. Somebody had a sense of humor. But it was the kind of humor that should be beaten out of him.

Slowly.

It was a long drive, especially in the storm. I turned on the radio, tried a few stations. I didn't recognize any of the tunes. There was talk about closing down the highways. She had some CD's. Classical stuff, mostly.

It took me a second to figure out the CD player and I stuck some Bach in. When I went in, CD's weren't around yet. Now, everything was on CD. It was just one of the ways the world had changed while I was marking time. There weren't any cell phones in 1980, but in 1990 everybody and his dog had one. There was no internet when I went in. Now they were launching the world wide web and even kids had computers.

Everything was on computer.

Even crime.

The world was still a mess, of course. Iraq, for example, had decided to re-annex its former province, Kuwait. And President George Bush (pere) was trying to show everybody how big his dick was. Crime was up, the economy was down. The rich were getting richer and you know what happens to the poor.

La plus que change, right?

It was slow going, but we made it to her apartment, which was on the north side, spitting distance from the loop. Half an hour after we landed, they closed the roads down.

There were a few final papers to sign.

"I took the liberty of picking up a few things for you," she said. "Just until you get set up."

"Thanks. That's very thoughtful of you."

"Sorry," she shrugged, looking out the window at the winter wonderland. "Doesn't seem right for you to spend your first night of freedom trapped inside, but it looks like you may have to be my guest for tonight."

"I've had lots worse company."

She smiled and adjusted her goggle-like eyeglasses on her tiny nose. "I also have a little Christmas present for you."

"I think you've already given it to me," I told her.

But she produced a large box, wrapped in paper festooned with candy canes, finished with a bright red bow. I opened it slowly. Inside was a classic leather car coat. Black, of course. I tried it on. My shape had changed in prison. I had done nothing but work out and read, just like everybody else did, except for the reading part. So I didn't expect the coat to fit, but it did. I hugged myself in it, just to hear the leather creak.

"Merry Christmas, Mr. Flynn."

"I don't have a gift for you," I said. I felt awkward.

"Look at it this way," she said. "I'll be getting a third of the settlement. I've published in the Law Review and already gotten partnership offers from five of the six firms on my dream list. Couldn't have done it without you."

She went into the kitchen, came back with a bottle of champagne and a couple glasses. It was Asti Cinzano. One of my favorite things. Hadn't tasted any in ten years.

"You could've made your bones on another case," I said. "You told me you were considering some other cases."

"Oh. Well, actually," she said sliding her over-sized eyeglasses back up into place again, "actually, I lied a little bit about that. Yours was the case. *The* case. An honest police officer framed for murder by corrupt police officers. Hard to top that one."

"A little early to be anointing me for sainthood," I cracked.

She filled up our glasses.

"Here's to you, Saint Jack."

"Ho-ho-ho," I said.

I drank my glass dry in a single sweet throw, letting the sparkling wine tickle its way down my throat and into my balls like Tinker Bell on a pixie dust binge. She refilled me immediately.

We killed that bottle and another one just like it.

Outside, the storm was still going strong. Everything was cancelled and everyplace was closed. Fortunately, Alice Burton, Esquire, kept her pantry well stocked. She whipped up a couple of steaks and a salad. I caught a reflection of myself in the bay window, eating it in a hurry, huddled over my plate to guard it like an old mongrel dog.

I was out of prison.

But would I ever get prison out of me?

I forced myself to slow down, sit back. Enjoy.

It was a hell of a meal and I can tell you one thing for sure: even chewing on shoe leather on the outside, tastes better than the best meal in the world on the inside. She had a TV, but I declined an offer to watch it. TV was a big deal in the joint, but I never watched any inside, either. Maybe because everybody else did. Fought over it like a bone.

So we sat on the cool leather sofa, listening to some soft big band jazz, way down low. Sinatra. Tony Bennett. The kid had great taste.

And we talked.

And talked and talked.

Long into the night.

Not about my case or the settlement or prison or any of that. Just normal things a man and woman might talk about any time. Unimportant important things. Favorite books (At Play in the Fields of the Lord); movies (a Bogart fan). Who were you, what did you do, and what did you think, huh?

I began to notice subtle things about her. The way she'd look at me and then suddenly avoid eye contact. Reminded me of a little girl who'd had a crush on me a million years ago. It was sweet.

There was a lull in the conversation just as Tony started to croon about leaving his heart in San Francisco.

"I owe you," I said, taking her hand. Her fingers were long and slender. There was a distant scent on her wrist, like the memory of a summer night. I pressed her hand lightly against my cheek. "You saved my life."

On impulse I leaned over to kiss her on the cheek. But she turned and met me with her lips.

It was like the world's first kiss.

It wasn't *my* first kiss.

But it was a kiss that was soft and light and gentle and it filled me with sunlight and laughter. When it had run its lazy, ambling course, we both headed back toward our senses.

"You're a good man, Jack," she said. It was the first time she didn't call me "Mr. Flynn."

I liked the way my name sounded when she said it.

"And I... I mean, I find you very... " she was sputtering and stuttering like an old Chevy. "It would be a serious breach of the cannon of legal ethics to have a personal... an intimate relationship with you. I'm your attorney and, well, regardless of any personal feelings I might have, it would be inappropriate of me to... I take my obligations as your attorney very seriously. And I can't just... "

"Ms. Burton," I said.

"Yes?"

"You're fired."

She looked at me a long time, balancing on the edge of her ethics. "Oh," she said. "That's different."

She removed her glasses and set them on the coffee table.

Sometime later, as she pulled her pink turtleneck sweater off, I started to feel butterflies of apprehension. It had been a long, long time since I'd been with a woman and it was both wonderful and terrifying.

"You know," I said. "I'm a little out of practice."

She smiled reassuringly. "It's like riding a bicycle, isn't it?"

"Yeah. It's embarrassing if you fall off."

That made her laugh. It was a good laugh, too. Honest. Unselfconscious. Something about that laugh put me completely at ease, all the anxiety laughed away.

That night, I discovered what I'd really missed most.

It wasn't coming. I was expert enough at getting myself off. What I'd really missed was making someone else come. Giving someone else pleasure, no strings attached. Just for fun. Just for its own sake.

I spent a long while re-acquainting myself with that, delighting in her scent, her taste, her every moan, every sigh, every wiggle of her hips, every shudder up her spine, every clutching of her hand for mine.

The first day of Christmas melted into the second day of Christmas.

And the third.

On the fourth day of Christmas my true love gave to me an unseasonable heat wave that started to melt off the snow from the three-day storm. The sun crawled out of bed very late and we were already up. I guess I made myself more or less at home. I went to make coffee. Toast some bagels. Cinnamon and raisin.

She sat across from me at the round glass table, and sipped coffee, wrapped in a blue flannel robe as grey light began to insinuate itself into the winter sky. Took her coffee black. Like me.

I brought in the papers, too — even the mailman had missed a couple of days. She read the Trib and the New York Times. There was an article about Nelson Mandela giving a speech somewhere. Mandela had been released from stir the previous February after being locked up as a political prisoner for 27 years. It put my measly 10 years in perspective. And, while not guilty of the crimes for which I'd been convicted, I wasn't exactly "innocent" either.

"You know," Alice said. "You're still going to be needing an attorney."

"You're probably right. Anybody you'd recommend?"

"Frankly," she replied, "I'd recommend me."

"There's nobody I'd rather have on my side, Ms. Burton," I told her.

"Thank you, Mr. Flynn."

We shook hands across the tray of bagels. It was more than a handshake, but it was a handshake. Even the most furious storms run their course and when they're over, they're over.

But we'd always have Paris.

Want some whiskey in your water?
Sugar in your tea?
What's all these crazy questions they're askin' me?
This is the craziest party that could ever be
Don't turn on the lights 'cause I don't wanna see

("Mama Told Me Not to Come," Three Dog Night)

CHAPTER TWENTY-TWO:
IRISH WAKE IN MEXICO

It seemed like a good idea at the time.
It was a well-laid plan.
You know what they say about mice and men.
It's true. And I know whereof I squeak.

I didn't need the money.
It wasn't about the money for any of us. It was about
fighting back. Getting even. Thumbing your nose at the whole
system. Tweaking the Devil's beard.
Shit like that.

It was Crazy Eddie's score. His plan. His funeral. We
stayed up all night while he laid out the why's and wherefore's.
It took all night and a lot of tequila to convince me, but I think,
in my heart, I wanted to be convinced. To this day, I don't
know for sure how it went sour. I have some suspicions. If
I knew for sure, I'd arrange some payback, but I don't.
When I crossed into Mexico I carried with me a suitcase
full of cash, and the memories of three dead amigos. Hard to
say which was heavier.

The actual expenses of the job came off the top, so the first order of business was to check in with the people who had given Eddie the seed money. They had assumed that I had also bitten the proverbial dust and were both surprised and pleased to hear from me. Maybe it was partly because, as they assured me, they "liked" me. But it may have been more that they had been contemplating the unenviable task of reporting back that both the seed money and the anticipated profits were gone with the wind. Not the kind of message you'd like to deliver in a business with a long tradition of killing the messenger. Maybe I could stiff them by playing dead, but if they caught on, I wouldn't be playing. Besides, a deal with the devil is still a deal.

I got 20 cents on the dollar. And 20 cents on the dollar was still a big chunk of change. Using a numbered Swiss account I'd set up before the job, I immediately put the money to work, as we had previously agreed. The first donation went to "Habitat for Humanity." I hoped they would build some better places to call home than the ramshackle cockroach palace I grew up in. I sent a chunk to a drug rehab program in my old neighborhood on the south side of Chicago. It was run by a couple of former Black Panthers. Maybe if it had been there when I was a kid, my sister would still be alive. I kicked in some for the ACLU, some to Greenpeace, and some to the War Resistor's League.

That last one was especially for Crazy Eddie. For all these years after the Viet Nam war had ended, he had continued to be tormented by nightmares of the napalmed children and the other murdered civilians he'd seen. I never asked him what he personally had done. But whatever it was, it had eaten his soul alive. I figured it had probably been him who'd decided to go down swinging.

He'd choose that over more time in the joint any day.

So would I.

So would you.

I also sent a modest amount to a Native American group that breeds buffalo. There's an old prophecy that when the buffalo returns, it will signify the end of the whole putrid, polluted, cannibalistic, capitalistic wasichu circus. Anything I could possibly do to hasten the demise of such a corrupt and ignoble system would be a pleasure. Go, buffalo, go.

That was the last of it.

As I said, I didn't need money. Had plenty already. Enough to live very comfortably in the States, and a couple lifetimes like a lord in Mexico, if I wanted to stay there. That had some appeal. Maybe I would do that. Or maybe I would buy a boat. Buy a boat, stock it with good scotch and take off. Maybe I'd just bag it all, and sail around the world. And around. And around. And around. Where she stops, nobody knows.

There was a thing I had to do first.

I knew just the place to do it, too. The Casa del Gato was about the best brothel around, reputed to have very clean women and a proprietor who was famous for keeping his mouth shut. If he thought I was exaggerating when I told him I intended to do enough drinking and fucking for four men, some cold gringo cash persuaded him to take me completely seriously. I told him that the dramatis personae would include three women and one man for the party and that more money was no problem. He was on the case like Columbo and soon rounded up a variety of potential companions for me to choose from.

Choosing was tough. Maybe I should have done one potato-two potato. But I finally decided on a young lady with huge breasts in honor of Mickey who'd probably had the largest collection of tit magazines in the known universe. I don't remember her name.

A young man they called "Rickie" was my next recruit. He had a slender but muscular physique. Just Bert's type.

I had no idea what Crazy Eddie's tastes had been. I chose an older woman who looked very strong. I don't know why I thought Eddie would have dug her. Just a hunch. I think her name was "Ruby." Or maybe "Rubia," but she wasn't blonde.

My choice for myself was easy. She made the others look like cardboard cut-outs. Small, Muscular. Long, blue-black hair. Coarse Indian hair, like mine. High cheekbones. Almond-shaped eyes with a suggestion of the orient in their angle, and a glimpse of death in their coal-black depths. Skin the color and texture of melted chocolate ice cream.

Unlike most American women, she was unshaven, dark tufts under her arms, her pubis crowned by a luxurious ebony forest. She smelled of cinnamon and clove. She said her name was "Linda." In Spanish that means "beautiful."

I began drinking damiana liqueur laced with a hint of the coca leaf early in the afternoon. Damiana being a notorious aphrodisiac that makes Viagra look like lemonade, and I trust you know about the coca leaf.

I killed some time playing poker with a gang of local cut-throats. By evening I was down a few hundred. I'm not really a very good card player, anymore. I can't resist going for the long shots. My new-found pals didn't seem to mind.

At the appointed hour, the party moved upstairs.

I was generous with my crew. I told them that, just between us, I would double whatever cut they were getting from the proprietor. With bonuses, too, for duty above and beyond the call. Also, I wanted them to feel free to enjoy themselves, too, if they were so inclined. The food, booze, and the cocaine were on me.

"What are we celebrating, querido?" Linda asked me.

"It's a wake," I told her.

She didn't believe me.

I explained the ground rules. I asked the big-breasted girl to call me "Mickey" while I was fucking her. For the bread I was paying her, she would have been glad to call me "Mr. President" or to howl like a coyote, for that matter. Likewise, I asked Rickie to call me "Bert" and Ruby — if that was her name — to call me Eddie. They took my odd request in stride, as if it were as common as a crooked cop. I suppose they'd all had far more outrageous requests.

"And what should I call you, querido?" my hirsute Amazon asked.

"You can call me whatever you like," I told her.

"What's your name?"

I made up one for her and she seemed satisfied, but never used it after all. A real take-charge sort of person, she somewhat assumed the role of ringmaster for the ensuing sexual circus.

Some of it's pretty fuzzy, but a few things do stick in my memory.

It didn't take much to get me started. My ex always said I was a walking hard-on. At the time I'd thought she meant it as a compliment. Maybe she was right. I'm sure she's happier with Mr. All American White Bread. Not that I'm bitter.

Anyway, in any room full of naked flesh I would expect my needle to point north, and this was pretty good flesh. After some preliminaries, Mickey's date began massaging my cock between her breasts, as if she had read my mind. Or his. Personally, I don't have a particular tit fetish, but this was for Mickey. And he'd have been in heaven. So to speak. That girl got a nice bonus.

I didn't know how I would do with Rickie. I'd never fucked a man before. Not even in the joint. But a short time later, while I was sampling the salty taste of Ruby's cunt, I discovered that the person sucking me so expertly was indeed him. Bert had always teased me that nobody sucked a cock as sincerely or as well as a gay man. After all, having an instrument of his own just like it, it makes sense that he'd learn to play it well.

Okay, Bert, wherever you are, man: Salude!

I'd had anal sex with women a time or two. But this was — different. When I pressed my cock against the dark rosebud between Rickie's buttocks, I slipped into him as easily as into a moist cunt. He rhythmically flexed and released the tight ring of his sphincter muscle, something no woman had ever done, and I was greatly impressed. It felt like the hand of a tiny munchkin jerking me off. He stood, half bent over, bracing his hands on small bureau, and as I came inside him, I could see in the mirror that semen spurted from him, too, almost as if it were mine. It gave me the oddest sensation of being in two places at once, which is somehow very close to being nowhere at all.

I was stretched out recovering, when Ruby began to caress my balls, gently stroking the soft, sensitive spot between my scrotum and my anus, probing it with the tip of her tongue. At the same time Linda was breathing hotly in my ear, saying things I, myself, might have said but had never heard.

She whispered something to Ruby, and Ruby turned onto her back and deftly brought her legs up to her shoulders, locking her ankles behind her neck. She reached down to spread her thick, meaty lips out, rub her ponderous clit — not so much a little man in a canoe as an admiral on a battleship.

"Look at that pussy," Linda whispered to my cock through my ear. "Nice, eh? I want to watch you fuck her. You fuck everybody else first, Baby. Save me for last because you won't be able to do anybody else after me. I'm going to fuck you to *death*."

With her hoarse voice putting spurs to my cock, I was up and kneeling against Ruby, with Linda guiding my cock past the purple folds of those lips. Then I felt her wrap her fingers around my balls to squeeze and tug down gently on them with each stroke. Having ejaculated twice already, this time it took longer. Perhaps it was Rickie suckling my nipples that added enough fuel; perhaps it was whoever began probing into my ass with a finger. Coming lasted a long time, now, a dozen pulses. Maybe more.

Whether I made a face or an amusing noise, something seemed to entertain my paramours; they grinned, laughed a little, ooooh-ed and aaaahhh-ed, and Linda bit my ear lobe. I fell back against a safety net of huge breasts behind me and enjoyed riding the surf of that climax all the way to shore.

Sometime during eternity, I woke up on the beach with Linda re-waxing my board. I sat up to see her take a deep swig of our damiana witches' brew. Then she leaned over and kissed me and we shared the mouthful of aphrodisiac through the kiss. But calling it a kiss is like calling Jaws a fish.

Yeah. There are kisses and then there are kisses. It wasn't a kiss, it was *the* kiss. It was hard and hungry. It was a deep-probing, tongue-sucking, lip-biting kiss. The way you kiss when you haven't had a good one in a long time, and your whole body is one giant cock-ache, and nothing but disappearing into a deep, warm, wet cunt will assuage the pain.

And now, having fucked farewell to three bone-loyal, fuck-it tough, irreplaceable prison pals, it was time to deny my own mortality by dying a little.

I pulled away from Linda's mouth and looked into her bottomless eyes. It was like looking in the mirror. And I had a gut feeling she was thinking the same thing. So it was like a mirror reflecting a mirror, reflecting a mirror, reflecting a mirror and on into infinity. Which was exactly where I wanted to go with her.

I licked the salty sweat from her throat, briefly sucked on the plum-purple nipples of her tiny breasts, continued down her lean belly, and then pulled her over on top of me. She straddled my mouth, the musk of her cunt sending a river of fire up my spine and back down to my cock. Her lips were enormous, thick and heavy, and dripping wet and I took them into my mouth like a suckling baby, darting my tongue inside for more. As she rocked her hips, rubbing her pubis hard against my chin, she swallowed my cock to the hilt, pulling on my balls, working a fingertip into my ass, stroking it around in a slow circle. I inserted a fingertip into her ass, too, and felt her thighs quiver when I did it. It was 69 to the 69th power.

Linda continued to play the role of M.C., directing the others to act in diverse and sundry pleasant ways for my amusement, and the crew racked up a lot of bonuses during the course of the night.

When the dark outside the window finally turned a lighter shade of pitch-black, those just tuning in found me standing, legs wide apart, bracing myself by leaning against a chair or something. Ruby was poised under me, sucking on my balls, which felt like they were hanging down to my knees; Rickie was kneeling behind me, rimming away and giving my anus deep tongue and finger massage; the queen of breasts was playing the side of my cock like a harmonica and Linda herself was sucking and licking the head of it with both skill and enthusiasm.

My previous existence had never been one that could be described as "monastic" — not with a straight face, anyway — but I had never come the way I did that dawn, just as a warm breeze, like a lover's breath, swept into the room through the open window and turned my sweat-laden skin to goose flesh. Vesuvian jolts of ecstasy seemed to originate somewhere deep down in my belly, squeezing my balls in an invisible fist (or was it Ruby?) like a paramedic working a resuscitation bag, sending out tsunamis of semen far greater than my cock could accommodate, making it stretch and throb with every pulse. The spasms refused to stop, racking me from the tip of my cock, up the length of my spine, to spatter sizzling pleasure on my white-hot brain.

Sometime later, after the end of eternity, I was awakened by the trill of a swallow outside the window. I listened awhile and remembered the words from a song:

Eclipse of the Heart

Ave querida amada peregrina
mi corazón
al tuyo acercare
voy recordando
tierna golondrina
recordare
mi patria y llorare

Linda was gathering herself up; the others had already gone.

"Hey, querida," I asked her, "you have someplace important to go? Somebody important to go to?"

She considered a moment, then shook her head. We looked into each other's eyes again, a pair of lone, lonely predators bumping into each other by accident over a gazelle carcass.

"I could eat a horse," I told her, punning with the feminine form of the word to see if she would catch it and she did. "Why don't you have breakfast with me?"

She accepted.

We spent some more time together. Off the clock. In addition to guiding me to the "petite mort" a few more times, she nearly introduced me to the big one.

Maybe I'll tell you about it sometime.

Anyway, I didn't buy a boat.

Adam Adrian Crown

Don't know the reason,
Stayed here all season
With nothing to show but this brand new tattoo.
But it's a real beauty,
A Mexican cutie,
How it got here, I haven't a clue.

("Margaritaville," Jimmy Buffet)

CHAPTER TWENTY-THREE:
AN EYE AND A TOOTH

Clarence Allen Macy was a murderer.

And everyone knew it.

Everyone.

The cops knew it.

The DA knew it.

His own attorney knew it.

The family of his victim, the judge, and even the jurors who acquitted him knew it.

There was no "reasonable doubt" about it. Not even a "shadow" of a doubt. His guilt was an utter and absolute certainty.

And, just as certainly, there was nothing anyone could do about it.

I had been a free man for nearly a year. It was like returning from the dead. I didn't realize how much prison had changed me until I got out and walked once again among the living. Or maybe that's not quite right. Maybe everything I ever experienced, in my family, in school, in the service, and as a cop was teaching me the same lesson over and over again. Slightly differently angle each time, but essentially the same. Prison was just deja vu all over again, as Yogi Berra would say. Same old tune, different key. I didn't have the melody quite yet, but I was getting to the point that I could find the rhythm, anyway.

For a year, I had done nothing, "giving myself time to re-adjust" to life outside a cage. But it seemed to me, that most people were no less prisoners than I had been. They just had a slightly bigger yard to exercise in. They spent their lives working for someone else who was getting rich while paying them chump change. If they scrimped and saved they could afford a week or two of desperate annual fun at Disneyworld. And if they lived long enough to retire, and if the boss didn't cheat them out of their retirement benefits, they could look forward to a meager, meaningless decline to the grave.

As good as that sounds, it just didn't appeal to me.

I had some money, I had time, but I had no particular direction. I couldn't seem to find anything that made me feel joyful and alive. Perhaps I'd dreamed of freedom for so long that actually being free was anticlimactic. So I dabbled. I took a class in this and that, here and there. I worked out and practiced various martial arts, more out of habit than desire. I even flirted with following a life of crime, for which I was now impeccably well-suited. I drank quite a lot. Cavorted with women. Played a little music. Lay in the sun. I was the poster boy for terminal indolence.

I was stretched out on the sand, on a secluded Mexican beach, watching another celestial intromission as the sun slipped itself into the water on the horizon, going slowly as with a tiny, timid virgin. I let the glow burn into my retinas until it was all I could see.

"Hello, Mr. Flynn," she said. I couldn't see her — unless she happened to be round and bright red-yellow. But I recognized her voice.

"Hiya, Counselor," I replied. Alice Burton, Esquire. I hadn't been in touch with her for a while. She wasn't dressed for the beach. She was wearing a very conservative grey business suit. Hair in a French twist. Eyeglasses perched on top of her head. Briefcase in one hand, low-heeled shoes in the other. Barefoot. No panty hose? No stockings?

"How are you?"

"Great. Just working on my tan. I'm going to challenge George Hamilton to a duel. What's new with you?"

"Can we talk?"

It was a good question. I was pretty sure she could manage it, but I'd started drinking early and it was getting late.

I indicated a patch of sand next to me. "Step into my office," I told her. Her skirt wasn't exactly cut for it. She managed to sit down, but not without opening the sky blue crotch of her panties to my gaze. The material was pulled tight across her vulva, revealing the shape of her lips. It was a pleasant sight because it brought to my mind the sweet time we'd had together. I mentally waxed nostalgic.

We were practically alone, it being a Wednesday. All the good people were elsewhere, nose to the grindstone. A quarter mile away, a couple was necking on a blanket. Farther away in the opposite direction, a guy was tossing a stick into the water, teaching his dog to fetch. Or maybe the dog was teaching him to throw. I had a brief fantasy of us fucking there on the beach, with the sound of the waves, the warmth of the sun… I mean, me and Ms. Burton, not me and the guy. Or the dog.

"Margarita?" I offered.

"Why not?"

That's the spirit. I dug into the ice chest behind me, brushing the remains of lime slices off the lid. I had a half-gallon jug of hooch all made up — well, maybe a quart left. I poured some into my paper cup for her. I drank from the jug. It was cold enough to make my brain ache.

"Social call?" I asked her as she sipped.

"No."

Didn't think so.

"There's a certain party who wants to meet with you. Are you available for lunch on Monday? At the Palmer House."

"I'll check my calendar." Maybe I could squeeze something in between my morning workout and my afternoon drinking. "What's it about?"

"I believe that's a confidential matter for your ears only."

What the fuck did *that* mean?

"What the fuck does *that* mean?" I asked her.

"It means be there at noon. Number 1120."

Oh. A private lunch. Okay, now I was getting a little curious.

"Who's this meeting with?"

"Sorry. That's all I can say. Will you come? I'd consider it a personal favor."

I owed her. Big time. So it was a no-brainer.

"I'll be there," I promised.

"Um, sober?"

"If I have to be."

"You have to be."

I arrived a little early. Room 1120 proved to be a luxurious suite, bigger than most apartments I ever lived in. Fireplace. Terrace looking out toward Lake Michigan. It was Alice who opened the door to my knock and ushered me in, offered me a drink. I took a scotch. It was a good one. Single malt.

A moment or two later, my host emerged from the bathroom. I was reminded of a haiku that loosely translated, went:

On a pretty girl
A funny nose
Makes her more beautiful still.

That's pretty close. Anyway, you get the idea.

Nearly two intervening decades had put some lines on her face and some silver in her hair. But it only made her even more striking than I remembered her. When she looked at me, I felt my heart beat a little faster. When we shook hands, her palm was warm and soft, her grip strong and sure.

"Hello, Mr. Flynn" she said. "Thank you for coming."

"Hello, Your Honor."

"You look well."

"Thanks. You, too."

"Thank you. Please, make yourself comfortable."

Her voice was like a sultry desert breeze, languid with a subtle almost-drawl. The almost-drawl made me almost-drool. I wanted to pounce on her and ravage her like a wild beast. Tear her clothes off. Lose myself in the warmth of the deepest recesses of her body.

I sat down instead.

Alice Burton excused herself. And when we were alone, The Judge told me all about Clarence Allen Macy.

Macy was a moderately successful new & used car dealer in a little town not far from Waxahatchee, Texas. He met Linda Lee Simmons in his bank where she was a teller, and they began dating. Macy was fifteen years older than Linda and her family didn't like the age difference much. But they were glad to see her getting some attention. She was on the plain side and heaven forbid she should wind up an old maid. She was already thirty.

For two years she continued to date Macy. Things progressed until they were seeing each other daily or almost daily. He seemed polite. Considerate. He lavished her with expensive little gifts, mostly jewelry, tokens of his growing love.

Macy began referring to her as his fiancee.

But according to her closest friend, a co-worker at the bank, Linda Lee was intent on breaking up with Macy. He had become increasingly obsessive and controlling. He had to know where she was every moment of the day, who she was with, who she spoke to. He was jealous of every minute she spent away from him, even with her family. He began to dictate how she should do her hair, how she should dress and began demanding she move in with him, becoming sullen when she declined. Linda confided that Macy had also begun to press her to have group sex, to have sex with a roomful of men while he watched, to include another woman, even to have sex with animals. He advised her that she was too inhibited and needed to "loosen up." If this were not enough, Macy had recently flown into a rage, berating Linda because she had torn toilet paper from the roll unevenly.

She planned to tell him at their next meeting that it was over. Perhaps Macy sensed it, the way a shark can smell a drop of blood a mile away.

According to Mary Beth Hart, Macy's previous girlfriend, whom he'd dated for nearly ten years, Macy had made a plan and recruited her to assist him. Why did she help him? She didn't know. She was "under his spell." Enslaved by his powerful personality, his "charisma."

Under the pretext of showing off some of her jewelry, he lured Linda Lee to Hart's house, located on the sparsely populated outskirts of town. It would be a perfect place for what he had in mind. He'd previously "scream-tested" the house, standing outside while his ex-girlfriend screamed as loud as she could inside. It would not be heard.

Once at Hart's house, Macy dead-bolted the door and announced that Linda was going to get a "sex therapy" session to get rid of her "hang-ups." But he already knew how the session was going to end. Five days earlier, he had dug Linda's grave in the woods behind Hart's house.

He forced Linda to undress, to do a slow strip-tease at his direction, and he instructed Hart to document each step with Macy's polaroid camera. Then he tied Linda to the coffee table and raped and sodomized her, again instructing Hart to take photographs. But that was not all. He'd made up a list of things he wanted to do to her, and he checked them off as he went along. He had assembled a collection of objects which he inserted into Linda's vagina and rectum, taking note to see the largest item she could accommodate. He masturbated into a spoon and made her "take her medicine."

He did other things.

Worse things.

Much worse.

When he was finished with his list, he strangled Linda Lee Simmons to death. He wrapped her body in green garbage bags and, with Hart's help, buried her.

When Linda did not return home that night, her family immediately notified the police. Macy came under immediate suspicion and eventually the authorities were able to convince Mary Beth Hart to turn state's evidence and testify against Macy in return for a plea to a lesser charge. Hart agreed to wear a wire and provoke Macy into an incriminating conversation. And she led police to Linda Lee's body.

Unfortunately, when Hart took the stand, she proved to be an unsympathetic witness. Her too-short skirt, her make-up and her attitude advertised exactly what she was: a "trailer trash whore." At the most inappropriate times during her detailed description of the torture, rape and murder of Linda Lee Simmons, she would crack a smile. The jury loathed her and could not find her very credible.

Macy's defense attorney claimed that Hart was "a woman scorned." Jealous of Linda Lee, she'd murdered her and then blamed it on Macy just to get revenge on him for jilting her. The jury could certainly believe she was capable of that.

The authorities had no physical evidence connecting Macy to the murder. No hair or semen. Nor could police locate the missing jewelry or the stacks of polaroid photos Hart claimed to have taken.

As for the taped conversations with Hart, Macy never once actually said "body" or anything specific enough to be an unmistakable admission of guilt. The jury found sufficient reasonable doubt to bring back a verdict of "not guilty." Though some of them felt "in their hearts" that Macy was guilty, they were obliged to decide only on the evidence as presented.

Macy was a free man.

It takes a lot of money to beat a murder rap and Macy had been obliged to sell his boat, his cars, his business and his house to raise funds for his defense. About the only thing of value that he kept was a gold serpentine ring that he wore on his little finger.

A few months after his acquittal, the new owners of his house hired a carpeting firm to come in, remove the old carpet and replace it with something more to their taste. In pulling up the carpet, one of the workers uncovered an unused heating vent. Stuffed in the vent he found a large plastic bag. In the bag he found several pieces of jewelry and seventy-odd gut-wrenching polaroid photographs confirming Mary Beth Hart's testimony in every detail.

He immediately turned his discovery over to the police.

But it was too late.

In the law there's a thing called double jeopardy. It means that, once acquitted of a crime, a person can never be tried again for the same offense no matter how compelling any new evidence might be. This was intended to protect citizens from being harassed by the state, from being tried over and over and over again as the state fabricated new "evidence." It obliges the state to be sure they have a strong case in the first place because they only get one bite at the apple. It's a good law.

But sometimes a good law can benefit a bad person.

That was the situation with Macy. He could never again be charged with the kidnapping, rape, assault or murder of Linda

Lee. The authorities tried to get at him another way, charging him with perjury — he'd denied under oath murdering Linda Lee Simmons. He pled guilty to that charge and confessed to the crime in open court, even elaborating on some of the details, in exchange for a reduced sentence. He got seven years. Minus eighteen months time already served. Minus a year for "good behavior." Macy served a little over three years.

As The Judge finished her story, I could feel an old familiar rage. She'd conjured up a demon with her tale, and while pathetic images of the tortured woman whirled through my mind, the demon ran wild in my gut. It sent a sharp pain through my heart. Then I realized that the sharp pain was not in my heart, but in my hand. I had unconsciously squeezed my highball glass until it had broken. A piece of it had sliced into my palm. I gazed at the hand from a distance, marveling at the blood welling up from it like lava from a volcanic crater and nearly as hot.

The Judge produced a handkerchief and bound it around the cut.

"Why are you telling me about this?" I asked her.

"I thought it might interest you."

"Why should it? It doesn't have anything to do with me."

"No, I suppose it doesn't. I thought you might find it interesting anyway. It's terrible, don't you think?"

"Of course, it is. Terrible things happen all the time."

"Very true. Yet, not quite like this."

"Can't the feds get him? Civil rights violations or something."

"No."

"What about civil court? A wrongful death suit?"

"Even if the Simmons family had the necessary resources to pursue it, he really has no remaining assets. He sold everything to pay for his legal fees. No, I'm afraid he's beyond the reach of the law. Yet, something... cries out to be done, don't you think?"

"Such as?"

She poured us another scotch.

"I believe he should be punished for what he did. That he should be able to walk freely among us with impunity seems intolerable. If it were in my power, I would have him know the pain and anguish that poor girl knew before he finally killed her. I'd inflict on him what he inflicted upon her. He claims to have found salvation in Jesus, in the bible. I seem to recall something about an eye for an eye and a tooth for a tooth in there somewhere."

"What is it you're asking me to do?" I already knew the answer, but I couldn't really believe it. I needed to hear it.

"Why, I'm not asking you to do anything at all, darlin'," she replied. "I think you're a man who decides for himself what he's going to do or not do."

"Funny," I said. "Sounds awfully like solicitation of a felony, doesn't it? How does that square with your oath of office as a judge?"

She smiled, but it was a forced, mechanical smile with nothing pleasant behind it.

"As it happens," she said, "I have resigned from the bench. I haven't been a judge for..." she studied her wristwatch, "nearly seventy-two hours now. I would never violate my oath. But I'm no longer bound by it, you see."

Resigned from the bench. She said it as casually as if she were talking about having given away an old sweater. But the law was her life. Had been for nearly all her life.

Some people suggested that one day, there might be a chair on the Supreme Court with her name on it, and her name had frequently come up in discussions about who might become Attorney General of the United States.

So much for that.

"If someone were interested," I began, "do you know how they might be able to locate Mr. Macy?"

"Surely. In fact, I believe all the information that might be required is in here." She handed me a large brown envelope. "He's living completely out in the open, not in hiding or anything of that nature. Why should he? He's untouchable. And he knows it."

I stared at that envelope a long time. It weighed a ton in my hand. I felt like I was on the brink of something, and once I went over the edge, there was no way back again. But I kept seeing Linda Lee Simmons face, hearing her screams, the screams that no one else had heard. If a woman screams in a house and there's no one there to hear it, does she make a sound?

Not one the judge and jury can hear, I guess. Then it dawned on me.

"You were the judge at Macy's murder trial," I said.

"I was."

I slipped the envelope into my pocket and reached for my drink. The Judge lay her hand lightly on mine and we studied each other without a word. What could we say? We were going over the edge together and into the abyss and we both knew it.

At that moment, room service arrived with our lunch. We didn't say anything more about Macy.

Alice Burton, Esquire, re-joined us just as we were having coffee. The Judge and I made our farewell's and I rode down in the elevator with my lawyer.

"I'm curious about something," she said as we passed the seventh floor.

"What's that?" I asked her.

"How do you know my mother?"

What the hell was she talking about?

It hit me just as we jolted to a halt on the ground floor. She was talking about The Judge. She was the Judge's daughter.

Life is just full of fucking surprises.

About a month after I met with The Judge, Clarence Allen Macy disappeared. Not a word to anyone. Didn't pack a bag. Didn't notify his landlord. Didn't tell anyone at his church. Presto. Vanished.

The police went wild. They had been hoping to find some way to get him for something. No doubt Macy decided not to hang around waiting to see if they succeeded. Or maybe he just got tired of the isolation, the malevolent looks from the good people of Lutee, Texas, their icy shunning. Probably decided to start a new life someplace, some say.

Yeah. Probably.

But there's been not a trace of him. Since no one has filed any kind of a missing person report on him, and he has not been charged with a crime, the police are not actively searching for him. They are keeping an eye out though, just in case he shows up.

He won't.

What I remember most about him was his cheesy little mustache and the world's worst toupee, looking like a hair-gel laden muskrat clinging desperately to his head. I gave a great deal of thought to exactly what I should do and exactly how. A quick death seemed too easy. He really ought to have time to reflect.

So I gave him plenty of time.

In the end, he was begging and blubbering like an infant. It didn't surprise me. Scratch the surface of a bully and not far underneath, you'll find a coward.

Every damn time.

Mary Beth Hart was living in a trailer park when the UPS delivery man brought her a festively decorated package with a big label that said "Your FREE CD player is inside."

"It's some kind of special promotion," the UPS man confided in her. "I've been delivering quite a few of these. Me, I never get anything free. So you just have to sign, Ma'am."

His pen proved to be out of ink and he patted his pockets to find another, to no avail.

Fortunately, Mary Beth had one handy and she popped back inside to grab it.

He followed her silently in.

"I have something else for you, too," I told her. "From Linda Lee Simmons."

As I had done with Macy, I let her experience some of the things she had helped him do to his victim. Then I put a small caliber bullet into the back of her brain. I left her mostly nude body, splayed and open in the most disrespectful pose I could imagine and tossed the place just to add to the confusion. The police would take it for a robbery, sexual assault, and murder.

That would be all right.

George Simmons still lived in the house his grandfather built, though it was far too empty now, and had taken on the air of a mausoleum since the death of his sister, and his parents, both of whom had died while waiting for "justice to be served."

One morning, a postman came to the door bearing a special delivery package, a postman unfamiliar to Mr. Simmons. Nor did he notice that the parcel bore no postmark of any kind.

In the small package was a sympathy card, a Hallmark card. Onto the inside was stapled a typewritten note that said:

"My sincerest condolences for the loss of your sister."

There was a little white box inside the envelope, too.

It contained a finger.

A little finger.

Around the finger was a gold serpentine ring.

Oh, when the shark bites with his teeth, Babe
Scarlet billows start to spread
Fancy gloves wears old Mac Heath, Babe
So there's never, never a trace of red

("Mack the Knife," Bobby Darin)

CHAPTER TWENTY-FOUR:
LEX TALIONIS

The killing of a human being by another human being is called "homicide."

Ever since Cain smote Abel, the killing of another person has been considered the ultimate crime. There are very few universals in human behavior — true for all human cultures in all times and all places — but this one comes about as close as you can get.

Some places cross the t's and dot the i's differently, but in a general way it boils down to this. There are different kinds of homicide. A given homicide may be innocent or criminal, depending on the circumstances.

Criminal homicide comes in two basic flavors: with malice aforethought, which means "premeditated" or without malice aforethought. Homicide with malice aforethought is called murder; homicide without malice aforethought is called manslaughter.

For a homicide to be murder, the killer must have had a pre-meditated design to kill, or he must have intended to kill or do the victim grave bodily harm, or he must be engaged in an act that is so inherently dangerous to others that it reveals a wanton disregard for human life.

One of the variations on this theme is sometimes called "felony murder." This includes any death that occurs during the commission of a felony such as rape, robbery, burglary, sodomy or aggravated arson.

Suppose you go in to rob a bank. A guard shoots at you and you shoot back, killing him. That ain't self-defense; that's murder. Suppose that guard grabs for your gun and it goes off "accidentally." Still murder.

Suppose one of the tellers has a heart attack during your robbery?

Felony murder.

Pre-meditation doesn't require that you formulate a strategic plan to rival the Normandy invasion. It just requires that the intent was formed sufficiently before the act was committed. It can be conceived and executed within a short period of time.

Since, absent evidence to the contrary, we presume that a person intended the natural, probable and foreseeable consequences of his deliberate actions, if you do something that is very likely to result in grave bodily harm or death to another person, we will presume that you intended to do exactly that. No pre-meditation required.

If you take a shot at somebody intending only to wound them, but you kill him with that shot, your alleged intention to only wound doesn't mean squat.

Murder.

What if you close your eyes and randomly discharge a firearm in a room crowded with people? You may not intend any injury to a particular person or to any person at all.

Too bad for you.

When you kill someone by an act that is so inherently dangerous as to evidence a wanton disregard for human life, that's murder. Down you go.

Murder could be generally described as "cold-blooded."

Manslaughter, on the other hand is more of a "hot-blooded" thing.

When a person kills in the sudden heat of passion caused by adequate provocation, that's called voluntary manslaughter. The provocation must be of such a nature as to arouse uncontrollable passion in a reasonable and prudent person.

As a rule, words alone are not considered adequate provocation. It's the "sticks and stones" principle, even though we all know that some names can hurt deeply. Nevertheless there is the notion, mostly out of fashion these days, of "fighting words."

These would be utterances which, by the manner and context in which they are made, may inflict injury or cite an immediate breach of the peace.

A old pal of mine — a nearly full-blood Lakota — "just happened" to be in a bar where certain members of the US Army — the 7th Cavalry — "just happened" to hang out. At one point he loudly reflected on what a misbegotten cocksucker General Custer was. This immediately stopped the murmur of conversation in the place. Then my friend loudly apologized — for offending cocksuckers. The scene, right out of a John Ford western, was completely predictable — which was exactly why my friend said what he said.

It also might be that such utterances might create a reasonable apprehension of imminent harm in the person or persons so addressed, and may even be considered assault, even though assault usually refers to physical contact with the intent to cause injury. Suppose, for example, a dozen armed neo-nazi skinheads crash the Friday evening services at a Jewish temple and announce to the congregation "Jews are sub-humans that should be exterminated!"

That goes a little beyond the sticks and stones thing, wouldn't you say?

Personally, I'd smoke every one of the Aryan shitheads and not ask too many questions later. If the rabbi does just that, the law says it can't be self-defense, since no attack was imminent, but it's probably sufficient provocation to make it manslaughter instead of murder.

Certain outrageous acts can be considered sufficient provocation, too. Somebody rapes your pre-teen daughter? Or lynches your little brother? Or murders your spouse? That might do it.

But adequate provocation isn't enough, by itself, to make it manslaughter. You need that sudden heat of passion. That doesn't mean you don't know what you're doing while you're doing it (the Whacko Defense), just that your actions are governed by passion rather than reason. The hot tap is on, the cold tap is off, bloodwise.

As in so many things, timing is critical.

Would a reasonable and prudent man have "cooled off" in the time that elapsed between the provocation and his response? While no specific time limits have been recognized, the sooner is definitely the better.

Still, it depends.

It depends, it depends.

If it sounds like a whole lot depends on the specific circumstances of a particular situation, you're absolutely right. That's what juries are for.

Involuntary manslaughter generally stems from "culpable negligence," which is legalese for "incredibly fucking stupid." They say you should never ascribe to malevolence that which can be adequately explained by stupidity. In this case, it's an act or omission with wanton disregard for the foreseeable — though not necessarily probable or natural — consequences of your actions. Suppose you pick up a gun, a semi-auto, pop the magazine out and, just as a joke and point it at your buddy. "Don't worry," you say, "it ain't loaded." And to prove it you squeeze the trigger — sending the round that you had negligently left in the pipe right through your friend's brain.

That makes you incredibly fucking stupid and you should put the next one in your own ear, dimwit. But it isn't murder.

Innocent homicides, killings that attach no criminal guilt, come in two flavors, too: excusable homicide and justifiable homicide.

Excusable homicide may be accidental or an act of self-defense. For the homicide to be accidental, you would have to be doing a lawful act in a lawful manner and without negligence. For example: Bubba goes out a-deer huntin'. He fires at one and brings it down with one well-placed shot. Bubba has no way of knowing that cousin Billy Joe Bob has also gone a-huntin' and has cleverly disguised himself as a deer, the better to sneak up and get the drop on his deadly prey. So that homicide is excusable — at least as long as Bubba doesn't commence to field dressin' his cousin.

Or suppose a surgeon performs a legal operation for a fully informed patient and exercises all due care and skill, but the patient double-crosses him and dies anyway. Not the doctor's fault. Excusable homicide.

Killing in self-defense may be excusable when the killer reasonably believed that the killing was necessary in order to protect his own life or the life of another innocent person. Even if the grounds for his reasonable belief turn out to be false, but believed for good cause to be present, the homicide is excusable.

Let's suppose Joe Citizen is confronted by Mack the Mugger who brandishes a pistola in his direction and threatens to shoot. From all those apparent or subtle cues of facial expression and body language that we all instinctively know, Joe believes Mack is sincere and responds by pulling out his own trusty weapon and shooting Mack dead. Afterward, top-notch scientific detective work reveals that that Mack's pistol was just a very realistic non-firing toy.

Now even though it turns out that Joe was in no actual danger of being shot, Joe had no way to know that Mack's piece was a phony, and thus his belief was reasonable. Wrong, but reasonable. Therefore, the homicide is excusable.

The key element here is the reasonableness of Joe's belief. If Mack had threatened him with a bright fluorescent green water pistol, Joe's belief may not be so reasonable. If Mack had made the same death threat while aiming only his index finger, though gun-like, in Joe's direction, Joe would be on his way to setting up house-keeping in a 10x10 bachelor pad.

With excusable homicide, we're saying you weren't right to kill him, but we can see how any reasonable and prudent person under those circumstances could make the same mistake.

If Mack's gun had been real, the homicide would have been justifiable homicide.

Justifiable homicide is killing that is authorized or commanded by law. Killing an enemy on the field of battle in accordance with the rules of war is justifiable homicide.

Killing to protect yourself — or another innocent person — from the imminent threat of grave bodily injury or death is justifiable. Killing to prevent a violent felony such as rape or robbery or another crime against the person is justifiable.

When we say a homicide is justifiable, we're saying, yes, you were right to kill him. We don't go quite so far as to say you would've been wrong not to kill him, but it veers pretty near to that edge.

Executing a death sentence pronounced by a competent authority is justifiable homicide, too.

And as far as I'm concerned, The Judge is about the most competent authority you'll ever run into. She's a woman of impeccable integrity, profound compassion, and knows the law better than all nine of the Supremes put together. Her judgment is never biased. Not racially. Not politically. Not no way, not no how. If I had a conscience, it might look like her.

After Macy, the Judge and I fell into the most beautiful friendship since Ric and Louis decided to skip out of Casablanca and join the resistance.

I would get a call.

We'd meet.

She'd tell me a story.

Then I'd decide what to do about it.

Sometimes we'd agree that there was only one thing to do, and I did it.

Other times, there was another possibility.

So I did that instead.

I was comfortable with it.

Comfortable with myself, with her, and with what we were doing.

I had found my niche.

Had myself all figured out.

Or so I thought.

Adam Adrian Crown

When you're weary,
feeling small,
When tears are in your eyes,
I will dry them all...

("Bridge Over Troubled Water," Simon and Garfunkel)

CHAPTER TWENTY-FIVE:
WHERE THE ARROW POINTS TO THE RAINBOW

When the student is ready, the master appears.

That's a very old saying. But what does it mean, exactly?

I can think of two possibilities. It *could* mean that as the student reaches a certain level of accomplishment, he attracts exactly the teacher he needs to take him to the next stage of development. Law of attraction. Cosmic magic. Ain't life grand?

Or it *could* mean that the student is stumbling around, groping haphazardly along, with his head way up his ass, rendering him unable to see the master who's been there all along, trying to reach him. The student trips over a big rock, accidently jerking his head free, and suddenly finds the master has "appeared."

I can tell you from personal experience which one of those interpretations is the most plausible.

I think I told you about French-kissing an electric lamp cord when I was a little kid. Not something I can recommend. And I told you about The Dream, right? The Indian dream. With that old Dream Chief telling me "Go where the arrow points to the rainbow." Something which was nothing but dream jibberish, as far as I was concerned. Had that same dream, with slight variations, quite a lot during my recovery. And now and again in years after. Seemed to be at random times. Never could make any sense of it. No dots to connect. But the feeling of that dream was powerful. I knew in my gut that it was important somehow. I just couldn't figure out how.

OK. Fast forward a bunch of years.
I was dating this girl named Casey.
Casey at the bat.
Except she never struck out.
One night in that warm post-coital languor that often makes you say really stupid things, she mentioned that she used to have a pony when she was a kid, but hadn't ridden a horse since childhood, and would love to do it again sometime.
I liked Casey.
So I looked into it and found out there was a place, not too far away, with a couple of hundred acres to ride and State Forests on three sides, with even more trails. So just for fun, I arranged for us to have a lesson and go on a trail ride for her birthday.

Walking into the barn, I was assailed by the combined scent of hay, manure, horse sweat and leather. To some people this is an unpleasant odor. For me it seemed like some long forgotten ambrosia wafting on the summer wind.
Very relaxing.
Welcoming.
And because I wasn't accustomed to relaxed welcomes, it put me a little on edge. I didn't know what I was feeling, but something was definitely up.
I was introduced to a grey Arab-Quarterhorse gelding named Moonshine. Our riding teacher and host, Jill, showed us how to tack up, explained this and that. Some of it I seemed to remember from some way-back-when that had never been.
Moonshine sniffed me. Nuzzled my hand very delicately with his nose, wiggling his lips side to side like Samantha on

Bewitched. His unclipped whiskers tickled my hand and made me smile.

But what really struck me, what completely fascinated me, astounded me, awed me — and a whole bunch of other synonyms — was the look in Moonshine's eyes.

He didn't look *at* me.

He looked *into* me.

I felt like I was standing there completely naked, being examined by a vastly superior alien being, infinitely wise and of impeccable spiritual character. Nothing judgmental in that examination, mind you. There was only a softness. A comprehension. Compassion. Acceptance. And no guile at all.

The reflection of myself in his eyes was someone I didn't recognize. Like looking in a funhouse mirror. You know it's you, but it doesn't look like you. At least not the you that you've grown accustomed to seeing. I felt hot and itchy all over and I could feel inexplicable tears boiling over.

"Are you all right," Jill asked me. "You look a little — sick or something."

"I'm fine," I said. "Just allergies."

Liar.

When I stepped up and swung effortlessly into the saddle, I was swept up by a tsunami of long lost memory. I recalled how, as a child, I'd dreamed about riding horses. How high up I was. How far away the world seemed from horseback. It was almost like flying. I remembered the dream sounds of hoof beats and leather creaking. The scent of horse. The hot sun on the back of my head.

And I remembered, suddenly, Jan Johanson.

Jan owned a small dairy farm in Wisconsin, just across the Illinois border. Like most small farmers, he was gradually sinking into the quicksand of debt and it was his job with the railroad that kept him afloat. I can't quite recall whether he was a conductor or what.

I think he was more or less in charge of the tiny Illinois Central station at Englewood, Illinois, about a 30 minute train ride from the Chicago loop. I don't know how he knew my father, but they were pals of some kind. Maybe Army buddies. Maybe jail mates.

Jan would stop by our place for a coffee or a beer from time to time and always brought a little something for each of us kids — piece of candy or something like that.

And he always called me "Best."

"Where's Best?" he'd ask. "There he is. Come on over here, Best. How'd you get to be such a good kid, huh? You're the best boy I know." And so on.

That may not seem like a very big deal. But when people beat the shit out of you every day and tell you what a rotten, worthless bastard you are, having someone express such a contrary opinion — well, there aren't really any words that can describe it. Imagine if somebody had taped a plastic bag around your head and you were suffocating. Jan Johanson poked a hole in the bag so I could breathe. Remembering his kindness now, even after all this time, I can feel myself wanting to cry.

Can't help it.

At least one time, probably several times, we visited Jan's farm. My dad did some work for him, I think. Worked on his tractor, maybe. My dad was good with machines. Too bad I hadn't been one.

That was when my horse-riding dream came true.

When Jan Johanson lifted me up onto the back of one of his horses, it was all just as I had dreamed it. The sights, the sounds, the smells.

Everything. Exactly.

At some time or other, Jan was in the stirrups and I was riding in his lap, though he pretended I was actually doing the riding. "Ask him to go this way, Best, look over there..." and we went. "Ask him to trot, Best," and brought him up to a trot for me.

"That's the way! How'd you learn to ride a horse so good, Best?"

We cantered, too. It's an exquisite feeling, hips rolling forward and back in synch with that triplet hoofbeat, wind in your ears, horsemane flying.

It's like being weightless. Invisible. A ghost.

Beyond time.

Unlimited by space.

One Christmas, I got a special present from Jan. It was a toy horse, like a rocking horse, only it was suspended from a frame by four heavy springs. A golden pony with a white mane and tail, if I recall. I spent every waking moment on that toy horsie that I could. I'm told that I would even climb up on that plastic palomino in cowboy hat and jammies, and go to sleep in the saddle.

Another memory flooded in.

As a young teenager, I had once dated a horsewoman.

One day, when I hitch-hiked over to her house I found that the whole family was gone. But a neighbor was there. Marilyn was her name. Pale skin, brown eyes, straw-blonde hair, extremely buxom, the more obviously so due to her petite stature. She was dressed in dirty, faded Levis and cowboy boots. Plaid shirt knotted at the waist to show off her belly. It was a nice belly.

She explained to me that some horses had gotten loose and had been spotted out near the beach at Lake Villanova and everybody was out after them before something awful happened. Lots of tourist traffic around there in the summertime. She was about to take off and join in the search.

"You want to come? You could ride Sweet Sioux."

Sweet Sioux was her horse but she boarded it temporarily at my girlfriend's place. Marilyn peered up at me skeptically as she asked, chewing on a stalk of grass.

Well, hell, I was a teenager and I was suffering from all the signs of testosterone poisoning, including transient idiocy.

Maybe not so transient.

"Sure," I said.

In no time, we were in the saddle, crossing the back pastures in a straight line toward Lake Villanova with me trying to pretend I knew what I was doing, desperately trying to remember everything I'd seen my girlfriend do on horseback and imitate it. I doubt Marilyn was fooled for a second. But the testosterone poisoning syndrome allowed me to believe she was. Forced me to believe it.

Fortunately for me, Sweet Sioux knew pretty much how to horse and more or less walked along with Marilyn's horse — just as she would have done if I hadn't been there at all. But I got feeling quite good about myself. I was a natural.

I felt like the Lone Ranger — or, rather, Tonto.

At a *walk*.

Without sighting hair or hoof of the missing horses, we emerged at Lake Villanova about a block from the public beach. We could see it from there. Crowded even on an overcast Tuesday. But even crowded, that beach looked pretty inviting. Lots of bare skin. I wondered what Marilyn was wearing under her jeans.

But I wasn't going to find out right now.

At that moment, Marilyn spotted the missing horses, both of them, far across the fields, maybe a quarter mile away, and picked up a trot in their direction. Sweet Sioux, without so much as consulting me, did likewise.

Now, the trot is a more difficult gait to ride than the walk is. More difficult than the canter, I'd say. It's particularly difficult when a complete lack of balance causes you to bounce on your testicles on every alternate diagonal beat. My testicles are veterans with their fair share of bumps and thumps, but there's nothing to compare with getting them between you and the saddle and landing on them with your full weight. I believe that's how posting was actually invented. In any case, nothing like it to teach you to sit back on your pockets.

The dizziness and nausea that accompanied full contact testicle squashing subsided just as we caught up to the errant steeds. But they wanted to play.

Great.

One of them, the chestnut, took off to the left and the bay took off to the right, initiating the ever-popular chase-me game. I wish I could take some credit for catching one of those horses, but I can't. What I will take credit for is hanging on and staying in the saddle while Sweet Sioux caught one.

Seems that somewhere in her checkered past, Sweet Sioux must have worked cattle, because she cut off the ring on that chestnut time after time until she finally got her to quit and stand still. The escapee's halter was still on, so it was a simple matter to snap a lead rope on her and pony her along behind me. Marilyn had easily grabbed the bay and was leaning on her saddle horn squinting at me as I approached.

"That was some pretty fancy riding," she said.

"Shucks, 't'warn't nothin' ma'am," I said. Ok, maybe that's not what I said. But that's what it sounded like. It's the effect of testosterone on the tongue.

So back to the present.

Casey and I had about a 20 minute lesson with Jill, long enough for her to decide we'd be safe on a trail ride, I guess. Jill was going out with us and so was another woman named Stevie, who was a veterinarian, and was married to a classical guitarist. I think I had one of his CD's of Villa-Lobos etudes.

We were out about three hours, I think. Most of it through pine forest. It was peaceful there. Quiet. Hoof-beats muffled by a thick carpet of pine needles. Crossed tinkling streams. Up and down hills. Jumped an old log. Startled once by a half-dozen deer sprinting across the trail. That is, *I* was startled. Moonshine took it in stride. Finished up with a nice canter home.

It rained a little, while we were out. Just enough to cool things off pleasantly after a string of hot, muggy days.

While we were cooling our horses down back at the barn, we happened to walk through a few puddles and in one of them something caught my eye, just as Moonshine stepped in it.

"Look, Jack!" Casey was pointing skyward. A rainbow stretched brightly from horizon to horizon, one end disappearing into the forest we'd ridden through.

That's what I'd seen reflected in the puddle.

The rainbow.

But there was something else, too.

When Moonshine stepped in that puddle, he left behind a clear hoof-print. The arc of his toe lay perfectly along the arc of the rainbow. The impression of his frog was clear, too. And that frog was shaped just like an arrowhead.

An arrow.

Pointing up at the rainbow.

The world reeled in a Hitchcock tilt, and the Twilight Zone theme ran through my head, and I gasped as if old Moonshine had kicked me in the gut.

"Go where the arrow points to the rainbow," I mumbled.

"What?" said Casey.

"Uh, nice rainbow."

I couldn't tell her what was really going on. I didn't have the words to convey it. Still don't.

It was like dying.

And it was like being born.

It was like losing yourself.

And finding yourself.

All at the same time.

It was like looking in the mirror and removing a Halloween mask and seeing your own face for the very first time.

I felt whole. Right. Good. Clear. Clean.

And for the first time in my life, I had a real sense of belonging.

I was home.

I could have sworn I heard my old Dream Chief cackling with delight.

.

Well the weeks went by
and spring turned to summer
And summer turned into fall
And it turns out he was a missing person
who nobody missed at all

("Goodbye Earl," The Dixie Chicks)

CHAPTER TWENTY-SIX:
FINISH THE JOB

It was no big surprise to Keri Lamorie when her husband tried to kill her.

In the four years they had been married, he had become progressively violent. At first Keri had been flattered by his tinge of jealousy, certain that it was, as he said, just proof that he loved her. But that jealousy had increasingly darkened into a need to control her every step, where she went and when, who her friends were, who she spoke to. He had pressured her, with his jealous rages, to gradually distance herself, one by one, from family and friends, like a sailor washed overboard drifting away from a life ring, until they were eliminated from her life. Until he alone was in her life. Until he *was* her life.

And even that was not enough.

He became more and more intolerant of her tiniest fault. From folding his shirts just so, to arranging the cans on the kitchen shelves to suit him, by size, labels facing out, and, of course, right-side up. He required absolute obedience to his every whim without the merest deviation. And the slightest transgressions were punished. Grabbing, pulling and pushing had led to slapping and then to punching.

And kicking.

Kicking was the worst, and the scowl of utter contempt that twisted his face when he kicked her hurt more than the kick did.

I understood about that.

On four different occasions in the last year, she or the neighbors had summoned the police. But there wasn't much they could do, the cops explained. She didn't really want him to go to jail, did she? This was, after all, a private matter. As long as he did not "disturb the peace," they warned him sternly. Nowadays, of course, most police departments have a policy, if it is not a state law, of a "mandatory arrest" in a domestic dispute. But at that time not enough women had yet died at the hands of boyfriends, lovers and husbands.

Finally, Keri tried to escape.

She contacted an old friend who offered her a place to stay. But HE came home unexpectedly and discovered her as she was packing a few essentials into a suitcase. That time she went to the hospital. She also went to court, filed for divorce and got an order of protection prohibiting him from coming within one hundred yards of her. Unfortunately, paper is inadequate armor against a hunting knife with a seven inch blade.

When Keri ran screaming and bloody from the house, with her hands cut to the bone, once again her neighbors called the police. Within moments, a patrol car, nearby on another call, arrived on the scene.

The officers rendered first aid to Keri, who was bleeding profusely from deep cuts on her face and neck, as well as the defensive cuts on her hands. He had come within a few centimeters of severing her carotid artery, had just grazed her windpipe.

The police confronted her husband, who turned over the gore-covered knife without resistance. They did not immediately handcuff him or even place him under arrest.

That was when he stepped in and kicked Keri in the head, stomping down on her with the heel of his heavy work boot. A jolt of searing pain ran along her body like a ripple of molten lava and then she no longer felt her arms or legs. It was only then that the police actually took her husband into custody, cuffed him and ushered him into the back of the squad car. The last thing Keri saw before passing out was her husband's face, looking back at her over his shoulder, sneering smugly.

Nathan Lamorie was convicted of attempted murder and was sentenced to twenty years in prison. Keri sued the police department. Her suit claimed that the police were required to provide "equal protection" for an assault victim, regardless of the fact that the assailant was her husband. She claimed that the failure of the police to promptly arrest and charge her husband as they would have done if her assailant had been a stranger, resulted in her suffering a disabling injury.

A jury agreed. They awarded her more than a million dollars in damages.

In my opinion, it wasn't enough.

Keri's face was permanently disfigured. She lost most of the use of her right hand.

Mercifully, the paralysis she'd experienced from the kick to her head had been temporary. Though she was still weak on her left side, which caused her to drag her left leg a little when she walked, she could at least walk.

It could have been much worse.

Much worse.

At least she had survived. Many other women were not so lucky.

Nathan Lamorie would be eligible for parole in fourteen years, assuming good behavior in the joint. His initial activities weren't cause for optimism. He lost his letter-writing and phone privileges by using them to make death threats to Keri, and he told everyone who would listen that he would one day "finish the job." She was his and his alone "til death do us part."

Eventually, I suppose, after he was turned down for parole enough times, he learned to keep his mouth shut. He became silent and sullen.

Prison is an unbearable existence for a human being. To withstand it, you need something to keep you afloat. For Nathan Lamorie, it was the determination to "avenge" himself against his "betraying" wife.

The Judge contacted me nine days before Nathan Lamorie was scheduled to be released, having served his full sentence in prison. There was no parole or probation now. He was a free man. No one would be checking up on him.

Keri — now Keri Vincent, with a husband of ten years and two beautiful sons — was afraid that, even after all this time, her former husband would come after her. She had received several odd phone calls. No threats. Just quiet breathing on the other end of the line. It could have been anyone.

But she knew it was him.

Some people would ascribe her fear to hysteria.

Those people are stupid.

If there's one thing I've learned it's to trust your intuition.

So I told The Judge I'd take care of it. I would ensure that Nathan Lamorie would do neither Keri nor her family any harm and that he would be out of her life forever. Usually, by the time I hear from The Judge, it's too late. Irreparable damage has already been done. I was glad to get a chance to step in a little earlier for a change.

When he was released, I was there.

He never knew it, but I was never farther from him than his shadow. I was there when he found a studio apartment on the west side, only five blocks from Keri's new home. I was there when he got a job with a sanitation company. I was there when he bought the knife.

All the while he was stalking her, I was stalking him.

It's a recurrent theme in my work: the predators never realize that they, too, might be prey. There's a lesson there someplace.

He continued to phone her, never speaking, just listening, then hanging up. I could feel the anticipation mounting in him. In the way he stood, walked, watched her. It was building to an almost sexual climax — perhaps for him it was a sexual climax. He was approaching the point of no return.

It was a sunny afternoon, unseasonably warm. The seventeenth day after his release.

Keri's husband was at work. Her sons were in school.

She was all alone.

He approached the back door of her house, cut through the screen door with his knife, and reached around for the lock inside.

I placed a single blow carefully between his third and fourth cervical vertebrae.

The dislodging of the bones severed his spinal cord and he collapsed into my waiting arms like a marionette whose strings had been cut. I took the knife easily from his now limp hand.

He seemed quite perturbed.

He gasped and tried to speak, but couldn't.

"You said it was "til death do you part," I told him softly. "This is good-bye."

I disposed of his body in the city dump.

His disappearance didn't arouse any interest.

My folks were always putting him down
They said he came from the wrong side of town
They told me he was bad
But I knew he was sad
That's why I fell for the leader of the pack

("Leader of the Pack," the Shangri-Las)

CHAPTER TWENTY-SEVEN:
THE CICERO KID

I can't resist betting on the underdog.

My bookie doesn't seem to mind.

Nick Dimusio. Known as "Nick the Mouse." I think I've probably put both his kids through college. They ought to call me "Uncle" Jack. I've played so many long shots that a couple of times Nick, himself, even tried to warn me off — to no avail. Now he just shakes his head in resignation.

Take for example this fight.

I was grabbing some quality time with a 21-year old by the name of Balvenie. Nick's was normally a quiet place. But on this particular occasion, there were some tourists on the scene. Young guys in the 18-22 range who appeared to think that they were, and should always be, the center of attention. College boys, no doubt. Frat boys, I strongly suspected. They were drinking beer and it was having a negative effect on their ability to judge the volume of their voices. It made Nick wince as he refilled my glass. He was embarrassed for them.

Because they were bullhorn loud, I couldn't help "overhear" their conversation. Actually it wasn't conversation so much as it was a litany of clichés in adulation of the current

359

heavyweight champ. It was the sappy, overblown adolescent praise typically spouted by those who had never, themselves, ever been in the ring. Too many other opportunities available thanks to Daddy's money.

To be fair, the champ was a bruiser, all right. Promoters were having a little trouble finding opponents for him who could last a few rounds. Or even one round. He was compiling an impressive record of knock-outs, and truth is, nobody wanted to be his next victim. But they managed to scratch up somebody for another match. A journeyman boxer who had had some fine fights — and some unmitigated disasters. His weight fluctuated dramatically, as did his commitment to training. But I guess he needed the payday and was willing to take a beating to get one.

The fight was widely condemned as a terrible mismatch. Last I checked, the odds were fifty to one in the Champ's favor. So, yeah, the Champ was going to kill the challenger, maybe even in the first round. And yeah, the Champ had never been knocked down — in fact, he'd never even gotten a standing 8-count. And yeah, and yeah, and yeah, it was all true.

But the champ was also a punk, a small-time mugger and all-around bully from the projects, and character-wise hadn't changed his stripes one iota. I was tired of hearing about how great he was, and these kids were starting to grind on my nerves like Lawrence Olivier going into Dustin Hoffman's tooth.

"Would you gentlemen care to make a small wager?" I heard myself ask.

Nick the Mouse rolled his eyes heavenward, but heaven didn't say anything. Didn't have to.

I put up a grand between these four kids. I suggest that, if they were so confident, they should be willing to give me five to one odds.

"Hell, make it ten to one," the kid with shaggy blonde hair said.

"You could make it twenty to one," his be-spectacled pal chimed in.

"Shit," said their pudgy partner in pugilistic prognostication, "Let's make it a *million* to one. It's not going to matter." That got some laughs, lots of nods, and a high-five.

A million to one was tempting.

We settled on half of the last official odds.

"Twenty-five to one, then," I said. "If you insist."

Nick the Mouse witnessed the bet. The boys went back to their beer. Nick went back to washing glasses. He leaned across the bar to whisper to me. "Jack, Jack, Jack," he said, "why the fuck do you *do* shit like that?

Back in 1965, back before Chicago sprawled its scummy tentacles north almost to Wisconsin, Wolf Lake was a beautiful place in the fall. And the long Indian Summer meant that kids at Liberty Junior High School could still duck outside during free periods and lunch hours to shoot some hoops in t-shirts.

Liberty Junior High was a tiny school that fell, by geographical accident, into a basketball conference that pitted the teenage "Wolves" against teams from much larger schools, from far wealthier environs, including George Washington Junior High School, the villain of the piece. A more jaded person might suspect, what with the strange and irregular borders, that those school districts were drawn up specifically to contain the urban spillage of "niggers, spics and dagos," in a geographical quarantine to protect the blonde, blue-eyed and button-down crowd. But who would do such a thing? Right?

The George Washington kids were all lily-white, upper upper class. All college prep. No "vocational" classes were even offered at GW. Their sport teams were all very good, but basketball was their pride and joy. And why not? They were conference champions 6 years running, completely demolishing their opponents. But then, they had a lot of talent to choose from and carried twenty boys — *twenty* — on their squad. They had a fulltime coach and two part-time assistants — *paid* coaches, not just teachers or parents volunteering their time.

It might seem odd these days for an all-white team from an all-white school to do so well, but back in the bad old days, there still weren't that many black players in the NBA. The Boston Celtics had drafted the first Black player in 1950, and had started all five of their Black players in '64. Still, as far as most people were concerned, there were only two Black players in the NBA: Wilt Chamberlain and Bill Russell — and these gents were viewed as aberrations. It would be a long time yet before any black student would even attend George Washington.

The Liberty Junior kids were losers in the socio-economic olympics. Few if any of them ever went to college. Fewer finished. Fewer still ever returned to tell the tale. Most of them followed vocational training curricula, designed to assure them of a place in the work force — and keep them in it. These were the kids who would build elegant homes, but never live in them; they would service Mercedes Benz's, but never drive them, and they would be conscripted to fight and die in wars, but never reap windfall profits from promoting them.

Albert Katz was a possible exception.

A fat, wheezy child, he'd learned to read practically while still in the womb and had read voraciously ever since. He was embarrassingly good in Latin and Math. Science was a breeze. And English was scarcely enough to keep him awake. In short, he was in grave danger of becoming a real geek.

362

Albert played forward on the Liberty Junior basketball team — not because he played well. He played — how to put it charitably?

He sucked.

He could dribble adequately — right-handed only — sometimes he would be standing where he couldn't avoid the rebound, and he didn't wear out many nets with his shooting. But he was certainly not going to flunk off the team, and that was something, anyway. So the coach, Mr. Lubanski, who was also the principal and an English teacher, kept Albert on. When you only have about ten kids going out for the team in the first place, you pretty much suit up everybody you can.

Albert's main function on the team, in fact, was to play the foil for the "star" of the team — if a team without a single victory can indeed have a star — Bruce the Ace. Now Bruce could play ball and was dedicated to it, too. He could dribble, he could shoot, he could rebound (even his own shots). He was a one-man team. Visions of pro basketball danced in his head. He would score, maybe 20 or 30 points a game — and so Liberty Junior would lose, like 95 to 30. Before games, Albert would play a little one-on-one with Bruce, getting utterly trashed, but dutifully "warming up" the star. Between games, it was understood that Albert would also "study together" with Bruce, making sure Bruce remained eligible to play.

As a reward Albert was entitled to stand very nearby when Melanie Johnson, Bruce's counterpart on the cheer-leading squad, sidled by, taking her precociously developed breasts for a walk like a pair of pure-bred Great Danes straining against her sweater anxious to make a kill. Albert, rendered invisible by Bruce's aura, would sometimes imagine that Melanie's coy (Tits? Who? Me?) come-hither glance was for him. Was it possible to get laid by osmosis?

One early October morning, before class, Albert was outside shooting baskets. (Well, chasing the ball.)

Unnoticed by him, three of the rudest, crudest juvenile delinquency candidates at Liberty circled him like sharks sniffing out blood. Ralph, Jeff and Johnny D. (who proudly proclaimed that his very initials stood for "juvenile delinquent"). They were like the three stooges of small-town punkdom. They were as inseparable as Susie Lewandowski's fat thighs and were in and out of trouble — mostly in — most of the time. Serious trouble; not kid stuff. Not just youthful hijinks. These three clowns were headed for the joint.

When one of Albert's shots careened way back, his ball landed in the hands of Johnny D., the leader of the pack, and a pick-up game of keep-away immediately ensued, in which Albert, of course, was "it." He dutifully chased after his ball, running from one goon to the other as they came on like low-rent Harlem Globetrotters. But shortly, the amusement provided by merely taunting Albert began to wane. They had to increase their fix. A push here, a trip there, and Albert was lying on the ground with Ralphie's foot on his back, pressing his face down against the blacktop, their taunts blurring in his fuzzy, hot ears.

At that moment, Albert heard THE VOICE.

"Hey. Let's see the ball," it said. It was a smooth, cool, casual who-gives-a-fuck voice.

The three hoody stooges exchanged looks and then Jeff grudgingly tossed over Albert's ball.

Albert, with great effort, managed to twist his head around and squint in the direction of the voice. Though his glasses had been knocked askew, he could make out boots. Engineer boots. With a length of chain — a dog's choke-collar actually — circling one ankle. Those boots were nowhere near the dress code.

"How's about a game?" Me'n him." The voice said.

The foot withdrew from Albert's back and he gathered himself up, replaced his glasses and beheld the dashing figure who had unexpectedly descended from Olympus to dally with the fate of mortals and, in a moment of caprice, keep Albert from getting his ass kicked.

The Voice belonged to a Stranger whose almost-black hair was swept up into a pompadour that broke into a wave washing onto his forehead like the surf at Maui.

He wore jeans so tight that his dick and balls swelled against the faded denim like a blister. Under his Brando-esque black leather motorcycle jacket, he wore a black t-shirt — *both* of which were against the school dress code. Pinned to the lapel of the jacket was a campaign button that said, "Don't knock the twist." He chewed elegantly on a match and examined his nails with deep interest.

"You're a man short," said Johnny D.

"You're like two men short, man" said Ralphie.

The stooges sniggered as Albert got to his feet.

"We'll stand yuz," the Stranger said with complete confidence.

"You and him?" queried Ralphie in disbelief.

"We get first outs," the Stranger crooned.

The two minor stooges waited for Moe's decision.

"Take it out, kid," pronounced Johnny D.

Albert and the Stranger went to half court to confer as the stooges set up a zone defense.

"What's your name, kid?" The Stranger asked.

"Albert."

"Albert? Jesus. Take it out, okay?"

"But..."

"Just pass me the ball, pal. Okay?"

Pal. Did he say "pal?"

"Okay," Albert agreed.

Albert put the ball into play and then witnessed a display of artistry and effortless technique unequalled before or since. Ralphie and Johnny D. immediately double-teamed the Stranger as Albert plodded toward the basket. Spinning low, the Stranger elbowed Ralphie in the nuts. Ralphie grabbed his crotch, opening his mouth wider than the laws of anatomy formally allow, issued a silent howl and sunk to his knees.

The Stranger then turned to Johnny D. and passed him the ball.

Really hard.

Right in the face.

It bounced off Johnny D.'s nose and right back into the Stranger's hands.

"Ow, fuck!" protested Johnny, squinting around his suddenly smashed and profusely bleeding beak. "Fuck!"

The Stranger drove toward the basket, the cleats on his heels clacking out a joyful rhythm. Jeff, still not fully comprehending what had just happened, was foolish enough to try to guard the Stranger as he made his lay-up. The Stranger went up for the shot — and raised his knee nonchalantly into Jeff's gut, eliciting a grunt of sharply expelled air that was worthy of any mambo champion. But instead of shooting, the Stranger passed the ball over to Albert.

Albert caught the pass reflexively, out of self-defense, and was too stunned to do anything but stand there.

"Shoot it!" the Stranger laughed. "Shoot it! And don't you fuckin' miss!"

Albert shot it.

And he didn't fuckin' miss.

Just as the ball hit the pavement, the bell rang for class. The Stranger got Albert to give him some skin. "Way to go, Daddy-o. Nice shot, Albert, baby."

Then the Stranger picked up the ball, tucking it under his arm like the head of Medusa, and strolled to where Johnny D. was leaning against the brick wall of the gym, unsuccessfully attempting to staunch the flow of bright red blood by stuffing Kleenex up his nostrils.

"I guess we win," announced the Stranger. "Nice game. Let's play again sometime."

"Fuck you, jerk-off" muttered Johnny D. under his breath, and he turned his back on the Stranger.

Now that was a mistake.

The Stranger heaved the ball — I mean really heaved it, overhand, like a major league pitcher — right at the back of Johnny D.'s head. The force of it slammed Johnny D.'s face against the rough red brick, and if his nose wasn't already broken, that probably did the trick. Raised a nice lump on his forehead, too.

Impressive.

The balled ricocheted off Johnny D.'s bonehead, bouncing way out into the grass, someplace.

Who cared?

"Albert," the Stranger was saying to himself as he and Albert headed inside. "Albert," as if tasting it. "So Albert. What's the scene?"

Thus, as if on a pale horse, came the Cicero Kid to Liberty Junior High School.

Nobody knew much about Derek Mueller, not even his name. Except that he was a "bad" kid from Cicero who lived with his mother. (She was reputed to be a whore, but the sources of this information were themselves quite suspect.) No apparent father present.

He was at first referred to as "that kid from Cicero," then as "that Cicero kid." Finally, one day at lunch, Derek overheard a whispered conversation about himself.

"Hey," he interrupted. "I ain't that Cicero kid. I'm *the* Cicero Kid." And he strode proudly away leaving mouths agape in his wake. Albert immediately followed after him, happy to play the unofficial role of "Pancho." He was, after all, comfortable as a remora fish, having been assigned a similar relationship to Bruce the Star. But Bruce disdained Albert as social company and wouldn't hesitate to participate in group derision of him. Albert sensed that the Cicero Kid would do no such thing. And so they soon became, for all intents and purposes, friends. Their companionship had a profound effect on each of them, as if their characters interacted synergistically, the strengths of one filling in the weaknesses of the other.

The Cicero Kid was no dummy. Indeed, he was a perfect example of a bright child so bored by the snail's pace of so-called education in public school that he found it smothering to be forced to keep that pace. He turned his frustration outward, into action, which got him in trouble. Albert suffered from a similar problem, but turned his energy inward, to day-dreaming, which meant he was quiet, which meant they left him alone.

One of the things the Cicero Kid learned from Albert was to write down his ideas instead of immediately putting them into action, and sometimes this helped.
Sometimes.
For Albert, The Cicero Kid was the sure-cure for shyness.
One day, at lunch, The Kid noticed Albert gawking at Melanie Johnson's tits as she sashayed by, each step precisely measured to effect maximum jiggle and bounce, while confidently pretending that she was unaware of the fact that everyone was watching her.

While every *other* male eye in the room followed her as eager as a cat to catch cream, The Kid chuckled out loud.
"C'mon, Albert, don't tell me you're in love with that little cunt."
"You don't think she's pretty?"
"Pretty stuck up. Listen man, like my old man says, you don't ever have to let a chick lead you around by your dick as long as you got one good hand left." He pumped his fist as if

pretending to shake a can of whipped cream, but that wasn't what he was pretending.

"Your *Dad* told you that?"

"What? Like you don't jerk off?"

"Me...?"

"C'mon, man. Everybody does it. You *got* to."

Before Albert could protest, The Kid pointed out Rita "Cookie" Charles across the room, snapping her gum expressionlessly, yet her eyes darting quickly around taking in everything. "Now *there* is a cool chick," The Kid said. "And I think she digs you, too, man."

"Oh, she does not."

"Yeah, she does. You should see how she looks at you when you're not looking. She thinks you're cool."

"Get out of here... Really...? Should I talk to her?"

"Sure. But you gotta let her see who you really are."

"What do you mean?"

Thus The Cicero Kid undertook to tutor Albert in the social graces.

They began Albert's tutelage with something easy: unbuttoning the top couple of buttons of Albert's shirt. This violation of the dress code made Albert feel like he was leaping up onto the roof of the school and yelling "Top of the world, Ma!" waiting to be gunned down by irate teachers. He was a bit disappointed when nothing happened.

Next, Albert attended TCK's school of good grooming and learned how to use pomade and a comb to force his cowlick into submission. He slicked his hair back tight on the sides, left a pompadour on top. He had to admit, it made him look a little like James Dean.

They found Albert a black leather car coat at the Salvation Army store and with what Albert made from his paper route plus a loan from The Kid, it became his. He wore it as if it were a Crusader's mantle.

Which it was.

But the best of all was one afternoon, after school when they were at The Kid's house. His mother was out, waitressing at Inga's Restaurant. In the basement, The Kid had set up his old man's weight-lifting bench and barbells. Why these were in his mother's possession, Albert didn't know. The Kid's dad had taken off a long time ago. But his Mom still carted his dad's stuff around everyplace they moved to, as if she actually believed that one day he'd show up again.

Albert had just completed a set of biceps curls when The Kid surprised him by suddenly sticking a magazine in front of his face. And not just any magazine. It was in Swedish and had a lot of pictures. Close up, full color pictures.

Of girls.

Naked girls.

And I mean *completely* naked.

The unexpected sight of an actual naked girl hit Albert like a bolt of electricity. He jumped nearly straight up in the air and back-pedaled as if the magazine might strike at him with venomous nipples. He tripped over a chair, spun around, managed to keep himself from falling, but knocked over a lamp. Like an all-star catching the winning pass, Albert was miraculously able to catch the lamp not an inch before it would have hit the floor.

The Kid laughed so hard he cried.

"Wow, man I didn't know you could fuckin' dance...!" The Kid practically choked. He gasped. He coughed. He laughed some more. He held his sides to keep them from splitting.

Albert could feel his face burning. Then The Kid did an impression of Albert's antics that was so ridiculous that Albert, in spite of himself, started to laugh, too.

"I can't believe it," The Kid gasped. "You looked just like a fuckin' cat! And you caught it! I can't believe you actually fuckin' caught it!!!"

A moment later, they were both laughing and couldn't seem to stop. Albert got a stitch in his side from it. It seemed like forever before they got a grip on themselves, wiped the tears from their eyes, got enough air to talk again.

"Albert the Cat," The Kid mused. "The Cat. The Cat-man. Never seen such a big cat get so scared by such a little pussy..." and they were off laughing again.

Thus it came to pass that Albert was transmogrified.

And became "Cat."

The Easter Invitational Basketball Championship. They called it an "invitational" but every school in the North Shore Conference was invited. It was a direct elimination tournament; one loss and you're out. The winner is undefeated. There were 16 schools so you had to win four games to take the championship. George Washington had won for the last three years, and was once again the favorite.

Opponents were drawn by lot. Liberty drew George Washington. The worst team in the league, without a single victory to its credit, would face-off against the undefeated league champions.

The news fell on the ears of the Liberty players like a damp, woolen shroud. If they had drawn Antioch, or even McNeil, they might have stood a chance — albeit a small one. But against George Washington? This was like a kid on a tricycle playing chicken with a Sherman tank.

"Well, fuck me," said The Cicero Kid, speaking more or less what everyone was thinking.

"Listen up," Coach Lubanski told them, pretending not to have heard the Kid. "You guys have had a tough season. You played some close games that could've gone either way. You're a lot better than the record shows."

Who the hell was he talking about?

"We've got another couple of weeks to get ready," he continued, "and we're going to work on our DEfense and..." He went on, never realizing he was now talking to himself.

Cat and the Cicero Kid walked home together after practice, as usual. It was nippy out and Cat huddled down in his jacket and pulled his stocking cap down over his ears. The Kid refused to wear a cap — ruined his hair, you know, and he'd rather freeze his ears off. He sported the same leather jacket in the dead of winter that he wore in summer — worn unzipped even now, in defiance of the cold. His sole concession to winter was a bulky turtle-necked sweater, but turtle-necks were cool, anyway.

They were quiet a long time, sharing a Lucky Strike as they sauntered along. Finally, The Kid took a last drag and flicked the butt over the Merle Street Bridge onto the frozen Wolf River below.

"Fuck," said the Kid. "This is the way it goes, you know? Guys like us, man we just get fucked over all the time and we're just supposed to lay down and take it, take it, take it. Well, fuck 'em. Cocksuckers. Fuck 'em all. You know those mother-fuckers at GW are celebrating right now. Easy win for round one. They think all they have to do is show up and we're gonna just shake in our fuckin' boots..."

"They beat us 120 to 40 last..."

"I know what the fuckin' score was, man! I was fuckin' there, too! Fuck the score." He took Cat earnestly by the lapels and put his face so close that, for a fleeting moment, Cat thought that The Kid was going to kiss him. "We got to make those candyass, mother-fuckers bleed for every mother-fucking point, man. We *got* to. It's like a moral imperative, daddy-o."

"How do we do that?"

The Kid let out a long sigh, his breath forming a solid white cloud. Cat almost expected the Kid's words to appear there, like in the comics.

"I don't know. Bribe the fuckin' tooth fairy, I guess."

They stopped at Woolworth's for fries and a coke. There was a lovely dark-haired waitress there who served them.

372

Diane Something. Deep brown eyes, teeth a little crooked, one eyebrow and could have had a mustache with no problem. But her smile was bright and her laugh was like ice tinkling in a glass of lemonade on a hot summer day. She immediately put The Kid's little speech completely out of Cat's mind. He wouldn't think about it again until the day of the game.

As usual, it was Albert's job to warm up Bruce the Star. They met at the gym early Saturday morning, a full hour before the bus would leave to take them on the 30-minute trip to the North Waukegan armory where the game would be held. Time for some good old one-on-one.

But from the moment Albert took the ball out, he knew that something was terribly, terribly wrong — he sank a shot from about the free-throw line.

First shot.

Swishhh.

Nothing but net.

Albert could not recall such an odd phenomenon ever happening before and stifled an urge to apologize.

Bruce was a little miffed, but shrugged it off the way you do with any freak occurrence of nature. He quickly took the ball out while Albert was still stunned — and missed an easy lay-up. The rebound sprang into Albert's arms. He dribbled a step or two closer to the bucket. Bruce, knowing that Albert couldn't shoot, guarded him only perfunctorily, making ready to pull in the rebound this time.

Swishhh.

Nothing but net.

It took a moment for Albert to realize that he'd just hit two in a row, and that last one was from what he always considered the wrong side of the basket; he'd just made that lay-up *left-handed*.

If the laws of gravity had suddenly been suspended and Albert had actually begun to fly, what followed could not have been more aberrant, could not have violated the natural laws governing the proper order of things more profoundly, nor could it have been more unbelievable to either of the two lads who experienced it.

For whatever reason — sunspots, the alignment of the planets, or the interference of leprechauns — Bruce the Star just couldn't sink a shot. He couldn't hit the basket with a sledge hammer. And Albert the Cat, presumably under the same influences, just couldn't miss. It was crazy. As if the polarities of the universe had flipped; hot was cold, black was white and Albert was Bruce and Bruce was Albert.

It was so crazy, in fact, that Albert almost literally couldn't believe it. It must be Candid Fucking Camera or something. To test the situation, Albert, at about the free throw line, turned his back to the basket and tossed a shot backwards without even looking.

Swishhh.

Nothing but net.

What the *fuck*?

Albert could only laugh.

The effect on Bruce was unflattering. The more Albert scored, the harder Bruce tried, and the harder he tried, the worse he did, and the worse he did, the more Albert scored. And Albert's giddy laughter didn't help matters.

When Coach Lubanski told the boys it was time to board the bus, Bruce let the ball bounce away and turned his back on Albert, without even the customary hand-shaking and "nice game." For a moment, Albert once again felt like running after Bruce to apologize, to re-assure the star of his talent and skill. To resume his rightful place as Bruce's foil.

Behind him, Albert heard the sound of dribbling. He turned just in time to see the Cicero Kid, who'd come in the side door, sink a smooth jump shot.

Swishhhh.

Nothing but net.

Albert took a breath to launch into the tale of the cosmic practical joke he'd just been part of, but the Kid cut him off at the pass.

"Fuck him," the Kid dismissed the star. "That punk ain't never been your friend, daddy-o. He was way over-do for an ass-kicking. You did him a fuckin' favor."

Maybe so.

One thing for sure: after that, Bruce never spoke to Albert again.

The second sign of the apocalypse came on the bus en route to the armory.

It was normal for there to be transistor radios playing (preferably not tuned in to the same station) joking, talking, singing — all marks of pre-game anticipation. But on this occasion, not a sound. Not a word, not a laugh, not a song. Though there were nine players, five cheerleaders, and three members of the band who, for their own twisted reasons, still attended games, it was as silent as stone.

It was weird. So unspeakably weird, that Joe the Bus-driver kept looking back in the rear-view mirror to check things out. He exchanged nervous glances with Coach Lubanski, who was sitting in his customary front seat. You can imagine the unspoken cinematic dialogue in that glance:

"Mighty quiet out there."

"Yeah. Too quiet."

The funereal mood continued unbroken when the Liberty team reached the armory, and as they filed, just as grimly, into the locker-room. No grab-assing, or jock-snapping, or other normal signs of male teenage life, were in evidence. Locker doors slammed open, uniforms were roughly pulled on and locker doors slammed shut again. No condemned criminal ever went to the chair with more resigned resentment than that of the Liberty players as they each made their way to the game floor.

By the time Cat and the Cicero Kid made their entrance, ambling last out of the locker-room, the George Washington team was already on the floor, doing their warm-up drills. They were dressed in slick white satin warm-ups suits with red and blue trim that matched their white satin uniforms. Each player's name was embroidered on the back. They had formed into three lines and in teams of three did a passing drill culminating in somebody sinking a shot — sometimes actually *dunking* a shot, since a number of their players must have hit that growth spurt early being six feet tall or better. By comparison, the Liberty center, a gangly black kid named Tom Murray, was just a hair under six-feet tall, and the tallest player on the Liberty team by a fistful of inches.

The George Washington half of the gym was over-flowing with their fans, parents, families, students (wearing red-white and blue George Washington sweaters), ten cheerleaders and what appeared to be about a fifty piece brass-band.

What, no fucking firing squad?

There were so many George Washington supporters, in fact, that many had to find seats on the Liberty half of the gym. This was no problem since it was only occupied by the Liberty team, the five cheerleaders, the three band members, the coach and Joe the bus-driver, easily contained in one section of the pull-out bleachers.

The George Washington cheerleaders were as perky and peppy as hummingbirds on cocaine and led the crowd in one roar after another, as happy as if their team had already won.

The Kid surveyed the all-American display of spirit that the George Washington mob put on, roughly equivalent to a lion salivating a little before biting off a nice hunk of zebra. He compared it to the Liberty High entourage, with its collection of three Blacks, two Puerto Ricans, a Jew and three Polish-Italian also-rans. He leaned close to Cat's ear and said, "Jesus Fuckin' Christ. Ain't we the fuckin' mutts of the universe."

Cat shrugged and said, "At the Battle of Thermopylae, 300 Spartans faced off against about a zillion Persians. Xerxes was trying to get the Spartans to fold. He told them that if they didn't, he'd have his army fire such a storm of arrows, that it would block out the fucking sun. Know what the Spartans said to him?"

"No, what?"

"They said 'Good. Then we'll fight in the shade.'"

The Cicero Kid grinned and nodded. "That's cool, man," he said. "That is real cool."

The Liberty High warm-up routine was a striking contrast to the crowd-pleasing antics of the George Washington squad. The Wolves simply lounged on the bench and watched the George Washington players do their stuff. Bruce the Star stared at his shoes. The Cicero Kid puffed on a Lucky. Occasionally, his searing glance would shift from the opposing team to their cheerleaders as their skirts flew up to reveal bright blue curve-clinging undershorts. The rest of the Wolves just sprawled and stared.

Not even the Liberty cheerleaders could rouse themselves. After one routine, drowned out completely by the hullabaloo from the George Washington side, they found a place on the bench and were still, sad as clowns when nobody comes to the circus.

"Okay, let's get on the floor," Coach Lubanski said with strained enthusiasm and he tossed a ball to center Tom Murray — who gave the coach a dead-pan stare as he let the ball hit his chest and roll away. Nobody went after it. The coach sat back down.

When the ref blew his whistle to summon the starting fives, the George Washington lads leaped into place like randy goats; the Liberty players pushed themselves up and dragged themselves onto the floor. The Kid paused to take one last drag on his Lucky, exhaling the smoke, if not in the ref's face, at least in his general direction.

"When those Spartan cats made the scene at Thermopylae...?" he asked Cat.

"Oh," Cat shrugged, "they all got killed."

The Kid laughed out loud.

Up went the ball, for the tip-off, tipped easily to GW. Dribbled down court to set up an easy...

Wait a minute. What the fuck?

As the GW number 17 dribbled past Gil Sanchez, starting a drive to the basket, The Cicero Kid darted out a hand and picked the ball away so deftly that GW17 took a few more steps dribbling the air before realizing he no longer had the ball. The Kid chased the ball down court, picked it up, dribbled twice and shot.

Two points.

In the gulf of surprised silence that followed, the ref gave outs to GW and number 17 said to the Kid, "I hope you enjoyed that shot, kid; it's your last one."

The Kid's reply is not recorded, but it inspired the GW player to grab him by the jersey. The ref stepped in just in time to prevent a scuffle.

"Okay," yelled coach Lubanski, "set up your zones." He was calling for a 1-2-2 defense, not because GW couldn't shoot from outside, but because he didn't know what else to say and he had to say something.

The Liberty players seemed not to hear. Instead of falling back into defense, they stuck to the GW players like a bad reputation, doing an impromptu full court man-to-man press. In frustration, the GW guard drove down, passed to his left forward, who spun a hook shot, not a bit shy about giving Big Tom Murray a knee in the process that doubled Tommy up. The ref called a foul — on Tom. As if they'd been waiting for that precise cue, players of both teams suddenly sprang at each other's throats and it took both refs and both coaches to separate them.

And that's how the game went, minute after minute. Like pulling teeth — provided the dentist was reaching your molars by way of your rectum. Both sides trading baskets; both sides fouling heavily. Bruce the Star fouled out at the end of the third quarter, but it hardly mattered. Something odd had happened to the Liberty team, something had energized them beyond all plausibility, and kids who hadn't so much as held the ball except in practice were actually scoring. Yet there remained an odd mood among them. As if taking their cue from the Cicero Kid, they were not jubilant, they were not smiling. It was more like desperation. They went after the ball like a drowning man goes after his next breath, with a singleness of purpose that is awesome to behold.

And so it came to pass that with three seconds left on the clock, the Liberty Wolves trailed the exasperated George Washington Patriots by a mere two points.

One single goal.

No one had come this close to beating GW in a long time and as remarkable as that was in itself, the game wasn't yet over.

It was Liberty's ball and Coach Lubanski called a time-out. As the team huddled around him he outlined a plan that was a marvel of Euclidian geometry and esoteric philosophy, the gist of which was incomprehensible to anyone listening. As the team took the floor, the Cicero Kid whispered in Big Tom's ear and got a nod in reply. The other members of the team fanned out trying to elude the GW players guarding them. The ref handed the Kid the ball and blew his whistle. Liberty had only seconds to put the ball in play or they'd turn the ball over to GW and that would be the end. But none of the Wolves could get free, and if GW intercepted or even stalled for just a few seconds then the game would be over, too.

With time almost up, the Cicero Kid did a strange thing: he shot the ball toward the basket. It was a nice high arc and it was clear that it was right on target. Except you can't do that;

it wouldn't count. The Kid had apparently gone nuts under the strain.

Then, just as the ball finished its descent into the hoop, Big Tom made a mighty leap, the leap of a Watusi warrior, caught and held the ball for the briefest moment and then slammed it into the bucket just as the buzzer sounded. The mere fact that he fell on his ass afterwards, looking more like the Scarecrow on the Road to Oz than Chaka Zulu, detracted nothing from the effect.

Some GW players fell to their knees, some struck the air with disbelieving fists. GW cheerleaders covered their mouths, eyes wide. One actually screamed. The rest of the stadium was silent. The ref signaled a basket. Two points. Liberty had tied the score and the game would go into over-time.

And indeed it did.

Not *one* over-time period, but *two*. And as the remainder of the game unfolded, the event was transformed from sport to struggle, from athletics to ordeal, from game to fight.

By the end, five Liberty players (and seven GW players) had fouled out and in the final seconds of the second over-time period Liberty was obliged to play with only the four remaining men on the floor. GW now led by a point and the exhausted Liberty kids fell back to half court on defense as GW brought the ball down. They did it slowly, passing a lot, crossing over half-court just in time to avoid a penalty. Their strategy was clear: protect that one point lead and let time run out.

And that was when the Cicero Kid rode in once more. He feinted toward one GW guard, making him pass the ball, then as he did, The Kid hurled himself at it to try for an interception. He stretched out barely grazing the ball with a fingernail — but enough to send it bouncing away. Both teams converged on the loose ball and engaged in what appeared to be a frantic game of hot potato. In the end, it was The Kid who grabbed it and bolted for the basket. But three GW players were on him. All over him. He not only missed the shot but in the frenzy, caught an elbow squarely in the nose.

No bucket. No points. Two seconds on the clock. Face it. Game over. The GW crowd started cheering, as much from relief as anything else.

Not so fast.

The ref was calling a foul. And it was *against George Washington*.

Somebody brought out an ice pack and put it on the Kid's face. The ref looked the Kid over, but the Kid brushed him off, insisting that the bright blood streaming down his mouth from his swelling nose and his bloodshot eyes were nothing but the merest inconvenience. He tossed the ice pack away with clear disdain and did his best saunter, though unsteadily, to the free throw line where he would get two shots.

The Kid shook his head to clear the bees out, squinted at the basket and tossed the ball casually into the air.

Swish.

Nothing but net.

Cat got the rebound, walked it to the ref. The ref handed the Kid the ball and Cat leaned over to whisper into the Kid's ear.

"Don't you fuckin' miss," he said.

The Kid grinned a bold, bloody grin, wiped his nose and mouth with his arm, bounced the ball twice and shot.

And he didn't fuckin' miss.

George Washington took the ball out and with one second left on the clock, their number 8 made a full court last ditch overhand heave at the bucket — and nearly made it. It rattled in and out as the buzzer ended.

It was over.

From the GW crowd, much moaning and wailing and gnashing of teeth. Some GW players crumbled, emotionally and physically exhausted, to the floor. Cheerleaders cried, hugging each other. A couple players cried, too. The GW coach looked like he was going to cry but had the stones to cross the floor to Coach Lubanski, who was clearly struck completely dumb by what had just happened. They shook hands.

"Your boys played one hell of a game there, Coach," the GW coach said.

As for the Liberty players, no cheers of exaltation. No jubilant hugging, huddling or shoulder slapping. Ignored by the George Washington players, they simply walked off the floor, into the locker-room.

And into legend.

It didn't matter that they would lose their next game against so-so St. Michael's. It didn't matter that their victory over George Washington was the only game they won all season. All that mattered was that David had, for once, beaten Goliath.

Unfortunately, Goliath didn't take it very well. The game was followed by a virtual riot, with George Washington students smashing all the windows on Liberty's bus, slashing the tires for good measure. It looked like a rumble might become the main event of the afternoon. But somebody called the police and the mob grudgingly dispersed. Liberty was allowed to borrow a George Washington bus so they could get home, and was more or less escorted out of town by the cops.

Meanwhile the three geeks from the Liberty marching band had been on the phone calling everybody they could think of with the incredible news. The announcement was generally followed by "No, this is *not* a joke; I'm serious!" A fair number of students and parents were gathered in the gym to welcome the victorious Liberty team home.

They took The Kid off the bus and right over to see Dr. Freedman. The Kid's nose did, in fact, turn out to be broken.

Cat was suddenly alone on this uncomfortable sea of people and started edging for the door.

"Hey, Albert."

The honey-smooth voice and the succulent scent of
Melanie Johnson stopped him in his tracks.

"Hi," he replied.

"You sure played good today," she said. Played *well*, he
mentally corrected her.

"Thanks."

"How come some people call you 'Cat'?"

"Umm. It's just a, you know, nickname."

"It's cool. I like it. Can I call you Cat?"

"Sure."

She turned on her high beams.

"There's gonna be a party at Silvia's. You're coming
aren't you?"

Albert thought a moment. Well, fuck. Here she is, tits and
all.

"*I'm* going to be there," she added to close the sale.

"Thanks, but I don't think so," Cat said. "I have something
else I have to do."

For a moment, Albert regretted being the cause of that
kicked-puppy look that fell across Melanie's face. Clearly, no
one had ever said anything to her before that had even
distantly resembled the word "no."

That night, Albert crashed at the Cicero Kid's house. The
Kid was pretty out of it, nose all taped up and everything.
Hung out with the Kid's mom, who was very cool, herself.
The three of them watched TV and told jokes, ate pizza. And
they never said one single word about the game.

Oh, yeah. About that fight.

Well, you know what happened, right? It was such a mismatch that nobody in the States would sanction it. So they
fought it in Japan. Underdog challenger James "Buster"
Douglas fought the fight of his career and beat Iron Mike
Tyson to a pulp. Knocked him out as clearly, cleanly,
undeniably, indisputably, unequivocally and irrevocably as if
he'd dropped a house on him in Munchkinland.

David doesn't beat Goliath very often but when it happens,
it's sweet.
And you just never know.

To the credit of those college boys, they paid up.
That was 25k to me.
I didn't need the money, but I took it.
They needed the lesson.

Star Dancer, fly me away
Ride me off to a better day
Your hooves barely touching the ground
I don't care if we never come down

("Star Dancer," Spartacus Jones)

CHAPTER TWENTY-EIGHT:
STAR DANCER

Some say that when the Taino Indians first saw the Conquistadors on horseback, they thought horse and rider were one being. Now, having known Star Dancer awhile, it's easy for me to understand how you could make that mistake. He responds to the merest knee pressure or shifting of weight so immediately that it's almost like telepathy.

Hell, maybe it *is* telepathy.

Star Dancer is an 18-year-old Appaloosa gelding. He's gray with patches of black like an approaching storm. Like most Appaloosas he has a marvelous combination of speed, stamina and toughness. The rolling rhythm of his walk is a mantra for relaxation, soothes the stiffness from hips and back. His canter is like soaring. But what really sets him apart is his unique shuffle, "Indian shuffle" some people call it. It's a four-beat gate that's smooth and easy on both horse and rider, a gate that eats up the miles so effortlessly that his kind were sometimes referred to as "hundred mile a day" horses.

There's something I don't understand about horses. They're so powerful and yet so gentle. They could easily buck us off, bludgeon us into gory pulp with those hooves. I wonder why they don't. Why do they let us ride them? Why have they carried loads, dragged plows, pulled wagons, carried us into deadly battle, lived and died with us and for us?

A guy I know says that after the Creator made humans, he saw how small and weak and stupid we turned out. He was pretty depressed about it. The Horse Chief asked the Creator why he was so sad, and when the Creator told him, the Horse Chief took pity on us. Don't worry, the Horse Chief promised the Creator, we'll look after them. And horses have been trying to help us get our heads out of our asses ever since.

I haven't known Star Dancer very long, but we seemed to have a certain rapport right from the start. I enjoy his company — maybe I enjoy the company of anyone who can tolerate mine. I spend more time grooming him than I absolutely have to, delighting in the warmth of him, tracing along the contours of his muscles with the brush, following with my hand, combing out his tail and mane — even when I know he's going to go right back out and frolic in the mud. I've sat in his stall for long times, just being with him. Talking to him. Listening to him. Seeing what I can learn by osmosis.

Horses know secrets.

But they don't proselytize.

Once, I fell asleep, stayed there with him, stretched out on the hay, my back propped against the gate. Awakening to the soft, warm nuzzle of his nose, just before dawn.

I turn him out on warm nights, leading him out to his paddock, navigating along the rutted path by starlight. After I walk him in past the gate and slip off his halter, sometimes I climb up on the fence and stay awhile, breathing in the soul-refreshing combination of earth smells aloft on the breeze, looking out at a billion other worlds that have got to be better than this one, and feeling about as important as a fly speck. Often Star Dancer will come and stand near me, nudge my leg with the side of his face until I pet his brow in long strokes

from between his eyes, down to his nose. Or the side of his
neck. He likes that.

And carrots.

Some horses prefer apples, but Star Dancer is a carrot man.

I always bring him some nice carrots. Sometimes I munch
one along with him. I figure I hate to drink alone, so maybe...
Once in a while, I put a carrot in my jacket pocket and let him
ease it daintily out with his teeth. He'd have made a great
pickpocket.

Maybe, if I'd met him earlier, when I was a kid, I'd have
turned out to be somebody different, too.

One evening, I was playing with Star Dancer in the indoor
arena, and I had the feeling something was different. He
seemed nervous, on edge, like a guy who's been on a cocaine
binge. Walking out and trotting, he kept sidling, turning his
head to watch me out of the corner of his eye, as if he didn't
want to takes his eyes off me. The way you'd keep your eye
on a guy you thought was going to give you one right in the
back.

It puzzled and disturbed me. I decided to ask Jill what she
thought the matter was. Jill and her wife owned the place and
had grown up with horses. I figured she might know.

Then, it dawned on me that my keys were still hanging
from my belt. There are quite a few keys on that ring, attached
to a big brass hook that's a souvenir from the couple of years I
spent on a ship. Used to carry my bos'n keys on that hook. I
usually leave them with my coat in the tack room because
losing them in the arena would mean a search through dirt and
dung that would make finding a needle in a haystack seem as
easy as bottom-dealing an ace.

I wondered if the jingle of those keys might be distracting
Star Dancer. I asked Jill to hang on to them for me and tossed
them over to her. The keys jangled loudly as she fumbled
them and with the sound of it Star Dancer snorted and bolted. I

spoke to him, reassuring him and in a moment, he settled back down. And for the rest of the time, he was perfectly fine, back to his old self again.

We did some easy cantering — he knows how to do it but I need the practice — then sprinted around a few barrels — he loves barrel racing — and then walked a few laps. I slid off his back, but he was still not cooled down completely so I walked him around the arena a few more laps, slow and easy. Jill kept us company and I asked her what she thought about Star Dancer's aversion to my keys.

"Horses are smart. Something new and unexplained in their environment, and they get their guard up, ready to run. That's how they survive. Being really aware of potential threats."

Sure. But keys?

"Sometimes a horse will have a pet peeve like that. Usually it's from a bad experience. In Dancer's case," she added, "it may have something to do with his being abused some back before we got him."

"What do you mean, 'abused'?"

"Well, there was this guy. Hired hand. A real Marlborough man cowboy, if you know what I mean."

I knew what she meant.

"One time he laid into Dancer with a shovel."

"He did *what*?"

"Didn't hurt him real bad or anything but..."

"A shovel? " I said. "He hit him with a fucking *shovel*?"

"He didn't last long," Jill nodded. "When Bonnie — you met Bonnie right?"

I had. Bonnie was the B in B&J Stables.

"Bonnie told his boss about it and they canned his ass right away."

"Not soon enough," I said.

"No, I guess not."

"You think Dancer's carrying a scar from that?

She shrugged. "All I know is that this guy had a big old key ring, kind of like yours. It jingled when he walked. You could hear him coming."

No wonder Star Dancer and I got along so well. We had some history in common. We walked another lap or so in quiet. Off in one corner, a pair of tabby barn cats were hunting for a mouse in a small haystack to the amusement of Sheba, a grand dame German Shepherd whose only remaining duty was to enjoy her retirement. Finally, as we headed for the paddocks I said — very casually — "So this shovel guy. You remember his name?"

I don't know why they called him "Red."

There was nothing red about him. Except maybe where hard drinking put blotches on his cheeks and bloodshot in his empty blue eyes. He was skinny as an ice pick and he had the look of a man who was just as dangerous.

When your back was turned.

He liked to hang out in this roadhouse called "Cactus Jack's Saloon." The place was so old they still had a jukebox over by the pool table, even though on weekends they might have a DJ come in — on rare occasions a live band — and people would jam the place for country line dancing, which, as far as I could tell, was an unpleasant form of close order drill.

Okay, I'm not a real big country fan. Per se.

Beer bellies and fancy belt buckles. Imitation alligator or ostrich skin boots — or, worse real alligator or ostrich skin. Skoal tucked into the lip. Cowboy hats apparently nailed to their fucking heads. And those were the women.

Somebody had selected an ancient recording of Hank Williams Jr. doing his dad's tune, "Your Cheatin' Heart," and it started up just as I slid onto a barstool a couple seats down from Red. I almost laughed out loud to see myself in the mirror: a ragged camo vest over a faded Levi jacket; black chamois shirt, jeans, work boots. "John Deere" baseball cap tilted down over my eyes, partly to hold my wig on. Most of my attire was from a Goodwill Thrift Shop.

It wasn't my style. But then, what color is a chameleon, anyway?

And it matched up well with the uniform that Red was wearing. He had a woodland camo baseball cap pushed back on his head, revealing sandy hair that matched the scruff of beard on his chin. Undershirt stained around the neck. Plaid flannel shirt, hunter orange vest. His shirttails hung out under the vest. Levis. Harness boots. And hanging from his belt, a big old truckers' key ring on a heavy chain.

I order a beer, sipped it from the bottle, just like he did, putting a stretch in my vowels that might suggest I was raised somewhere south of the Manson-Nixon Line. Just like he did, I leered at the buxom waitress who showed lots of cleavage above her ruffles. I made a comment about her breasts and he sniggered.

And that was the start of a beautiful friendship.

We got to talking. Bought each other a few beers. Made crass comments about pussy. Mostly I listened. Nodded a lot. Asked him what he thought about this, what he thought about that.

It was almost too easy.

I worked it into the conversation that my daughter had a birthday coming up and that I wanted to get her something really special — something my cunt of an ex wouldn't be able to top. Maybe a horse of her own. I told him I knew of a horse for sale that sounded like a pretty good deal, too.

Then I led him to questions he could ask me, letting him think it was all his idea, showing him how stupid I was when it came to horses, letting him flaunt all he thought he knew. Letting him walk into the trap all by himself, using just his ego and a little greed for bait.

It usually does the trick.

By the end of the night, my new pal had agreed to meet me the next morning to go out and have a good look at this horse I wanted to buy. Give me the benefit of his expert opinion for fifty bucks. I noticed, when he left, his keys jangled loudly at his side as he walked, like spurs.

I had already picked out a good place.

It was empty and for sale and the nearest neighbors were more than a shout — or scream — away. I had checked with the realtor to find out if I could see the place, but there was no way anyone would be showing anybody a house on a Sunday, they informed me rather indignantly. Obviously speaking to an infidel. I had tucked the "for sale" sign out of sight, behind the barn.

I met Red at the appointed hour. We drove out in my pickup truck — a "borrowed" truck. Told some jokes on the way. Some dirty ones. Some racial ones. Sipped some Jack Daniels from a pint bottle. I explained that the owner wouldn't be home — he and the family would be in church, but he'd said I was welcome to come out anytime.

I pulled way in the driveway so nobody happening by would spot the truck. We got out and headed for the barn. I let him go in first.

I think there was a moment when, on some level, he became conscious of how quiet it was in there. He might even have suspected that something was amiss.

He didn't see any tack, or gear.

Didn't see a horse trailer.

Didn't see any horses, for that matter.

And he didn't see the shovel I had left just inside the door.

Adam Adrian Crown

You had your way
Now you must pay
I'm glad that you're sorry now

("Who's Sorry Now?" Connie Francis)

CHAPTER TWENTY-NINE:
LAY BACK AND ENJOY IT

There's hardly anyone in Onondaga Lake Park at two o'clock on a Wednesday afternoon. Lunch hour is over. The kids aren't out of school yet. So it's a good place to meet discreetly.

It was a battleship-grey day and the chilly northeast breeze smelled like a storm coming. I stood a couple of feet from the slabs of rock along the lakeshore and tossed greasy popcorn to the ducks. I pretended not to hear the car door slam in the deserted parking area. Just for practice, I listened to The Judge's footfalls as she approached across the twig-littered grass, and estimated the distance between us from the sound.

"Hello, Mr. Smith," said The Judge. "Smith. Not very original, is it?"
"Just have a peek at how many Smiths there are in the phone book," I said. When you do what I do, you don't want to be original. You want to be invisible. But she knew that. "Smith" is good. I use it a lot.

The Judge handed me a manila envelope. Inside were a few photos, some newspaper clippings. I felt like Mr. Phelps from the Impossible Missions Force. I glanced at them and then watched her gaze out at the approaching fog. She was a striking woman with a no-nonsense air of command about her. She was lean and looked like a very fit fifty — but I knew she was a good deal older than that.

"The girl is Christy Jacobsen," she said. "Daughter of Peter Jacobsen, a plumber, and Sherry Jacobsen, home-maker."

I looked at what appeared to be a photo xeroxed from a high school year book. A plain, but pleasant blonde with an overbite that gave her a pixie-ish quality.

"On or about September 30," The Judge continued, "she was working at the Dunkin' Donuts over on James Street. When she got off work, it was late — around eleven p.m. She just missed the last bus, and it was starting to rain. The three young men were waiting for her and offered to drive her home."

The photos of the three boys were better. One kneeling proudly in a football uniform. The other two, equally cheesy headshots. Graduation portraits, I guessed.

"They took her out behind the old Bowl-Mor and raped her repeatedly for several hours."

I nodded. "Cops?"

"Oh, yes. She filed a complaint. Went through the entire charade."

"What happened?"

"A working class townie girl versus the cream of the college crop, complete with indignant parents and very expensive lawyers. What do you think happened?"

"I think they walked."

"You're very perceptive, Jack. Have I ever told you that?"

"All the time. How's the kid doing?"

"PTSD, of course. She's getting counseling at the Rape Crisis Center. I think, eventually, she'll recover from it, for the most part. But such things leave deep scars. They took something from her she can never restore."

"Understood," I said.

"Do you know what they said to her?" The Judge took some popcorn from my bag and tossing it casually toward a pair of ducks. "Might as well lay back and enjoy it. Can you imagine anyone actually saying that? Lay back and enjoy it. "

There was something in the Judge's voice that sounded tight, barely under control. I wondered if she had some personal connection with this case. But I didn't ask her, and she wouldn't have told me anyway.

"I'll take care of it," I said.

"I know it's awfully close to home."

"It's all right."

"Are you sure? I don't want you to compromise yourself."

"I'm sure."

I tossed the popcorn dregs onto the ground, crumpled up the bag and stuck it in my pocket.

"Particulars?" I asked.

"I'll leave that to your creative imagination. Lex talionis." That was her way of saying "make the punishment fit the crime."

"Consider it done," I told her.

When I was a kid, we moved out of the city to the "Chain o' Lakes" area. The place we lived in was right on Fox Bay. I mean right on the bay, too. Our house was only about 50 yards from the water's edge.

The place we lived in had been intended as a summer cottage, but, of course, we lived in it year around. It was built way before the building codes were in force, when they're enforced. So, being a summer cottage, there was little or no insulation in the walls. Summer was fine, but winter?

Grim.

Old oil stove shivering out heat. Plastic taped over the windows. The larger cracks in the walls we stuffed with rags.

The water pump was located in an added-on "back room," the floor of which was mostly rotted away. It was an old pump that quit on us frequently. On those occasions, while it was waiting to be fixed — my old man spent most of his time working for the landlords in lieu of paying rent — us kids, my little brother David, my older sister, Kay and I, would be obliged to carry armloads of milk jugs to the landlords' broken down hotel next door, and beg to have them filled from the tap. These were my half-siblings. I have an older half-brother somewhere, too, whom I've never met. None of us had the same father, and possibly my old man wasn't really my old man, which might explain some of the beatings.

The landlords had quite a scam going on my old man (if, in fact, he was my old man). They calculated his wages at a fraction of what they would have had to pay anyone else for the same work and after they deducted his bar bill and the rent, there was little, if anything left. Lots of times he would come out in the hole and wind up putting in hours for free, just to pay for his booze. Doing any repairs on our house came last, after putting in his time for the landlords.

My old man spent most of his free time drunk. And when he was drinking he had two favorite pastimes. One of them was conjuring up some "reason" (in his alcohol-twisted mind) to beat my brother or me, or both, with whatever he had handy.

Sometimes it indeed was his hand, though he much preferred his heavy leather belt, using the buckle end if he felt particularly irked. But he'd settle for using his feet, too, for that matter. He loved to grab fistfuls of hair then drag us across the room and heave us into a wall.

He'd have been a hell of a bowler.

His other hobby was molesting my sister.

I was around seven or eight when I first witnessed one of those awkward, uneven wrestling matches. It was in the summer. I was supposed to be asleep on the living room couch. The house was dark except for the light from the TV screen. Alfred Hitchcock Presents. I pretended to be asleep so I could watch it.

My old man called Kay over to him. She was probably thirteen or fourteen at this time. Once she came close enough to the easy chair, he grabbed her wrist and pulled her onto his lap, entwining her with his arms and legs. She fought to get loose, but he was too strong for her. He was a strong guy.

I couldn't help watching, even though I really didn't know what it was about. It looked completely goofy to me. My old man must've caught me looking then, because he laughed. Big joke.

Reflexively, I gave a little laugh, too.

My sister looked up at me, right into my eyes. A strand of her auburn hair had fallen down across her nose, but it didn't hide the feral gleam of combined despair, fear and anger that burned in them.

"That's right, you bastard," she said to me, "Go on and laugh."

My heart sank and I felt my cheeks flush red. My stomach churned violently.

Something was wrong here.

Very, very wrong.

I wasn't sure what it was.

But I didn't do anything to help her. Maybe because I didn't know what to do. Maybe because I was afraid of what would happen to me if I gave the old man an actual reason to beat on me for a change. Whatever it was, I didn't try to help her, and I can't seem to forgive myself for that. My therapist says it's unfair for me to judge myself as a child by the standards I have as a man. She says I need to forgive myself, but I can't quite manage it.

I know I'll never forget the look in my sister's eyes.

Everything I needed to hatch a plan I found in the materials I'd gotten from The Judge. She's nothing, if not well-organized and methodical. There were school records, police records, DMV information, copies of statements and court transcripts. It was a lot more than I needed. I like to keep things simple.

My first stop was "Captain Jack's," a biker bar just outside Solvay. Sounds very jaunty and nautical unless you know that "captain jack" is an old euphemism for heroin. Lots of leathermen frequent Jack's along with the more mainstream bikers, if we could call any biker mainstream.

Harleys by the dozen.

Troubles by the score.

Springsteen on the jukebox, prison tats galore.

Reefer smoke in the air. Lots of weapons in plain sight. Anything goes. Cops don't go in there; they pretend they don't know about the place, or that it's in somebody else's jurisdiction.

I waited outside for Bulldog, standing in the leeward side of a tree so I'd blend in between its shape and its shadow. No hurry. He'd be out sooner or later. I'd met Bulldog in prison. He was in for possession and resisting. He resisted some cop right into the emergency room. One day Bulldog was undiplomatic enough to refuse an invitation to join the White Aryan Brotherhood, posing his refusal in very amusing, though anatomically unlikely terms. Some neo-nazi geek tried to shank the Bulldog in the shower. I happened to be there and saw it coming before Bulldog did.

It also happens that I don't care much for that nazi shit either. But maybe I just felt snubbed that they didn't invite me to join up.

Anyway, the shank never made it into Bulldog and the neo-nazi geek never made it out of the shower. In one of those twists of fate that the gods love to laugh about, a guard — who happen to be black — testified to the self-defense nature of my actions, and I was acquitted of any wrong-doing in the untimely demise of the aforementioned Aryan asshole.

As a result, Bulldog felt he owed me a favor.

Now I had come to collect.

It was just after 2 a.m. (bars are supposed to close at 1 a.m.) when Bulldog emerged, tugging at his zipper. He ambled unsteadily toward his chopper and I stepped out of the shadows toward him. He spun into a crouch, whipping out a knife and clicking the blade open in less time than it takes for C4 to go from solid to gas.

"You want somethin' moth'r-fucker?"

"How about a little kiss, Petunia?"

He relaxed, stood up and favored me with that grimace that few people other than his mother would describe as a smile.

"No shit. Long fuckin' time, man."

We shared a jailhouse handshake and spared each other the "what've you been doing with yourself" bullshit. Instead, I explained what I needed and he was more than agreeable and certain he could set it up for me.

"After this," I offered, "we'll be even."

"No, we won't, brother."

The first guy was easy. I spotted him at Friday afternoon football practice. Allstar bone-crusher. 6'5", had to be 250 if he was a pound. Blonde and blue. Jarhead buzzcut. Had the tell-tale acne and chipmunk jowls of a steroid sissy. I already knew the kind of car he drove and the plate number. I used a slim-jim to pop the lock and waited for him in the back seat. When I slipped my arm around his throat, I could see his eyes in the rearview mirror, wide and wild as the eyes of a trapped animal, which, of course, was what he was. Putting judicious pressure on his carotid arteries with my biceps on one side and forearm on the other, in a few seconds I had squeezed him out.

I cuffed his hands behind him, smoothed a piece of gray duct tape over his mouth and pulled a ski cap down over his eyes. Shoving him over, I got behind the wheel and drove him to the spot I'd lined up. I made sure he could breathe, duct-taped him to a chair, which in turn was secured to an old water pipe, and left him.

The second guy I had to hunt down. He'd cut football practice — he was the super-hero quarterback so he was apparently entitled to blow it off from time to time. It probably didn't hurt that his father was a big wheeler & dealer in Albany where he had been a member of the state legislature.

No problem. It was easy to pass for his uncle and get his class schedule from the half-witted freshman work-study clerk.

The kid's self-absorbed nature was evident in his perfectly sculptured hair and his expensive chinos. Unfortunately, even though I tailed him all over hell, he was a very gregarious lad and seemed to always be in a crowd. Finally, in the late evening, he was sprawled out in a secluded spot with joint in one hand and a co-ed in the other, getting high and putting in some serious make-out time. More serious, in fact, than the lady in question really wanted. Their necking turned into an ever-escalating contest of slap and tickle as I watched from the cover of immaculately manicured shrubbery about 25 feet away. My subject was determined to get the young woman's panties off while she adroitly countered with body shifting to make it impossible. I had a feeling it was going nowhere and started closing in.

Finally the young woman sat up and re-arranged her clothes.

"Damn it, Steve, I said no!"

"Aw, come on, Tanya..."

"No. And I mean it."

"Okay, okay," he shushed her, and drew her back into his arms. About a second later, his hand was at her panties again. That did it.

Tanya stood up sputtering and stormed off in a huff and a half.

"Hey, Tanya," he called after her. "Come on, will ya?"

No answer.

"Fucking cunt," he muttered to himself. "Tanya! Come on, Baby, I said I'm sorry..."

He laid back and sighed, plans ruined.

"Shit," he pronounced. "Fuckin' lesbo."

Then the shrubbery rustled a little and he brightened, shaded his eyes with one hand so he could look toward the lights, toward the direction Tanya had gone, certain that she had decided to return to his irresistible self.

"Hey, Baby..." he began.

It wasn't Tanya.

The third guy, the last of the bunch, rode a Honda. Guys like Bulldog, who ride hogs, consider a Honda one step above training wheels. The bike was in the shop for repairs and when the owner came to pick it up several friends were waiting. But they were my friends, not his.

Actually, Bulldog's friends.

The ancient remains of the gas station was an eerie reminder of another place and time, like a relic of a lost civilization. It was the Sinclair brontosaurus sign that lay rusting out front, leaning against an antique coke machine — the coke you sip, not snort — now an apartment complex for rodents, that sent me off into a rush of déjà vu. Maybe karma is like musical chairs. Until the music stops you never know who's going to be the good guy and who's going to be the bad guy.

The place was so far off the beaten path you had to know exactly where it was and exactly how to get there or you'd never find it except by accident. There was nothing for miles around. Not even a phone.

It was perfect.

I got there at about 11 p.m.

Inside were my three guys, taped and gagged, sitting back to back, more or less, in a circle on the floor. Bulldog was there, and about six or seven other bikers — and a couple mamas, too. Lounging around on their choppers, joking with each other, drinking Jack Daniels, snorting coke, and a couple were pumping up.

If you're a fitness nut, I suppose you might think that by "pumping up" I mean they were lifting weights.

Not exactly.

There are men who have a real fetish about penis size and enlarge theirs by regularly putting them in a vacuum tube for various lengths of time. Apparently this increases blood flow to the penis and increases the capacity of the spongy tissue inside to hold more blood, thereby gradually thickening it. At the same time, the process stretches the suspensory ligaments, allowing more of the shaft of the penis to emerge. Over a long period of time — years, I mean — the accumulated effect on some of these guys can be impressive.

Grotesque, maybe, but impressive.

Take, for example, the mustached bear wearing leather chaps. I didn't know his name. He was certainly at least nine or ten inches long in the pumping tube, and filling it wall to wall, at least 7 or 8 inches around. And he was definitely not the biggest guy there. Of course, I have no idea how big his cock was to begin with. It might always have been huge.

The Viking-looking body-builder, right next to him, who was presently being jacked off in the tube by a stiletto-lean red-head with a Harley tattoo on her arm, was substantially larger in girth, if not in length. I was in no mood to get out my tape measure. But some of the others called him "fireplug."

The three guests of honor were observing these preparations with wide-eyed terror as I approached and stood over them. I made a slow, casual circle around them, looking each one in the eye real hard. In my favorite short story, The Cask of Amontillado, Edgar Allen Poe gave a pretty good model for revenge. The mark has to know who's punishing him and why, and he has to know there's nothing he can do about it.

"Christy Jacobsen says hello," I told them.

The effect of hearing their victim's name was profound. The steroid giant growled and struggled vainly against his bonds. The quarterback began to cry and a dark, wet spot appeared on the front of his chinos. The third boy squeezed his eyes tightly shut and hung his head low.

"Listen carefully, gentlemen," I said and kicked the foot of the third boy to get his undivided attention. "Here's what's on the agenda. I'm going to give you the opportunity to fully comprehend the ramifications of your actions. You're going to feel what Ms. Jacobsen felt when you raped her. And you're going to feel the after-effects, go through just what she's going through now. Afterwards, if you feel like you're entitled to some kind of payback, I'll tell you right now, if you go anywhere near that girl or her family in any way, I'll know about it. And then I'll come back. And then I'll kill you. Slowly. Am I clear?"

The third kid seemed resigned to it more than the others. I think he knew he had done wrong and that he had it coming. I almost felt sorry for him.

The gang had their pumps off now and were jacked up to cartoon proportions. They began smearing heavy layers of vaseline onto their erections.

"So," I told the football heroes. "That's what's going to happen. And there's nothing you can do about it. So my advice to you is, hey, lay back and enjoy it."

I nodded to the waiting crew and headed for the door.

A couple of guys grabbed the steroid giant and dragged him out, none too gently. He fought it, but he was about as successful as a shy and diminutive 17-year-old girl had been against three college jocks.

They didn't bother to take off his jeans, just sliced the crotch seam with a wicked-looking Bowie knife and tore the legs down. His flanks were acned and there were definite needle tracks on his glutes. A couple of whacks to the testicles took the fight out of him. Mr. Leather Chaps came over while a couple of others leaned the kid over the saddle of a bike. He slapped the boy on the ass.

Hoots and whistles from the crowd.

"Slam 'im, Hon," hissed the red-head.

"Ride him, fuckin' cowboy! Yeehah!" called out somebody in the back.

"Go, Marco," encouraged the Viking. I think Viking was into Marco.

Marco poised over the kid's flanks and started fitting his cock to the job.

"Hey," chirped the red-head, "I think he digs you, baby."

Bulldog was leaning against the doorjamb, elegantly cleaning his fingernails with the point of his knife.

"You ain't stayin' for the party?" he asked me.

"Not my cup of tea," I said.

"You want copies if I take some pictures?

"I don't think I'll need them, but thanks." We did the jailhouse handshake. "Now we're even, brother."

"No we ain't, brother," he snorted.

It was cool outside. Autumn was lingering before making way for winter. The moon was up and there was a soft, southerly breeze. It felt soft and warm on my face.

This is the point from which I could never return
And if I back down now then forever I burn
This is the point from which I could never retreat
Cause If I turn back now there can never be peace
This is the point from which I will die or succeed
Living the struggle, I know I'm alive when I bleed

("Point of No Return," Immortal Technique)

CHAPTER THIRTY: BENNY

I have a photograph.

It's a railroad station in Germany in the late 1930's or early 1940's. All down the track, disappearing into the horizon, is a line of cattle cars with people crammed in like sardines. There are hundreds, hell, maybe thousands more people swarming outside the train cars, trying to climb up into them, getting a boost up from one another. Men, women and children. Elderly and infants. On many, the yellow Star of David is visible on their clothing.

Now the hell of it is, I can only make out six or seven, maybe eight German soldiers. There's a couple of guys with grease guns on top of the train cars, about three or four cars apart. There's a guy who looks like an officer pointing out into the crowd and he's flanked by a couple more bullyboys with machine guns. That's about it. Now, I don't know, maybe there's a full brigade just out of frame. It's possible.

Here's what bothers me: Why didn't somebody jump the guys with the guns, beat their brains in and make a run for it? Maybe you'd still wind up getting killed, but at least you'd go down swinging, maybe even take a couple of those Nazi supershitheads with you. Wouldn't that be better than meekly getting on those trains?

I'm not saying this to suggest there's anything cowardly or stupid about those Jews. Maybe they hadn't heard what was going on in those camps. If they'd heard, maybe they didn't believe it. It would be hard to believe. You wouldn't *want* to believe that anyone was capable of doing such horrible things to so many innocent people.

Still, in your heart of hearts, you must know that nobody rounds you up in the middle of the night and packs you into a train car at gunpoint for your own good. Wouldn't you just *know* something bad was up?

I spent a lot of late nights puzzling over that one. Finally, a friend and mentor explained it to me. He was a 16.2-hand leopard appaloosa gelding named Benny.

I was in the barn grooming him, getting ready to tack up for a ride. He was good at ground-tying, and would stand there for you until hell froze over or you asked him to move.

It happened that one of the barn cats had just had a litter, and one of the kittens was wobbling down the center aisle, on the prowl. A tiny grey puffball. Tail sticking straight up like she was giving the world the finger, eyes watery, not having been opened for long. She paused at the feet of this giant beast I was brushing, and looked up at him. Being intelligent, and therefore curious, he lowered his muzzle by degrees to investigate. And as soon as he got his nose within range, that puny, only weeks-old kitten hissed and gave him a swat of her mighty paw.

With a snort, Benny crow-hopped his 1100 pounds backwards and sideways about two feet, oblivious to the fact that that's right where I was standing. He knocked me into the tack-room door, and rolled his eyes, pretty sure he was about to be the kitten's dinner. The kitten sauntered off, maybe to pick on someone her own size.

Despite getting a huge bruise on my ass where I hit a doorknob, it was so ridiculous I had to laugh.

Benny turned to me and stared balefully.

He was not amused.

It took a little while for the lesson to sink in because I'm only a human being, and human beings are not as smart as horses. But it finally got through my thick skull.

What my equine mentor had so brilliantly demonstrated was this:

If you conceive of yourself as prey, then any predator, no matter how fragile or puny, is a threat to you.

If you conceive of yourself as a predator, no prey, no matter how big or powerful, frightens you.

What you are is important. But what you *believe* you are is even more important. So you have to be very damn careful what you believe about yourself.

Adam Adrian Crown

And she'll promise you more
than the Garden of Eden
Then she'll carelessly cut you
and laugh while you're bleeding
She'll bring out the best
and the worst you can be
Blame it all on yourself
'cause she's always a woman to me

("Always a Woman," Billy Joel)

CHAPTER THIRTY-ONE: DOROTHY'S SIX-SHOOTER

Life is just fucking full of surprises.

The nature of most of those surprises would seem to suggest that god has a sense of humor that's half Woody Allen and half Charles Manson.

I was killing a little time, browsing porn sites on the internet. One of the few legitimate and benevolent uses of a computer, in my opinion. From the number of porn sites there are, and the amount of money they're making, it looks like I'm not completely alone in that opinion.

Many of these sites are quite alike, and some even have the same images, licensed from some porn image wholesaler. A typical array of image categories would include such standards as "big breasts," "oral," and "anal," in addition to good old fucking, with a few lipstick lesbian shots tossed in for good measure.

On this particular idle day, I was in the devil's workshop, and I happened upon a site called "antique-eros.com," which claimed to have "the largest exclusive collection of unpublished amateur erotica from the 1890's through the

1950's." With my penchant for the off-beat and unusual, I just had to have a peek.

I was particularly attracted by the "amateur" part. I find the professional porn queens to be a bit ho-hum. Mostly ho. Their sexual activities are about as believable as the flying chop-sockey stunts in kung fu b-movies, and just about as engaging. As much as I might admire Jackie Chan's acrobatic skills, there's no question that the fight choreography lies somewhere between caricature and comic book, and much the same could be said of actresses' performances in x-rated films. The sex is so cliche that a viewer with average intelligence and a modicum of experience can just about tell you the exact moment they'll switch from blow-job to butt-fucking. I have a feeling there's a guy just out of frame with a stop-watch and a whistle.

"*Tweet*! Position 22!" he yells, and the talent whips through the Karnal Sutra on command. Or maybe he uses hand signals like a third base coach, or a New York cop directing traffic.

This order of the sexual routine is as predictable as a 12-bar blues in E, or the next line in a pop lyric, when the first line ends in "love." (You know, "It came from above," "fit like a glove," "didn't need a shove" "soft as a dove.")

Worse yet, the cheesy un-spontaneity combines with a few of my other least favorite things:

Like ruby red lips and six-inch long fingernails to match.

Like lacy "French" underwear — apparently you could hang this crap on an oak tree and the average guy will try to fuck the knotholes.

Like 84GGG silicone tits that are as soft and nuzzlesome as chunks of concrete duct-taped to a woman's chest.

Like a woman in bed naked except for spike heeled shoes and a scarf around her neck — Amelia Erhardt Does Dallas.

Or like a woman who grimaces and contorts her face to utter unconvincing "ooooo's" and "aaahhhh's" and "fuck, yeah; fuck, yeah; fuck, yeah" like she's counting "one-two" for calisthenics.

That's only when she's not licking her lips and generally wagging her tongue around like a rattlesnake on acid. Maybe it's just because I've never gone to bed with a woman who left just her shoes and scarf on, or who went into fits that make Linda Blair in The Exorcist look like Julie Andrews in Mary Poppins. If you have, let me know.

Amateurs, I like much better. With them, it's sex gratia sexualis, fucking for its own sweet sake. It may not be polished or highly skilled, but it's enthusiastic and honest — unless those amateurs try to imitate the pro's. Then it's bad porn done badly. Enough to make a penis weep.

The folks at antique-eros.com turned out to be as good as their word. There were indeed hundreds of photos to peruse. A few could truly have been late 19th century vintage, but most were from the 1940's and 50's.

The contrast with newer porn was fascinating.

Most of the antique stuff was quite tame by comparison, not what we would call "hardcore" today. Lots of breast and leg and thigh. Some asses. In most, a hand or crossed leg, or an article of clothing was strategically placed to avoid revealing the pubis.

Many were series' of photos, strip-tease sequences in which the model went from wearing little to nothing over the course of a half-dozen shots. While there were a handful of really explicit images — made less so by shadowy lighting and grainy film — most of the collection were, in a strange way, almost innocent, like a little girl putting on her mummy's high heels.

It was one of the exceptions that caught my eye: a dozen or so extremely hardcore photos, all featuring the same woman.

Perhaps it was the exceptionally explicit nature of these photos or that they were less grainy and shadowy, and the clarity made them stand out.

Perhaps it was that in some of these photos this white woman was with a black man — or several black men, and that was the kind of behavior that could have spelled the bitter end for all parties in question back in the America of the 40's. And in some places it'll do the trick even now.

Perhaps it was something about the model herself.

She appeared to be in her mid or late twenties. Her breasts were pendulous and despite her high cheekbones, there was a certain roundness to her face, the suggestion of a little extra fat under her chin. A well-fed fullness to her hips, buttocks and thighs. Not quite a Rubens pin-up but certainly working the zoftig side of the street. Voluptuous, some would say. Plump, others might call it.

Her hair was dark, swept up into a skyscraper pompadour in front, the back hanging down in well-regulated curls to just past her shoulders. It was a style that the Andrews Sisters had made de rigeur for young women in the WWII years and just after. Her make-up had been applied in the same paint-by-numbers fashion of that time. Inexpertly done, it resembled a clown's death mask. Her full lips were sharply delineated in what I knew in my heart was the arterial red I detest. What she had done with a tweezer to her natural eyebrows, the Germans had done to Poland. In their stead were two drawn-in versions that started where her real brows did near her nose, then arched high and away into left field. The arch was not only too high, but was angled crookedly in the middle, giving her an oddly jack-o-lantern appearance. Her dark eyes were shuttered by lashes far too long and thick to be her own. On one side of her chin — the right side — just below her mouth she had decided it better to embellish a mole, rather than try to hide it, thus transforming the blemish into a "beauty mark." She'd succumbed to the same frailty of judgment with another mole located high on her left cheekbone.

In one photo — the most modest of the collection — she was slumped back in a chair, her heavy breasts hanging almost to the waistline of her panties — but then the panties were a style that put the waistline higher than her navel. She had enormous nipples and the aureolae spread out from them like the shock wave of an atomic blast.

On closer examination, I detected scars on the left side of her chest. They were molten in appearance, swirling and pock-riddled like the surface of the moon.

Burn scars.

The kind a little girl might get if she approached the stove in an unsupervised moment, reached up and spilled down onto herself a pot of boiling water. Or at least, that's the tale she might tell.

In the first few photos, the woman merely displayed herself, splaying her legs, reaching down through the morass of dark curls between her thighs to pull her labia wide apart, peering up demurely into the lens, one side of her lip curled up slightly, Elvis-style.

In another pic, she was kneeling with her back to the camera, a hand on each buttock to open the crevice between the halves as widely as possible, looking back at us over her shoulder.

In the remainder of the pictures, she displayed impressive feats of sexual derring-do.

The piece de resistance was one in which she coupled with six men simultaneously. Four of the men were obviously black — the two others, also quite dark, could have been.

She accomplished this ambitious task in the following manner:

One gentleman was seated on a low bench — perhaps a piano bench. She sat on his lap with her back to him, admitting his cock into her ass. The second gentleman stood facing them and introduced himself into her cunt. The third gentleman, who also deserves some credit for acrobatic skill, stood on the bench, was straddling her chest, pressing her breasts around his penis. By leaning backward, she was able to suck on the cock of the fourth man, who was standing behind the bench. Two other men were near the ends of the bench, one standing, the other kneeling on the bench with one leg. Our heroine was thus able to grasp a cock in each hand, too. All the men used limbs not otherwise engaged to support her and steady themselves.

It was, in all, quite a stunt.

And one hell of a sturdy bench, too.

Oddly enough — or maybe not oddly at all — the faces of all the men in all the photos had been obscured, blackened-in to render them unidentifiable. But the woman's face, of course, was not.

In some photos she is very aware of the camera, as if her particular intention is to tease or taunt the photographer. In others, she clearly couldn't care less. In every case, there is something dark and bestial in the woman's expression, a feral gleam in the eye suggesting that she is feverishly consumed with lust.

I have seen that look only rarely.

Too rarely.

Chuckling to myself, I downloaded the photos onto a disc to save them and printed out copies, too. The group photo — which I think of as Dorothy's Six-Shooter — I tacked up on the wall above my desk. I may get a nice gold antique frame for it. Maybe I'll frame them all, make a nice grouping near the fireplace.

They are, after all, the only pictures of my mother that I have.

And we go where nobody else can go
See things that nobody else can see
And we fly like a shooting star across the sky
My Rainbow Pony and me.

("Rainbow Pony," Spartacus Jones)

CHAPTER THIRTY-TWO: OSCAR

I once read a piece written by a French knight who fought in the Crusades, I forget which one. He describes a battle with some Moorish cavalry in which the European Crusaders were victorious. They were particularly delighted at the prospect of taking the Moors' magnificent horses — Arabians, of course — home as "spoils of war."

But everywhere a Moor had fallen, his horse remained by the body and refused to be led away. These horses fought so fiercely that, in the end, the crusaders put them all down, and didn't take a single one as a prize.

On the first clear day after a summer storm, I went to Max's farm to have a look at a saddle he was selling. A 1904 US Army McClellan. That's the one with the spider rigging, before the Army switched over to an English-type girth. It proved to be a size 12, which was what I needed. It had just one little place along the cantle where a couple of stitches had given up the ghost, but I could repair that easily enough. Like the weathered leather of Max's face, it was well-used, but well-maintained and well-worth the asking price. Cash, of course. No need to get Uncle Sam mixed up in the deal.

Naturally, after spending 10 minutes on the saddle, we spent the next couple of hours generally talking horses and sipping coffee that would take the curl right out of your hair. I also got the twenty-five cent tour of his place.

Max's farm was about 10 acres' worth. Had a barn with four stalls and a hayloft, a 12x12 tack room jam-packed with saddles and tack and old lariats. One stall was empty. In another was an appaloosa belonging to his wife (who was at least 30 years younger than he was, incidentally). In another, was a fine bay quarterhorse. In the last was a sway backed old boy with swollen fetlocks and who appeared to be blind in both eyes. Seemed to suffer from heaves, too. His stall had a Dutch "back door" that opened out into a separate paddock.

"That's Oscar," Max told me. "He's coming up on 36 years old." There was something special in his tone when he spoke that horse's name.

Now, not many people would keep a wheezy, blind, thirty-five-year-old horse with arthritis. A lot of people would put him down or sell him off to the butchers when the price of horsemeat was high. I remarked on it to Max. I told him I admired his loyalty.

"Let me tell you a little something about loyalty, son," Max said. He offered me a chew, which I declined. Then he told me.

"I was working at this little spread outside McClusky, South Dakota. Years back, it had been a working cattle ranch; now it was a dude ranch. I guess they had 40 or 50 horses. Something struck me about Oscar. He was way down on the pecking order. Maybe I took a liking to him because I've been down there myself. He was just the gentlest, calmest horse — bombproof, some people like to call it. He was always first pick to be some little kid's first ride. Kind of an ambassador of good will.

I don't want to make him sound like a tired old plug. He was about eight at that time and could show some spark if you took him out and let him know you wanted to do some running. He had real good feet, too. I'd bet he had some Arab in him. He needed shoes like we need more half-wits in congress.

One particular day, after a hellacious storm, I was going out to ride one of the trails, just to see what's what, and I decided to saddle up Oscar for the trip. I figured it would take all morning anyhow, so I packed up a lunch to take along. It was a cool, windy day, the kind that often follows up a period of heat and humidity like we'd been having, and it was a lovely ride. Oscar and I got along right away and I was riding him just by thought.

Or maybe he was riding me; he sure knew the way as well as I did.

About mid-day we come to a nice spot where there was a little meadow and some woods, and I decided we'd take a little rest. I ground-tied Oscar to let him graze — he ground tied like he had an anchor on the end of that rein — and I took my lunch over to a bit of shade.

I remember sitting there with little gusts of wind blowing in my face, carrying the sound of Oscar's munching along to me. Most peaceful sound there is.

Well, I always sort of blamed them sardines. Had a couple of sandwiches loaded with sardines and French's mustard. I can just imagine the scent of those sardines wafting right over to that bear's nostrils.

She wasn't forty yards away.
Stood up on her hind legs and bellowed. I pert near wet my pants. I jumped up and looked at her, saw her looking right at me. She was a giant, even for a Grizzly. When she bolted toward me, I got an impression of a ripple of muscle from her nose to her rump, a ripple of power.

417

People see bears lumbering along at an easy waddle and they think bears are slow and clumsy. It ain't so.

A Grizz can cover a hundred yards faster than the fastest human being on earth, change leads better than the best reining horse you'll ever see, climb a tree like a cat.

It couldn't have taken her ten seconds to get to me. Probably more like five.

Your mind can do a lot of racing in five seconds. I tried to remember all that bear advice I'd heard.

Turn and run like hell? No, that's prey behavior for sure, and I couldn't outrun her anyways. That would've been my instinct though, if I could have made my feet move.

Play dead? That just seemed like I wouldn't be playing for very long.

About the time she was nearly on top of me, I got unfrozen, threw my sandwich at her and starting digging at my belt for my knife while I back-peddled as best I could. At a time like that, if there's something you can trip on, you'll find it. I did. Fell on my ass, twisted my ankle hard — pretty sure I heard it go, or maybe just felt it pop. Couldn't get to my knife now — I was laying on that hand. Only thing left was to cover my face and throat with my free arm, curl up my free leg to cover my belly, or maybe to kick at her with.

When that bear bellowed and charged, I could hear Oscar give a long, shrill whinny followed by the thud of his hooves on the soft ground. You might think it strange, but I took some comfort in that. I thought to myself, looks like my time has come, but at least Oscar is getting away to safety. I was pretty certain he'd head right back to the barn, too, which meant that people would come looking for me. If there was anything left to find.

I think I started a little chat with God as I squeezed myself into a tight, hard ball and waited for the impact of that enormous body, the tear of those six-inch claws, the clamp of those powerful jaws.

But it never came.

A shadow fell across me like a cloud crossing in front of the sun. At first I thought it was the bear, but it wasn't.
It was Oscar.

He screamed and snorted and stood over me flailing at the bear with his front hooves then spun and kicked out at her with both hind feet. Kind of amazing, I guess, that he didn't trample me.

I heard it more than I saw it. I could hear him connect with those hooves. Sounded like somebody slapping a tree with a sockful of wet sand. I can't give a blow-by-blow account. I was feeling shocky, you know — dizzy, cold sweat and like to puke. I don't know how long it lasted. Could've been two seconds. Could have been two hours.

Somewhere along the line, I felt Oscar's soft muzzle gently nudge my cheek and I came around. The bear was gone. Ankle throbbed and hurt like a sonovabitch, but other than that, I seemed to be all right. Soon as I propped myself up on an elbow, Oscar nickered and grabbed up a mouthful of grass. I think he saw that I was basically ok and when it's over, it's over. Time to eat.
You can learn a lot from horses.

With the help of a lot of swearing and sweating, I got to my feet and Oscar stood close by while I climbed up into the saddle. Had to mount from the Indian side, which was awkward, but he was steady as they come. I saw then that he had some deep tears, like plowed furrows, on the side of his rump. Real deep. That bear had landed one good swipe of her paw, anyway.

I had my ankle in a cast for six weeks, during which time I became a champion one-legged manure shoveler. I told my boss I'd be real interested in buying Oscar. Turned out, she gave him to me as a gift."

Max and I watched Oscar sniff his way over to some clover and nip it down to the roots. He raised his head up while he chewed. His ears pivoted back toward us. Maybe he knew we were talking about him.

"That's one hell of a story," I told Max.

He nodded and spilled out the dregs of his coffee onto the ground. "I've never quite understood it, myself. It's a horse's nature to run from danger. That's how they've survived. And Oscar wasn't even *my* horse at the time. Not like we'd spent a lot of time together or anything like that. I don't know why he adopted me as his herd to look after. Maybe he'd have done the same for anyone. Or maybe he just didn't have no use for bears."

Max spat out a stream of tobacco juice and leaned on the paddock fence, watching old Oscar eat. I had to agree with Max; horse munching is the most peaceful sound there is. We stood there together listening to it for a long time.

I took that saddle home with me.

Alone from night to night you'll find me
Too weak to break the chains that bind me
I need no shackles to remind me
I'm just a prisoner, don't let me be a prisoner.

("Prisoner of Love," James Brown)

CHAPTER THIRTY-THREE:
PRISON CHANGES YOU

Here's kind of a funny story. I think it's funny, anyway.

See, prison changes you.
And not for the better.
It changed me.
And not for the better.
I spent just shy of a decade behind bars. Nearly ten years out of what most people refer to as the "best years" of their lives, I spent buried alive. More than 3000 days of lifeless, soul-sapping, regimented routine. Everything by the minute, by the numbers. The same drill day after day after day after day after day after day after day after day…
See what I mean?
Prison never changed anybody for the better.
Never.
You're locked up 23/7, continually brutalized mentally or physically by both inmates and guards, unless you decided to be one of the brutalizers, because those are the only two choices you get.
Prison never rehabilitated anybody.
Never.

421

Every once in a while you get the Bird Man of Alcatraz going on and it might appear, as some would claim who have never themselves been behind bars, that being locked up "straightened him out" or "taught him a lesson" or, yes, "rehabilitated him."

Bullshit.

Any time you see some decency emerge in a prisoner it's either because the guy had it in him all the time and it came out in *spite* of prison, or it's a way to deal with the terminal monotony of incarceration. Guys in the joint would be more than happy to work around the clock to find a cure for cancer — not because they care if anybody gets cancer, but because it's something to *do*, a way to break up the boredom of the endless sameness that spells death to the human soul.

No doubt someone, sometime, somewhere will bend your ear with that double-talk of prison being about "rehabilitation." When that happens, smack them real hard and tell them it's from me.

Prison changes you.

And not for the better.

It changed me.

And not for the better.

The fact that I was innocent didn't help — made it worse, if anything.

The fact that eventually I was exonerated and released didn't help.

I got a citation from the police commissioner along with an offer to get my old dusty badge back.

I got a handshake from the mayor, and a letter from the Governor, all very compassionate.

I got a whopping out-of-court settlement from a civil suit for wrongful imprisonment, after my ferocious young Amazon of an attorney scared the pants off the lawyers representing the police department, the district attorney, et al.

You know what I didn't get?

I didn't get those ten years back.

And I didn't get myself back, either.

All the king's horses and all the king's men couldn't put Jack together again.

I had all this money.
And now I had a horse. Hell of a horse, too.
I'll tell you about him sometime.
But I didn't have a place to keep my horse.
So I thought I'd better get one.

I looked around, found a hundred-year-old horse farm on the market in Darby, just about 5 miles and 20 years from Ithaca. Ninety-nine acres, instead of bottles of beer, and no wall. About half in pasture, half wooded. A pond. Couple of streams. Bordered some State Forest land on one side. Farms on two other sides, one of them a horse farm. 150 feet of frontage on State route 79 a quarter mile away down the driveway, and on the other side of that, hills and gorges no one would be developing any time soon. The house, a Greek revival, was built at a time when people had big families that stayed together, several generations worth in the same house. Five bedrooms. 2 ½ baths. An eat-in kitchen, plus a formal dining room. Living room. Full basement. Set up to heat with oil, but I could change that.
There was a monstrous barn with a loft. A wood shed. A small storage barn that looked to have been used as a garage. A recently-added 20-stall horse barn.

The previous owners, who had gone out west to take over a sibling's dude ranch when that person met his untimely demise, had built that nice, new barn. I was taking the grand tour of the place with the real estate agent, who was also a very popular singer locally, but that's another story. She was showing me around, yada-yada-yada and led the way into the barn.
Naturally, I followed her in.
Down the ten-foot wide concrete center aisle I sauntered, past rows of barred doors and behind them dark, 10x10 stalls.

10x10.

About the size of that cell I had lived in for a couple of forevers.

Without warning, I felt it all close in on me, and I was suffocating, my heart was racing, beating so hard that the noise of it in my ears made my head hurt. In an instant I was bathed in clammy sweat, clawing my way along to get out, out, out. It took a terrifyingly long time.

But I scratched my way out of the coffin, up through the damp earth and finally reached the open air, the sunlight, gasping for breath. I vomited and waited for my head to clear. Eventually, the dizziness and the tachycardia and the sweats all subsided. And eventually my guide, who had presumably been talking to herself for several minutes now, must have noticed my absence, and she came looking for me.

"Are you all right?" she asked. Bewildered.

"Fine," I lied. "Getting over the flu."

At least she'd missed the puking portion of the program.

When you pay cash for real estate you can go from offer to closing faster than a Maserati can go from zero to sixty.

Downhill.

With a tailwind.

I paid cash.

The night of the day the farm became mine, there happened to be a full moon. There also happened to be an unfortunate accident — somehow a fire started in that nice new horse barn. One of my good neighbors must've called in the alarm because the Darby volunteer fire company stumbled out in force about forty-five minutes later. By the time they showed up, of course, the structure was pretty far gone. I intercepted the first-on-scene, an assistant chief who looked like he was about 14 years old.

"I don't think we can save it," the fire-fighting honcho told me.

"No shit," I said.

"Pardon me?"

"Fuck it," I said. "Just let it burn."

And so they did.

I watched it until there was nothing left of it but bad memories.

Silly, I suppose.

But there you go.

Prison changes you.

Adam Adrian Crown

Someday we'll live like horses
Free rein from your old iron fences
There's more ways than one
to regain your senses
Break out the stalls and we'll live like horses

("Live Like Horses," Elton John)

CHAPTER THIRTY-FOUR:
THE BREATH OF ALLAH

Summer hasn't left just yet, but the signs are unmistakable that she's been seeing somebody else.

She still comes over, but she arrives later and later and leaves earlier and earlier. Even at times when she may feel as warm as she ever was, she seems somehow distant. Her body's here, but her spirit is somewhere else. Her smiles become forced. She laughs too loud and too long at your jokes, which aren't nearly that funny, trying to pretend nothing's changed, but being a lousy liar.

You want to tell her it's all right. That everything runs its course and when it's time, it's time. Move on.

But you don't tell her.

Partly because you can't bear the thought of the look it will put in her eyes, and partly because, somewhere deep inside, you know it's better if she figures it out for herself.

So maybe you go out to the paddock one night, just after moonrise, the light from that huge pearl turning night almost into day. As soon as the languid wind carries your scent up the hill, he prances over to you, knowing full well you always have an apple in your pocket. He munches his tribute in two slobbery bites, and, that formality concluded, gives his mane a shake. You hold your face close to his a moment or two, breathing into his nostrils and breathing in his moist breath in return.

"What's up, Jack?" he nickers.

A sigh is the only appropriate reply.

"Got the blues, huh?"

You say nothing, gaze up at the full moon, feeling in your every cell the profound appropriateness of the word "lunacy."

He nuzzles your elbow. "Want to go for a ride?"

The thought of going back, dragging all that tack over and putting it on, suddenly seems like an unreasonable chore, demanding far more energy than you have.

"Fuck it," he says, as if reading your mind. "Come on, let's just go."

And "let's just go" is exactly what you need. Where doesn't matter.

You strip off your clothes, tossing your stuff carelessly against a fence post, until you're down to bare skin. Your nakedness stirs up the wind's curiosity and a gentle breeze comes over and kisses all the places that the breeze usually doesn't get to kiss, making them vibrate with life. There must be rough debris under your feet, but you don't feel it. As far as you're concerned, it's like walking on a plush carpet.

He offers you his mane and you grab a handful of it, pivot back for a good lead-off, and swing up onto his back. You find your spot, letting your legs go into those places behind his shoulders, where they fit so perfectly that you'd think they were created with this in mind.

Who knows? Maybe they were.

You sink deeply onto him, into him, feeling the soft ravine of his spine between your glutes, and against the back of your scrotum. The heat of him seeps into your thighs and fills you up, the air, being so much cooler, alighting on your skin like a butterfly.

And you just go.

Eclipse of the Heart

The thud of his hoofbeats shinnies up your spine and your insides begin to vibrate to that rhythm like a tuning fork. The vibrations create heat, and you start to melt. Like a candle left in the hot sun. But this sun is coming from under you. Your legs melt into his legs, pounding the earth in a sacred dance; your hips melt into his hips and you can feel the powerful surge of your rump, your maleness swaggering with every step; your arms melt into his neck, your hands become his head. Now, you're just a little lump on his back, feeling the wind in your face as you fly through the night like a witch to the sabbat.

Along the old logging road you race, instinctively ducking and dodging to avoid tree limbs, splashing through the shallow stream in the ancient riverbed, sailing effortlessly over the trunk of a rotting tree, bent low in homage across your path. Up Bald Hill you climb, up, up to the very top, like Rocky running up those stairs, and once there, you snort and blow, your heart pounding like a war drum, and you dance with the sheer joy of doing so well what the creator made you to do.

In that moment, it isn't just that you *know* God.
In that moment, you *are* God.

Adam Adrian Crown

Blame the angels, blame the Fates
Blame the Jews or your sister, Kate
Teach your children who to hate
And the Big Wheel turns around and around

("Little Wheel Spin and Spin," Buffy St. Marie)

CHAPTER THIRTY-FIVE:
A WHITE ROSE FOR JACOB

The word "holocaust" comes from Greek. It means devastation, especially by fire, or a religious sacrifice. A burnt offering. Most people think of that word in connection to the genocidal campaign against the Jews by Nazi Germany, and as holocausts go, that was a pretty good one, I guess.

But it wasn't the only one, that's for sure.

The destruction of Carthage by Rome in around 146 BCE certainly qualifies.

Genghis Khan wiped out the Tata Mongols, among others, in the 13th century. Tamerlane, in turn, massacred Christians, Shi'ite Muslims, Jews and heathens alike. An equal opportunity destroyer.

Between 1492, when Columbus sailed the ocean blue, and 1900, the indigenous population of America went from around 50 million people to around 2 million. Scholars like to point out that this was mostly due to European diseases like small pox, as if that made the Euros innocent of genocide. I would remind those scholars that the Europeans used small pox as a biological weapon on more than one occasion. The Brits used this same tactic against the aborigines in Australia. Between

431

that and lead, that population went from half a million down to about 50 thousand.

Just after World War One, the Ottoman Turks killed off a million and a half Armenians. They didn't spare the Assyrians or the Greeks, either.

Stalin starved more than three million Ukrainians to death.

Between slavery, lynchings, rape and terrorism, some researchers would say that Black people in the United States suffered a holocaust.

Cambodia, Rwanda, Sudan...

Look, you could write a book about all the genocides the world has seen. It would be a thick one, too.

But I'm not going to write it.

I don't think there's any point in arguing over which genocide was the worst. All the folks who fell victim to one died in equal measure, and whether it was 20 million dead or a mere 20,000 dead, to me it's the same. You don't measure that kind of thing in numbers of victims. You measure it in brutality of the killers.

Trust me. Brutality is something I know about.

Hitler and the Nazis — the political party, not the punk rock group — sure as hell weren't the first to perpetrate a "crime against humanity," and they weren't the last, either. But there's something especially disturbing to me about the way they did it. It was so scientific, sanitized, industrialized. Assembly-line murder. They approached genocide with workman-like efficiency and they were proud of their achievement. They kept meticulous records, took photos, even made home-movies. Satisfaction in a job well done.

That makes my skin crawl. I hope if someone kills me, it's because he hates my fucking guts, personally, and not because he's just doing his fucking job.

If the records are accurate, the Nazis murdered somewhere between 6 and 12 million people including Jews, Gypsies,

Slavs, intellectuals, dissidents, homosexuals and anyone else they found it a drag to have around.

That's a staggering number.

I can't get my mind around that. So I try to come up with ways to understand it, render it less abstract. Here's one:

There are 60 seconds in a minute, 60 minutes in an hour, 24 hours in a day. That makes 86,400 seconds in a day. If you killed one person a second, around the clock, day and night, it would take you two years, five months and eighteen days to kill eight million people.

But that's still just numbers. It's meaningless unless you can put a face on it.

I found one.

It was the face of a young man, mid-20's, I'd guess. Not bad looking in a working-class sort of way. No matinee idol. Just a regular guy. His was one face among many faces. I don't know why it stood out to me. Something in the eyes. Something different from the resigned sorrow of those around him. Something still strong and alive. Maybe even defiant. A kindred spirit.

His name was Jacob Rosenfeld. He had played soccer and the violin and was in medical school in Berlin where he was in the top 20% of his class. He had a wife named Gretta, and I believe he had a daughter, but I haven't been able to verify that.

He's cradling a little girl to his chest in one of the photos. She's hiding her face against his neck.

The number that the Nazis tattooed on his arm was clearly visible. Jacob Rosenfeld and his wife and daughter were murdered at Dachau in April of 1943. He was just one of 6 to12 million. But knowing details about him made him more than a number to me.

The internet has made communication a lot easier for the people who use it.

Not all of them are nice people. Every crack-pot hate group seems to have its own website. There must be a couple dozen of them or more. If you're so inclined, you can find just the right group to join. Don't like Blacks? You hate Jews? You have it in for left-handed homosexual Irish midgets from Mexico? You can find a group that custom-tailors their irrational hatred to just your size.

Thanks to the internet, it's easy for these hate-mongers to flock together. It's easy for them to find each other.

On the other hand, it makes it very easy for me to find them, too.

These guys held regular meetings in what used to be a church, a building owned by der oberfuckinazi of the group. He had a website, published a blog in which he called on White people to "rise up" — because White folks have historically been so down-trodden, right? — and exterminate the "mud people," the mongrels that were polluting and out-populating the White Race. Blacks, Hispanics, Jews — all had to go. Gays, the mentally ill, and other "social parasites" had to go, too. And the "liberals" who were in cahoots with them. I assume he would include people with flabby hands and irritating laughs. God, according to the neo-nazi gospel, had made the world for White "Christians," and there was no room for anybody else, including "race traitors" who disagreed. Had all the bases covered.

I guessed he'd sure as hell be putting *me* — half-breed Indian with a bad attitude — on his little list.

Me, I think it's the height of stupidity to hate someone for the color of their skin, the shape of their eyes, the religion of their ancestors, or the place where they were born. I've always found that most people, if you just give them a fair chance, will give you much better reasons to hate them.

It's not the things over which they have no control that makes them deserve a good ass-kicking, but the things they do have control over. It's not what they *are* that I despise, but what they *do*.

You don't see a difference between that and the Nazis? Then fuck you.

Inside the erstwhile church, there was still an altar, but now it was consecrated to something other than the Prince of Peace. The pulpit was flanked by flags — the red, white and blue on one side, blood red cum-swastika on the other. Hitler had replaced Jesus as the centerpiece, and his portrait was flanked by another pair of Nazi flags, hanging from high up.

I wish I could say that all the guys in this group were glue-sniffing skinheads with swastika tattoos and combat boots. Would that it were so.

Take Herr Oberfuckinazi, for example. Local businessman. Boy Scout leader. Sponsored a Little League team. Family man. How all-American can you get? Maybe that should tell you something.

You'd never make him for a neo-nazi hate monger. He was 40-something. Not a misled teenager with misplaced angst. Pudgy, red-faced little guy. Tight mouth and pudgy little lips. Graying at the temples. Only his eyes gave him away. They were feral eyes, vicious and cruel.

His congregation — not a terribly large congregation — was similarly nondescript. Mostly just regular, working class guys, from all outward appearances. A butcher, a baker, a candlestick maker. And several cops. They weren't in uniform, of course, but they were unmistakable. They weren't there to raid the place.

Lots of propaganda literature lying around, pamphlets written by the meisterblogger. I was disappointed that there was no Wagner playing in the background.

During the meeting, some of the members recounted how they had "carried on the struggle" since their last circle-jerk. A swastika painted here, a Jew beaten up there, a Black shot somewhere else. It all added up, and they were proud to share. At the end, they sang.

I parked my van down the street, sat in the back and watched guys come and go. I use magnetic signs on the doors so I can change them whenever I want. Painting. Carpeting. Plumbing. Carpentry. Catering. I can even be the cable company. Sometimes I'll rent a van. Or "borrow" a vehicle from long-term parking at the airport. But I'm probably overcautious.

Time and again I've seen it happen; predators don't see themselves as prey.

And that makes them easy targets.

The oberfuckinazi was the last to leave after closing up shop for the night. Like Adolf, himself, this guy didn't do his own dirty work. He got others to do it for him. But he was responsible. That's called "the burden of command." Everybody wants the authority, but nobody wants the responsibility.

I approached him casually; said good evening.

He squinted at me, trying to place the face, but I didn't look much like the guy who'd attended their meeting.

I took out my photo of Jacob Rosenfeld and showed it to him. "Do you know this guy?" I asked.

He studied the photo with furrowed brow. He knew something was wrong but didn't quite get what it was. Finally, he pulled a face and shook his head "no."

"His name was Jacob Rosenfeld," I told him. "He says 'hello'."

Then I shot him precisely between the eyes with a .32 automatic. Now, a .32 isn't necessarily a man-stopper. But I do the cartridges myself. Half-loads to cut down on the noise. I file the nose so that when the bullet hits, it breaks apart and turns to shrapnel inside your skull. It makes scrambled eggs out of any grey matter that gets in the way.

One quick look at him told me he was an ex-oberfuckinazi now.

It was mid-April. I drove through a predominantly Jewish neighborhood on my way back and noticed a good many yellow candles burning in the windows. Special candles. A day of remembrance for victims of the holocaust. Sandwiched in between two upbeat holidays because mourning for the dead should never outweigh the joy of living. I respect their way.

But I like my way better.

Adam Adrian Crown

He is the horse of the years to come
And I will get me down
Before this steed upon my knees
And sing to him the sorrows of a thousand centuries

("Three Horses," Joan Baez)

CHAPTER THIRTY-SIX: BANNERBOY'S HERD

Like me, the Judge is a horse-lover. It's almost a state law in Texas, where she grew up, but not everyone who owns horses loves them, they just love owning them. A lot of people seem to think that a horse is just a hair-covered motorcycle, a toy to play with when the mood suits you, to be tossed aside when you get bored.

"You know," I said to Mr. Huntington, "there is always some pathetic bastard who finds some way to put his own particular group at the top of the hierarchy, so he can feel superior, instead of weak and afraid, which is what he really feels. And it lets him justify what he does to the ones at the bottom."

I was feeling loquacious, I guess.

"The defeated and disgruntled Germans put themselves at the top, Jews at the bottom. That way they could justify what they did to the Jews. Whites put themselves at the top, Blacks at the bottom; that way they could justify what they did to the Blacks.

439

"You know, most people put the value of a human life at the top of the hierarchy, ascribing lesser value to the lives of other animals. Imagine that. The life of a child-rapist-murderer on death row is innately more valuable than the life of the most gentle, loyal, loving, noble dog? There are a lot of people who would say so. I'm not one of them."

At this, Mr. Huntington strained against the ropes that I'd tied his hands with. Tied them up high. Very high. So he was on tip-toes, just barely. He mumbled something, but what with a sock stuffed into his mouth and duct tape over it, I couldn't tell what it was. Didn't much care, either.

I cut his belt off and sliced away his urine-dampened chinos and boxer shorts, exposing his limp, white buttocks. Then I took up the cane and hefted it. It was bamboo, similar to the kind used in some Asian locales for public floggings. I picked up my pistol, too, placed it against his temple, cocked it and fired.

Click.

"At first," I told him, as I put the pistol aside, "I thought I'd just blow your miserable fucking brains out. But someone talked me out of that. You don't know her. But as of this moment, you owe her your life."

"Then I thought, one stroke for every day of Bannerboy's life? Or one stroke for every day he probably had left, if you hadn't sent him to the slaughterhouse? He was 15. Stallion. Probably would've lived another 10 years, anyway. Maybe more. That's a lot of strokes, Mister. But we have plenty of time. So then I figured, oh what the hell, it'd be a pain in the ass — no pun intended — to keep count anyway. I'll just whip you until I get tired of whipping you. It's a hard decision. What do you think?"

He mumbled something else. What? Who cares.

"I agree," I said. "We'll just play it by ear. Or by rear, I should say, huh? Maybe I'll be able to tell when it's enough."

It took a long while. He passed out a few times and I splashed water on his face to bring him around. I rested from time to time, to let the feeling seep back into his flesh — there's a limit to the amount of punishment the body can take without going numb. I had learned that myself at the hands of experts. I don't have the vaguest idea of how many strokes I actually gave him. But no matter how many, it wouldn't give Bannerboy even one more hour to prance in the sunshine, or munch on timothy and clover. It could not undo the ignoble death of a noble horse, who was killed, not because he was terminally sick or even unsound, but merely because his owner had grown bored with him. Bought a new sports car instead.

When I thought about that, it gave my weary arm renewed strength.

It took a long, long while.

When it was over, I revived him one more time, cut his raw wrists free, letting him fall heavily onto the ancient oak plank flooring of the long-abandoned barn. When he was conscious enough, I squatted down near him and picked his chin up so he could see my eyes.

"I've kidnapped you, assaulted you and battered you," I said. "You want to go to the cops? Go to the cops. Before they can get to me, I will get to you. And then you're going to be dead. Understand?"
   I believe he did.

"Here's what you're going to do, brother. You're going to rescue twenty horses. You're going to pay for their

441

rehabilitation, medical expenses, feed, board, whatever they need until they get a decent permanent home. Understand?"

His eyes nodded "yes."

"Same deal. Fail to do it and you're going to see me again. And I'll be the last thing you ever see." I took out a list I'd compiled. "You can start with these."

He was too weak to reach up for it, so I set it in his hand. His fingers curled around it lightly, like a spider on a hot stove.

I bent down close to his face, close enough to smell the sour stench of fear on his breath.

"Remember, I'll be keeping tabs on you. You don't ever want to see me again."

He has three horses left to go.

You are the beating of my heart
You are the chords of my guitar,
You are the freedom in my soul, my Corazon.

("My Corazon," Spartacus Jones)

CHAPTER THIRTY-SEVEN: CORAZON

I call her "Corazon."

Her actual name, in the record books, is "Cora's Own." I don't know who gave her that name or who Cora was or how this wonderful chestnut mare wound up half-starved, worm-ridden and dead lame on her way to the slaughterhouse. Probably just as well that I don't know that.

I went to my first and last horse auction with the wife of an acquaintance of mine. Stevie is her name. She's an equine vet — and would turn out to be my own long-term vet. Among other things, she rescues horses whenever she can. Sometimes former race horses who just weren't fast enough to earn their keep. Sometimes horses too old, lost, broken down or abandoned. She has a network of people with places that could accommodate some of these animals, but not nearly enough. A hundred thousand horses go to slaughter every year. I didn't know that then. I wish I didn't know it now.

She was huddled down against the rail of a holding pen, head hung low, ears slack, ribs sticking out, gaunt hipbones, mane and tail ratty and soiled. One of dozens in similar condition.

443

When I approached the pen, she raised her head, which clearly took some effort, and she looked at me. Her deep brown eyes were large and round and soft, even in her wasted condition. I noticed that she had a heart-shaped blaze on her forehead.

Against the rules, I climbed into the pen and went to her. She leaned against me, nuzzled my hand with her soft nose, like a kiss good-bye. Then there was some guy at my shoulder, saying something to me about the auction procedure, or something. I don't know exactly what I said to him. But I think I made it clear that I was taking this mare home with me and I didn't really give a fuck about his auction procedures any more than I gave a fuck about whether he himself were to keep on breathing. Something like that. He didn't get belligerent or call the cops. Good thing for him.

I don't go to auctions anymore and I bet nobody misses me. I let Stevie do the going for me.

Anyway, I brought Corazon home with me. I figured, if nothing else, I could give her a place to die where there was sunshine and sweet grass.

For a long time, I didn't think she was going to make it. There were times when I slept in her stall and woke up three or four times during the night to check on her, see if she was still alive. Spartacus Jones looked worried, too. He stayed close to her, nickering encouragement. She had abcesses no one had bothered to treat and every parasite in the hit parade, aside from being so underweight you could play boogie-woogie on her ribs like a xylophone. Even Dr. Stevie didn't give her much of a chance, and she's saved a lot of beat-up ponies in her day.

But Corazon fooled everybody. Now, I'll tell you, I was completely green. I didn't know nothin' 'bout birthin' no babies. But I followed Stevie's instructions to the letter. I treated the abcesses, the rain rot, got her teeth floated so she could chew, dewormed her, and added every supplement in the known world to her diet, along with plenty of Dr. Green — good pasture. Gradually — very gradually — she started to come around, started getting stronger.

On the day when she staggered out on her own to graze on a little grass — just a little at first — I felt like I'd just stepped down on the surface of the moon. I thought I knew something about being tough, about never giving up or giving in, about going down swinging. But she taught me I didn't know shit about it.

I call her "Corazon." I doubt the people who named her appreciated the pun in Spanish. As I got to know her, I came to realize we shared the same heart. Pride, defiance, whatever you want to call it. She's not my horse; she's my sister.

We have something. A connection I can't explain. Some people describe communication as a "V" shape. The bottom of the V, the narrowest part at the crotch, represents the softest, quietest, most subtle communication. The top, the widest spread, represents the hardest, loudest, most overt. A good horseman, they say, communicates at the bottom of the V. Corazon and I, we operate below the V.

There's more than one horse who comes to greet me when I come over to their paddock. Among themselves, I'm sure they refer to me as Mr. Apple and Carrots. But when I go to see Corazon, she's already there, waiting for me. We go for long rides. Almost always bareback. Don't need a bridle. Often I either loop a lead rope around her neck, or just hold her mane, which is now thick and luxurious. I don't steer her with reins or lead rope. I don't even steer her with leg pressure. I don't steer her at all. She reads my mind. I only think a thought and she responds, unerringly. And sometimes, I let her drive. We go where she wants to go and how she wants to get there and somehow it always seems to be where I want to go, too. That may sound spooky or crazy. But it's not much of a trick.

It's natural.

When you share the same heart.

Hello darkness my old friend
I've come to talk with you again
Because a vision softly creeping
Left its seeds while I was sleeping
And the vision that was planted in my brain
Still remains
Within the sounds of silence

("The Sound of Silence," Simon and Garfunkel)

CHAPTER THIRTY-EIGHT: THE LAST OF BRAVO

It was mid-morning.

Darby was engulfed by the rainy gloom that passes for autumn.

I was in the round pen doing free lunging with Dulcinea, Dulcie for short. She was five years old, a grey Arab, just a hair under 15 hands. She's from the Polish line though, so she hasn't the pronounced dish-face that the pure Egyptian line has.

Dulcie was the first foal I ever delivered. From birth, I handled her gently, touching her all over, in her ears, in her nose, tapping the bottoms of her feet. I also straddled her, standing over her, without any weight on her, of course. As soon as she was able, I'd walk her around the place, let her hear noises, walk over a little wooden "bridge" I have laid out on the ground. I'd walk her past saucepans clanging on the fence, flags flapping in the breeze. All the things most likely to spook a horse, she accepted as a normal part of her world from her first breath, and nothing to be particularly concerned about.

I think there's no such thing as a "bomb-proof" horse. Any horse might spook. It's their finely developed instinct for self-preservation. But you can help a horse become more "bomb-resistant" by exposing them to a variety of things while taking their cue from you — as leader of the heard of two — not to be afraid. It isn't so much the "desensitizing" to various stimuli that does it. It's developing leadership trust. Your pony learns to trust you more than they trust their own instinct. You have to earn that kind of trust. You don't deserve to be the leader just because you have opposable thumbs.

Dulcie's smart, even for a horse. She learns quickly and seems to enjoy conquering new challenges. And she's sensitive, too. Sometimes I wonder if she's the one looking after me, instead of the other way around.

When The Judge came by, it was Dulcie who sensed her arrival first, long before the Judge appeared at the arena gate. Dulcie would be a hell of a bodyguard. I gave her some extra pieces of carrot.

I'm always happy to see The Judge. We've known each other a long time. Had our times together. She's one of a tight fistful of people whose company I can tolerate, and right at the top of an even shorter list of people I give a fuck about. I guess, to me, people are either strangers or family, and it's a real small family.

Generally, when I hear from The Judge, it means there's something that needs to be done that won't get done unless I do it. Still, sometimes it's just a social call.

Not this time.

She followed me to the pasture as I turned Dulcie out and for a while we watched her join the other horses to graze and play the "move out of my way" game. Dulcie, as usual, was the big winner. She was on her way to becoming the boss mare of my little herd. Good thing she didn't have to play against The Judge.

"I've come to ask you a personal favor," she said, after watching the horseplay for a little while. "There's a very dear old friend who needs help. I thought you might be willing to talk with him about it. It's not the usual kind of thing though, so if..."

"What kind of thing is it?"

"I should probably let him tell you about it himself," she said. Not like her to be cryptic.

"Can't say no to an old friend," I said.

"No," she replied. "After all, I don't have too many left." The Judge was past the seventy mark. Most 50-year-olds would fuck the devil himself to look half as good.

Dulcie and Shashka took a few turns at the bite-me game, then cantered across the pasture, slowed to a trot, forgetting each other for the lure of lush grass.

"The friend of my friend is my friend," I said, quoting in Arabic.

No need to translate.

Fred Hoffman was an amiable fellow and, like The Judge, in his late 70's. But in his case, every day of it showed. He lived a twenty minute drive up the coast from San Mateo. Cozy little place overlooking the ocean where he spent a lot of time looking for beach glass. Retired police detective — that made my gut a little tense. But he welcomed me as if we were old pals, offered me coffee, sweetened it with a tipple of good brandy.

I liked him immediately.

And I don't like many people, immediately or otherwise.

We sat on out on the deck he'd built himself, and chatted for a long time about all kinds of random topics. His wife of fifty years was away visiting his eldest son, who'd taken over her family's construction business. He had another son, and three daughters scattered around the country, and nine grand-children, one of whom was due to make him a great-grandfather any minute now.

He had photos of them all displayed proudly on the walls. Among them was a faded photo of a young G.I. and his blushing bride.

"This you?" I asked.

He nodded. "Our wedding day."

"Quite a dish."

"Was and is," he said with a grin.

There was one other old photo that caught my eye. Group portrait. Young soldiers. Mugging for the camera. I studied the photo more closely.

"Guys in my platoon," he said.

Since his retirement, he'd had time to indulge in his favorite pastime: wood carving. And he was good at it, too. He'd created countless carved figures. He favored nudes and animals.

Lions, tigers and bares.

Oh, my.

I particularly admired a nude on horseback that he'd done out of walnut. Horse at the gallop, a woman straddling his back, her hair flowing out behind just like the horse's mane. The muscular detail was remarkable. I complimented Hoffman on it.

"Thanks," he said. "I kind of picked it up from a buddy of mine. Back in the Army. Good old Al. A real Tennessee ridge runner. Give him ten minutes, an old stick, and a pocketknife and you'd have a miniature of the Queen Mary. He said it kept him calm, so I started whittling, too. At first I was just turning little sticks into *real* little sticks. Made a lot of toothpicks. But it was something to think about besides getting blown to pieces. After a while he showed me a thing or two. So there you go."

We talked another long while. About everything but my reason for being out there a-having fun in the warm California sun. He needed time to get around to it, and I knew not to rush him. No hurry. It was his agenda, not mine.

There finally came a lull in the conversation, following a reasonably dirty joke he apparently loved to tell, and in the center of that calm, he suddenly and quietly asked me if I would be kind enough to kill him. He explained that he was facing the prospect of a prolonged and painful end from a disease for which there was no cure and no real treatment.

"I'm not bitching," he grinned. "I've had a good long run. Hell, by rights I should never have made it off the beach back at Normandy, anyway. So I've been on borrowed time for half a century. Can't complain about that. But I have to think about Norma. What it will be like for her. I don't see any point in putting her through that. No point at all. So there you go."

I let him talk it through awhile, until he'd said everything he needed to hear himself say. I knew when he was finished because he asked me if I'd like some more coffee.

He made good coffee. I passed on a second snort of brandy, but he went ahead.

"So you were in the war, " I said. "World War Two."

"Oh, hell, yes. The Big One. Went right down and enlisted the day after Pearl Harbor, just like about a thousand other dummies."

"You regret doing that?"

"Yes and no. I was just a kid, you know. I didn't know all the ins and outs of it, all the political bullshit behind it. I just knew the Japs had attacked us and Hitler was running amok in Europe and the simple answer was to shoot back. I didn't look any deeper than that. It seemed like the right thing to do. Everybody said it was, anyway. So there you go."

"See a lot of action?"

"Enough to last any sane man a hundred lifetimes. Normandy. Bastogne," he shook his head in wonder and gave a little laugh, the way you might if you did something really stupid and lived to tell the tale. "Me and Crazy Jerry," he said. "We were like Siamese twins, joined at the rifle. From the time we got out of boot camp until the day we got home, we weren't more than an arm's reach apart. We did it all together. Shared foxholes, frostbite and French floozies. He must have saved my ass a hundred times."

"And you saved his."

"I don't know. Maybe. Truth of it is, I wasn't much of a soldier. But Jerry, now, he was the one. I can't imagine a better soldier. He was always in the thick of it. First one up, first one out. First one out of the frying pan and into the fire."

"With you only an arm's reach away."

Fred chuckled. "There you go. Sometimes I hated that crazy fucker. But I had a feeling about him, too. It sounds foolish, I know. But I just had this feeling that he was going to get through this mess all right. And if I stayed close to him, why, maybe — *maybe* — I'd get through it all right, too. Foolish. But you have thoughts like that sometimes. Something to believe in, to help you believe you'll make it. I was hoping his crazy luck would rub off on me."

"Did it?"

"I suppose it must have. Jerry and me, we went from D-day to V-E day without so much as a shaving cut. Unless you count frostbite."

"Good for you," I said.

"I suppose. We made it home. A lot of other good boys — good men — didn't." He paused, long and thoughtful. "The truth is, nobody really made it home. One way or another, we all died over there. We weren't the same people when we came back. I know *I* wasn't."

"How'd your pal, Jerry, make out?" I asked. I had to know.

"It changes you. It's unavoidable. You do things you never imagined yourself doing. Shooting somebody. Killing somebody. It's an awful thing. You never quite get over it, even if you don't have any choice because that somebody's trying to kill you." He looked suddenly embarrassed, as if he'd called a Black guy a nigger without meaning to. "Oh," he stuttered. "Um, no offense intended."

"None taken," I said. "But it was for a good cause, wasn't it? " I wondered if he'd heard my other question.

452

"There are no causes in battle, son. It's just about staying alive. Trying to keep your buddies alive. That's all the cause there is. Day by day, hour by hour — hell, minute by minute survival. Whatever it is you think you're fighting for, whatever your good cause is, that gets left on the beach with all the other worthless shit they have you stuff into your pack — worthless because you don't need it to survive at the moment. You might need it later, but later doesn't exist if you don't make it through right now. You kill because you'll get killed if you don't. Or your buddies will get killed. You kill because you want to go home. You kill because you want the killing to be over. But killing itself, it's still an awful thing. For the killed and for the killer."

He looked at me as if he'd slipped again

"I mean," he added quickly, "It's different for some people, I guess."

"Maybe," I conceded. But maybe not. "You were saying about your pal...?"

"Huh?"

"Your buddy Jerry...?"

He thought a long time about that one.

"You've got to understand. The thing about Jerry was, he was indestructible. We all thought so. He thought so, too. We'd go through some — some hell — and come *this* close — and five seconds later he'd be cracking jokes about it. He was always joking around. Sometimes I think that was the only thing that kept us going. The unofficial morale officer. And in action, you'd swear he was bullet-proof. My god. It was like he was a kid, playing soldier in his back yard. It was something to see. But that was before."

"Before what?"

"You want a little more coffee?"

"Sure, thanks."

He topped us off.

453

"This was right near the end. It was almost all over. We were taking a lot of prisoners, by then. I mean, whole companies of prisoners. It was getting to be pretty quiet. So when we heard some gunfire one morning, Jerry naturally volunteered us to go check it out. We found one of those — camps, you know. One of those... camps. When we got there — hell, we didn't know what it was. I'd never heard anything about *this* shit going on. Nobody had, as far as I know. Most of the krauts had already taken off. The gates were left open.

"When Jerry saw these people, the inmates, come out — Jesus, he just turned white. Like all the blood drained out of him, like he was going into shock, you know. He looked like he was dead. Walking dead. These poor bastards, you can't imagine. They were skin and bones. A lot of them were so weak they couldn't move. Just skin and bones. Some of the stronger ones, they hugged us. They kissed us. They held onto us like we were their life-jackets and letting go would be the end. I remember carrying one guy over to where our medic could look at him. He weighed nothing at all in my arms. Like he was hollow. And the stink. The stink of death and dysentery and burned flesh. My god."

Hoffman paused to catch his breath. I could see how hard it was for him to recount this to me. He steadied himself with a belt of that sweetened coffee and lunged ahead.

"We gave them everything we had — our rations, our water, whatever. We sent a runner back to battalion for more help, more supplies. Most of them didn't look like they would make it. But some did.

"Around the far side of the barracks, we found piles of bodies. I mean, there were hundreds. One or two were still alive among them. Starved and shot, but still alive. And there were maybe a half-dozen guards still there. Just hanging around waiting for us.

"Already had their hands up when we came around the corner. You see, I didn't get it at first. These guys weren't regular Wermacht grunts. One of the camp inmates started

454

jabbering at us — I could hardly understand him — and my German was pretty good thanks to Grossmutter Hoffman. Anyway, I finally got him to slow down, speak more clearly and this guy explained to us that this morning these guards had killed as many of their prisoners as they could until they ran out of ammo — can you imagine that? They knew the damn war was lost and gone, but they were *still* trying to murder as many of these poor people as they could. Then the bastards turn around, put their hands up and say 'Don't shoot! I surrender!' Literally with the smoking gun still in their hands. It was beyond me. I just couldn't understand that."

He shook his head hopelessly. "Einsatzgruppen," he said, as if that explained everything. And, in a way, I suppose it did.

"Jerry was in a daze. I thought he was on the edge of breaking down. Like he was fighting back the tears. Jaw was clamped down so tight, you could see this muscle right here, stand out." He pointed to the muscle on his own cheek.

"All the shit we saw together, all the heart-breaking shit, I never saw him like that before. He tried to talk to the guards but got frustrated, fouled his little bit of German all up. So he had me do the talking. He made them get down into the mass grave and pull out people who were still alive. There were maybe a half a dozen. We had the guards carry them over to the side of the barracks. Then he said to me, in this real distant voice, 'Take a walk, Freddy,' he says to me. I told him I wasn't about to do that.

"He says 'Get out of here, Freddy. I meant it.'

"But I wouldn't go. He remembered enough of his German then to order these guards to get down on their knees. He told them to put their hands on their heads. I remember one of them still had his hat on and Jerry slapped it off his head. Jerry took out his .45 and went down the line, one after another. 'Look at me, you cocksucker,' he told them. And they looked up and he looked them right in the eye and said 'Fuck you.' Then he shot each one of them. One round, right between the eyes. I don't remember how many. Six. Eight, maybe. Enough that he had to reload. When he did, the last one, an officer, made a run for it. Jerry shot him in the back, down low, dragged him back and shot him again like the others.

"He stood there a long time, staring at those dead Nazis, as if he was waiting for one to move so he could shoot him again. After maybe a minute or so, I don't know how long it was, an inmate came over and put his hand on Jerry's gun, lowering it down. He wrapped both his arms around Jerry's arm, laid his head against Jerry's chest and cried. That's where my friend Jerry died. There in that stinking camp. No more jokes. No more laughing. So there you go."

It was hard to listen to, but I did. I had to. And I had to be sure.

"Is he still around?"

"No. We lost touch. Then I decided to track him down, but... he passed a while back."

"What unit were you in?" I asked him.

"99th Infantry," Fred told me. "Why?"

I took good care of Fred.

According to the cops, he was the victim of a robbery and was shot by the intruder. I tossed the place pretty well, made it look good. Took some things he suggested I take to help sell the cops on the robbery angle. They're usually happy with the obvious. The insurance company paid off a huge death benefit to Fred's newly born great-grandson.

They didn't like it much.

But they never like paying off.

They thought it smelled fishy.

But they couldn't prove a thing, so they had to pay.

Me, I took in payment two items.

The first was that beautiful walnut nude on horseback.

The other was a photo. A bunch of young guys from Bravo Company, 99th Infantry, circa 1944.

Right in the middle, mugging for the camera, was a twenty-year-old version of Fred Hoffman. Next to him was his crazy pal Jerry, helmet tilted at a cocky angle, broad, devilish grin on his face, cigarette dangling rakishly from the corner of his mouth, pencil-thin Errol Flynn mustache tracing along his upper lip.

It was the face of a man I'd hated all my life.

A man who turned out to be, in many ways, more like me than I had ever imagined. Or maybe it was that I was more like him than I'd ever wanted to be.

Yeah.

My father.

Adam Adrian Crown

And the pattern still remains
on the wall where darkness fell
And it's fitting that it should
for in darkness I must dwell
Like the color of my skin
or the day that I grow old
My life is made of patterns
that can scarcely be controlled.

"Patterns," Simon and Garfunkel

Acknowledgments.

Thanks to everyone who read all or part of this and gave me feedback on it along the way: Richard Alvarez, Kim Strauss, Felicia Rivers, Skye Brown, and Hanita Blair.

Special thanks to Linda Wyatt, who read the original work, edited, proofread, and formatted the final version, and was a sounding board for ideas.

Thanks also to Artist Richard Turylo who designed the cover.

The following are songs I quoted. While I was using these quotations in a transformative way as the raw materials for a new work, you might want to track down these pieces and give them a listen.

Some of them are pretty damn good.

Opening: "Patterns" Written by Paul Simon.

1. "Ain't No Sunshine" Written by Bill Withers.
5. "Passion" Written by Rod Stewart, Phil Chen, Gary Granger and Kevin Savigar.
15. "Aquarius" From the Rock Musical "Hair." Written by James Rado, Gerome Regni, and Galt MacDermot.
28. "Besa Me Mucho" Written by Consuelo Velasquez.
37. "Hey Jude" Written by Paul McCartney.
51. "Jumpin' Jack Flash" Written by Mick Jagger and Keith Richards.
83. "Bad Leroy Brown" Written by Jim Croce.
85. "Papa Was a Rollin' Stone" Written by Norman Whitfield and Barrett Strong.
90. "Green Door" Written by Bob Davie and Marvin Moore.

93. "He's a Rebel" Written by Gene Pitney.
101. "I Enjoy Being a Girl" From The Flower Drum Song. Written by Richard Rogers and Oscar Hammerstein.
107. "Dream a Little Dream of Me" Written by Fabian Andre, Wilbur Schwandt and Gus Kahn.
113. "Coward of the County" Written by Roger Bowling and Bill Ed Wheeler.
117. "We Didn't Start the Fire" Written by Billy Joel.
125. "What's New, Pussycat?" Written by Burt Bacharach and Hal David.
129. "Ramblin' Gamblin Man" Written by Bob Seger.
139. "Trouble" From the motion picture "King Creole," starring Elvis Presley. Written by Jerry Leiber and Mike Stroller.
147. "California Dreamin' " Written by John Phillips and Michelle Phillips.
165. "Ride Away" Written by Roy Orbison.
168. "Baby Let Me Bang Your Box" Written by Teddy Mac Rae and Sidney Wyche.
175. "Me and Julio" Written by Paul Simon.
187. "Hit the Road Jack" Written by Percy Mayfield.
201. "That's Life" Written by Dean Kay & Gordon L. Kelly.
243. "Brandy (You're a fine girl)" Written by Elliot Lurie.
269. "Jailhouse Rock" Written by Jerry Leiber and Mike Stroller.
303. "Silver Threads and Golden Needles" Written by Jack Rhodes and Dick Reynolds.
311. "Mama Told Me Not to Come" Written by Randy Newman.
319. "La Golondrina" Written by Narciso Serradell Sevilla.
321. "Margaritaville" Written by Jimmy Buffet.
335. "Mack the Knife" Written by Kurt Weill and Bertolt Brecht.
343. "Bridge over Troubled Water" Written by Paul Simon.
353. "Goodbye Earl" Written by Dennis Linde.
359. "The Leader of the Pack" Written by George "Shadow" Morton. Jeff Barry and Ellie Greenwich.

385. "Star Dancer" Written by Spartacus Jones.
393. "Who's Sorry Now?" Written by Ted Snyder, Bert Kalmar Harry Ruby.
405. "Point of No Return" Written by Immortal Technique.
409. "Always a Woman" Written by Billy Joel.
415. "Rainbow Pony" Written by Spartacus Jones.
421. "Prisoner of Love" Written by George Astasio, Jerry Wayne Gaskill, Doug T. Pinnick, Bruce Kulick, William S. Taylor, Ty Ryan Tabor, Russ Columbo, Clarence Gaskill, Gene Simmons, Leo Robin, Jason Andrew Pebworth.
427. "Live Like Horses" Written by Elton John and Bernie Taupin.
431. "Little Wheel Spin and Spin" Written by Buffy Sainte-Marie.
439. "Three Horses" Written by Joan Baez.
443. "My Corazon" Written by Spartacus Jones.
447. "Sound of Silence" Written by Paul Simon.
Closing: "Patterns" Written by Paul Simon.

Adam Adrian Crown

www.ingramcontent.com/pod-product-compliance
Lightning Source LLC
Chambersburg PA
CBHW030535260626
47157CB00006B/2036